FOLLOWERS

Megan Angelo

ONE PLACE. MANY STORIES

This novel is entirely a work of fiction. The names, characters
and incidents portrayed in it are the work of the author's
imagination. Any resemblance to actual persons, living or
dead, events or localities is entirely coincidental.

HQ
An imprint of HarperCollins*Publishers* Ltd
1 London Bridge Street
London SE1 9GF

This edition 2020

1

First published in Great Britain by
HQ, an imprint of HarperCollins*Publishers* Ltd 2020

Copyright © Megan Angelo 2020

Megan Angelo asserts the moral right to be
identified as the author of this work.
A catalogue record for this book is
available from the British Library.

ISBN: 978-1-84845-763-8

MIX
Paper from
responsible sources
FSC **FSC™ C007454**
www.fsc.org

This book is produced from independently certified FSC™ paper
to ensure responsible forest management.

For more information visit: www.harpercollins.co.uk/green

Printed and bound by CPI Group (UK) Ltd, Croydon CR0 4YY

FOLLOWERS

For Mom and Dad, who taught me what is real.

What? You seek something? You seek to multiply yourself tenfold, a hundredfold? You seek followers? Seek zeros!

Friedrich Nietzsche

I know how influential I am over my fans and followers. I feel like everything I do, my hair color, my makeup, I always start these huge trends, and I don't even realize what I'm capable of.

Kylie Jenner

PROLOGUE

Marlow

New York, New York
2051

So she still believed in mail, this woman, whoever she was. The first thing Marlow saw when she walked into the building was a grid of metal boxes, each with its own window and cobwebbed keyhole.

Most of the boxes had only blank spaces where the names had once been. But the one for 6D still had a label, and the name on it was the same one Marlow had written down in eyeliner at the Archive. She could see, behind the small square of glass, the white slant of a waiting envelope.

Marlow slid a bobby pin out of her hair, ignoring the wave that sprang free and clung to the sweat on her neck. Ellis had taught her how to pick a lock on their third date. "Why do you know how to do this?" she'd asked, watching him bend the pin. Though she didn't know him well yet, she was sure he had never needed to steal. They had grown up the same way.

"I like exploiting the flaws in things," Ellis had answered.

And Marlow, twenty-two and in a hopeful phase, had laughed and let the omen sail high over her head.

Now she jiggled the crimped bit of metal in the keyhole, listening for the seize as he had taught her. Finally, the little door popped open and the envelope jutted toward her. She slid it into her back pocket, shut the box, and walked toward the elevator.

The stoned superintendent stared at her as she waited. His desk was tall, pointedly designed for someone to stand behind, but the man sat, his bloodshot eyes at the lip of the walnut veneer. He must have seen her pick the lock, but he didn't say a thing.

On the sixth floor, the doors were painted jade, the color the carpet looked like it had been before it turned trampled brown. Marlow found the door with the oily brass *D* and knocked. No answer. She tried the knob. It turned, and then she was inside, her feet falling on a gaudy doormat—black rubber, with hot-pink stripes. Marlow winced. Now that she was seeing colors clearly again, she could not get over how many of them she disliked. She saw, in a flash of memory, the roses stuffed into her mother's bathroom, just before she ran. That had done it for pink, she supposed. She'd be avoiding it the rest of her life.

No one was home. The apartment smelled like air that had been sitting undisturbed. To Marlow's left, as the front door swung shut behind her, was a narrow kitchen wrapped in cheap white cabinets. Three stools sat beneath the gray counter that divided the kitchen from the rest of the long, charmless room. The place dead-ended twenty feet or so out, in a naked window overlooking Eighth Avenue. The walls were dull handyman white, the color of a place between people.

The couch was the thing that made her feel like something was off. It was plump and lived-in-looking, the color of melted chocolate. But on the cushion closest to the window, a precise rectangle of fabric had been bleached beige by the sun. It was not the kind of thing, Marlow thought, with a tweak in her stomach, that anyone just let happen. Staring at it, she felt the way she would if she was sensing an intruder, though this was the opposite: an absence, just as sinister.

She wasn't sure how long she lay shaking on the couch, trying to recover from the chase. After a minute, after an hour, she sat up and looked at the mail she'd stolen. The envelope was soft with age. The faded stamp on its front claimed it had been sent from Los Angeles. Marlow scratched at the yellowed seal, scraping it upward bit by bit. She could never remember how to open these things.

The paper inside was child's stationery, embossed at the top with a chain of daisies. Above them, in all capitals, was a declaration that made the skin on the back of her neck prickle: FROM THE DESK OF MARLOW. She had never seen the paper before.

Each sheet—there were three—had the same crazy look. Filled back and front and end to end, margins forgone. Words compressed, begging to be heard out, at the edges where their writer had misjudged the space left.

She was reading for several seconds before she realized: she wasn't. She couldn't. The letter was in another tongue, one with its own strange alphabet—lilting loops, curving tails, linked letters forming something both foreign and familiar. There—that word reminded her of *free*. But was it?

She'd have to take the letter with her. As if she didn't look suspicious enough already, now she'd have three pages of paper on her person. She practiced fixing her face in a way that made this seem like nothing—*Yes, I'm carrying a bunch of paper, casually. What's the problem? People still have it for plenty of reasons.* She was the last person who would have bought her own explanation. Paper had occupied a nervous place in Marlow's childhood. There was a shredder in her house, kept on a high garage shelf, that each of her parents brought down and used when the other wasn't home. Her mother used it to destroy the department store receipts she still insisted on cashiers printing for her, so that Marlow's father couldn't trace her greedy habits as easily. Her father fed the shredder wrinkled cocktail napkins, after he memorized the names and numbers on them.

She had grown up seeing paper as synonymous with secrets. It was why it still surprised her, how light it felt in her hands.

Her fingers still gripping the letter, Marlow looked up. She heard footsteps in the hallway, getting closer. She waited for the click of another door, the sound of someone who had every right to be here going home. But the footsteps kept getting louder until, finally, they stopped. She watched the steel handle of the apartment's front door beginning to turn—slowly, soundlessly, like the person on the outside didn't want to scare her yet.

She put the letter down on the counter carefully. Eyes, then balls? Balls, then eyes? She wished that she and Jacqueline hadn't gone to happy hour before their self-defense class. "It's just for fun, anyway," Jacqueline had reasoned, lips pursed on the rim of her vodka martini. "If you ever get jumped for real, your device will walk you through what to do."

But Marlow's device was gone.

There had been a part in the self-defense class, too, Marlow recalled, about how to disarm a rogue bot. But bot-on-human violence almost never happened, and so that was the lesson she and Jacqueline paid the least attention to. If memory served, they had talked off to the side throughout the demonstration, admiring the instructor's exquisite biceps.

If it was a bot, she would go for the hip area, where the controls were usually hidden.

If it was a human, she would go for the balls. The thought of her thumbs on someone's eyes made her queasy.

The doorjamb gave way. Marlow braced herself up and down. She tried to look indestructible, like she was made of more durable stuff than whatever lay inside the thing or person in the hall. Stronger than heartless steel, stronger than menacing bone. Just as the door started out of its frame, the word for the language the letter was in came back to her. *Cursive.*

CHAPTER ONE

Orla

New York, New York
2015

Orla left for the bad salad place without her phone, so it took her a while to find out that Sage Sterling had finally died. Sage was found on a poolside chaise at the Los Angeles hotel where she had been living for a year—never mind the fact that she was so broke, she often tipped the staff not from her handbag but *with* old handbags: scuffed-up Louis Vuittons, old Balenciaga totes with half the fringe worn off. The bellhops would make a big show of thanking her, then place the purses in the lost and found.

Sage was erratic and filthy and sporadically mean, and she kept a pet ferret named Mofongo in the room with her. Yet everyone felt compelled to treat her gently, because outside the stucco walls of the hotel complex, the world was waiting, teeth bared, for her to fuck up again. So it was not strange, as the staff would tell the police later, that no one stopped Sage when she let herself into the pool around three in the morning. And it was not strange that no one disturbed her when the sun came up and she was still there, sleeping soundly. She was, after all, known for her impenetrable naps. Paparazzi had captured Sage snoozing in roped-off sections of exclusive New York bars, on a ski lift in Gstaad (she rode it around for hours), and during the premiere of her own latest film, an expensive animated adventure based on the phone game *Candy Crush*. (Sage played a lemon drop.) Head back, Sage snored loudly through the whole terrible movie. Someone at the premiere captured her snuffling on video. It went viral instantly, via a website called Lady-ish.com. Orla was the one who put it there.

Sage had lain still at the pool until around eight in the morning, when a towel boy watched a seagull shit directly onto her stomach. Sage didn't even flinch. The towel boy—"towel maintenance associate," as he would later correct a reporter—walked over, wondering what the most tasteful part of her body to jostle was. He saw that her lips were blue. Her eyes were still, but just slightly open, watery slivers cast down through brittle lashes. He touched her shoulder, the one directly in the sun. It was cold.

Orla was in the middle of ordering her salad when the news on the flat-screen over her head cut to an aerial view of the hotel. The shot circled its gray slate roof, hovering above the oblivious billboards on Sunset, and informed viewers that, somewhere down there, Sage Sterling was dead at twenty-seven.

The girl behind Orla, who wore dingy flip-flops with her skirt suit, looked up from her phone and said, sounding bored, "I literally thought she was dead already."

The stout Guatemalan man on the other side of the counter sighed as Orla gaped at the screen, ruffling brown-edged romaine with his tongs. He was waiting for her to choose another topping. Orla always spent a long time pretending to consider vegetables before saying, as if it had just occurred to her, "Actually, just double croutons, please."

The man in front of Orla was tapping out a missive on his phone in all caps: **SAGE STERLING DEAD!** Like no one would know it had happened, Orla thought, if this guy didn't tweet it.

Not that she was much different. Back at the Lady-ish offices, Orla's intern would be looking over the obit Orla had written for Sage eighteen months ago, the one she had marked with a warning: DO NOT PUBLISH UNTIL. Sage had been Orla's beat at Lady-ish for most of the time she'd worked there. Ingrid, Orla's boss, had identified Sage as a source of "bonkers" traffic early on, when a post Orla tried about her nail art drew ninety thousand views in ten minutes. From then on, every move Sage made, every boy and girl she kissed, every gown she put on was Orla's to write up. The clicks flooded in, even more so when it became apparent that Sage had a temper. Sage grabbed photographers' cameras and forced them down to the sidewalk. Sage scratched a bouncer, nearly blinding him. Sage pushed her boyfriend off his own parents' yacht. Orla received small bonuses for stories that clocked more than five million views in a day; Sage's boat rage had paid for her laptop. She tried now, very hard, not to think about what the star's death might bring, pushing away the thought of a pair of boots she had seen in a shop window recently—soft gray suede and knee-high, meant to be worn in weather that was still weeks away. Maybe months, with this heat.

Orla apologized to the Guatemalan man and left. The intern would have published Sage's obituary by now, Orla's name at the top of it. The clicks would be raging, Ingrid ecstatic. No one on the internet would care about anything else today. Orla could afford, in terms of time and money, to go to the good salad place now.

———

That night, Orla wrote three hundred ninety-six words of her novel while watching a dating competition show. She had been aiming for six hundred words, but the episode had been too engrossing. Dabbing at her nose with a tissue, a finalist had confessed that she was bipolar. The oatmeal-faced host had raised his eyebrows and said, "Wow. This is a first for us."

Orla promised herself she would write more tomorrow. Three hundred ninety-six words, she figured, would turn easily into six hundred once she went back and filled in some of the parts about the Orthodox Jews. She didn't know any Orthodox Jews. She kept meaning to google them. But along with themes of self-discovery and female sexuality, along with tiny doodles and charts she drew herself, she felt that, to be edgy and relevant, her book needed an Orthodox Jew or two. For now, she marked the passages about them with the same shorthand they used at work for "to come" where they didn't yet know what to say in a story: "TK." Then she went to bed and lay awake, thinking she should have done more.

The frustrating part of it, writing a book she wasn't really writing, was that she had been good at this once, when she was young. Orla would spend her afternoons curled over the electric typewriter that sat on her bedroom carpet, her shins beneath her and still encased in the blue knee socks she wore to school. She didn't have time to change; she was filled with urgent, grotesque tragedies, like the one about the murderous lunch lady who ground her child victims into the taco meat, or the one about the baseball player killed by a wild pitch, a fastball that orphaned his nine frilly-named daughters. She was prolific.

There was one main difference between writing now and writing when she was in second grade: back then, she didn't own screens. Now, whenever a sentence of hers unfurled into something awkward or just never began at all, she gave up. She let her eyes jump from her drab Word document to the brighter planes of her phone and TV. Suddenly it would be 1:00 a.m., and she would be tapping out half-dream run-ons—into her manuscript if she was lucky, Facebook if she wasn't.

All of the scrolling and staring was delaying her grand life plan, the one she had always had. Orla had never not known she would move to New York. That was where authors grew, and she would be an author. She thought, when she walked into a bookstore as a kid, that the novels on the shelves had been emitted, nearly automatically, by the grown-up iterations of each American high school's best writer. In her high school, that was her. She was always winning prizes for her persuasive essays, written on things that didn't matter anymore. She had a ribbon from the governor for her paper on Napster, and she imagined, serenely, when she was young, that New York was holding her place. Then she got to New York and found out that it wasn't. No one cared about her ribbon. She learned what former teen composition all-stars actually did when they got to the city. They blogged.

She had been blogging at Lady-ish now for six years, and trying to do something bigger—write a book—for just as long. She tried to ignore the old teachers who found her on Facebook, who remarked, between *FarmVille* moves, that they couldn't wait to see what she did next.

Not that it was their prophecies that haunted her. No: it was Danny's. That was all part of the pressure, too—a part that grew, strangely, as the years since she had last seen him counted up. Orla thought that perhaps she was striking a bargain with herself: if the whole world wasn't meant to believe she was special, then maybe just him thinking it would be enough.

And now, at twenty-eight, with her brain wrung of thousands of Lady-ish posts and her body sick of being pounded by New York, she was—though she couldn't admit it directly, not even to herself—in search of a shortcut. A way to be someone who had done something without having to actually do it.

A former Lady-ish colleague of hers—she was one of the older women, thirty-three, maybe—had quit the site after selling a compilation of her dating app exchanges to a large publisher. "Now I just have to actually write the damn thing," Orla had overheard the woman say in the ladies' room, the day before she left Lady-ish for good. Her agent, she added, had sold the unwritten book on a single chapter. Orla's ears had perked at that: she had a chapter and then some. Now she just needed an agent. But she had no idea how to get one.

And then, one morning, an agent turned up on the floor outside her apartment.

Orla wouldn't say that she had stolen the business card, really. For one thing, what was a business card these days but a collection of information anyone could find online? For another, Florence was never going to remember dropping the card. She was so drunk when she came home the night before, she could hardly remember which apartment was theirs. Orla had awoken to the sound of her stumbling down the hall, ramming her key into different locks, before finally their door swung open and Florence bellowed from the doorway, "Six! Motherfucking! D! I live in 6D!" A raft of smells—rum, shawarma, Florence's thick cotton-candy perfume—pushed under the fake door in Orla's fake wall, the dinky partition that cut the living room in half, making the one-bedroom two.

It had been three weeks since Florence moved in, and she had never come home before last call. Orla had barely caught a glimpse of her new Craigslist roommate since the day she arrived, braless in a tight white tank top, her long dark hair straying into her armpits. Florence slept all day and woke at dusk to start primping, the odor of her burning hair mixing with the fumes from Orla's microwave dinner. She left each night just after Orla went to bed, returned around dawn, and settled in to sleep just as Orla left for work, picking her way through the living room aftermath of Florence's night out: shoes shipwrecked in the entryway, clutch forsaken on the kitchen linoleum, credit cards half under the oven, keys still swinging from the door.

But on that morning, there was something else: at least a dozen business cards, strewn across the living room's linted rug.

Orla gathered them up and read them all. Modeling scouts, TV producers, beauty company underlings, and one man calling himself a "personal brand cultivator and 360-degree image guru." Orla shuffled the cards together, placed them on the counter, and walked out the door.

On the matted, jade-colored carpet near the elevator, faceup, there was one more card. Orla could read it without picking it up: Marie Jacinto, literary agent. The card was not impressive. The name of the firm it advertised had the ring of something small, and its stock was so flimsy that it shuddered slightly when the elevator came and split open.

Orla stepped into the elevator, then put her hand against the door and got back out. *Couldn't hurt* was the phrase skipping around in her mind. She had no reason then not to believe it. She was already composing the email she would send Marie Jacinto as she scraped the card off the carpet and slid it into the gut of her purse.

———

The apartment was dense with new silence in the mornings, at least between the banshee wails of the fire trucks racing up Eighth. Though she was the one who had lived there for years, Orla found herself trying not to wake Florence up. She watched the morning news on mute, let her hair air-dry, and started picking up coffee after she left instead of grinding beans in the kitchen. Orla told herself that it was better for her brain to have quiet, that her damp waves helped keep her cool in the underground heat of the August subways, that holding a paper coffee cup as she marched into her day was the New York thing to do, anyway. But this was just what she did, and she knew it. Orla had always been the sort of person who let brazen classmates borrow her clothes, the sort of person who said "sorry, sorry" when someone ran into her on the street. The sort of person who could not speak up at Lady-ish team-building tapas, who let her colleagues order awful things, octopus and duck, then failed to secure any carbs for herself. Orla hated tapas. She hated so much about food in New York: six inches of meat in the sandwiches, block-long lines for mutant pastries, the way people talked about chefs as if they knew them intimately. ("That's one of Boulud's places," Ingrid had said casually the other day, as if she sometimes played pickup basketball with him.) Most of all, Orla hated brunch, how it went on all day, pulling everyone out of their apartments and dumping them on the sidewalk, making her seem glaringly alone as she passed by with her solitary bagel.

But there was one good thing about brunch: on Sundays, Florence left to go have it. Orla would hear her in her room—the apartment's real bedroom—agitating her phone into an endless flurry of chimes before finally using it to call someone and rave about her hangover. Vowels stood in for each other at random. "Hay gurl hay," she would whine. "Faaaack. I'm hungover as fuuuuck." The call would conclude with Florence agreeing to meet someone somewhere in twenty minutes. "Getting in a cab now," she would sign off. Then she'd sleep for another hour before clattering out the door.

The Sunday after Orla took the business card, she heard Florence through the walls, braying her way through one of these exchanges. Suddenly, Florence stopped talking, so abruptly that Orla was scared her roommate might be choking. She crawled to the foot of her bed and pulled her laptop from her desk to the comforter. She was googling the Heimlich maneuver when she heard Florence say, in the unmistakable manner of someone getting another call: "Shit. Call you right back." Orla closed her laptop. She stayed very still. There was something about the way Florence sounded that made Orla wonder who was getting through to her.

"Hi, Mommy," Florence said. There was a flinch in her voice, but a steeliness, too, like she was ducking something sharp before it could be thrown.

"What's wrong with her?" Florence went on, worry leaping into her tone. "Oh. That's no big deal. You scared me. Her paw's always like that." A pause. "Are you kidding? Put her *down*? She's not even sick. You just don't want to take care of her—"

The air-conditioning unit under Orla's window rattled into action. She leaped up and switched it off.

"Just don't do anything, please," Florence was saying, "until I can afford a flight home. I'll come and get her and bring her back with me—please, Mom."

Orla imagined, rather than heard, the tinny hum of someone protesting on the other end.

"I know you don't believe me," Florence said, "but I'm getting real traction. People out here love my voice. They get me. I'm meeting so many— Give me a few weeks, okay? Forget airfare to Ohio—if things keep going like this, I'll have a record contract soon. I can buy you a new house."

Another pause, then Florence rushing her words out like she regretted it, in a voice so small and beaten Orla almost ran down the hall and hugged her. "No-no-no," Florence said. "I love our house. I didn't mean it like that. It's just something famous singers do."

This time, Orla was sure she could actually hear mocking on the other end.

"Well, *I* think I could be," Florence said quietly.

After that, there was nothing—no sign-offs—and then Orla heard Florence pacing. Orla lifted herself off her bed, avoiding the creaky pit in the mattress, and came to sit on the ground beside her door, one shoulder and ear leaned against it.

Florence was making more calls—short ones.

"I sent you my demo a few months back— Oh, you did?"

"And you thought you might have a spot in the showcase— Oh, it was?"

"I saw your posting about needing models for— Hello?"

"Yes! That's *so* sweet of you. I mean, I've been working on those songs since— Oh. No. I'm sorry, I have to stop you—I'm not blonde. No, I was the brunette. Sure. I understand. I'll be at this number if you want to— Okay. Bye."

Orla held her breath, waiting for things to resume. She could picture, vaguely, the sort of people Florence must be calling: the so-called promoters and producers who were always male, who claimed to know everyone and have a hand in everything, who did all their business from their cells rather than an office, who picked up the phone on Sundays. The sort who only ever seemed to see potential in pretty girls, sidling up to them at bars to set meetings which, invariably, took place in the man's apartment.

After a minute of silence, she heard Florence murmur, in the stilted tone of someone leaving a voice mail: "Following up on the entry-level programmer position. *Fuck*," she finished softly. Orla hoped she had hung up before that last part. Ten seconds later, Florence left for brunch.

———

After an hour of enjoying being alone in the apartment, Orla got bored and went to the office, walking directly into the sun as she moved east on Twenty-Third Street, toward the not-old, not-new Gramercy building Lady-ish shared with dentists and accountants. She wanted to get a jump on her posts for the week. Sage had been dead six days. The slideshow of celebrities walking into her funeral had gotten nine million clicks and counting, but the pace was tapering off. Orla's follow-up, a trend piece on a hat three stars had worn to the services, had done about twice that, despite everyone on the internet pretending to be horrified by it. **SO INAPPROPRIATE!** a Lady-ish reader had screamed in the comments, echoing Orla's original thoughts on the post. Ingrid had only said, "If we didn't do it, someone else would have."

Orla liked the office on weekends—the half-light, the natural coolness it took on when jittery bodies weren't packed along the tables. She sat down and closed her hand over her mouse, nudged her computer awake. She was scanning social media, looking for actresses who might have cut their hair over the weekend, when she saw Ingrid's office door sliding open out of the corner of her eye.

"Hey," Ingrid said when she reached Orla's desk. Orla looked up. Ingrid's hair was even greasier than usual. Her boss had a six-step lip routine involving liners and glosses and setting powders, but she seemed to only wash her hair roughly once a moon cycle. "How was your weekend?" she said, like it was already over, and without waiting for an answer went on: "Can you cover a red carpet tomorrow? It's this what's-her-name who's going to be there, her publicist's always bothering me, and we need to keep the publicist happy because she also reps that—you know, that YouTube girl, with the harp?"

"Tomorrow?" Orla rolled her eyes sideways, grasping for an excuse.

"I just thought you might have some extra time," Ingrid said meaningfully, "now that the Sage stuff is going away."

Orla nodded. She would do it. The year before, a handsome European prince who was constantly falling down outside clubs got sober, joined the armed forces, and largely disappeared. As a result, one Lady-ish blogger lost her job. Orla was determined not to lose hers—after all, if she lost it, she would never get to leave it. And this was something she fantasized about constantly: her quitting Lady-ish after selling her book, just like her Tinder-star colleague. In the fantasy, she carried a box of her things, though she didn't have things at the office. Her desk was just a two-foot section of a long cafeteria-style table shared by nine other bloggers. No one had drawers or plants or picture frames—they barely had supplies. "Where's the pen?" one of them would cry out a few times a day, and whoever had it last would send it skidding down the row.

She knew she wasn't the only one who dreamed about quitting. When she and her colleagues sat in the conference room, watching Ingrid run her laser pointer over a screen filled with top-performing headlines ("You Won't BELIEVE What This Megastar Looks Like WITHOUT Her Extensions"), Orla would think about how every one of their minds was somewhere else, lusting over their next moves, reminding themselves they were better. Better than this job, and better than the girl in the next seat doing it, too. That last part was important. Orla believed it fiercely: she would be gone someday, on to greater things, and the next girl down would still be in her chair. She better still be in her chair. Someone had to stay to be who Orla was before.

But before what? That was the question in her mind at dawn, when Florence slammed over the threshold and woke her, and at night, when she lay staring at her phone while she should have been writing or sleeping. More than anything else—to be an author, to have a boyfriend, to learn how it felt to breathe without being forty thousand dollars in debt—she wanted the answer to the question. She was living in the before of something, and she was getting tired of it. The dangerous thing about the way she felt, Orla knew, was that she didn't know exactly what she wanted to happen, and she didn't care that she didn't know. Almost any change would do.

CHAPTER TWO

Marlow

Constellation, California
2051

The morning was for numbers. Marlow woke at seven to take one pill in front of—she gave a mental glance at the dashboard that kept track of her followers, blinking on the screen inside her mind—eleven-point-six million people, as of this moment. She hooked the quilt beneath her armpits in two places—wardrobe malfunction prevention had installed loops on all her bedding, had sewn prongs into the lace edges of the short silk gowns she wore to bed. Then she sat up and took three deep breaths, opening her eyes on the last one. She blinked four times, unhurried. Smiled twice. The first smile was meant to look sleepy, to hint at consciousness emerging. The second was meant to look spontaneous, giddy, as if she had just remembered that she was alive and felt unspeakably blessed.

To look, in other words, as though the pill worked that fast.

Lately, Marlow had been adding some movement to this second smile, sighing and stretching her arms over her head. But the network had sent her a clucking note yesterday, reminding her to *aim for consistency wherever possible. Departures from long-held routines can seem to the audience like signs of emotional trouble.* Her followers had other concerns. After Marlow lowered her palms this morning, she closed her eyes just in time to see a comment scrolling: **Is it me or does Mar have kinda chubby armpits?**

Marlow looked at Ellis, sleeping stomach-down beside her. She couldn't ask him if he thought her armpits were fat. To bring it up on camera would be to acknowledge the follower's comment, to acknowledge the existence of followers at all. This was against employee policy. Which was a total farce, of course; her followers knew she knew they were watching. They knew she could see them talking about her. But the fact that she and the other talent never let on, that they pretended to just be *living*— this was what her followers wanted. They liked to feel like voyeurs; they didn't want to be looked in the eye. And so, as her contract stated: *The Constellation Network has a zero-tolerance policy on spell-breaking.*

She got up and padded across the bedroom, listening to the faint saw of the cameras in the shiplap wall's grooves sliding on their tracks to follow her.

The writers had been editing her closet again, Marlow saw when she pulled its doors open. Yesterday, as the day stretched empty before her, Marlow had reclined in her backyard cabana, let her eyelids close behind her sunglasses, and intuited lazily, just for something to do: *vintage fashion images.* The browsing turned into obsession; the obsession turned into a wardrobe request that was filled within the hour. As Marlow sat cross-legged in her sarong on the dove-gray cushion, eating a spinach salad with strawberries, a drone descended from the sky and landed on the deck. It unfurled its arms to release a metal bar hung with the clothes she had asked for: jeans with the knees cat-clawed out, shoulderless blouses that billowed in the breeze as they settled down in front of her.

When she put everything on, Marlow grinned at herself in the mirror, feeling like a twenty-teens pinup. But then she saw her dashboard throbbing with feedback. **Those pants just made me second-guess being on the same meds as her**, someone wrote.

That night, as she lay in bed, Marlow heard the overnight drone making more noise than usual. After it cleaned and filed the dishes, after it folded the blankets she and Ellis left slopped on the couches when they ambled to bed, she heard the drone pushing its way into her closet, clattering around. Sure enough, this morning, all her vintage looks were gone.

Now she pulled a lime-colored hoodie and matching leggings off a hanger. If the network cared so much about what she wore, let them green-screen it in themselves.

Such a bold floral on that cardigan, but she's pulling it off! went the follower comment that appeared a moment later. **Clicking to buy!**

Marlow fought the gag that rose inside her at the phrase *bold floral*. She swore someone in wardrobe had it out for her.

On the other hand, she thought as she went into the kitchen and opened the fridge, she had a guardian angel in craft services. Science had definitively linked caffeine to anxiety recently, and the network had immediately freaked about the optics of Marlow consuming it. But someone in crafty had come to the rescue, developing a coffee, just for her, that could be dyed to look like cold-pressed juice. Now Marlow uncapped a plastic bottle with a label that read Carrot Apple, took a sip of terra-cotta-colored liquid, and tasted the bitter cool of iced espresso. The sensation loosened her instantly; her shoulders retreated downward, her heart rose, her face relaxed. She could sense herself having an attractive moment, and, as if on cue, she heard a muted snap. The camera in the brass knob on the cabinet door across from her had detected, and captured, a still image perfect for the Hysteryl ad that would be patched onto the corner of her live feed in—Marlow counted—three, two—

She DOES always look so content though, someone piped up on her dashboard. **Next time they do a promo code for Hysteryl I might give it a shot.**

Doesn't anyone think it's weird the way she drinks that juice, someone else said. **She's like SAVORING the tiniest sips. I bet she's on coffee and they're CGI'ing shit.**

Marlow froze with her lips on the bottle. She waited a beat for the comment to clear, then tipped her head back and forced herself to take a giant gulp of her drink. She exhaled discreetly, to keep from releasing the telltale coffee char of her breath. Then she stifled a smile; her followers couldn't *smell* her. Her heartbeat stuttered as it always did when she came up with another thing, though sometimes she could go years on end without adding to the list: *Things I Have to Myself.* The hour before 3:00 and 4:00 a.m., when the network broke for ad interruption. Dressing rooms and doctor's office chambers and bathrooms, in her home and all over town. Her favorite was a toilet stall in the vegan gastropub downtown—as a teenager, she used a nail file to scratch mean things about some of her ruder followers into its enamel walls. And now: her smell. Something small, but hers alone.

———

This was how it had gone, at Jacqueline's parties, for nearly a decade: Marlow sat on the cantaloupe-colored sofa, against its right arm, her good side facing camera east. Ida slumped opposite her, on the daisy-patterned club chair, droning unbearably. Marlow had once liked being across from Ida, back when the woman was a bawdy, sloppy drunk. But these days, Ida was sober, and a stay-at-home mom, and she spent most of Jacqueline's parties performing small dramas about her allergies. Marlow had seen Ida walk around an ottoman like it was a land mine, sniffling, "Oh, God, is that mohair?" Ida routinely flung herself across the room to close a window, whining, "Sorry, pollen, I have to." Once, failing to detect Ida's allergy profile from her device, a server bot had extended a tray of shrimp cocktail her way. Ida had gone to City Hall the next week, made a twenty-minute speech about her hives, and insisted that the network decommission—and *dismember*, Marlow recalled, with a scandalized chill—the offending machine.

But tonight, Ida was missing, recast without explanation. A new girl—olive-skinned and sleek, formidably cheekboned, with bronze lipstick and black hair parted into pigtail braids—sat in Ida's chair with her bare feet pulled up under her, like she had been here forever.

Marlow looked at Jacqueline, who stood in the center of the thick sand-colored carpet, holding up something called a "scrunchie." At these parties, Jacqueline pushed things that, according to her invites, *changed her life*: ab gadgets, smoothies, ugly quilted handbags. Marlow knew—they all knew—that none of these things had really changed Jacqueline's life. The network chose the items based on sponsorship agreements. Then Jacqueline threw parties where she raised them up and gushed about them to her dozen in-person guests and her roughly nine-point-nine million followers—plus all of her guests' followers, too. The items the network chose reflected Jacqueline's core audience demo: married mothers across America, aged twenty-eight to forty-four, who tuned in while folding laundry around 9:00 p.m. on weeknights. Though Jacqueline fit squarely in with her followers—she was thirty-eight, with two daughters—she was always embarrassed when someone mentioned her demo. "It makes me feel so old and boring," she told Marlow once. "It's better than mine," Marlow had said. No one would argue with that.

"Where's Ida?" Marlow called to Jacqueline, raising her voice above the scrunchie-induced *oohs* and *aahs*.

Jacqueline ignored her. She pushed the scrunchie onto her wrist and waved her hand around for all to see. "And it's super-cute as a bracelet," she said.

"Jac?" Marlow repeated. "Is Ida on vacation?"

The end of her sentence slipped under the clatter of something breaking on the ground. The women turned to see a server bot bent over the shards of a wineglass. Marlow watched the lilies in the coffee table vase twist in the same direction, their scarlet pistils stretching to train their tiny cameras on the action. She could swear the bot had dropped the glass to drown out the sound of Ida's name.

When she looked back at Jacqueline, her friend nodded once and dabbed at her lips. It was their signal for *Tell you off-camera*.

An hour later, as Marlow passed the powder room, Jacqueline's arm shot out of it and pulled her inside. "Ida's gone," she said, as she pulled the door shut.

"Gone?" Marlow saw herself in the mirror. One of Jacqueline's hair drones, its silver talons clacking near her ear, had pinned a ridiculous silk bow barrette into her dark waves.

"Yup," Jacqueline said. "Just up and left Mike and the kids. Blew right through the perimeter. Left the fucking *state*." She walked her fingers on an invisible path through the air. "Check your map. She's in *Denver*. And for God's sake, Marlow—don't mention her on camera again."

"But what about her contract?" Marlow said. "I thought she and Mike were doing the whole on-the-rocks thing this year." She unlatched her barrette and massaged her scalp, ignoring Jacqueline's puffed breath of protest.

"They didn't even stage a hunt for her, supposedly," Jacqueline said, adjusting the pearl comb at her temple. She sucked her cheeks in and glared at herself in the glass. "How shitty would *that* feel? It's like they don't even care she's gone. I honestly think the network was glad to get the chance to sub in that new girl. Diversity and all."

"Jacqueline." Marlow spoke in a firm voice. This was something she had been trying to do more since she turned thirty-five—the age felt, to her, like a cosmic deadline for being strong and self-possessed. Complete. "Hunts aren't real," she said.

"They certainly are," Jacqueline returned, in a tone that trumped hers effortlessly, and Marlow let it go. Jacqueline was an incorrigible know-it-all. It was what Marlow loved most about her. Her friend's brazen authority always made her feel safe.

Jacqueline's eyes flitted away for a moment. She nodded, but not at Marlow. Her device was telling her something. "Gotta get back out there," she said. "Talk later."

Alone in the bathroom, Marlow twiddled the twigs in the diffuser on the sink and closed her eyes. *Find Ida Stanley*, she intuited.

In her mind's eye, California shrank and plummeted away, making Marlow's stomach flip, like she was the falling thing. Her map shifted, streaking past hundreds of her neighbors' symbols in a blur, and brought her down again in Denver. Ida's symbol—the red stiletto that had always depressed Marlow—hovered over the city. There she was, proudly gone, in the state of—Marlow had to zoom out to remind herself what state Denver was in—Colorado. Marlow pictured Ida on a purple-flowered mountain. Sneezing.

The black gem at her wrist nicked her gently. *I have a message from production*, came the voice in her brain. *I should return to an on-camera space. I have now been off camera five minutes. I have lost seventy-eight followers during this off-camera time.*

Marlow watched herself blush with guilt in the mirror. It was as if the network knew what she was thinking about just then: what it would be like for her to leave, too.

I have lost eighty-nine followers during this off-camera time, the voice followed up.

Eighty-nine followers was nothing. Marlow averaged an audience of over twelve million. And that was why Ida could run, she thought, and get away with it, whereas she wouldn't. Ida had, what—one, one-point-five million followers? Hardly a fan favorite, especially after she transitioned from the party-girl ensemble to a standard housewife arc. She didn't even have a sponsor. Marlow, by contrast, was the most looked-at woman in the room, presented by a marquee partner: Hysteryl. Her followers—the people who observed every move she made—were spread across the rest of America and various races and age groups. What they had in common was that they were troubled. This was how the network marketed her: as the poster child for troubled, the Constellation star who got what they were going through. The network mined public data, looking for adults whose devices clocked too much crying or eating, for kids whose heartbeats surged to panicked levels during gym class. *Meet Marlow*, went the ad the network would beam straight to their devices. *She knows just how you feel.* The sad people, glad to be talked to, would opt right in and start watching her. They would see that she moved through her days with buoyant normalcy, and they would be reminded, every so often, that Hysteryl had made her this way. It was Jacqueline's job to show America what they could buy to keep them happy. It was Marlow's job to show them what to swallow.

She calmed herself at the sink, willed the redness to fade from her cheeks.

I should return to an on-camera space.

Marlow's hair was bent and snarled where she had pulled out the bow. She dug the clasp back in, even tighter this time, and went back out to the party.

CHAPTER THREE

Orla

New York, New York
2015

The red carpet Ingrid sent Orla to was at a terrible club on a terrible block. Bits of trash stuck to the filthy red carpet slapped down at its entrance. A bouncer stood at the doorway, staring straight ahead, as if trying to block out the Container Store directly to his right.

Orla scanned the ground and found her place, a square of sidewalk the size of a cereal box, marked with a laminated printout: ORLA CADDEN, LADY-ISH.COM. She elbowed her way in next to an anxious waif who wore a gown that plunged to her belly button. She was dressed, Orla knew, like she was hoping to be invited inside later. A chubby Hispanic guy in horn-rimmed glasses held his phone up to the waif, filming her as she said: "We're here at the launch of Hilaria Dahl's dog sweater line, and all the hottest celebrity animal lovers have tuned out for the occasion."

"*Turned* out!" Horn-rimmed Glasses shrieked as if he had just caught fire.

Hilaria Dahl was a judge on a reality show that pitted cancer survivors against each other in baking contests. By the time she made her way to Orla, Hilaria had submitted to eighteen other interviews, and the corners of her mouth were caked with spit. She smacked her lips together. "I love Lady-ish!" she squealed, her long earrings jangling at either side of her jaw.

Orla nodded and stretched her face into a smile. "So, dog clothes! What inspired this project?"

Hilaria shifted in her heels. "Well, it's really close to my heart."

"What is?" Orla said.

"AIDS," Hilaria answered.

"AIDS?" Orla looked to Hilaria's publicist, a black-clad woman in a headset.

"Ten percent of the proceeds from the line benefits AIDS," the publicist snapped.

"And I love animals," Hilaria added. "I loved the idea of putting my name on something that would keep them warm, the way they keep *us* warm."

Next to Orla, the waif was nodding fiercely, a hand pressed over her heart.

"We're just targeting dogs right now," Hilaria went on. "But I'm also really passionate about cats. So we're looking to expand into the cat market as well."

Orla couldn't stop herself. "Couldn't cats just wear the clothes you make now?"

Hilaria looked at her publicist. "I guess cats could wear the small ones, right?" she said uncertainly. "Like the alpaca cowl-neck?"

"Cats could wear the small ones," the publicist confirmed, glaring.

"And every piece is one hundred percent vegan!" Hilaria shouted.

"Didn't you just say something's alpaca?" Orla said. "An alpaca is an *animal*. It's kind of like a llama."

"That's all the time she has," the publicist said, taking Hilaria by the elbow and guiding her toward the doors. She looked back at Orla. "Fuck you," she said plainly. "Not you," she added, into the headset. "But maybe you, soon, if you don't find out where Isabelle went."

There was a lull in the arrivals. The waif was complaining to Horn-rimmed Glasses, claiming her improv teacher had called her too pretty for comedy, when Horn-rimmed Glasses waved his hand in her face and bellowed, "GIRL SHUT THE FUCK UP HERE SHE COMES."

Orla perked up and craned her neck toward the SUV that had just pulled up. Hilaria's publicist had likely emailed Ingrid already, demanding that Orla apologize. Maybe Orla could redeem herself with a quote from whoever was making Horn-rimmed Glasses clap tiny, overjoyed claps.

Flashbulbs popped so brightly that Orla had to look down. Then she could only see the pair of legs coming toward them, oiled and deliberate. Next to her, the waif leaned forward and said breathlessly, "Floss, it's like the *hugest* honor."

Standing in front of the waif, Orla saw as bursts of light cleared her vision, was her own roommate. Florence.

Orla stared at her from the side. She was closer to Florence now than she had ever been in their apartment. The skin that ran from her ear to the corner of her mouth shimmered with such pearlescence that Orla could see her own shadow in it. Florence's eyes, dark and liquid, blinked slowly, sleepily, beneath the weight of her thousand-legger eyelashes. She had more hair than she did at home, and they were laughably bad, the extensions—limp, and shiny, and stinking of something chemical. Florence had on the same things Orla wore on formal occasions: a strapless, nude bra and stomach-slimming nude panties that continued down the thigh. But Florence wasn't wearing anything over them.

She was beautiful, the type of beautiful that made Orla wish that she knew more of Florence's bad qualities, so she could soothe herself by listing them out loud.

Then, suddenly, Florence was air-kissing the waif goodbye and stepping into Orla's little space. "Hi," Florence trilled. Orla startled at the sound of her public voice. It came from somewhere high in her nose. "Oh," Florence went on, "I love Lady-ish."

"Florence," Orla said.

"Call me Floss!" Florence giggled. She pulled all of her hair over one shoulder and stroked it like a pet.

They were at an impasse: Floss didn't recognize Orla, and Orla didn't know who Floss was supposed to be. As Orla tried to decide what to say next, Floss's publicist—she had a *publicist*!—jumped in.

"Jordie from Liberty PR," he said. "You of course know Floss Natuzzi from the reality competition *Who Wants to Work at a Surf Shack*." His voice had a defeated sort of hum, like he no longer got up in the morning hoping people would take him seriously. Orla could envision the half-finished law school application on his desk at home. "She's also a fixture on the Akron fashion scene," Jordie added, "where until recently she lived with Columbus Blue Jackets star Wynn Walters."

"The Athens fashion scene?" Orla said.

"Sure, let's go with that," Jordie sighed, at the same time Floss said loudly, "No, Akron. Akron, Ohio."

Jordie shot Floss a look, then laughed and threw his hands up. "Yes, Akron," he said wearily. "It's mostly, ah, underground. Very avant-garde. LeBron James…" He trailed off purposefully. It wasn't a lie; he had merely said the words "LeBron James." Orla nodded appreciatively. He would do well at law school.

She looked at Floss, who seemed not to be listening. She was peering down at the printout Orla was standing on, then back up at Orla's face. As Jordie tugged her toward the next reporter, Floss seemed to realize something. "Wait," she said, blinking, looking back. "Omigod."

Orla waved at her stupidly.

"Come inside, then," Floss called over her shoulder. "I want to talk to you." She tottered off on her heels. Orla watched as Jordie stepped forward to pull something off Floss's wrist. It was Orla's own yellow hair elastic. She had left it on the sink that morning.

"What, you know her?" Orla heard the waif say, sullenly. Out of some instinct, Orla didn't respond. Floss was only the last to arrive at a party for dog shirts in Midtown, but she was clearly someone to someone, and she had told Orla to come inside. Orla didn't have to talk to the waif anymore.

———

The girl at the door with the list was unimpressed. "I'm a personal guest of Floss Natuzzi's," Orla said again. "She'll be so upset to hear about this." The girl just looked behind her, waving someone forward. Orla stepped back to let an Afghan hound in a beret and its handler walk through.

She walked along Fifty-Seventh Street and found she could see into the event, which spilled into a courtyard fenced in by wrought iron. Floss was just a few yards away, talking to a short, sweaty man with his shirt buttons mostly undone.

Orla put her face to the bars and hissed into the party. "Floss!"

Floss looked up. She turned away from the man while he was still midsentence and came trotting over to Orla. "What are you doing? I said to come *inside*."

"They wouldn't let me," Orla said. "Can you get me in?"

Floss looked down at Orla's scuffed ballet flats and murmured, "Those, probably." She took a glass of champagne from a waitress and slid it through a gap in the fence to Orla.

"You can't—" the waitress began, and Floss fixed her with a cold smile. "Did they resolve the oyster situation yet?" she asked the waitress. "Would you please find Gus and find out? I'll wait here." The waitress scurried away.

"Who's Gus?" The champagne glass felt so delicate in Orla's grasp, she had to focus on not crushing it.

Floss rolled her eyes. "There's no Gus." She drained her champagne and motioned for Orla to drink hers down. "Wait there," she said.

Three minutes later, Floss was walking toward Orla, one arm in the air, hailing a cab. When one stopped, she stood there blinking at it until Orla stepped forward and opened the door, then stepped back to let her in first.

Jordie skidded out of the club toward their cab, the soles of his needle-nosed shoes slipping on the pavement. He stuck his head through the window. "Where the hell are you going?" he said to Floss. "Do you know how I had to beg to get you into this party? You're nobody, honey." A drop of sweat eased out of a crease in his forehead and landed on Floss's thigh, right where the nude shorts disappeared into the boot that stretched over her knee.

Floss dabbed at the mark. "If you had to beg that hard," she said calmly, "I guess you're nobody, too."

The light turned green. As the cab pulled away, Orla glanced over her shoulder at Jordie. She thought he'd be staring after them, reeling from the exchange, but he was already back on his phone, skating toward the party.

Perhaps it was because Orla remembered how he looked from that distance—freckles you could sense a block away—that she recognized Jordie's photo on the cover of the *New York Post*, more than a year later, while she was still walking toward it. She would never forget him. Nobody would. Jordie was the very first to die in the Spill. The story about his death didn't mention his working with Floss, which surprised Orla at first. By then, even a minor interaction with Floss would be the starriest thing that had ever happened to most people, and any reporter with a brain and a LinkedIn log-in could have dug up Jordie's connection. Then Orla remembered: the reporter who wrote about Jordie dying wouldn't have been able to see his LinkedIn page—wouldn't even have been able to google him. The reporter must have had to rely on word of mouth and yearbooks. Jordie's aunt was quoted as saying that he had just been accepted to law school. When Orla read that—her snarky prediction in print—she let out an actual howl, and crushed the paper in her hand. The newsstand attendant, who had been staring at the white grid on his useless, frozen phone screen, startled. "One dollar, you know?" he said to Orla. But he sounded scared, like he was only suggesting it. Orla dropped the paper and kept walking, kept crying. This was back when things had gotten as bad as everyone thought they would get, and when no one knew yet how bad things would actually go on to be. There were still jokes about the chaos on the late-night shows. There were still late-night shows.

———

When Orla and Floss got back to Twenty-First Street, the doorman grinned at them in a way that let Orla know they looked drunk, and the smile she gave back to him made her feel like she was someone else, someone used to being part of things. In the elevator, Orla reached for 6, but Floss batted her hand back and sent them to the roof. Orla hadn't been up on the roof since a few weeks after she moved to the city. She had gone up there one night with a book and a glass of warm white wine, because she was twenty-two and didn't know to chill it yet. The roof was a disappointment. There was nothing to see from the one bench rooted next to the cluster of air handlers. A neighboring, newer building stood in the way of the view. Orla had spent fifteen minutes rereading the same page before she gave up and went in, imagining the people whose windows faced the courtyard laughing at her over their dinners.

The one corner that escaped the adjacent building's shadow was reserved for residents of the penthouse. But Floss walked straight toward the gate to the penthouse's private patio and rattled it open. She stepped inside without looking back to see if Orla was following. She was.

The patio had a modest outdoor dining table and a row of hostas in wooden planters. Floss kicked at a red-and-yellow toddler car in her path, then reached into one of the planters and pulled out a bottle of whiskey. Above the top of the patio fence, the view stretched, uninterrupted, toward New Jersey. The sun was already gone, dragging the last of its light down over the Hudson. Orla sensed another glow behind her and turned to see, beyond a pair of sliding glass doors, a giant television flashing out the news. Opposite it, a man leaned back on his couch. His feet, in black socks, rested on the coffee table. Without smiling, he raised his glass to Orla.

"Jesus Christ," Orla hissed. "Floss, he sees us."

"It's okay." Floss took a sip of whiskey. "He lets me use the deck. It's just his crash pad anyway, 'cause he works here. He really lives in Delaware." She passed the bottle to Orla.

"But…" Orla looked at the toddler car, then back at the man in the penthouse. He was still watching them. "But it's weird."

Floss shrugged. "Whatever. He's, like, Ukrainian."

They drank and talked, but did more of the former than the latter, the conversation stalling constantly. Orla sensed that Floss wanted both of them drunker before she said what she wanted to say. Finally, as Orla answered Floss's demand to know who had lived in her bedroom before her—big-haired Jeannette, with the sportscaster ambitions, then shy Priya, with the endless visiting relatives—Floss cut her off to confess something.

"So, like, I know who you are," she said. "I mean, I know your name. I just didn't know that *you* were my *roommate*. To be honest, when we met that first day, I forgot your name as soon as you said it—you know how that happens? I decided it was Olga." Floss spread her hands, swinging the whiskey by the neck. "And here, all along, you were *Orla Cadden*. I know your work."

"My work?" Orla repeated. It seemed too grand a term for blogging.

Floss didn't hesitate. "Sage Sterling," she said. "Pretty sad, her dying and all."

"It was sad," Orla agreed. She actually, absurdly, did kind of miss Sage.

"You wrote about her one hundred and twenty-three times in the last year," Floss said, swiping her manicured finger over her phone. Orla could see her own name and headshot atop the list of headlines on the screen. "Here's the one where you listed what was in that salad the paparazzi always snapped her eating," Floss murmured. "I liked that."

"It was the best traffic anything on her ever did," Orla said. "Even better than when I wrote she died."

Floss waited for a siren to fade, then said: "Do you think you could do that—what you did for her—for me?"

"Um," Orla said. "I just called the salad place, and they told me what she got. It was just a standard Cobb with edamame, if you think about it."

"Not that." Floss took a swallow of whiskey and set the bottle on the edge of the roof. "The first time you wrote about Sage," she said, "she was just the daughter of some studio executive. She was nobody."

"Right, but then she started to act," Orla protested. "She got the *Some Like It Hot* remake pretty much right away—"

"No." Floss shook her head hard. A segment of her fake hair was starting to come loose, its sticky root sagging into view. "No, she did *not* get it right away. First she was in that photo, when all those models went to one of those dumb strip mall places where you drink and paint the same paintings. They Instagrammed it, and you did that post identifying everyone in the picture."

Orla had forgotten that that was how it started.

"That, just that, was enough to get her a publicist," Floss went on. "And the publicist got someone to send her those boots, the white leather ones with the rainbow laces. And she wore them, so the boot people sent the pictures to bloggers. You remember getting those pictures?"

Orla nodded. The post she had turned them into was headlined "Sage Sterling's Boots: Trippy Or Trippin'?" "I don't think we should say 'trippin'," Orla had protested to Ingrid, before she hit Publish. "I think that's like a black thing? And we shouldn't appropriate it? It might seem racist?" Ingrid had overruled her. "*You're* the one being racist, trust me," she had said.

"So then you did a post about her boot style, with photos of all the boots she'd ever worn." Floss smeared the gloss off her mouth with her palm and wiped it on the back of a cream-colored chair cushion. "You called her a boot icon. A couple months later, the boot people named a style after her, which you covered, which made the boots sell out. So some fashion line invited her to curate—" here, Floss raised her fingers and made air quotes that punctured the air so forcefully, Orla winced on its behalf "—a whole *line* of boots for them. That got her to Fashion Week. She was supposed to sit in the second row, but her publicist brought sheets of paper with her name printed on them and stole the seats of front-row girls who didn't show up. That was smart. I liked that move."

It had grown dark. A floodlight tacked up over the sliding doors went on. It was too bright for the small space, meant to shine over someone's endless suburban backyard. It might have made Orla homesick, if she wasn't busy wondering whether the Ukrainian man could now see up her skirt as she leaned over the rim of the building, into the night. She felt thirsty and picked up the whiskey, found it didn't help.

"You put her in a roundup of Fashion Week It Girls," Floss went on. "A reader asked you who she was, so you did a post with, like, facts about her. Remember?"

"9 INSANE Facts About Sage Sterling." Never ten facts—

readers hated the number ten. It was too perfect, too choreo-graphed. Suspect.

"And you found that old photo of her with the kid from that boy band, the one who's hot now," Floss went on.

"Yeah," Orla said. "I thought they dated in high school."

"Wasn't true," Floss said, "but it didn't matter. You wrote it, and then you corrected yourself, but someone had already put it in their Wikipedia pages. I bet you it's still there now. And the publicists were into it, so they went with it. They made them date." Floss hugged herself and shivered. It was August, warm enough to be out on a roof near the water, but not warm enough to do it in just shapewear. "And then you *really* wrote," she said.

Orla remembered. "Sage and Finn—Uh, We Mean SINN—Step Out Together for the First Time." "Every Sinn-gle Thing Sage Wore On Tour With Finn's New Band." "Sinn Has a Sexy Hawaiian Veterans Day—Pics, Right This Way!"

"And then, Jesus Christ," Floss said. "She got that haircut, the grandma haircut with the platinum and the curlers."

"Erm, Marilyn Monroe WHO? Come See Sage Sterling's New 'Do." Ingrid had added the "erm" after Orla left the of-fice for the day.

"*That's* when she got *Some Like It Hot*," Floss said bitterly. She pointed at Orla. "After you said she looked like Marilyn Mon-roe. She looked like a goddamn Golden Girl!"

Floss sounded so upset that Orla almost apologized. Instead, she reminded Floss that the movie was made by the studio Sage's dad ran, that she probably would have gotten the part even if he was the only one who knew who she was. "Besides," she added, feeling suddenly defensive of Sage, patron saint of her dispos-able income, "are you trying to tell me you're jealous? She got addicted to heroin and *died*."

Floss waved it away. "She got sloppy. I'm not like that."

Orla stared at her. She thought about going downstairs and into her room, about putting the flimsy fake wall between her and this strange, scheming girl. She thought about telling her super, Manny, about the weirdo in the penthouse, watching young women on his deck when he should have been home with his kid in Delaware.

"This is the part," Floss said patiently, "where you ask what's in it for you."

Orla shook her head. "What could possibly be in it for me?" she asked. "Also, no offense, but you're a little old to start trying to be famous. I mean, you're, what...?"

"I'm twenty-eight," Floss said. "Just like you, right?"

Orla straightened herself with what she hoped seemed like authority, with the air of someone who had put Sage Sterling on the map. "And you're just *now* getting into dog apparel parties," she said.

Floss smoothed her hair away from her face, flicked it over her shoulder. "At least I'm not working at them."

The line was cruel, but Floss made it sound like a joke they'd had for years. And that was what got Orla—Orla, who had told herself on the day she moved to New York that the hollow way she felt would subside once the cable got hooked up, and who had gone on feeling empty every day for six years.

She said, "What's in it for me?"

"If we do this right," Floss answered, "whatever you need. I'm sure you don't want to blog forever. I'm sure you have, what? A book? So you need an agent. If you help me, if I get as big as I think I can, they'll want to talk to you just because you're standing next to me."

Orla thought of her laptop sitting closed and cool, untouched in the dark of her room. She told herself that as soon as she finished this drink, she would go downstairs and write a thousand words without the TV on. "I don't need your help with my book," she said. "I can get an agent on my own."

Floss laughed. "Oh, really?" she said. "Are you sure? You better be sure. You better be sure that you're in, like, the top five writers in New York City, and that you know all the people they know, and that *those* people like you better, and that those people are the right ones to begin with. Because look, Orla." Floss placed her hands on either side of Orla's head and pointed it at the building next to theirs, the one that blocked the sky from the rest of the roof. "It's 10:45 on a Monday night, and everybody in that building has their lights on. You see? They're all still up. Just like we're still up. What do you think they're doing?" She aimed Orla's head, roughly, at another building beneath them, a low-rise in pinkish-gray brick. "More lights," she said. "How about them?"

Orla saw a girl in her sports bra bent over her computer, drumming her fingers on her chin.

"I've done the math," Floss said. "I've done the actual math. There are eight million people here, and all of them want something as bad as I want what I want, as bad as you want what you want. We're not all going to get it. It's just not possible, that all these people could have their dreams come true in the same time, same place. It's not enough to be talented. It's not enough to work hard. You need to be disciplined, and you need to be ruthless. You have to do anything, everything, and you need to forget about doing the *right* thing." She released Orla with a little shove and put her hands on her hips. "Leave that shit to people in the Midwest."

They were quiet as the atmosphere sucked up her monologue. Orla steadied herself and looked Floss over. She would never make it as an actress, she thought. She went a little too big, wanted a little too hard. But Floss, it seemed, didn't want to be an actress. She wanted to be what she already was, even if nobody knew it yet: a celebrity. A person, exaggerated. And her point—the cold slap of the eight million dreams around them—unhooked something in Orla.

"I don't know," she said, shakily, finally. "That kind of sounds like bullshit to me." She tried to hold back a burp and found that it wasn't a burp at all. She leaned over and threw up on the deck. The whiskey burned twice as hot coming back up. Orla kicked her purse toward Floss. "Can you get me a tissue?" she gasped.

Floss dug through Orla's bag. "Ohhhh," she breathed after a moment, tugging something out. "This looks familiar."

Panting, hands on her knees, Orla squinted up and saw Floss holding, between two egg-shaped nails, Marie Jacinto's cheap business card. The one Orla had found by the elevator. Orla would never forget that: Floss standing there, grinning at her, flicking the card. She would think of it on that awful last day, as blood bloomed through her shirt and Floss said in a low voice, for once trying not to be heard, that *this was the deal, and you know it.*

And they did have a deal by then, with lawyers and seals and duplicates, but Orla never felt that the scrawls she made numbly on those documents were as binding as her failure to argue with what Floss said next. Floss put the card back in Orla's bag carefully, like she wanted it to be safe. She pushed the kiddie car away from the puddle of vomit and walked Orla off of the roof, leaving the mess untouched and the gate wide open behind them. Inside, as they waited for the elevator, Floss grinned and put her face in Orla's hair. "I don't think it does sound like bullshit to you," she said into Orla's ear. "I think you are like me."

CHAPTER FOUR

Marlow

Constellation, California
2051

When Jacqueline's event had wrapped, Marlow told her car to take the long way home, hoping she could put off arriving until Ellis had gone to bed. The car obliged and turned onto Clooney Street, which wound lazily through Constellation. Marlow reclined her seat and lay on her side, watching her hometown float by. She was mistily struck, after two cocktails and a glimpse of how stupid-old she looked in a hair bow, by how different Constellation had seemed to her when she was young, when she didn't know what so much of it was. As a kid, she had seen trees draped with ruby-red leaves in the fall and pure white blooms in the spring. She had seen gentle green hills loping along the back of the town, jutting up into pale coral sunsets that were always on time and spectacular. But the sunsets, she later learned, were staged—lit, from below, by colossal rose-colored lamps in the ground, because the network liked continuity and could not rely on the weather. The hills she had sprawled on as a teenager, bikini'd, enjoying being the only kid in town whose mother let her tan—those were actually fortified shelters, for hiding talent in case of an attack. As for the trees: they turned out to be fake, and fireproof, their mineral wool trunks wrapped in vinyl laminate bark. (Constellation had been built, after all, on top of the scorched wreckage of a county-leveling wildfire.) The leaves and flowers Marlow so loved, she found out, would never have coexisted in one natural species, especially not in California. Their foliage was laser-cut from modacrylics and melamines. When they flooded with color, they did so at the push of a button, at the whim of the network.

But even with all that was choreographed for the cameras, Constellation still had more realness to it than its fans believed. Though Marlow knew people thought the opposite, her life wasn't technically scripted. There were writers, of course—they lived in the gray-block high-rises on the edge of town, buildings so ugly they seemed designed to remind the writers who they weren't—but they didn't decide what came out of Marlow's mouth. The writers were more like overbearing aunts, giving Marlow broad pep talks on how to be, weeding out her wardrobe. The network execs were both more mysterious and more direct. They lived among the talent, rotating and functioning as watchful extras—not long ago, Marlow had been startled to find the Head of Storyline himself behind the juice bar's counter, handing her her usual smoothie. They never spoke to the talent out loud, not with the audience watching, but they were constantly in Marlow's head, bossing her through her device. They let her choose things for herself, but they also closed off plenty of options. It was a little like being a mouse in a maze. She could run as fast as she wanted, but she wasn't picking the turns.

It took Marlow a long time to see that this was how she had come to marry Ellis. The network had nudged him into the path they knew she'd have to take, a lonely corridor she had been racing down since freshman year of high school, when Hysteryl started sponsoring her and the network began forcing kids to sit with her at lunch. Marlow knew her classmates' parents had threatened and cajoled them—*be nice to her or we'll get a fine, next semester you'll be back with your real friends*—and the kids always listened. They were always kind. But she could feel the resentment over their assigned seats rising like heat from their skin. No one had sat with her just because they wanted to since Grace. No one had been her friend out of choice since the night she became, as the network put it, "a good fit" for the Hysteryl campaign.

After graduation, everyone else in Marlow's class was issued their vocational arcs—outdoorsy chef, promiscuous nurse— and sent off for their year of training. But all Marlow got was a memo, telling her she was free to spend her days in any way that kept her happy. So she trailed her mother to the spa. She rearranged the furniture in her room and pretended that it meant she had a flair for interior design. She kept going to ballet class, even though every year the girls got younger and younger than her. Marlow never liked the actual dancing but loved posing in formation with the others. She loved the tiny *heh* of the shared breath they took just before they started moving, the synchronized *thunk* of their pointe shoes as they finished a combination. She would let herself imagine that these girls were really her friends, standing close to her on purpose. After class, she would pay attention as the other dancers rolled their tights up to their knees and talked about their classmates. Over time, she learned all the names, all the stories, every corner of an ecosystem she was not a part of. Sometimes, when she was out, she would recognize someone from the ballerinas' gossip, someone she had never met but felt like she knew so well, it was hard not to say hello. It was the first time she understood the way her followers must feel about her, and the line that came into her mind, as she gazed at these strangers, was always the same: *Oh, it's one of you. From my collection.*

Finally, Marlow turned twenty-one and was eligible for real romance. Twenty-one was the age at which the young talent's random dalliances with each other were replaced with dates staged by the network: amber-lit restaurant dinners of vibrant food that sat untouched, lest the sounds of chewing muddy the audio of the two stars at the table. The network sent Marlow matches each Friday morning, the smirk of a straight, single, network-approved man appearing in her thoughts over break-fast. *Would I like to meet him?* her device would prompt, and Marlow always said yes. Even though she never ate, Marlow always ordered dessert, just to prolong the experience of being in a place full of happy-looking couples her age. It felt nearly like having friends.

She met Ellis on one of those bad dates. Marlow couldn't remember, now, the face of the boy she had come to the bar with—this was fourteen years ago—but she remembered that her followers were not enthused by the way he blabbered on about his family's vineyard. She remembered that, when she let her mind wander and checked her dashboard, 61 percent of her audience thought that she should ditch him immediately.

Over her date's shoulder, she watched a knot of people orbit a tall, lanky boy with a shock of reddish-brown hair and a stubbled, strong jaw. He wore a T-shirt with tiny holes at the shoulder seams. Eventually, he pushed through a segment of the people around him and joined the line for the bathroom. His friends watched him go, holding their drinks against their chests. When he tossed a joke over his shoulder, they laughed in hearty unison. They held the space where he had been standing open, for when he came back.

"Excuse me," Marlow said, after watching this scene. She ducked under her date's arm. "I'm just going to the bathroom."

She went and stood behind the boy. His face was turned in

her direction, but she could tell he was lost in his device. She tried to think of something to say, a way to flare her eyes, that would make him see what he was already looking at. The song that was on in the bar, a woman sounding anxious over bitter guitar, flooded the space between them.

Before she could speak, Ellis snapped to. "I know you," he said. "I've got a poster of you on my wall." Then he went red, and she laughed. "My cubicle wall," he clarified. People loved this part of the story, and Marlow had once, too. Now when she looked back on it, she only thought: *Of course.*

Marlow always said she fell in love that very night—and she did, but not with him. It was the group Ellis drew her into when she followed him back from the bathroom. His hand on the small of her back, he guided her into the space his friends had saved for him. "Everyone, Marlow," he said. "Marlow, everyone." Everyone's faces turned warmly her way. Everyone's hands clasped hers without hesitation. One boy passed her a beer like it was a napkin, the essence of no big deal. The girls pulled their hair away from their faces and told her their names.

Ellis leaned through the driver's side window of her car and kissed her before she rode home, hugging her knees to her chest and giggling the whole way about her good fortune: she had met a new crush and all of his friends. As soon as she got home that night, slamming her door on her mother's questions, she plugged each and every one of them into the neighbors list on her map. Up their symbols popped, all around hers. It astonished her: they had been right there, all around her, these friendly people. And despite her past—despite her breakthrough moment, the thing they all must know she was known for—every one of them treated her like she was normal. Ellis Trieste standing next to her instantly undid years of shunning.

That night, as she lay on her bed, she researched him. She learned that his parents were on the board of the network. They were part of the original group of old-Hollywood producers who invented Constellation, who had moved quickly, in the twenty-twenties, to purchase the stretch of ash it would be built on. She learned that he was business-class talent, which meant he had a real job, not just a few tricks for making it look that way on camera. He was even approved for travel beyond Constellation's borders; he worked in marketing for a company outside town called Antidote Pharmaceutical, which—more research, propping her legs up on the headboard, jiggling one knee impatiently—happened to be a valued network ad partner. Beneath the stone-faced profile photo of Ellis that Marlow held in her head, scrutinizing each pore, was a tagline. *Ask me about Hysteryl.* The pill that kept her even, and kept her on the air.

What she told herself as they began to date was: So what? So what if her relationship had been dreamed up by people in a meeting? So what if some ambitious Antidote intern, having studied up on Marlow, had pointed out that she seemed lonely, that she would probably love to date someone who came with a group of friends? So what if some VP of something or other had nodded at the intern's suggestion, then turned to Ellis and said, "Trieste, you're single, aren't you?" So what if Ellis had nodded sagely, ever the company man, and answered, "Sure, I can run point on this."

So what if these things that she imagined were true? No matter how things had begun, Marlow decided then, she was glad to be with people. Happy to have friends, and proud to have won the unwinnable Ellis Trieste. He confessed to her, early on, that he was a "personality snob"—that his standards were probably too high, that he found most women too dramatic. The frame of reference he gave made it even sweeter, then, when he began to compliment her lack of feeling. He noted how cool she was, for a girl—how even-keeled, how unaffected. But for Marlow, it was no challenge, looking like she didn't care. Hysteryl kept her emotions like clothes in a neat dresser drawer: stored where they belonged, unfolded only when appropriate, and put back

54

with ease, in order. She was so pleased about earning the label of cool—her, the girl whose reputation could not, for so long, outrun one violent impulse—that she missed what a stupid thing it was, marrying someone to celebrate impressing him.

At their wedding, they were surrounded by the people from the bar the night they met. When the ushers went to seat their friends—bride's side, or groom's?—the friends all flapped their hands. They said it didn't matter; they said they loved them both. Marlow had never been so content.

Then the people went home, and the marriage began. Marlow realized she had been naive to think that they would see their friends as much afterward; they were all marrying, too, and Ellis began to grow tired of, as he called it, "the scene." Even when he withdrew, Marlow kept up with everyone. She played tennis with them, got massages and manicures with them, helped them plan brunches and showers and parties. She did her best to not be alone with her husband, because a frightening truth was beginning to peel itself back, like paint off a wall: she didn't like being married to Ellis. He was always on his device while she spoke, working on other things in his head as he stood there, pretending to listen to her. The only time he paid attention to what she was saying was when she talked about her medication—the thing they had in common, the thing he was keeping tabs on. There were small things she hated about him, too, and those were somehow worse, their symbolism metastasizing as the years passed. This one drove her insane, a permanent mental hangnail: he hid the snacks he liked best beneath their bed, so that he didn't have to share them with her. He would rather risk eating unrefrigerated cheese—cashew cheddar he stashed in the dark next to his snowboard—than let her have some, too. It all added up to an obvious correlation, one she had no business being surprised by: the man with the air of not-caring actually didn't care.

It went on like this for ten years. Sometimes Marlow thought—

from a detached, theoretical distance—about screaming or breaking a dish. But mostly she would call up her map with its crop of contacts, her busy social schedule for the week, and remind herself: *Small price to pay.* Sometimes she thought it so forcefully, her device mistook it for an intuition. *Small price to pay,* the soundless voice would repeat. *An English expression meaning: a minor sacrifice. Worth the trouble.*

The marriage had gone flat, and so had the content they made together. More than once, the network had chastised them for their long dinner silences, their heavy sighs side by side in bed. For Ellis, the matter was doubly serious. Like all network talent, he was obligated to be interesting. And as an Antidote employee, he felt pressure to make sure that his wife—the face of Hysteryl—looked content. But these days, Marlow made no attempt to look content with Ellis. She secretly hoped that her marriage would become so boring to viewers that the network would have to cancel it.

And now Ida, who was supposed to get this season's divorce plot, was gone.

Someone would have to take over that narrative—the network needed breakups. Ratings on the hetero ones were particularly good, especially with women in the flyover states, forty-five to sixty. The network lavished real budget on such arcs: if Marlow got one, she might even get to go on a trip, despite the no-travel stipulation in her contract. (It was too hard to control her environment beyond Constellation's borders, to ensure that nothing would dent her mood and, by extension, Hysteryl's reputation.) She could imagine the ending perfectly, could see herself giving Ellis a poignant goodbye, taking one last look around the home they had shared. She wouldn't sob or heave, the way her mother would in such a scene. She would stand straight and tall—with a fresh blowout, maybe. She would radiate class and faint optimism. Now, *that*, she bet, would make her feel thirty-five. She was ready for a new story.

One evening, not long after Jacqueline's scrunchie party, Marlow and Ellis sat on the couch in silence, watching different films in their heads. Suddenly, their devices perked in unison. Midseason assignments were in.

Divorce c'mon divorce, Marlow begged silently. *Divorce, with temporary relocation to Anguilla and personal fitness trainer. Male.*

She and Ellis sat forward on the sofa.

Congratulations! Marlow heard in her head. *We will be having a baby this season.*

Marlow broke the word down into syllables—*bay, bee*—and found she couldn't make sense of the term in this context, the context being her life.

Egg storage for female lead Marlow Clipp, aged thirty-five, has reached its expiration date. More details about our baby design process and sowing celebration will be forthcoming.

Bay. Bee.

Marlow tried to picture herself in a hospital bed, Ellis at her side, an infant being lowered onto her chest. She couldn't imagine them smiling at each other the way the parents always did in these scenes. All at once, Marlow got what this storyline meant. For the first time in her life on camera, she would have to act.

She looked at Ellis, to see how he was taking the news, and found him one step ahead of her. His eyes were wider than she had ever seen them, his smile unfamiliar, with too many teeth on display. He raised a hand and smacked his forehead theatrically.

He knew, Marlow thought. *He's not surprised.* And neither was she, when she thought about it. When she remembered the Liberty deal.

Six months earlier, Ellis had come home with a new account. He was overseeing his first merger, he told Marlow proudly. Antidote was acquiring Liberty Family Planning, the company that had long overseen Constellation's babymaking. Liberty was expanding across the country, and it was Ellis's job to up their profile on the network, to convince Constellation fans that they should have babies the same expensive way their favorite stars did. The process had three stages: egg reaping, baby design, egg replacement.

"Huge for me," Ellis had said that day, rapping a rhythm on the table. "Huge for us."

Marlow had opened some champagne, feeling conspicuously wifelike. As she poured their drinks, she thought of her own trip to Liberty. It was where she and every other teenage girl in Constellation had their eggs siphoned out of them at eighteen, to be frozen until the network green-lit their pregnancy arcs. "This will give you total freedom from your biological clock," Marlow could still hear the nurse saying. "Freedom to grow and achieve." (Lazy writer guidance, there, Marlow thought later—Liberty's actual motto was "Freedom to grow. Freedom to achieve. Freedom from your biological clock.") The network worked closely with Liberty to plan the births of their stars' babies—to prevent viewers from being torn between Jacqueline's second C-section and the bursting forth of Ida's twin boys, or to ensure that offspring could be quickly defrosted for couples the audience responded to.

Or for couples, Marlow thought, whom the audience had grown bored of. Whose stories were in dire need of a twist.

She got up and went into the master bathroom. Ellis followed her in, closing the door behind them. He seemed somewhere else entirely for a moment before he looked to her and grinned. "A baby!" he said. "Man, I can't wait to be a dad. I can't wait to tell the client."

He said those two things, Marlow thought, like they were perfectly related, and equal in weight. She heard herself laughing, heard the way the drugs in her bloodstream smoothed desperation out of the sound. Her laughter sounded joyful. Normal.

Ellis thought so, too. "Hold on!" he said, waving his hands. "Save it, Mar. This is your authentic reaction to becoming a mother. You've gotta share it with your followers." He opened the bathroom door and prodded her out, to where she could be seen.

———

Her followers were thrilled, of course. Followers loved babies.

The next day, Marlow and Ellis drove to the same blush-colored, circular building where Marlow's eggs had been harvested. Liberty's waiting room hadn't changed. The furniture was all cut from that frosted plastic that had been everywhere in her youth, the past's idea of future, all of it yellowing now.

"Have you decided on a gender?" the chipper nurse asked in the exam room. She handed them six genetic input kits, for each of them and their parents. They were to return them dirty, full of swabs and hair, so that the designers could begin sorting Marlow's and Ellis's gene pools, marking the things they wanted their child to have, striking the things they didn't. This was stage two: design.

"We don't know yet," Marlow said, at the same time Ellis said, "A boy."

The nurse smiled. "You don't have to be coy," she said to Marlow. "Exam rooms are off camera. There won't be any spoilers."

"I'm not," Marlow said, aiming her tone at her husband. "We aren't done discussing it."

Ellis held his tongue, for the moment.

"This is a special case, of course." The nurse flattened her hands on the desk, splaying her elbows as she looked at her tablet. "While Hysteryl is a miracle drug, it's still not safe for baby's development. So we'll be weaning you off, Marlow, a bit at a time, before we replace your eggs."

"She'll still be the face of the drug," Ellis broke in, as if this was the important thing, as if this mattered to the nurse. "She'll be on a short cleanse, yes, but her campaign will go on. We're testing some new ads that focus on the baby—like, what could be a happier ending for a troubled girl, growing up into a perfectly normal mother?"

Marlow watched the side of his face as he talked. His ears were red. He seemed so eager for the nurse's approval. "You didn't tell me that, honey," she murmured. "I had no idea that marketing had already met to decide my happy ending."

Ellis didn't turn to look at her. "See how she jokes?" he said to the nurse. "She's going to be fine."

The nurse nodded uneasily. "Right," she said. "Well, it's incredibly important—" the nurse trailed off, like she was listening to something come through her device, then nodded and squinted threateningly at Ellis "—that Marlow avoid stress completely during this time. Because she won't have her normal defense system in place."

That night, the housekeeping drone whirred into their bedroom and set only half a pill on Marlow's nightstand. Both of them looked at it. Ellis patted the blanket near where her leg was.

"Don't worry," he said. "You'll just have to be vigilant about self-care. All you have to do is stay happy."

———

A week later, Hysteryl was officially out of her system, the tiny dish beside her bed empty for the first time since she was fourteen.

"You're feeling good? Good girl," Ellis said, scrutinizing her over his coffee, when she came into the kitchen each morning.

And she was feeling good, at first. Then she began to feel strange, as if she was expanding, taking on new acreage too rapidly to keep up with her own topography. Feelings were returned to her like toys she hadn't seen since childhood, and she held them awkwardly, unsure of what to do with them as an adult.

Pettiness—at least, that was the best word she could think of for the sensation—came over her like hunger, several times a day.

Once, in the middle of taking a bath, she stood up and sloshed naked into her bedroom, tugged Ellis's snacks out from under the bed, and shoved every morsel down the garbage disposal. A few days later, she walked out of trivia night—a monthly outing with Ellis and their friends—after getting an answer wrong.

"What's the matter?" Ellis said, his voice deadly even, when he found her in the parking lot.

"I hate trivia," Marlow said. "I'm terrible at it."

Ellis ran his fingers slowly through his hair. He did this as often as he had when they met, though now he only had a third of the hair he had then. "You're terrible at it," he said, "because you're not cheating. Everyone else is, you know."

Marlow stared at him. "What do you mean?" she said. "Cheating how?"

Ellis held up his wrist. "We use our devices," he said. "We just ask them the questions, and whoever's fastest…"

Here it came, with a force disproportionate to the moment: her anger. She imagined it black and crinkling, peeking out from all the places Hysteryl had long hidden it—behind her pink organs, between the gray folds of her brain. The trivia master made it clear before every game: *No devices. Use the rest of your brain!* "Everyone's cheating?" Marlow repeated. "What's the fun in that?"

"The part where you win," Ellis said. "Come on," he added, somewhat sharply. "Don't be sad."

"I'm not *sad*." Marlow turned away from the window of the bar, so that her friends couldn't see her face, even if twelve million strangers could. "I'm pissed."

Ellis shrugged and dug into his jeans pocket. "Then why are you crying?" he said.

She took the tissue he handed her. She didn't know she was.

She went to Jacqueline's again, for a mud mask party, and found her lungs constricting in the middle of it, her brain suddenly rattling with the sensation that she had wasted too much of her life here, watching Jacqueline smearing on things. She backed quietly toward the front door, then out of it. On her way to her car, she stopped at the line of vintage lawn flamingos in Jacqueline's front yard.

"What is the *point* of you?" she hissed at them, glaring into their black button eyes. Her hand twitched at her side. She knew, if she gave in to the urge, what would be waiting for her when she woke up: a note from the network, idling in her mind, warning that *erratic behavior had been flagged on my feed*, that *commercial cutaway had been employed as a stopgap*, that *I should please restrict such behavior, in the future, to off-camera zones*.

She hauled off and slapped the plastic birds, every one of them, and felt savagely wronged when they didn't fall. Jacqueline had staked them in firmly, and so they only bobbed, beaks glinting in the haze of the illumidrones waiting in the sky for someone on the ground to need them. When an illumidrone sensed a person walking in the dark, it swooped down to light a path, looking, from a distance, like a shooting star in descent. When she was young, Marlow remembered, that was what she thought they were. Another pretty thing she had misjudged.

She toggled over to see what her followers were saying.

She's losing it again. Go bitch! Show them one-legged fuckers what's up!

What did those birds ever do to you Mar? LOL

NOOOOOOO NO ONE WANTS TO WATCH ANOTHER PILL AD—PUT THE MARLOW FLAMINGO SMACKDOWN BACK ON!!!!!

And:

What I don't get is how she's so unhinged over this pregnancy thing, like it's some big surprise. Course they were

gonna give her one, with Ellis on that deal or whatever and her being thirty-fucking-five. Saw this "twist" coming a mile away.

That was the thing about being the mouse in the maze, Marlow thought as the flamingos finished trembling, went still. She was the only one surprised by where she ended up.

CHAPTER FIVE

Orla

New York, New York
2015

Right from the start, it was suspiciously easy. At least, Orla should have been suspicious of how easy it was, two girls hijacking the public eye from the floor of their Chelsea rental. Her mistake was seeing the ease—the way things ribboned out in front of her and Floss—as a sign she was on the right path.

They started the way everyone did: they shared. Floss posted pictures online—of herself, her things, her food—constantly, as if she was someone whose meals became fascinating just by virtue of her being in front of them. Nobody ever said, as Orla worried they would, **With respect, what do you do for a living?** or **Who dis bitch?** Floss didn't even have a proper bio on any of her platforms, just a quote: "There is no security on this earth. There is only opportunity." She had attributed it to Britney Spears before Orla plugged it into Google and found that it had been said by General Douglas MacArthur.

One day, Floss prepared to post a Snapchat of herself explaining how to apply brow gel. "So fire," she rehearsed, as she ran the brush across her arches. "So fi-yah." A thought came to Orla, torn from the script of people more famous than Floss.

"You know what I think you should do at the end?" Orla said. "Say that you don't have a deal with them. The brow gel people. Say, like, 'I swear, they're not even paying me to say this.'"

"Why?" Floss jammed the wand back into its bottle and stretched her eyes in the mirror.

"Because then people will think that other brands *do* pay you," Orla said. "To talk about their stuff."

That was at seven thirty in the morning. As Floss mulled the idea, Orla showered, then went to work. She was at her desk when Floss posted the video, at 8:45 a.m. "I'm not getting any money for this, either, you guys," Floss sang dutifully. At 9:03 a.m., Orla sent the video to Ingrid, who popped her head out of her office thirty seconds later. Her lips were coral. Lady-ish had recently taken a firm stance on coral being the new red.

"Orla," Ingrid called, "why do I care this girl's doing her eyebrows?"

"It's Floss Natuzzi," Orla said. "She's big on Insta? Plus, you know that hundred-dollar brow gel, from that Korean beauty line that doesn't write anything on their packaging? It looks from the video like she might be one of the first stars here they sent it to."

It did look like that, because, just before stepping onto the elevator at home, Orla had run back to the apartment, scraped the lettering from an old Maybelline tube, and pressed it into Floss's hand.

"Fine," Ingrid said, and slid her door shut.

At 9:27 a.m., Orla published the post: "Sooo What Does The World's Most Expensive Brow Gel Actually Do? One Instagram It Girl Finds Out." Then she cupped her phone in her hands and swiped to Floss's Twitter account. As Floss, Orla tweeted the link to the post, tagging Lady-ish. She waited.

Two minutes later, Orla got an email from Ingrid: **Floss tweeted our post! What a SWEETHEART. RT from Lady-ish, pls.** That was the thing about Ingrid: every semifamous person disgusted her right up until the second they threw her a bone.

Orla used her computer to log into the Lady-ish account and retweeted the missive she had written as Floss. She quickly silenced her phone, muffling the incoming notifications of Floss's new followers. It was 9:30 on the nose.

That night, when Orla got home, Floss was waiting for her at the door. So was a crate of cream-flavored vodka, a pallet of whispery diet chips, and a dozen forty-dollar lipsticks, arranged like chocolates inside a black box.

"This one came by messenger," Floss said. "And he asked me for a selfie."

The more she tweeted, the less they spent. Orla found herself living almost entirely off Floss's loot. Their apartment filled up with the sort of things Orla never would have chosen for herself—gluten-free freezer meals with a pop star's face on the box, shoes downy with calf hair, purses pimpled with ostrich flesh—but she ate them and wore them eagerly, because they were free and they were proof: she and Floss were succeeding. The doorman never grinned at them anymore; "Package," he said wearily, over and over, rising from his stool when he saw one of them coming. Orla sometimes slipped him bags of free cookies or chips, removing the hopeful notes from entry-level PR girls. Almost invariably, the girls were named Alyssa.

Orla didn't have time, most nights, to work on writing her book. As soon as she walked in the door, Floss would hand her a bowl of Apple Jacks for dinner. They would sit cross-legged on the parquet, a laptop between them, and work. Before long, Floss would be begged to attend all sorts of events, dozens a week—but in the meantime, she had found a way to hack into several publicists' email accounts, to keep track of what invites were going around. She forwarded the invites to an address she made up for her imaginary publicist, Pat White. "Gender-neutral and forgettable," she said of the name. As Pat, Orla RSVP'd Floss to events she hadn't been asked to, saying she would be there, plus one. Floss made Orla swear she'd never tell anyone about the scheme. "I could get in trouble," she said. But Orla knew that wasn't it. Hacking required intelligence, and intelligence was off-brand.

Orla was in charge of writing about Floss on Lady-ish, and of breaking down the shipping cardboard the free things came in, and of maintaining Floss's Twitter account. She changed the password on it twice weekly, dutifully jumbling numbers and letters with asterisks and exclamation points. Of course, even as she concocted them, the passwords were already useless. It would almost make her laugh, later, after the Spill, remembering how she labored over those combinations. They all thought special characters would save them.

One day, Orla got Floss to trend worldwide by lashing out at a snack company's corporate account. The operative behind it had called a recipe for bruschetta made with its wheat crisps "an Italian wonder on par with the Sistine Chapel." As Floss, Orla bombarded them with claims that the comparison offended her on behalf of Italians and Italian Americans, a "group that continues to be underestimated in culture"—even though Floss was only one-eighth Sicilian, half-Latina, and a few other things she claimed not to recall. The whole time her online ego was battling crackers, Floss herself was at the gym, doing arm day with a famous trainer who was very expensive, if one wasn't sleeping with him. Orla didn't even run the stunt by her. Floss's identity had become a thing they shared respectfully, like the skim milk in the fridge.

As Orla sat at her desk at Lady-ish, stabbing out a call to boycott the snack company from Floss's handle, Ingrid instant-messaged her: **Did you see Floss going APESHIT about racist crackers? THREAD**, she wrote, linking Orla to Orla's own handiwork. **Go ahead and post. Dude, you practically invented her.**

Orla thought, *You have no idea.* She was electric with adrenaline. All these years in the city, she had been telling herself, in the bathroom mirror, that she was a modern woman, chasing modern goals. But sometimes, as her subway car went through the tunnel, she'd catch a glimpse of herself in its smudged glass window, and see herself the way the world did: another girl with a dream and a hemline set precisely knee-high, low enough that no catcaller should notice it, that no coworker should factor it into her credibility. There, on the darkest part of the ride, as the train nearly kissed the one running parallel, Orla often caught her breath at how dispensable she looked.

But now, with nothing but her job and her phone and her instincts, she had claimed a minor superpower: she had made someone famous just by saying it was so.

Better yet: she had made herself a friend. When they got ready to go out, Floss shouted from down the hall, over their deafening playlists, "What are we wearing tonight? I hate all my clothes!" When they ordered Chinese food, Floss let Orla have both fortune cookies. Floss thought they were bullshit, that her fate was hers to shape—plus, she didn't do carbs. But Orla still thought it was generous. Not wanting something didn't make it easy to give it away.

She would get back to writing her book soon, but for now she was busy being important, busy not being lonely. The change she had yearned for was dawning around her. She was waiting for just one more thing.

Danny.

———

One morning, as Floss and Orla napped off hangovers, the doorman rang the white phone on their wall. Orla picked herself up off the sofa and got it. "Be right down," she mumbled automatically.

"No deliveries, Miss Orla. It's Sunday," he said. "Your mother and father are here, okay?"

"Okay," Orla said. She hung up, and flew across the floor to Floss, who was curled on the love seat, one breast easing free of her black satin nightie. Orla squatted down. "Hey, my parents are here. Can you…?"

"Your parents?" Floss was awake immediately, gathering herself, making a break for her room. "Why?" she said harshly, over her shoulder.

Orla flushed with anger—not at her roommate, but at her parents, for puncturing their world. Orla was steering the tides of celebrity; she didn't need her mother to bring her Tupperwares of plain grilled chicken breasts, which Gayle would unbag while saying, "You need your protein, and I know you won't go to the trouble yourself."

Orla opened the door. Gayle and Jerry snapped their heads toward her as if she'd startled them, two pairs of eyebrows clutching toward each other with concern. This was how her parents had been greeting her since the days of them meeting her at the school bus: like they had spent all day discussing her worrisome behavior.

"Surprise!" her father said, grabbing Orla by the shoulders and kneading them.

"Hel-lo," her mother murmured, in her strangely formal way, reaching around Orla not so much to hug her but to lightly tap the base of her neck. She was wearing a hunter green long-sleeved shirt and an aggressively plaid vest. Orla's father wore beaten khakis, the black sneakers he passed off as dress shoes, and an old suit shirt with a drooping collar. When his dress shirts wore out, instead of getting rid of them, Jerry demoted them to casualwear.

"You should have seen us getting down here," Gayle sighed, smoothing back her dyed-cranberry bangs. "We sure stuck out."

"You mean because it's eighty degrees out?" Orla said, eyeing the vest. But she knew what Gayle meant. Orla came from Mifflin, Pennsylvania, a town smack between New York and Philadelphia—growing up, she had gone to the zoos in both cities on field trips. Mifflin had been nothing but fields strung together by farms until the 1980s, when families like Orla's descended, slapping up vinyl siding everywhere. Their neighborhood had sidewalks and young trees and a superfluous name, embossed on a concrete block at the turn-in: Hidden Ponds. (The one semiboyfriend Orla had ever brought home from the city had stood in her driveway, looking at all the short grass and macadam, and said, "They hid those ponds pretty well.") Still, Orla's parents pretended they had nothing to do with suburban sprawl. They did imitations of people who worked the earth. Gayle stomped around in rain boots all year and wore clothes she ordered from a catalog that had a mallard on the front. Her father puttered and fussed over their half-acre lawn and four tomato plants as if it was his job. "Frost tonight," Orla could recall Jerry, a CPA, saying wistfully throughout her childhood, as if they might not eat. Gayle would call Orla in from the yard for dinner by ringing a large bell she had nailed to a beam near the back door. "6:00 p.m., supper's on!" she'd shout. The kids in the adjacent yards would freeze, kickballs in hand, and blink at Orla. "Why does she do that?" one of them asked Orla once as they tugged at a tangle of Barbies. "So I know what time it is," Orla said. The girl pointed at the CoreStates Bank on the other side of the cypresses at the back of the development. The bank's tall sign blinked 6:01 at them in red. "The rest of us just use that," she said.

After depositing the chicken breasts in Orla's fridge, Gayle looked around the apartment, surveying the flattened boxes piled at the door. "What's all this?" she said.

Orla handed each of them a glass of water. Her dad pulled out his hankie, dipped it in, and wiped his balding head. "I don't know," Orla said. "They're my roommate's." In her room, Floss was soundless, not even her phone daring to chime.

Gayle lifted the flap on one of the boxes, trying to read the label.

"Mom," Orla hissed. "I said they're not mine."

"Just checking," Gayle said. "If you had a shopping addiction, you'd tell us, wouldn't you?"

"Yes, Mom," Orla said.

"Because you remember the year Aunt Diane gave us all those strange gifts? Your dad got the turkey fryer?"

"I liked that," Jerry said tonelessly.

"And you got those black pearl earrings," Gayle said severely to Orla, "but they *weren't* real pearls."

"I don't have a shopping addiction, Mom." Orla began the strenuous mental exercise of trying to come up with a restaurant that was inexpensive, close enough to walk to, and stocked with normal bread baskets, not focaccia or olive loaf or anything that might make her mother say, derisively, "Ooh la la."

"Because it's in our blood. That's all I'm saying." Gayle sniffed.

————

Ten minutes later: "Ooh la la," Gayle said as the waitress set down the bread basket.

Orla sighed. "But it's just rolls."

Gayle pointed at the dish next to the basket, which, instead of wrapped pats of butter, held a pool of oil and herbs for dipping.

"How's the job?" Jerry said to Orla. "Working on anything interesting?" Jerry had no idea what Orla wrote about, and they both preferred it that way. He could keep telling his coworkers that Orla was "a culture writer" if he didn't see things like "How to Copy This Socialite Goddess's Distressed Booty Jean Shorts in Just 13 Steps."

Gayle, who liked to share Orla's posts on Facebook, flapped her napkin at him. "Jerry, that's girl stuff," she said, like Orla's job was a box of tampons. "She doesn't want to talk about that with you." Gayle pinched a piece of bread between her thumb and forefinger. "Anyway," she said. "Guess who I saw the other day? Catherine. And Danny."

Orla's heart tripped. She made a show of chewing for a moment, then, when she trusted her voice to come out right, said: "And how are they?"

"To be honest with you," Gayle said, "they seemed extremely unhappy."

Orla could feel the blotches starting up her chest. She prayed Gayle wouldn't notice. She could never be sure, then or now, how much her mother knew about then. Or now. "What do you mean?" she said. "How could you tell?"

Before Gayle could answer, Jerry knocked his fork off the table with his elbow and looked at Gayle helplessly. Instead of signaling for the waiter, Gayle got up, approached the wait station, and retrieved a new set of silverware. "Well," she said, unwrapping the utensils for Jerry, "they made quite a scene at Chick-fil-A. Maybe it'd be nothing in these parts." She looked pointedly at two men holding hands across the corner table. "They were fighting, and she..."

"She what?" Orla jumped in, forgetting to act like she didn't care.

"She was screaming," Gayle said. "At the top of her lungs."

"*Catherine* was screaming?" Orla pictured Catherine, with her slicked-back soccer-girl braid, always pulling at Orla's arm as soon as they got to a party, whimpering *Let's go, I know the cops are gonna come.*

"Evidently," Gayle said, "she wanted Danny to pray with her over their meals. And he wouldn't."

Jerry swallowed and laughed to himself without looking up.

Orla had noticed a religious tinge to Catherine's online presence, the last time she browsed. This was the term Orla clung to—*browse* had a light touch, a whiff of the happenstance—as she bored through everything she could find on Danny, sucking her ice cream spoon in the light of her laptop. She recalled an Instagram photo of a sunset, shot from Danny and Catherine's backyard, just a few miles from her parents' house, and the photo's caption: **When something beautiful happens and you just can't help but thank Him. #nofilter.**

Gayle watched Orla carefully as she said: "When he got her calmed down, she said, 'This is why I can't be with you anymore.'"

Orla's fingers itched. She needed to get rid of them, get back to the apartment, get online. Since she and Floss began working together, she had been spending fewer nights looking up Danny. But it didn't really matter how much time she spent clicking around his life, how many times she entered his name into a search box or how many days she managed not to. She was always waiting, still.

Jerry shook the empty little cylinder and called out, "Salt?" The waitress came over to refill it and got trapped in Gayle's signature rant on allergies (she did not have any; she just wanted to establish that she thought people invented them these days. People needed to toughen up about peanuts and gluten, that was all). The waitress looked to Orla for aid, but Orla was glad for the distraction. She let the letters on the menu blur in front of her and thought about Danny, the last time she ever spoke to him.

———

They were at a party, the night before high school graduation. The party was at the home of a kid named Ian, whose parents were never there. Neither, usually, were Orla and Catherine. Gayle and Jerry never had to police Orla's whereabouts; her best friend was frightened of everything. But they were graduating, Orla insisted to Catherine, and they wouldn't want to look back and remember that they had spent the last night of high school making Cheez Whiz nachos and rewatching *Austin Powers*. "We'll bring Danny," Orla added, feeling bold. "Danny won't let anything happen." Finally, Catherine gave in.

Danny drove them. Catherine slid into the front seat, and he leaned over to kiss her on the cheek. He made sure her seat belt was clicked in right. Orla watched from her place in the back— behind Catherine, where she could see him.

It was simple: Orla had always loved him. She had loved him since the first day of ninth grade, when she and Catherine, allies from middle school, sat next to each other in English. Danny sat in a desk on the other side of the room. His arms were pale and muscled, folded across a wordless gray T-shirt on a day everyone else had picked their clothes like their lives depended on them. When he twisted around to look, at the teacher's urging, at a how-to chart on bibliographies, his dark blue eyes locked on Orla's pale brown ones, and that was what she would always remember: the way he was willing to stare, when so many boys nearly wet themselves from eye contact. Orla looked at him, and he looked back at her, and she wished the teacher would never shut up about how to cite sources.

Afterward, Catherine turned to Orla in the hallway, red as an angry infant, and said, "Did you see him?"

And Orla said, "I know."

They were talking quietly, because he was behind them, all of them shuffling toward next period, struggling to hold the map of the school in their heads. Catherine turned quickly, as if she needed to do it before she lost her courage. Her braid grazed Orla's face, a quick, bristling lash. "Hi," Catherine said to Danny. "Do you know which way Upper B is?" Danny glanced once at Orla, then nodded and started speaking to Catherine. Simple again: Danny and Catherine started dating that weekend, and never stopped.

Orla could have raged or cried or sabotaged them, but she was strangely content to orbit them instead. For four years, she joined Danny and Catherine for movies and camping trips and felt only shallow pangs when they went into one tent, and she went into the other. She dated plenty of his friends, was always happy to take on another for the pleasure of Danny leaning against her locker, grinning, his hand on her shoulder as he joked, "Be nice to this one." They spent high school in the same carpeted basements and starry parking lots, under the arms of different people. And as Danny and Catherine synced up their applications to state schools, Orla never tried a thing, never made an advance, never confessed. She was already writing him into the story of her life later on. She had it all planned: she was going to be a New Yorker, an author with chic glasses and a grip on what to do with her disorderly hair. At seventeen, she went to bed dreaming not of going to prom with Danny, but of him knocking on the door of her brownstone. She bundled him together with success and self-confidence—things from the future—and her ability to wait for them made her feel brave and pure and wise, like a monk. Catherine often told the story of how she and Danny met. "He stared at me all through freshman English on the first day of school," she would say, turning to her best friend for backup. "Ask Orla. She was there." Orla would nod and murmur, "It's true. I was there." But the truth, the smooth and immutable fact that propelled her through each day, was that Danny's gaze had been on her first.

At Ian's pre-graduation party, Catherine gulped Mad Dog too fast from a jelly jar with *Lion King* characters on it. Danny and Orla put her to sleep in the only untrashed room of the house, atop Ian's parents' plain navy quilt. Danny sandwiched Catherine between pillows, propping her on her side in case she threw up. When they got back downstairs, the other kids had all passed out or gone home, abandoning the strobe light that sat blinking on a card table. Orla was starving. Danny suggested they go back into town, to Wawa, for hoagies.

When they left the store, bags swinging, Orla thought they would head right back to watch Catherine, but Danny felt like a drive. Orla, sitting in the front seat for once, touched the gear-shift and said, "I wish I could drive stick." She wished no such thing; she couldn't have cared less. But she was always on the lookout for ways to seem interesting.

Without taking his eyes off the road, Danny had covered her hand with his and left it there as he guided the car through its powers. Orla hadn't said a thing, hadn't moved, hadn't breathed. He was driving too fast, she thought, drifting too close to the yellow line, getting careless on hairpin curves. She had never felt safer in her life.

When they got back, they sat on Ian's porch, eating and talking. Orla had given Danny a book a few weeks earlier, a whiny teenage manifesto she took as gospel at the time. "I loved it," he said. "I tried to get Catherine to read it, but I don't think she got it." He looked out past the porch rail as if there were a great vista in front of them, though the house across from Ian's was only thirty feet out. A string of Christmas lights, half-burned-out, still drooped from its eaves. "It'll be our thing," Danny said.

Inside, they found Catherine sleeping deeply. Danny felt for her breath with his hand, then crawled into bed beside her. Orla collapsed on the floor, and Danny pulled the pillow from beneath his neck and tossed it down. "Are you gonna remember us, Orla?" he said quietly.

Orla's heart pounded in her throat as she wondered, briefly, if she had done it all wrong, being brave and pure and wise, if she should withdraw from her fancy mountainside college, or beg him to come along. Like the seventeen-year-old girl she was, she believed him full of potential that was invisible to everyone but her.

"Who's us?" she said finally.

Danny was half-asleep when he answered. "All of us," he said. "You know, you're gonna be somewhere else, you'll be this writer, and..." He paused, gave a long moan of a yawn. "I'll be like, 'I know her.'"

The next morning, after the principal and class president were finished, Orla had to give a speech. She had served as class vice president after running unopposed, at Gayle's insistence, for the sake of her college applications. Onstage with her speech, a single-spaced printout of metaphors that didn't quite land, Orla spoke slowly, hoping Danny and Catherine might show up by the end. But their seats were still empty when she finished.

A few hours after graduation, the phone rang at Orla's house. It was Catherine. Though both girls had cell phones by then, they still called each other's homes, a habit both formal and intimate, proud proof of their long friendship. Catherine was shaky with guilt. She had been sick from drinking all morning, she said. Then she had gone to the car wash with Danny, to wait with him while he had his car detailed. She had vomited, on the way home from Ian's, all over the passenger seat.

"Was I awful?" Catherine said. "At the party?"

"Not *awful*," Orla said. She drew the word out carefully, as if Catherine had really embarrassed herself and Orla was sparing her the truth.

"I feel terrible I missed your speech." Catherine's voice was gaspy in the receiver, the way it got when she was headed for a cry. "Are we okay?"

"Sure," Orla said. Nothing else. She listened to Catherine's trembling sighs on the other end, the sound of her waiting for Orla to comfort her. But all she could think of was Catherine puking in Danny's car, on the seat that had been hers in the middle of the night. She tucked the receiver under her chin and stayed stingily silent.

When Orla hung up, she saw Gayle in her bedroom doorway, holding the lidded plastic tub that would live under Orla's bed at Lehigh. "You have so much going for you, Orla," Gayle said. "Let Catherine have what Catherine has."

Summer drifted past, and Orla made excuses not to see Catherine. They said shallow precollege goodbyes over the phone. Orla hadn't lied, when Catherine asked; they were okay. She wasn't angry. She just didn't see the point of staying close. Her feelings for Danny had been validated—*I'll be like, I know her.* He wanted to see how she was going to turn out. No matter where the story went from here, Orla thought, Catherine was destined to be a footnote.

College became the place she started watching him, because college was the place she started being alone. For no reason Orla could see, the girls on her freshman-year dorm floor looked around her as if by agreement. Her roommate mumbled something about a sleeping problem and transferred elsewhere in October, just weeks after she and Orla had agreed, with the rusty manners of two girls who have always had their own rooms, where to put the posters and the minifridge. After the roommate's furniture was removed, Orla vowed each day to plant her feet in front of one of her hallmates and say, "I have a single now, you know, if you guys want to drink in my room tonight." But— perhaps because they mostly saw each other while wearing only towels—she never found the bravery.

By the time fall break began, the borders of cliques were bonded and set. Orla could hear groups of friends moving outside the door she no longer kept propped hopefully open, as her orientation counselor had advised. She heard them going to breakfast late without her, going to dinner early without her, going to parties loudly without her. Her aloneness was so random, so total and unprovoked, that she almost thought someone from the school would come along to smooth it out, the way they might a housing mix-up, or a schedule snafu. Just before winter break, she tried to join a sorority, walking into an information session to find two hundred girls in the nearly same black pointed boots, ink-blue jeans, and tartan scarves. Only one other girl in the room was not wearing some version of this look: a girl from

India whom Orla recognized from her discrete math class. An eager blonde who had been talking to the Indian girl, enunciating loudly, turned to Orla when she sat down. She assessed Orla's Lehigh hoodie and sky blue denim, the plastic claw in her hair. "And what country are you from?" the blonde said loudly.

By spring, Orla was leaning into isolation. She sold her meal plan on the student exchange website and took to eating buffalo wings in her room. She worked her way through *Sex and the City* on DVD. She wrote: short stories, song lyrics, never-ending screenplays. And, as more and more ways to do it were invented, she kept up with Danny. She would write for four minutes, then refresh Danny's Myspace. She would falter on a passage, then toggle over to stare at his screen name on her Instant Messenger buddy list, watching the letters go from black to gray when he found something better to do.

The semesters turned into the next ones, and nothing changed. Once, Orla saw the Indian girl from the sorority meeting in the student union. She walked toward the girl, an opener gathering itself in her mind—*Remember that night, how crazy was that, like was there a Burberry memo we missed?* But as she got closer, a harried redhead ran up and punched the arm of the Indian girl. They found a table and unzipped their jackets. Orla saw that the Indian girl had on the right scarf, the right jeans and boots. And a crew-necked sweatshirt with Greek letters, denoting Alpha Phi.

When she went home on breaks, Orla would sometimes glance up at the ring of her parents' landline. But, after a school year's worth of silence, Catherine had started to text her. She would send Orla canned messages on holidays—happy this or that, and hi to your parents—and each girl would ask how the other had been. What could really be said that way? Twice, Orla snuffed out an exchange by saying, with a smiley, "Nothing new to report!" Facebook had not yet reached Catherine's lower-tier state school, but Orla didn't need it; she could picture how well her friend had moved on. She imagined Catherine's soccer teammates with tight stomachs and clean faces, fussing over Danny the first time he came to visit. She imagined them teasing Catherine about being a lightweight, and putting her gently to bed when she proved them right. There was only one thing she really wondered about her old friend: how long she and Danny would be together.

She got the answer she wanted a few weeks after college graduation. Orla moved straight back to Mifflin, to make good on a deal she had struck with her parents: she would live at home and work locally for one year, to save money before moving to New York. She had secured a job covering town council meetings for the newspaper that fell on Mifflin's doorsteps.

One night, a week before she was due to start at the paper, Orla ran into Catherine while picking up takeout at TGI Fridays. (Jerry was fond of saying that the chain's Jack Daniel's chicken was the best dinner on earth, that "you"—who "you" was had never quite been defined—"can keep your Michelin-star joints.") When their eyes met, Orla was holding her father's credit card, and Catherine was holding a drink with a flashing scrotum plunged into the ice.

"It's my bachelorette party!" she crowed, grabbing Orla's elbow to anchor herself. "Danny and I are getting married next month." Her eyes widened and she dug her fingers into Orla's arm. "Stay!" she pleaded. "Hang out." Orla phoned home, hoping for an out, but Gayle joyfully insisted that Orla forget about bringing home the food and enjoy herself.

Catherine's soccer friends—there were three of them—looked exactly as Orla had envisioned. They were bright and healthy, sculpted muscle covered in skin that was somehow tanned and freckled at once. They all had hair that looked like it was only worn down on special nights like this—too long, too limp, and vaguely damp-seeming, but somehow on the whole not unappealing. Catherine fit with them perfectly, Orla thought, though it was her old friend who, for once, had a good haircut. Catherine's braid was gone, replaced by a pretty bob, the golden ends of which twisted into her mouth as she spoke.

"This is Orla," Catherine said, and Orla didn't miss what happened next. The friends' eyes narrowed at the mention of her name. They looked at each other. They straightened. It was obvious: they had heard, at an earlier time, a memorable explanation of who she was.

Orla took her penis straw. She endured the torrent of inside jokes. She was careful not to let anyone catch her looking at the clock. Catherine more or less ignored her for the rest of the night, until it finally ended and the bossiest of the soccer girls jingled her keys. "Okay," she said to Catherine, taking the drink right out of her hand. "Let's get you home."

Catherine shook her head. "It's out of your way," she said. "Orla will take me."

Orla had her car from high school—the boxy, cat-eyed Taurus. She watched as Catherine popped open the glove compartment, an automatic reflex, and pulled out the little book of Orla's old burned CDs. "The one with the Incubus," she slurred, rifling.

"I forgot those were in there," Orla said. She was surprised to find herself suddenly on the edge of tears, and grateful that Catherine seemed too drunk to notice, her index finger swaying as she pointed out the turns.

The house was a small brick Cape with white metal awnings over the windows and a black horse and buggy embedded in the screen door. "Wait here a minute," Catherine said. She got out of the car and stomped toward the house, missing every bluestone paver in the path. Mulch splintered upward as her heels sank into the earth. The concrete stoop's metal railing wobbled as she gripped it.

He's in there, Orla was thinking, her eyes on the front window. *Danny is in there.*

And then she saw him, rising from the couch opposite the

window to answer Catherine's knocks. He rubbed his eyes as he ambled across the room. The light was behind him; all Orla saw was his outline, the shadows of his features. He opened the door and looked out through the screen, but Catherine prodded him back as she pushed inside the house and pulled the door shut behind her. Orla gripped the wheel. Was she still supposed to wait?

A minute later, Catherine reappeared. She stumbled back toward the car. In her hand was an envelope, rimmed in black-and-white damask. She got back in the car and thrust it at Orla. Orla clicked on the overhead light and disassembled it quickly. The card she pulled out began: "Together with our families, Daniel and Catherine…"

"Oh," she said. "Catherine, that's— You don't have to." She tilted the wedding invitation. Even in the dim light, she could see that the words were slightly askew, cocked toward the top right corner of the card. Catherine must have printed these herself. The lump in Orla's throat grew, and she realized suddenly why it was there: she did not want to go to this wedding, she did not intend to go to this wedding. But the gesture overwhelmed her; she had been so cruel, and Catherine was being so nice to her. At least, that was what she thought until Catherine started speaking again. Her voice was suddenly so intense, so oddly charged, that Orla looked up, as startled as if she had screamed.

"You were at the bachelorette party," Catherine said, "so it's only *proper* you're invited." Orla watched as she opened the glove compartment again and began to rummage through it. After a moment, she found what she was looking for—a pen—and handed it to Orla point first, stabbing the small glinting end at her palm. She nodded at the invitation. "Just pick your entrée now," she said. "Save you the stamp."

Orla swallowed and looked toward the house. The couch was vacant now, the room surrounding it dark.

"He's not coming out," Catherine said. She lifted her arm to the edge of the car door and rested it there, where the window was all the way down. She dragged her nails back and forth on the vinyl. She smiled at Orla—a knowing smile. "He's not coming out to see you."

The lump in Orla's throat dried up, chased away by a settling calm. She felt the same way she did when she sat down to an exam she was well prepared for. Whatever theory Catherine had, right or wrong, was just that: a theory, lacking evidence. Orla had been so careful not to create any evidence, and she was not going to stammer.

She looked at Catherine. "Of course he's not," she said evenly. "It's late." She looked down at the invitation and scratched her finger over the date. "I'm not sure I can make it, actually."

Catherine cut her off with a laugh. She clapped a hand to her mouth, like she hadn't meant to let the sound out, then dropped it and giggled again. "But where would you be?" she said. "I know you always *thought* you'd be somewhere else, but you're here. You're around." She grabbed the card back, then the pen. She clicked its point in and out, in and out. "Chicken or steak, Orla?"

"I'll have to check the date," Orla said.

Catherine snorted. She made a violent X next to the steak option. She got out and slammed the door, leaned down near the open window. "I'm glad you're coming, Orla," she said. "I think it's important you be there to see this."

But Orla wasn't there to see it. The Monday after she ran into Catherine, she emailed the newspaper editor who was meant to be her boss. Something had come up, she explained. Something undeniable. Gayle was apoplectic about Orla reneging on the offer; she left the editor her own rambling voice mail, spelling her full name and saying that she had raised her daughter better than this.

A week later, Orla agreed to sublet a room that didn't exist yet from a girl named Jeannette in Chelsea. Jeannette explained it over and over: the place was a one-bedroom, and she'd wanted to live there alone, but she found she couldn't afford it and needed someone else to chip in. Did Orla understand—she would have to put up a wall in the living room to box off some space for herself. Orla said she got it, she didn't mind, and yes, she understood: the cost of the wall was hers to bear.

On the morning of Catherine and Danny's wedding, Orla and Jerry set out in a U-Haul for Manhattan. Orla waited to call the bride until the skyline was close enough to touch, mirror gray on her right as the rented truck rumbled toward Jersey City. She told Catherine the same thing she told her parents: she'd gotten a job at a website. Soon enough it would be true— within months, she would find the job that would turn into the job that turned into Lady-ish. But just at that moment, it was a lie. Orla had funded the check for Jeannette by cashing in all her old savings bonds, the brittle peach stubs given by grandparents and godparents on the milestone days of her premillennium childhood: baptism, birthdays, eighth-grade graduation. "These haven't fully matured yet," the bank clerk warned Orla, "if you want to wait." Orla didn't want to wait. She asked for all of it in cash.

Let Catherine have what Catherine has, her mother had said years ago. But wasn't that exactly what Orla had been doing? She was letting Catherine have Danny until Orla became the person he predicted. And that *was* who she would become, she resolved: the person Danny thought she could be, not the one Catherine thought she was. She would be damned if she turned out to be someone Catherine could laugh at from down the road. She would be damned if she turned out to be *around*.

"This is really late notice," Catherine said when Orla called to say she couldn't make the wedding. Orla could hear the hot hiss of a hair straightener working on the other end. "We paid twenty-six dollars a head," Catherine added.

"Yeah, I'm sorry," Orla said. "I had to take the move-in slot the building gave me. They're really strict about this stuff in New York."

Orla never spoke to Catherine again, but she saw her plenty while she kept watching Danny, just as she had all through college. She wore out screens and acquired new ones, and all the time—though countless new ways to reach him bloomed around her—she only watched. She watched as he started balding and managing a cold-storage locker one town over. She watched as Catherine put on weight, her athletic figure retaining its contours but not its firmness, and started selling three-step skin care systems. She watched as the newlyweds renounced carbs and started traveling with friends from the gym, and she watched as they got sick of all that and started a blog about Catherine's slow-cooker shortcuts and Danny's home repairs. Orla didn't like a bit of their marriage, not online and not in real life. But she was curiously undeterred. She understood now, in a way that she hadn't in college, that waiting for him was just part of her life. That she would never really stop. When people bumped her on the street without seeming to see her at all, she brushed it off with the thought: *Someone is waiting to brag that he knows me.*

So it wasn't buried quite as deep as the back of her mind, the notion that maybe this business with Floss would prop her up at a height Danny couldn't ignore. Somewhere he could find her easily, and see that, all along, he'd been right.

CHAPTER SIX

Marlow

Constellation, California
2051

The morning after she slapped Jacqueline's flamingos, Marlow woke to a reminder from her device, one that filled her with fear and a deep longing for the chemicals that blunted her anxiety.

She was due, in forty-five minutes, to meet both her mother and mother-in-law at the dress shop, to try on her sowing gown.

She walked, taking Lohan instead of Pitt, so that she wouldn't have to pass her childhood home close-up. It was bad enough glimpsing it from three blocks away. The house's rooftop garden was overgrown, the mortifying jumble of vines and brown leaves indistinguishable from the tidy grass pigtails that had been there when they moved in. "The houses all have hair!" Marlow had crowed that day, as her father pulled the car up to the gray-sided Colonial Type 5 with the moss-colored metal roof. She had thought herself very clever, and her parents had laughed at the joke. By the time the sun set, though, most of the other children had said the same thing. A chorus of house-hair comments echoed up and down the fresh pavement, the opening chords of a town that had gone from soulless to settled in twelve hours. Marlow could still remember standing in the street that evening, as the town's first man-made sunset went off without a hitch and the banners unfurled ceremoniously from the streetlights. Welcome to Constellation, they said. Where Fame Is Our Patriotic Privilege. On went the cameras. The new neighbors cheered, introduced themselves to each other. Marlow's mother had turned to her, eyes shining. "You're officially famous, honey," she said, and laughed when Marlow asked why. "Because you're here," her mother said. "That's how it works now."

She reached the center of town and walked around the fountain, its jets firing high into the cloudless blue. The lilies floating in the pool at the fountain's base were mic'd, perfect for capturing the conversations of talent who stopped to sit there. On the other side of the traffic circle, Marlow stopped to let a wave of bots cross in front of her. They emerged like cheerful commuters, throughout the day and night, from a staircase that stretched underground, designed to evoke a subway station. But no train ran underneath it. There was just a quiet cave where the bots waited to be summoned for work. They mostly served as extras, filling out empty restaurants or sparsely attended parties, their voices set to mute, while the human talent shone in the foreground. The real train, a tubular high-speed, stopped at a station set away from the filming areas, just within the perimeter. It deposited, every day, domestic workers from the south, for Constellation stars who didn't like bots sorting through their laundry.

Marlow saw, as she crossed the street toward the dress shop, that her mother and mother-in-law were both already there. The sight of them together made her slightly sick to her stomach, but when she flicked over to her follower dashboard, she saw her total followers number skyrocketing, climbing toward twelve and a half million. The enmity between her mother and mother-in-law was the one ratings boon out of Marlow's marriage. She knew that, at this moment, lots of people—especially retired Southern women and gay men across the country—were settling in to witness gold. The preparations for Marlow's sowing party, which would celebrate her impending pregnancy and be four times the size of her wedding, had already been great for ratings—the mothers had fought twice so far. The first clash happened when Ellis's mother suggested using repurposed coffee bean sacks as table linens, and Marlow's mother replied that the line between rustic and "fugly" was a fine one. The second happened when both women decided they wanted Marlow's baby to call them Nana.

In the shop, Marlow stood in the three-way mirror, wearing the dress that had been altered to fit her body, and realized that her mother-in-law had been right, months ago, when Marlow first tried it on. The color was awful. Marlow could have sworn that it was close to buttercream, but now that she was no longer taking Hysteryl—one of the pill's biggest side effects was a color blindness that skewed all shades sepia—she saw that the dress was a greenish neon canary.

"I am sorry to say," she sighed, "that I hate this."

Her mother got up, batting down the chair that clung to her wide backside as she stood. She stomped toward Marlow. She was wearing sharp-toed calf-hair booties, a fur vest with padded shoulders, and lacquered black leather leggings. Her wig slid askew as she shook her head at Marlow in the mirror.

"Are you fishing kidding me?" Floss said. "You fishing chose it yourself. What the fish?" Long ago, after being fined the annual maximum for on-air profanity, Marlow's mother had retrained her cursing reflexes.

Floss ran her fingers over the silver embroidery that snaked around the waist of the dress. She fluffed the train of tulle and fanned it out behind Marlow. Then she got distracted by the sight of her face in the glass. Marlow watched as her mother forgot what she was doing and defaulted to her usual reflection-triggered motions: pursing her lips, turning her chin this way and that.

Marlow's mother-in-law, Bridget, recrossed her legs beneath her simple white tunic. Sitting in a chair identical to the one that was too small for Floss, she took up less than half the cushion. "I suppose I could see," she said, as if they didn't all remember that she had never liked the dress, "how you could hate it."

Floss sighed. "But yellow's your favorite," she said dreamily. There was a pause. Then her voice thickened. "We can choose something else, but your dad will kill me about the money."

Bridget half rose out of her chair, then sat back down. "Marlow, I think—"

Marlow nodded. She was already reaching for Floss's hands, helping her down from the carpeted platform. "I got her," she said. "It's fine."

"Will she be all right?" Bridget's voice was pitched at an impatient octave, and Marlow briefly imagined some massive force sucking Bridget's chair back—right through the window behind them, *smash*—and depositing her mother-in-law in some other dimension. Bridget had no room to be sniffy about Floss's fogs. Both Bridget and Ellis's father, Ryan, had to be secluded by their housekeeper bot immediately whenever their own fogs struck. Their spells were long and engulfing, leaving them in drooling stupors that would terrify children passing by, not to mention network shareholders. Marlow was one of the very few people who knew that her in-laws had quietly commissioned a room in their basement that would keep them safe from themselves and out of view when a fog took over. The walls were padded. The padding was green, not white, of course. Like all Americans of a certain age, white padded walls made Ellis's parents shiver.

By contrast, Floss was lucky, especially considering how much she had used the old phones with screens when she was younger. Floss's doctor had showed Marlow once, on a chart with bars that ran from pale pink to red, where her mother's mind should have fallen—the darkest part of the graph. But Floss's fogs were short and relatively mild, marked by glazed eyes and time travel. Anyone who didn't know better might think she was only high, or deeply nostalgic. "It's like smoking, if you've ever heard of that," the doctor said. "We can usually predict the damage by how much someone used screens, but there are exceptions. Your mother's lucky, for now."

Marlow's father, of course, was a different story.

Floss looked at Marlow without seeing her, her hands motionless in Marlow's fingers. "He yelled at me about the AmEx at breakfast," Floss murmured.

"Mom," Marlow said softly, trying to fit Floss gently back into the chair, "Dad didn't yell at you. He's not at home anymore."

Bridget was standing now, nervous, edging toward the fitting room's doorway. "Water," she said. "Let me get your mother some water."

"Can you help me unzip this first?" Marlow said, but Bridget was already gone. Floss leaned back in her chair and closed her eyes.

Marlow raised her elbows above her head and stretched her fingertips down toward the dress's zipper. She worked it far enough south to slide her arms out of the fabric, but then it got stuck between her shoulder blades. She tugged and twisted the dress, trying to pull the zipper to where she could see it, near her rib cage, and had just succeeded in exposing her torso when the curtain slid aside and the saleswoman bot stepped in.

"Just a second—" Marlow threw her forearm across her breasts.

"How are we doing in here?" the bot said. It was trim and vaguely Asian. Marlow could tell that its curves had been filed

90

down to look less sexual—it had probably once been a companion bot, neutered and repurposed for the dress shop. "That looks *gorgeous* on you," the bot gushed. Marlow saw that its filmy eyes were darting between Marlow's forehead and the spot where Floss slumped, trying to figure out which pocket of body heat belonged to the person with the spending power. Marlow dropped her arm from her chest, reminding herself: there were no cameras in the dressing room, and there was no reason for modesty in front of a machine, no matter how much it looked like a person. This bot—Kendra, its name tag said—was the kind they called client-facing, with a fine mist of body hair and its own human tics. It was subtly chewing on its inner cheek as it waited for someone to speak. But under the algorithm-driven authenticity, Kendra was no different than the ones they called back-office. Marlow had caught an eerie glimpse of one of those earlier, when Kendra went into the storeroom to retrieve her dress. The upright figure Marlow saw as the door swung wide had hands that looked just like her own—tapered fingers, soft palms, even dull fingernails. The hands plunged into a swath of white satin, drew a flashing needle out, and pushed it in again. But from the wrists up, the bot was all chrome and wires, shining steel limbs. Where Marlow had a face, it had a blank, black-glassed lens.

"Seriously. Gorgeous." Kendra's voice broke the silence. It cocked its head to one side, the mechanical whisper that went with the motion giving its nature away. "Have we found the dress?" it sang giddily.

Marlow was thinking that she would rather wear the yellow dress every day of her life than stand here topless with this perky bot for one more moment. She was thinking that all that stretched in front of her was doing things she didn't want to do. What difference did it make what she wore?

"We've found the dress," she said to the man-made girl. "You can go ring it up."

The three women left the gown, smothering in its garment bag, in Floss's car. Then they walked across the wildflower-flanked artery of the shopping center, toward the café. Ellis was waiting outside, the sole of one sneaker braced against the wall as he stared into nothing. His mouth puckered open and closed. Marlow knew that look: he was dictating something. An email, or, she thought with bitterness, a grocery list full of things to hide from her. Though it was entirely unnecessary to do so— and though Marlow had expressed repeatedly that it sort of repelled her, the fish-lipped habit, like chewing food with your gums flapping open—Ellis always mouthed the words he intuited to his device.

Bridget hated it, too—it was the one thing she and Marlow agreed on. As the women approached Ellis, Bridget tried to catch her son's eye with her disapproving own, clucking. "Well," she sighed, as Ellis ignored her, "it's better than the alternative, I suppose." Marlow knew what she meant. People her parents' age often spoke of the way things were when the old phones were still around: whole waiting rooms, whole planes, whole parties full of people with their heads bent chin to chest, staring at oblongs of blue light, as still and as oblivious to their surroundings as if a gas leak had put them to sleep. Bridget spoke of this phenomenon with distaste; Floss always talked about it wistfully.

Marlow had trouble picturing it at all. She had missed the era of the so-called smartphone by a few years. The Spill had killed those, too. In the chaos, in the aftermath that seemed like it would never end, doctors first mistook the alarming symptom cropping up in middle-aged patients—sudden, fierce forgetfulness—as a side effect of the country's collective shock. But the mental fog kept rolling in, thickening, spreading. Finally, a study was soberly unveiled. It linked the use of personal screens—phones, tablets, anything that aimed blue light at the human eye from point-blank range—to a rapid dementia doctors predicted would eventually devastate Marlow's parents' entire generation. The millennials. Overnight, a company called Apple went under, and its products went away. And shortly thereafter, a nineteen-year-old genius who had been taking apart her parents' phones since birth stood on a stage in a crop top and unveiled the thing that would replace them: the device.

On her seventh birthday, like everyone else she knew, Marlow had one of the blank, black square-inch gems pressed into the softer side of her wrist. The device did not make a sound; the device did not have a screen. It did everything the old phones had done, and all it needed was brain waves. It did all its work inside its user's head.

Marlow could still recall the sample prompts her device came with, could still remember working through them with her eyes closed. *Tell me where to find delivery pizza. Tell me the current weather conditions at the Great Wall of China. Show me a photo of the president in college.* The staticky nudge at her skin, and the sudden bubbling-up of the very first answer in her brain: *Flower Crust Express, two-point-one miles. Am I hungry? Would I like to place an order?* Then the instant doubt of: Her brain knew that already, didn't it? It was where she got pizza all the time. But after that came the swoon at her next thought, natural as her own name: *It is currently eleven degrees Celsius at the Great Wall of China.* And finally, materializing on a backdrop in her head she hadn't known existed: the sixty-nine-year-old president, many decades earlier. She stood jauntily on the Princeton quad, fingers curled into the belt loops of her high-waisted blue jeans, her hair rounded in a neat, soft afro. *Would I like to see more?* "It's so weird," Marlow had said to Floss, who was watching her daughter anxiously, as if Marlow had swallowed a party drug. "It's calling me 'I.' Or it's saying it's me." A week later, there was nothing strange about it. Gone was the line between who she had been before and who she was now, what she had known before and what she knew now. Which was, for all intents and purposes, everything.

Inside the restaurant, Ellis and Marlow ate quietly while their mothers engaged in passive battle.

"My maternal grandfather," Floss said, waving a forkful of dripping kale, "had a full head of naturally dark hair until he died. Never lost a strand of it. Never went gray." She cast a sympathetic look at the top of Ellis's sparsely covered head.

"Wonderful," Bridget returned. "I think they would be wise to use a lot of your family's *physical* attributes." She scraped the dressing off of a blade of her salad and turned to Marlow and Ellis. "Now, you two do know that my father was a distant cousin of Stephen Hawking's, yes? I'm told that the designers can go through Ellis's input and find his genes specifically."

"The skateboarder?" Floss screwed up her face. "From like, a million years ago?"

"The genius," Bridget said. She looked at Ellis, only Ellis, and laughed.

"Well," Floss said, patting Bridget's hand, "I agree that when it comes to you guys, it's best to concentrate on the brains. Marlow shared your story with me." Floss shook her head, maudlin. "About your buck teeth. It couldn't have been easy, being ugly as a child. But I'm sure it toughened you up, too. You have such a strong, almost masculine energy."

Marlow drew back her leg to kick her mother, but her foot only found empty space. Floss had seen the hit coming, and reeled back from the table in time. She flounced off to the bathroom with an arrogant pulse in her step, as if the followers who were no doubt fawning over her bitchiness were actually there in the room with her.

Once Floss was far enough away, Bridget looked between Ellis and Marlow, her face taut and disapproving. "When are the two of you going to tell her?"

"That's our business, Mom," Ellis snapped through a forkful of eggplant.

"We'll tell her soon," Marlow said. And she meant it. Guilt

had been gnawing her over this breach of bloodline protocol: no matter how Floss drove her crazy, Marlow didn't want to keep something from her that Bridget—not to mention anyone who had been watching Marlow's or Ellis's channels when they came to the decision—already knew.

"I hope so." Bridget set her silverware over her barely touched meal in an X. "Otherwise, things will get ugly," she said in a warning singsong.

Things would be ugly no matter what, Marlow thought, watching Floss push through the narrow space between the tables. The quivering mass of her backside brushed diners on both sides. Her baby would never have an ass like that, Marlow thought. Her baby would never share anything with her mother. They had arranged, after not much discussion, to ask the designers to ignore Floss's genes as they assembled the baby's DNA. To toss them out altogether. Marlow wished it had been Ellis's idea, something she could claim she had been talked into. But it hadn't been. It had been hers.

———

At 3:05 in the morning, Ellis's alarm went off. He shook Marlow awake. "Off-camera time," he whispered to her. He settled onto his side and punched his pillow into a ball beneath his face so he could see her. Briefly, she was worried that he wanted to have sex. She tried to calm her resistance to the idea. She could ask her device to call up photos of Constellation's firefighter talent.

But it wasn't sex Ellis wanted. "We've got to decide about the baby," he said. "The sowing's next week. This is getting ridiculous."

Marlow hugged the comforter to her neck. "I said we could do acne," she murmured. They had pored over the forms for days, reading the questions in their head and trading answers out loud. They drew up extensive family histories, reporting birthplaces, death locations, diseases, distinctions. This was how the baby would be built: the inputters would map a genome based on all the contributors' traits. Marlow and Ellis would choose everything they wanted their child to be from the DNA they had to work with. It was tempting to make the baby perfect, but studies, and Jacqueline, claimed that children who were programmed without any potential flaws ended up "psychologically disadvantaged," as the studies put it—"petri-dish weirdos," in Jacqueline's words. "You've got to mess them up a little," she had told Marlow, with a surreptitious nod at a mole on her daughter's neck. But even mild weaknesses seemed cruel. Marlow couldn't think of a glitch she could live with. Finally, Ellis suggested acne. "No one ever died from a couple zits," he said.

"Not the flaws," he said now. "The gender."

Marlow knew that Ellis wanted a boy. She knew he was already thinking of passing on the family fortune he had yet to inherit, and that despite the fact that he had a mother revered as a business legend and a vintage T-shirt that said WILD FEMINIST in frequent rotation, he had trouble imagining anything better than what he saw in the mirror.

It wasn't that Marlow didn't want a boy. It wasn't that she wanted a girl. It was that choosing the gender would finalize the child that had, so far, existed only in lab hypotheticals and overwrought party plans. There was a reason the fertility center needed to know their baby's sex before her sowing: at the event, a mock-up of the child would be projected on a giant canvas backdrop. Marlow was dreading the sight of it. She sensed that, more than the moment she got the pregnancy arc assignment, even more than the eventual implantation of the embryo, seeing that baby-to-be gurgling at her from a screen would feel like the moment of no return. What could she do, how could she contemplate wriggling out of things, once she had seen her child?

"Let's talk about it tomorrow," she said, and rolled over. She fell back asleep almost instantly. Sleep, off Hysteryl, was a wholly new sensation, at first blunt and black and deep, then followed by vivid dreams. The old ones were back, and jarring as ever: Grace pleading, Honey mugging for the dashboard camera, the water climbing over the car. But tonight, she dreamed of her sowing. She saw herself in the yellow dress and Ellis at her side. The two of them stood, as planned, in front of a smiling crowd in her mother's backyard. Everyone had their faces trained on a screen hung above the altar. On the screen was Marlow's baby, with chubby feet and dimpled hands, wispy curls springing up from its scalp. But where it should have had a face, there was only a bulb of dark glass, like the one on the bot she wasn't supposed to look at in the dress shop. Above the crush of the crowd's shocked murmurs, Marlow heard it clearly: the sound of her mother behind her, gasping, "Omigod, look. She's beautiful."

———

The fog facility was twenty minutes away on foot and hidden by the artificial woods, because the network didn't like it showing up in any footage. Marlow didn't mind the walk; she couldn't sleep after that dream. She went halfway there in almost pitch dark. Finally, just as she reached the forest, an illumidrone picked her up, its long beam turning the ground white in front of her as street gave way to dirt. She passed the matte black brick of a building where the network's servers were housed, avoiding eye contact with the armed guards who stood along its walls. It was awkward, since the guards were real people. The network took the task of protecting its data seriously. The humans, their long guns, the building's stealth-bomber paint job—it had all been there since the beginning, meant to convince the people of Constellation that securing their privacy was a priority. Marlow had never really gotten the logic: What did anyone in Constellation have that was private? They had to eat and cry and give birth on camera. But here was a fortress for their data—which, in her estimation, was just another word for boring stuff: how much they spent at the dry cleaner, the combination to their locks at the gym, the messages they composed to each other in their minds. Who was coming after that stuff?

"That's what we used to think, too," Floss had said dryly, once, when Marlow made that point.

Then Marlow understood: the fortress must have reassured her parents when they came here. Like the gleaming fitness facilities and the shimmering village swimming pool—there were so few in the state, now, after all the water restrictions—data security must have been an attractive amenity. Constellation was launched at the dawn of the new, government-run, government-supervised internet, when Americans were still too scarred and scared to use it. Marlow's town was a lure, a way to get them back online. The shtick was irresistible: come watch these beautiful people be on camera all the time. Marlow was old enough now to know her town's history, to read between the lines: the real talent from back then—Oscar winners and rock stars—wanted nothing to do with Constellation. But the B-listers, like Marlow's parents, were broke, and heartsick for their old fame, and susceptible to the pitch the network used to recruit them: *What you did back then, driving all those people to vulnerable platforms—do you think you had nothing to do with the Spill? Blood is on your hands.* So the old reality players and socialites and actors' dull siblings signed contracts. They moved in and lived. They shared all day and night—proving, with their fearless return to the form, that all-important American refrain: the terrorists had not won.

The sun was rising at Marlow's back when she reached the fog facility. A slippered man on the other side of the glass stared as she touched her device to the grid on the door. Even this early, the door slid open; she was next of kin.

Floss made a big deal of shuddering when she talked about the facility, but Marlow liked the place. It was the only spot in Constellation, besides anywhere people disrobed, that the cameras didn't roll. There wasn't an audience out there for fog-addled people letting their breakfasts fall out of their mouths. Marlow wasn't afraid of the patients, though. Her father had looked like them for years before she and Floss admitted it was time to move him here. She was accustomed to the blankness in the eyes, the stillness in the faces. The place felt peaceful and weighty to her—almost royal, somehow. These were wealthy people. The men always wore pristine cashmere robes; the women had jewels in their ears. Once, the nurse Marlow liked best, a chubby man named Sean who was as old as her dad, bought her a coffee and introduced her to some of his favorite patients. "I was Twitter-famous," one of the old men croaked at her, glaring, and Marlow just nodded and smiled, pretending to be impressed. She had never quite understood Twitter, though Floss still talked about it like a dead, beloved friend. Short messages, but to everyone, mostly pointless, with blatant lies allowed—Marlow could not imagine what had been the appeal.

As she stepped off the elevator on her father's floor, Marlow spotted Sean at his desk, the violet sky outside the window framing his head as he frowned over charts. "Early bird!" he said when he saw Marlow coming. "What are you doing here?"

Marlow grinned and shifted her bag on her shoulder, patted it. "Oh, you know. Brought the big guy all his favorites. Filet mignon, lobster. Strawberry shortcake bars."

It was a dark joke between them. Her father would hardly eat anything now.

"He's up," Sean said, nodding to the room behind him. CLIPP, ASTON read the nameplate.

Marlow found her father in the chair beside his bed, already wrapped in his own cashmere robe. Floss had rushed out to buy him one the same day they moved him in, like a nervous mother wanting her child to fit right in at college.

"Dad," she said, "how are you?"

When he didn't answer, she talked about the sowing. How she wished that he could go, or that she didn't have to. How Ellis wanted a boy, and how she didn't want Ellis. She said more than she had to just to hear herself being honest, enjoying that every word she said would live and die in this room.

"I'm fucked, Dad," Marlow said. "I'm thoroughly fucked." That was another thing she loved about coming here: getting to curse, the real stuff, no seafood substitutions necessary.

She thought she saw him lean forward, so she put the straw into his mouth. Her father pulled water in. Marlow felt glad, a bit of gladness so tiny she wouldn't have known it was possible until his sickness shrank her world.

It was her father, she remembered, her mind drifting, who took care of her after she had her eggs reaped, all those years ago. Her mother had double-booked herself, something that took her away for a few days, over the week of Marlow's surgery. Marlow's parents were barely talking then, she recalled, though the exact reason why eluded her. Marlow had lost count of how many times her parents had broken up and reconciled in the course of her life. Sometimes, when Floss told old stories, she referenced separations Marlow didn't remember. If Marlow said as much, Floss would softly exclaim, "Oh, yeah!" Then she'd explain the rift in the sort of misty, rueful tone one might use to describe a long-ago vacation where it rained.

But Marlow remembered this much about the week of her egg reaping: her mother didn't want her father to know that she wouldn't be home to take care of Marlow. So Floss asked their driver, Amadou, to supervise, and pitched in by waking her daughter constantly with guilty messages. *How are you, honey? Do you have enough grape Popsicles? I told Amadou to be sure he got them. Were you surprised when you saw the grape Popsicles? I bet you thought I forgot! I would never forget my girl's grape Popsicles. I said Amadou this is very important!* Marlow had not answered. This was the essence of Floss: not mother of the year, but mother once a year, working remotely, and wanting the same medal.

Finally, when Marlow cried from the way her insides rang with pain, Amadou had closed his eyes and made a call on his device, stroking her hair silently the whole time. Marlow's father had come immediately with an overnight bag, had told Amadou to take the next few days off, that Floss, he promised, would never be the wiser. He gave Marlow a little bell to ring if she needed him when he was downstairs. He spent her long naps milling around the place he used to live, running his fingers over splits in the walls and water spots in the ceiling. He summoned other men to come fix things.

"Dad, what should I do?" Marlow whispered now as she pulled the straw away. She looked at him, marveling, as she often did, at his dark, shining eyes, at his jaw upholstered in skin too young for him, too smooth and vital-looking for someone wilting down to nothing. How she would miss the sight of his face when he was finally done disappearing.

Her father blinked back without answering, and suddenly something came to her. This face she loved—it could outlive them both. She could code it right into her child, bypassing her own looks, which were such diluted versions of her parents', people sometimes looked at her with pity before they could stop themselves. Marlow's parents waved it away: they swore her blue eyes were shaped like her father's brown ones, that Floss's hair had been just like Marlow's—untamed and ashy—at her age. Marlow had never thought much of it. She knew that, back in the twentieth century, Americans would list the things in their bloodstreams proudly—*I'm a quarter Irish, half-Ugandan, part French*—but people never did that anymore. The fractions had gotten too complicated by the time Marlow was born, and the children who came after her had even more heritage to keep track of: noses and brows and chins were less predictable, less indicative of any one thing. Still, Marlow wondered on occasion where her parents' features were hiding. Sometimes she played a game in front of mirrors, jerking her head up before her face could prepare itself, hoping to catch a glimpse of her mother or her father. It never worked. When her dad was gone, there would be nothing in her reflection to remind her of him.

Maybe, she thought suddenly, with a pang of guilt, she could be a bit like Ellis, and see potential in this child. An opportunity to save her father's face—to start it over, really. She would get to see it younger than she had the first time. If she lived long enough, she might even see it again the way she did in her favorite memory of theirs. She pictured it now: the day he taught her how to ride a bike, jogging alongside her unicorn two-wheeler with the end of a rope in his hand. The other end was tied around Marlow's waist—a compromise. She wanted him not to hold her; he couldn't let go just yet. "Sweetheart, look where you're going," he kept saying. "Look straight ahead." But she felt better looking at his face, at his hair flopping wildly as he trailed her. She could still see it now, the sweat at his temples, the crinkles in his eyes as he laughed with her, at her.

How old was her father in this memory? She asked her device to do the math, and the solution gave her an existential jolt: *Twenty-eight.* Seven years younger than she was now.

"Oh, Anna," her father said suddenly, weakly, his voice pushing through the phlegm of many speechless hours. "You're all right."

Marlow didn't know who Anna was, but she'd come to feel familiar with her. Her father called her by the name roughly a third of the time. The rest of the time, he didn't call her anything. Marlow didn't correct him, now—he sounded so relieved. She just nodded, retucked his blanket, and focused on looking that way: all right.

———

She and Ellis struck a deal: the boy he wanted, with her father's face. They messaged the Liberty center, and someone replied that the designers would start the mock-up right away.

The last days before her sowing passed in a heady blur. Floss got into a fight with the caterer that ended in brief, light shoving. Bridget threw a fit regarding the carbon implications of the cake Floss had ordered from the other side of the country. Marlow hung her yellow dress at her mother's house, where she wouldn't have to look at it. She attended her hen party, a spa day planned by Jacqueline. The women were all subdued because hen parties were always dry; the mother-to-be had to abstain, so everyone else did, too. "Buck up, losers," Jacqueline snapped, stamping her foot in the pedicure tub. "At least we can talk about Tia behind her back." Tia was the only one from their group who wasn't at the party. Childless women were never invited.

"You guys must have talked a *lot* about me over the years," Marlow said. Everyone laughed nervously.

The morning of the sowing, Marlow sat at her mother's kitchen table, sipping hot water with lemon. Ahead of her egg replacement, they had finally cut off her coffee. Through the glass doors that led to the backyard, she watched drones lower gold-painted chairs into the grass as a writer and exec from the network looked on. The backdrop that her son's face would be projected on had already been unrolled from a bar high over the lawn. Around her, inside, three bots were in high gear. One steamed Marlow's dress in the hallway, one chopped fruit at the island, and a third dropped tea lights into wide bowls of water. They were all client-facing—it was a special occasion. People didn't dress up to look at wires.

Though the machines were right on schedule, the humans were running behind. Floss was in the house somewhere, probably doing her makeup-before-the-makeup act. She would show up powdered with bronzer soon, claiming to be bare-faced. Jacqueline was on her way, set back by a drama with one of her daughters. Ellis was surfing with his sisters' husbands at a simulator facility. Its website promised to make the men feel like they were riding waves on the Gold Coast, then in Oahu, then off the Canary Islands, all inside a warehouse fifty miles from the Pacific.

As Marlow sat waiting, a message cut through the noise in her brain. *Urgent, for Marlow Clipp, from Liberty Family Planning— Can you stop by the office ASAP?*

Sure, Marlow responded. She slipped out of the kitchen without saying anything to the bots. They went on working, half smiles in place.

She drove to the center and stepped inside, finding the office dark and quiet, the chipper nurse nowhere to be found. Someone was waving at her, backlit, at the end of the hall.

Marlow walked toward the figure, its features falling into place as she got closer: a serious-eyed woman her age, thick-limbed in her blush-and-gray scrubs, with warm brown skin. Her ponytail was tied back tightly. The second Marlow saw it, her fingers tingled with a deep-seated memory of what that hair felt like: thick in her hands because there was so much of it, but brittle in her fingers, each strand highly breakable. Marlow knew the feeling of trying not to snap a single one as she coaxed them into braids and then elastics at the end.

"Grace," she breathed. "You work here?"

Grace swallowed. She looked anxious. "We need to give you a quick exam," she said loudly. "Your Pap came back abnormal. Please follow me."

"No problem," Marlow said. And just like that, for the first time ever, she was in violation of her contract. There was a clause in it that forbade her to talk to any of the children who had been there that night. But they weren't children anymore, were they? She hadn't seen Grace in twenty years.

CHAPTER SEVEN

Orla

New York, New York
2015

"**H**ey," Floss said at brunch one Sunday, rolling the stem of her glass between her fingers. "You know that singer, Aston Clipp?"

"*Is* he a singer?" Orla said. She took a sip of her mimosa, tasting virtually nothing. The mimosas at their regular brunch spot—a cheesy rooftop bar in Midtown that still smelled of bleach and liquor when it opened for eggs on Sunday—were advertised as bottomless. But Orla and Floss were pushing it; they had been there for nearly three hours. The angry waiter had started bringing their glasses back a shade darker each time, until Orla was sure that there wasn't a drop of champagne in the cup. Now he was even cutting the orange juice, with water. At least, she hoped it was water.

"Whatever he is—" Floss shrugged "—I think he'd be perfect. Don't you?"

They had been talking for weeks about the next step: coupling Floss with someone who would up the wattage of her star. Orla thought of a recent, blurry video they had run on Lady-ish: Aston Clipp's fist rising above the scrum of a crowd in Ibiza, coming down on a guy he thought had jostled his manager. Except the guy turned out to be a fourteen-year-old girl.

"I don't know," Orla said. "He could be trouble."

"Oh, he's trouble." Floss did the thing that Orla had come to know as her attempt to wiggle her eyebrows. Thanks to the injections she got, it only made her temples pulse.

Orla imagined Floss at a party on Aston Clipp's lap, ducking her head to hear him whisper, and felt preemptive jealousy shoot through her. She was lost in thought as Floss stood and led her out of the restaurant. They were almost to the door when Orla realized they hadn't paid. She looked back, mortified, and caught the waiter's eye. He stared at her, but didn't come after them. He mostly looked relieved that they were gone.

———

Aston Clipp was born Austin Kumon, the fourth son of Lee, a Kentucky single mom who bleached her jet-black Japanese hair and dreamed of seeing her best-looking kid on the Disney Channel. She showed up in LA a couple of times a year, prodding Austin into rooms where boys his age ducked their heads and mumbled the lines of kid detectives with talking dogs, kid surfing prodigies with talking dogs, and kid computer geniuses with talking dogs. Austin had a terrible speech impediment. "Walph," he would say to the casting assistant playing the talking dog at auditions, "wanna come suwfing, boy? I'm heading down to Wedondo. You should see how the guys thewe whip!" Gently, the casting directors would ask Lee to stop bringing her son to these things, but Lee didn't listen. She registered Austin under fake names. She ran speech drills with him mercilessly on the thirty-hour drives. On one of these road trips, having had enough of Lee, Austin secretly recorded her nagging him, added some effects, and put it on YouTube. He called it "My Dumb Bitch Mom." Six million people watched Lee, a cigarette clamped in one corner of her mouth, swerving to avoid a tractor trailer as she prompted, "The rooster...crows...in the morning!" Austin kept making the videos, egging his mom into tantrums she had no clue were being filmed until a Hollywood manager, Craig, showed up at their Dixie Highway rancher. Six weeks later, Austin inexplicably had a record deal, and a contract with a network that specialized in crass content for men. They invited him to create and star in his own sitcom. By the end of the year, Austin and Lee were living in Malibu, and she was wearing ribbed tanks that said DBM everywhere. Austin was sixteen.

Things quickly imploded. The sitcom, about a boy plotting to kill his dumb bitch mom, was met with uproar. Cable news—particularly the channel that shared an office building with the male-network douchebags—delightedly booked outraged parents and scandalized reps from religious leagues. (Teenage girls, taken with Austin's blinding grin and soft black wavy hair, were tuning in to the show behind their parents' backs, coming away with catchphrases like "Ground *me*, bitch? Imma burn your corpse!") The male network canceled the show, apologized to the public, and found a way out of paying the Kumons. Scrambling to keep her new lifestyle, Lee moved to sue everyone in sight. She even hauled Austin into court on charges of defamation. Though the judge threw it out, the damage had been done to the relationship. Craig advised Austin to emancipate himself; Austin agreed, stuffed his jeans and phone charger in a plastic shopping bag, and moved into Craig's guest bedroom.

Shortly afterward, Lee tracked Austin and Craig down at a Pinkberry. She lunged at her son, who raced around the other side of the counter, hiding in the toppings. Lee followed, and when Craig stepped between them, she grabbed Craig's head and smashed it into the counter. He came up holding his nose, bits of crushed Fruity Pebbles sparkling in his blood. So many bystanders had cell phone footage, the news stations were able to put together a practically professional film of the fight, complete with facial reactions and alternate angles. Some "Dumb Bitch Mom" fans wondered whether the whole thing had been staged.

Which was what gave Craig, before his nose had even healed, the idea to pretend that it was. To spin all of Austin—from his earliest YouTube videos through his auto-tuned singles and the slurs he whipped at his mother—as one long experiment in media and morality. "If you think about it," Craig begged his department head, "he really is an artist. He challenges our notions about language and propriety." The department head snorted. "He's a bratty backwoods idiot," she said. "I'm only entertaining this because every teenage girl in the country wants to suck his dick. Go ahead, knock yourself out."

So Austin changed his name to one of the fake ones his mother had come up with—Aston Clipp—and declared himself an artist. He traded in his Jordans for sandals and traveled the world, mainly amassing a collection of beaded bracelets. He sat shirtless atop the Holocaust memorial in Berlin and bothered monks in Tibet for selfies. He went to explore his roots in Japan, where he got bored of the customary bows and began to invent spontaneous dance moves in response to them. (He also asked for a fork everywhere he went, because, as he put it, he did not "fuck with chopsticks.") On a trip to South Africa, he tweeted, while sitting in his Learjet on a Johannesburg tarmac: **My heart is heavy thinking of the genicide here in Rwanda—think of how many young girls (and guys! LOL) couldve become Clippers.**

Eventually, Craig insisted that Aston create something. A song, a book, a web series—anything he could monetize.

"I was thinking about a stand-up special where the whole time I act like an Indian," Aston said, while bouncing on a pogo stick.

"No," Craig said, trying to imagine which kind of Indian Aston meant, and which kind would sink the both of them faster. "Artist," he reminded him. "You're an artist."

Aston nodded. He did some coke. Seven minutes later, he had an idea: he wanted to stage an exhibition in which he would sit in a pitch-black room, completely naked but for a pair of glow-in-the-dark leg casts, like the ones he had to wear the summer before fifth grade, after he fell under a friend's ATV. Visitors to the exhibit would each be allowed five minutes alone with him, to sign his casts with black light markers. "Let's do it at a museum," he said to Craig. "Whichever one's gonna pay us the most."

"That's not how museums work," Craig said.

Aston, who had turned twenty-one the day before, shrugged and said, "Urban Outfitters, then."

Which was how, that night, Orla and Floss ended up walking to the store on the corner of Sixth Avenue and Fourteenth Street. They stood in a long line beneath a marquee that read: "Urban Outfitters Presents an Extraordinary Work: Aston Clipp's *My Legs, Your Canvas: On the Summer of 2005 Being Shitty as Hell.*"

"He's seven years younger than you," Orla reminded Floss as they shuffled forward.

"Yeah," Floss said. "But look at him." She gazed up at the story-tall black-and-white photo of Aston in the window. In the picture, Aston gripped an old Super Soaker in one hand, offered the lens the middle finger with the other. "He's totally an old soul," Floss sighed.

A black Mercedes sedan crept around the corner, came to a stop in front of them, and expelled a model. The model, whose towering shoes were made of slippery wood, walked toward the store haltingly, like each step was her first. She cut the line and was ushered inside by a man with an earpiece, in a blazer.

Someone behind Floss and Orla said, "Oh, I think they're dating."

Floss dug her fingers into Orla's arm. Tears were clinging precariously to her mink lashes, the ones they had saved up for, the ones that weren't supposed to get wet. "Don't worry about her," Orla said. She thought of Catherine talking to Danny first, sealing their fates forever. "Just go down there and get him like she isn't even there," she went on firmly. "Once he meets you, she won't matter."

———

After an hour of wandering the upper level of the store, touching dream catchers and face-sized hoop earrings, Orla spotted Floss coming out of the dark room where Aston sat naked. She walked to the top of the staircase to wait for her.

As Orla stood there, the model brushed by her and began descending the steps, carefully negotiating the slick teak of her heels. Orla's pulse quickened as Floss stopped where she was, her hand on the railing, and waited for the model. Her mouth curled into a shape that Orla knew meant she had just thought of something. When the model was only a stair or two above her, Floss raised the back of her hand to her mouth and, with great deliberation, wiped it.

The model cursed and spit at her, wobbling as she jabbed her finger in Floss's direction, but Floss only smirked and started climbing the stairs again. Just as the two of them met in the middle, the model's ankle buckled in her strange, dangerous shoes and her torso jerked to the left. She yelped and reached out for Floss to steady herself.

The motion Floss made was so small, so fast, like the flit of a hummingbird, and yet it was entirely unmistakable: she jerked her arm away. The model tumbled down the stairs. Her head knocked against the steps twice. She settled at the bottom in a shape that hurt to look at, one arm hooked unnaturally beneath the rest of her body. A gasp echoed through the store, loud but barely audible over the throbbing trance music. Floss looked up at Orla helplessly.

Orla looked back, her mouth dry and hanging open. She wasn't sure if the hollow thumps she had heard came from the model's shoes or her bones, which sat so close to the surface of her skin, Orla felt like she could see her whole skeleton struggling. The model groaned and thrashed her head. Nothing else was moving. "Paulina!" someone shrieked. Someone else yelled, "Call 911!"

Floss clambered up the stairs, knees bound by the hem of her bandage dress. By the time she reached the top, people were wedging themselves between her and Orla, screaming at them, trying to push Floss. Together, they ran—to the door, to the corner, to the cab they flagged down frantically. They did not see the other cab, the one the hysterical girls piled into, could not hear one of them saying to the driver, "Follow that car!" They did not see the driver, besotted with the girls' young cleavage, nodding at a command he usually would have laughed at.

"What the fuck were you thinking?" Orla said in their cab.

"I don't know, I don't know!" Floss covered her face. "She might have been trying to hit me, don't you think?"

"No, I don't." Orla bent at the waist. She was nauseous. "And neither do you."

They did not pay any attention when both cabs came to a stop in front of their building, the teens waiting in theirs as Orla and Floss got out and hurried inside. And they were already in their respective bedrooms, somber and pale, as the girls snapped pictures of their front door and blasted the photos out on their networks with vicious captions.

Home of the EVIL worthless whore.

Aston + Paulina forever payback's a bitch, bitch.

This is where that skank who hurt Paulina lives, if anyone wants to drop by and beat the shit out of her. C'mon world. Don't hold back.

———

The next morning, Orla awoke to her phone's persistent symphony. She rolled onto her stomach and felt beneath her pillow for it, swiping her thumb across its screen in an attempt to silence her alarm. It was only when she heard a tiny, tinny version of her mother's voice—"Orla? Orla, are you there? Orla *Jane*!"—that she realized the phone had been ringing.

She slid it between her cheek and the pillow. "Mom."

"Look out your window, Orla." Gayle's voice quivered on the other end. "Your building is on the news. Your front door."

"What do you mean, my front door?" Orla couldn't see the black-gridded double doors at the building's entrance. They opened onto Twenty-First Street; her window faced the avenue. "Is it terrorists?" Orla said. "Mom!"

"Tell her it's on channel ten!" Jerry shouted, as if such things were the same the world over. She felt around in bed for the remote to her bedroom TV, the glass-domed box that had followed her since her freshman year of college.

"Orla," Gayle said, "I need you to go lock your door. You know my friend Adele, from the scrapbooking place? Her son has a Twitter—"

Orla went to lock the dead bolt. When she got close to the door, she heard the rising voices of people near the elevator.

"*Tweeted*," Jerry said to Gayle in the background. "They call it *tweeting*."

"Some person in your building," Gayle wailed, "hurt a young woman, a model, Paulina Kratz? I know her from *Dancing with the Stars*. She survived the tsunami, and this is what she gets? She danced with Maks. She danced *beautifully*."

"Val," Jerry corrected her. "She danced with Val."

"This woman in your building pushed her down the stairs," Gayle said. "Can you imagine? It's all over the news. People are furious. Someone tweeted your address. They're outside your door. With signs. One paintballed your super."

Orla closed her eyes. Poor Manny. She hoped his son, Linus, who trailed him everywhere, hadn't seen that.

"Tell her the police just got there," Jerry called out in the background. "They're setting up a barricade."

As if on cue, there was a slap on the door. "Ms. Natuzzi?" came the voice from the other side, deep and urgent. "Open up, please. NYPD."

"Who is that?" Gayle demanded. "You're old enough to have gentleman callers, but—"

"Oh, for Christ's sake," muttered Jerry.

Orla watched the door shake in its frame from the second knock.

"It's not a guy, Mom," Orla said. "It's the police. They're looking for my roommate. She's the one who pushed the model. I have to go." She thumbed the red circle on the screen.

Floss, in a periwinkle satin camisole and briefs, ambled to the door. "Are you gonna get that?" she said, rubbing her palms over her eyes.

Orla stared at her. The door went on shuddering. Would the police believe Orla if she denied everything? If she let her jaw go slack like a frightened kid, and said that Floss was just her subletter? There wasn't a soul on earth who could corroborate their friendship. "I really don't know anything about her," Orla imagined herself saying. She froze in the middle of the thought. *I really don't know anything about her.* It was the truth. Where was Floss from, for real, before Akron? Had she gone to college? How had she learned to hack people's emails? When had she had her first period? Her first kiss? Did she have siblings? Friends? Enemies? A driver's license? A criminal record? Together, they had chosen her passions from the things that arrived on their doorstep, her dreams from the common denominators of the getting-famous playbook. They assembled the soulless army that made up most of her followers—the bots who applauded her pictures and disseminated her thoughts—on a web page they had to translate from Russian. What of the triumphs and loves, the fights and failures that predated their efforts? Floss had never offered. Orla had never asked.

And she never would. This, she was sure of. She had been sure since, a few days earlier, she brought up a package that looked like anything else from a publicist. Floss, paging through a magazine on the couch, barely glanced at Orla opening it, at Orla lifting, from a sea of weightless packing peanuts, a vase. The vase was strangely heavy and squat, marbled green, with a matching cap screwed on tight and rimmed in gold. There was a gold plate embedded in the cap, engraved.

"'Biscuit,'" Orla read out loud. "Weird name for a decor line."

Floss had been licking a finger to turn the page when Orla said "Biscuit." Now she slowly dropped her finger from her tongue and got up. She walked over and lifted the vase from Orla's hands, her arms buckling slightly as she took on the weight.

Floss said, with her eyes on the porcelain, "Biscuit's my dog."

"What?" Blood rushed between Orla's eyes and ears. She felt her pulse quicken in an embarrassed way, as if she had been caught doing something.

"My dog," Floss repeated. "I guess these are her ashes." As Orla watched, horrified, Floss moved the bristles of her ponytail away from her face and pressed her cheek against the urn. "I told my mom to wait. She was bitching about taking care of her," Floss said. "I told her soon I'd have the money to fly home and get her, but she didn't think I would. She didn't think I could do this. She didn't think I could do *anything*." Floss held the urn out and blinked at it, disbelieving. "It was so *not* Biscuit's time," she said. Then she turned her back to Orla and started to cry.

Orla licked her lips, preparing all the questions she knew she should ask—*But why would your mom do this? How could any mom do this?* Before she could say anything, though, Floss whipped around. Mascara was running down her face. It hovered, in dark drops, from her chin.

"Don't," Floss said to Orla, her voice patching out. "Don't ask me anything about it. This—" She raised the urn. "This is the end of something. And if you have shit in your past, I don't want to know about that, either."

So Orla let her tongue lie still in her mouth. She understood what Floss was saying: they would be, from here on out, only who they were from here on out.

And now, as they stood in the entryway, listening to the cop's knocks cross into hostile, Orla stayed quiet again. She watched as Floss pulled a robe on and cinched it tightly, nodded at the door. "Go ahead," she said to Orla. "Open it."

Had it ever really happened before? She was famous overnight.

CHAPTER EIGHT

Marlow

Constellation, California
2051

In the exam room, as Marlow sat down on the table, Grace told her not to take her clothes off. "Just needed to get you off-camera," she said. "I don't have access to Pap smear results. Hopefully it takes the network's weekend crew a second to pick up on that."

"I can't believe you ended up on a medical arc," Marlow said. "Remember the cat?" In seventh-grade biology, the teacher had shown the class a taxidermied feline, split open down the middle to reveal its pickled insides. Grace had thrown up immediately, in the aisle between their desks, prompting the teacher to put down the cat and pick up a bulk bag of sawdust.

"I'm nowhere near the blood and guts, trust me," Grace said. "I'm professional talent, science. I do genetic design here. I've been working on your baby." She grinned as Marlow's mouth fell open. "Yeah, I know," she murmured. "They don't let us talk, but I can build you a baby. Go figure. Guess they didn't think of that wrinkle when they revised a couple kids' contracts." Grace picked up a doctor's tablet, with its lightless, fog-safe gray screen, from the long shelf against the wall. She smoothed its smudged surface. "I need to show you something," she said.

Marlow watched Grace summon a diagram, a honeycomb of yellow twigs connected by blue and green and red dots. The heading at the top of the graphic said BABY #1217, TRIESTE. "I kept waiting to send in your mock-up," Grace said. "I didn't believe what I found, when I went looking through your genes. I thought maybe the network was up to something—a big reveal, or whatever. But here we are—your sowing's today, right? And they still haven't told you."

"Told me what?" Marlow said. A perverted hope, the size of a tender shoot, sprang up—what if the designers had discovered that she and Ellis were distant cousins? They'd *have* to break them up then.

"It's about your dad," Grace said. She leaned in and explained.

Grace, as she worked to turn Marlow and Ellis's preferences into a person, had come across something curious. The physical traits belonging to Marlow's father, the ones they had selected for their baby—brown eyes with an epicanthic fold to the lids, black hair with a thick shaft—did not match the DNA in Marlow's own genome. In all the places her father should have been, there were the genes of someone else. Someone whose hair and nails and spit Marlow and Ellis had not brought to Liberty.

"I'm so sorry to tell you this," she said, "but I can't find Aston anywhere. He's not your biological father."

"No, he's my father," Marlow said dumbly. "Did you look—could you look again?" She felt her breath quickening. This was a mistake. People made them all the time.

The first warning from the network sounded in her mind.

I should return to an on-camera space. Grace got it, too, Marlow could tell. She started to talk faster.

"I tried to do some research, before I got you all upset," Grace said. "And this was weird, too: I can't find your birth certificate on file anywhere. I know you hardly need them for anything these days, but still." She frowned down at her nails, shy in her accusation. "I mean, that *could* be unrelated, if you don't have one," she added. "It wouldn't be the weirdest thing, considering your birthdate."

Floss was always bragging about when Marlow was born. "The whole world's divided into born before or born after," she said sometimes. "Not too many people can say 'during.'"

Grace slid a scrap of paper across the desk to Marlow. Marlow startled at the sight of it, and picked it up quickly, automatically, as if to hide it from the cameras. But when she remembered that no one could see them, she looked at it closely. The paper was thick and plum-colored. A golden pattern was laced across it— the swirls rose off the paper, catching under her nails.

"It's wallpaper," Grace said. "Left over from my dining room. I didn't have anything else to write on." She reached out and turned the paper over.

There, on its yellowish-white side, was an address, scrawled in Grace's hand.

Mount Sinai West. 1000 Tenth Avenue, New York, New York.

"The hospital where I was born," Marlow said.

"Yeah," Grace replied. "I pulled the address from your file. Maybe someone there can tell you something. Maybe they have a record of your real—" She couldn't finish the sentence. She never did, Marlow thought, have a mean bone.

The pads of Marlow's fingers pawed awkwardly at the scrap. "Could you just message me this info?" she said.

Grace looked at her a long time before she answered. "I think

118

it's better if I don't," she said. "I'm just worried that…" She looked down, shook her head at her lap. "The network runs all our storylines by the Department of Info, you know," she said. "And the network clearly didn't mean for you to find out about this. If I message you, and the Department of Info flags it, I'm worried they'll…" Grace raised her eyebrows wearily. "Well, it's a discrepancy. We're going off-script here, Marlow."

An eerie jangle ran through Marlow. She had never had a secret from the network before. She had never really had a secret, period. She couldn't find a place in her mind to put it. It wasn't a comfortable fit.

I should return to an on-camera space immediately, the voice reiterated firmly.

"And I would pump your mom for information," Grace said. "Like, ask to see a picture of your dad, at the hospital when you were born."

Marlow already knew that there were no pictures from when she was born. She had asked about them when she was a kid; she wanted to see her mother bare of makeup. "I've told you this," Floss said when she asked. "We couldn't take any photos. Nobody's phones were working, and it was pitch black most of the time. Besides, sweetie, I assure you—I was wearing makeup."

Grace stood up. "We should go now," she said. She stopped with her hand on the door and turned back. "I really feel so bad, Marlow," she said, quietly. "About this, but about everything with Honey, too. That's why I had to tell you—I owe you. I always felt like it was my fault."

Marlow felt the start of tears. She pinched the bridge of her nose to stop them. "No, Grace," she said. "It wasn't. That's not how I see it at all."

Then the door was open and they were back in the hall, Grace telling loud, specific lies about test results, and things looking fine after all. Marlow nodded, playing along. In her mind she saw her father, young beside her bike. This time, when she remembered that day, she felt the rope slip from her waist.

———

The party was beginning, Marlow saw from her car. Guests were winding around the side of her mother's house, accepting drinks from a bot who nodded as each person made its tray a little lighter. Marlow looked up at the roof. Instead of bothering to weed, she saw, her mother had merely covered her whole overgrown roof garden in gaudy blue fabric.

It was Ellis who found her sitting there. He yanked the car door open, puncturing the pleather vacuum. "What are you doing?" he said. "You know my boss is here, right?" His hair was perfectly dry—Marlow recalled him telling her that, at the surfing simulator, no one actually got wet.

She let him pull her into the kitchen, where Jacqueline was dropping sprigs of mint and sliced cucumber into a pitcher of water. "*There's* the hot mama!" she sang.

Floss was across the room in a folding chair. She stood when she saw Marlow and stamped across the room. One of her eyes was sludgy with gunmetal shadow. The other was bare, vulnerable-looking. "Where were you?" she demanded. "You know it takes at least an hour to do *anything* with your hair, and people are *here* already."

The makeup girl stood poised with her brush in the air. She was the only real human hired for the day—no one liked bots so close to their eyes. "Should I keep going, Mrs. Clipp?" she said. "Or do you want me to start on the mother-to-be?"

Marlow straightened her spine. "I need to talk to my mom," she said, forcing herself to sound firm. She borrowed a phrase from Floss. "Can we have the room, please?"

It was amazing, once Marlow started talking, how quickly Floss's full range of dramatics kicked in. It was a symphony of fidgets, everything firing at once, like an emergency alert had gone out to her nervous system. Floss fluffed her roots like a maniac. She pursed her lips into a tight bud. She dabbed at her lower lash lines with her ring fingers. These weren't just antics for antics' sake, Marlow knew. Her mother had taught her the trick once: "When someone confronts you," she said, "don't respond right away. Give it a second, so that as many followers as possible have time to tune in." Now Floss was breathing in and out loudly, letting her eyes fill up.

"Don't you dare cry," Marlow snarled. She felt like she could shake Floss, could bang her head on the glass—oh, how her thoughts could startle her, without Hysteryl to keep them at an even chill—and she closed her eyes for a moment to drain the image from her mind. "I'm the one who should be crying, Mom," she said, when she opened her eyes again. "Me."

Floss ignored her, unleashing a long soprano sob. "Why are you so obsessed," she said, "with ruining this day? I worked *so* hard on this day."

"You lied to me all my life," Marlow hissed. "I don't care about a *party*. I have a different father? Who is it? Does Dad know?"

Floss eyed her, her lower lip trembling. "I've always tried to do what's best for you," she said. "And so has Aston. *That's* what makes someone a parent."

Marlow clenched her fists at the sound of the line. It was so accurate, so smooth, so out of sync with Floss's sputtering reflexes. The sentence must have been in the wings for years, Marlow realized, waiting for its cue. Its scripted patter gave her a horrible thought. The thought came out of nowhere and out of everything. It came from being used to finding out, again and again, that something she thought was real was not.

She had broken her contract once already today. Why not shatter the spell?

"Did they *cast* a different dad for me?" she whispered to her mother. "They can't do that, right?"

Floss gasped. She grabbed Marlow by the elbow and dragged her down the hall, to her master bath. She slammed the door. "How dare you?" she hissed at her. "How dare you talk about the network like that—and on camera? Shame on you. After all they've done for us, the life they've given us—" Floss stopped to catch her breath. Her chest was heaving beneath her dress, which was too tight everywhere, Lycra burrowing mercilessly between the soft shelves of her flesh. Marlow noticed, for the first time, that her mother was wearing a necklace with diamond-stacked letters, spelling NANA.

And she noticed something else: her mother's walk-in shower was crammed with vases, with hundreds of roses in a dozen different kinds of pink. There were roses the color of a shell's pale inside and roses the color of the scorching lipstick Floss wore in the summer and roses every shade in between. They had been shoved in here, to dry and wither, because Floss hadn't wanted to wait on the florist order for the sowing until Marlow and Ellis picked a sex. She had simply ordered both pink and blue, then cast aside the one she didn't need.

Strangely, that was what Marlow was thinking of—all those flowers cut and dying, for absolutely nothing, behind sealed glass—when she said it: "See, Mom, this is why we don't want the baby having any of your genes."

Floss was silent as she walked to the sink. She rummaged in her bin of endless products, found a pot of eye shadow, and finished what the makeup girl had started. Marlow could see, as she crept closer, that there were more tears in her mother's eyes, threatening to fall. And then they simply didn't. They went away on their own.

Floss snapped the eye shadow shut. "It's time," she said. She opened the door, pushed past Marlow, and went back out into the hall. A moment later, Marlow heard the French doors that led to the backyard clicking open, then closing with a slam.

Jacqueline had tactfully retired to the kitchen while Floss and

Marlow fought, but now Marlow felt her hand on her back. She looked up and saw her friend behind her in the mirror, holding the yellow gown open at the knees. Marlow stepped in, and Jacqueline zipped it up.

When Jacqueline led her back down the hall a minute later, Marlow could see her sowing beginning. Just beyond the French doors, at the base of the deck stairs she was to walk down, the string quartet was seated in their spots, bows sawing. She could hear the violins.

Jacqueline walked Marlow to the doors and rubbed her back. Once, gently, in a circle. Then she was gone, too.

Marlow took in the scene on the other side of the glass. This was it; she should be out there. The music had stopped and started again—Brahms, it was always Brahms, when the mother-to-be was about to appear. Jacqueline was in her place, up front and to the side, her floor-length hem circled by her children, standing with her as a reminder of what this was all about. Ellis stood in front of the crowd, waiting for Marlow beneath an arch draped in bluebells. He was smiling at the guests, cracking jokes that didn't seem to land. Bridget twisted in her front-row seat to note who was and wasn't laughing at her magnificent son. Floss sat across the aisle from Bridget, staring straight ahead, all clues to her expression hidden by the swollen back of her updo.

Come to think of it, Marlow thought, it wasn't just about her mother. She didn't want to make a baby out of any of them.

There was one bot left behind Marlow, sorting cocktail napkins in the kitchen. She turned and walked over to it. She looked it right in its crystal eyes. "Move," she said.

The bot stepped aside politely, and Marlow reached past it to grab the duffel she had stashed in the corner of the kitchen. The network had approved her and Ellis's request for a babymoon, only a short distance away, just past the Mexican border. It would help with her stress, Marlow had reminded the talent welfare officers pointedly, when she petitioned them to let her go. She had booked an in-room acupuncture treatment and a private session with a yogi who specialized in fertility poses. Ellis was going to learn to roll a cigar. They were all packed, slated to leave right after the party concluded.

Marlow tucked the slip from Grace into a small pocket sewn on inside of the bag.

There was only one thing left to do now, she knew, if she really wanted to go. If she really wanted to run, and have a fighting chance of getting away. She would not be like Ida, half-gone and traceable. She didn't want anyone following her.

Marlow hesitated with her fingers curled over the gem on her wrist. *Dad*, she intuited, squeezing her eyes shut. *It's Marlow. Are you there?* He still wore his device—though he never answered, the messages technically still went through. *I love you, Dad*, Marlow intuited. *Please try to eat.* She wondered if he could hear the words on some level, if he tried to figure out who she was. For the first time, she realized, thinking back to Grace at the clinic—she and Aston were even. She didn't know, now, who he was, either.

Marlow slid her finger underneath her device, easing it upward one side at a time, wincing as its powerful adhesive relented, taking a few strips of skin with it as it went. She dropped her device between abandoned drinks on Floss's countertop. An odor shot up into her nose: sweet and stomach-turning, the smell of skin she hadn't seen in years. She felt something dim in her brain.

How long would it take for the people outside to come looking for her? She was already one minute late. Soon it would be two. Her mother, Ellis, anyone who had her on their maps—they were likely shifting in their seats right now, checking for her inside their heads and confirming that everything was all right, they had proof: she was still here, in the house. How many minutes until someone decided to come inside and look, to trust their instincts for once, instead of their devices?

The violinists were still playing, chins tucked low. Their faces gave nothing away, like the song always went on this long. The people were standing, waiting, their gaze on the back door.

But Marlow was going out the front.

She hurried across the lawn to her car. The dress spread out like a single useless wing, tulle hissing behind her as it skimmed the grass. A man walking his small, wet-eyed dog stopped to stare as she pushed herself into the driver's seat, bundling the endless skirt in around her, slapping it down so she could see. She figured out, as she cleared the mess from her vision, why she didn't like the gown anymore. It wasn't just that she had seen the color wrong, that the yellow screamed more loudly now than it had when she chose it. It was that she didn't like yellow at all, she realized. She had always thought it her favorite color, but that was a trick of the pills. It was just that, before she saw everything clearly, it was the brightest thing.

CHAPTER NINE

Orla

New York, New York
2016

As someone who made a living taking down wheat-dull quotes from glossy somebodies, Orla had always thought she knew what fame meant, what it consisted of, what it promised and took away. She had met Floss in August, the melon-colored end of the New York summer, everyone trudging and dying for fall to arrive and remind them why they came here. By January—another month in which everyone forgot, again, what it was they liked about this place—Orla had learned that everything she thought she knew about fame was wrong. Adorably outsider.

For instance: the craziest thing about being famous was not the being recognized, mostly by the girls who spent their twenties in the East Thirties, but also, sometimes, by men, who cupped their hands and yelled down the block, "Yo! It's the roommate!"

The craziest thing was not the money, which landed in chunks in Orla's account, knocking it up to five figures and finally, unbelievably, six.

The craziest thing was not the parties, which Orla struggled to look natural at. She was terrible at dancing and even worse at drugs. "Holy shit," someone had said to her at a party recently, "go wipe your nose. There's coke on it. You look like an albino pig." The idea of snorting things made Orla queasy, so she tended to simply skim her face along the mirror instead of inhaling.

The craziest thing about fame was not the fact that she had a trick for wasting fine cocaine now.

It was not even the fact that the person who had noticed her powdered snout was an Olympic darling du jour, a javelin hurler with more DUIs than medals who had followed her into the bathroom, waited for her to clean up, and mashed himself up against her.

It was almost, but not quite, the fact that it seemed to exempt her from the weather. Winter in New York, for Orla, was suddenly no more difficult than any other season. Gone were the days of underestimating icy puddles and paying with damp feet all day. Winter was half-over, and Orla had barely buttoned her coat. The rain boots from Gayle stayed under her bed. She went out in silk flats and suede platforms, in all sorts of impractical, delicate shoes. If the street filled with rain, or a curb was blocked by snow, their driver and bodyguard, Amadou, would put his hands beneath her arms and lift her over the moisture, into his Escalade.

No, the craziest thing about fame, to Orla—who was never meant to have it in the first place—was that, deep down, she didn't mind it. She wouldn't have admitted this to anyone: when a perfect stranger looked at her twice or followed her on Instagram, she felt a flickering understanding of Floss and what she wanted. She knew how strangers saw her: as the cheapest sort of star, the tagalong friend of a TMI queen. But the point was: they saw her. She was visible. She was there.

On most red carpets, Orla would stand with Floss for ten seconds or so. Then, despite the way Floss sometimes called out over the camera shutters' soft gunfire—"that's my friend Orla Cadden, C-A-D-D-E-N, she's a literary talent on the rise"—Orla would be asked to move off to the side, so that Floss could be shot alone. She never minded. She liked to stand at the edge of the step-and-repeat, watching Floss give what they called, together, The Face. It was a thing to behold. Floss would suck in her cheeks, push her lips out in a pout, and make her eyes smolder like she was charging into battle. She would cast The Face down her nose, over her shoulder—it was a beam she could throw anywhere. Orla always felt mesmerized, watching her. Who cared that Floss was, essentially, just standing there? Orla knew now how hard it was to stay put in the crosshairs of so many flashbulbs. The instinct, when things got that bright, was to run, or at least to blink. But others who witnessed The Face in person were not as impressed. If Floss heard a camera click while she was talking to someone, she'd abandon her sentence cold and go right to work, posing. Whoever she was talking to would be left to stand there, perplexed and forgotten, until they saw themselves out of the moment—or until Orla did, smiling apologetically and trying to finish Floss's point. "Doesn't she know that, like, we can see her?" one of those people had whispered to Orla once. But Floss was not concerned about the people in front of her; Floss was concerned about followers. Her followers only saw the picture, and the picture always turned out.

One night, as Orla killed time out of frame, she looked down the press's side of the carpet and saw the laminated paper she used to stand on—LADY-ISH.COM. There was a set of delicate, neon-polished toes covering the name that had replaced hers, and Orla followed them up to the rest of a girl who must have just finished college. Only recently had Orla come to accept that there was now a whole class of people living and working in New York who were several years younger than her, that they were not interns who had overstayed their summers—they were here to stay and grow up and compete.

Orla walked toward the girl from Lady-ish. "Hi," she said, feeling radiant, generous.

The girl looked up from scribbling on her notepad. She had enormous black-rimmed glasses, perfect olive skin, and nude lip gloss, shiny and pearly, the kind Orla would have thought was out of style. Self-consciously, she touched her own lips, which were a thick red Floss had talked her into.

"Huh?" the girl said. She studied Orla. "Oh. Right. You're on *Flosston Public*. The bookish one, right? Orla."

It was her brand, but Orla still flinched at being called bookish. Not knowing what else to do, she trilled, feeling fake, "I *love* Lady-ish."

The girl broke into a knowing grin. "I guess you do," she said. "You worked there a long time."

Orla bristled. "Right," she said, reddening. "It's a great place to start out."

The girl shrugged. "I went to Yale," she said, as if this explained multitudes. "I won't be there that long. I'm writing a play. About— Well, I shouldn't say too much. My agent wouldn't want me to. I swear it's like her full name is Polly 'Top Secret' Cummings."

Orla nodded, teeth frozen. The girl had to be bluffing, she thought. There was no way she was repped by Polly Cummings. Polly was a lioness of literary agents, one whose name Orla had known since high school, when she checked a guide to the industry out of the local library. Her senior year, she had mailed Polly a short story she had written, the same one that now made up most of her manuscript. She remembered the day she got the response from Polly's office. Gayle had come running out to where Orla floated in their aboveground pool, waving the envelope—Polly's response came by mail, because it was only 2005—"Polly Cummings wrote back!" *I see promise here. Keep going!!—P,* said the Post-it on top of the packet Orla had mailed. Beneath the Post-it was another sheet, a half page of typed feedback. Now that she knew how these things worked, Orla understood that the letter had been written by an assistant—this was back when people Yale Girl's age were expected to be assistants, not self-ordained playwrights. Yale Girl was full of shit, Orla ruled. But something must have crossed her face, doubt or envy or fear, because Yale Girl smiled suddenly, like she had won a race between them. Just before she turned to see who else was coming down the line, Yale Girl looked at Orla with pity in her eyes. "Anyway, good luck," she said. "I mean it."

Orla was already shuffling away when she realized: the bitch hadn't even bothered asking her a question.

———

Floss had broken through, become known, back in September. What did it was Paulina's fall at the Urban Outfitters, and Floss looking on, not catching her. It should have ruined Floss's life. It might have sent her to court. But instead, she was saved by a sound effect.

There had been video, of course. At first, this was a bad thing. It looked somehow worse each time they watched it—Floss tugging her arm away, Paulina collapsing in a pile of wrong-way bones. They huddled together on Orla's bed as the Paulina fans who saw their address on Twitter stood outside their building, hurling overripe squash at the brick. (The internet had decided that Floss's face was gourd-like.)

Over the course of twenty-four hours, the video transcended web bedlam and landed on the news, local and national. Anchors shook their heads and talked about new lows. "You don't understand," Orla said, trying to impress on Floss how big and bad this was. "It's not just online. *Grown-ups* know about it now."

The little mobs kept coming. Orla and Floss were trapped inside. They quickly ran out of food. The police had stopped bike messengers from entering the building because of safety concerns, so there could be no takeout. Their neighbors all hated them for the fuss, so there was no one to beg for help or ramen. In a desperate moment, thinking the Ukrainian man might sympathize, they took a ride up to the roof. But all they found was a new padlock on the patio gate. Floss was furious. She took it personally. But Orla thought, as she stared at the lock, *Good for you.*

Gayle kept calling Orla and then refusing to speak to her, handing the phone to Jerry as soon as Orla picked up. But when Orla told her father that she and Floss were hungry, her mother went to work. Twelve hours later, the doorman held out a crazily markered-up box—FRAGILE!!!! PERISHABLE!!!—filled with cardboard sleeves of pasta and bubble-wrapped jars of Prego, Campbell's soup, Chex Mix, Oreos, a bunch of bananas, Maxwell House coffee, and the drip coffee maker that sat on the counter in her parents' kitchen. They had simply torn its plug out of the wall and would go without it, for her.

By the time they had eaten the provisions from Gayle, the strangest thing had happened: the video began to work for them. Someone, somewhere, had taken it and edited in a sound. *Womp-womp*, went the sound, as Paulina careened. Perhaps it was because the news said the model was healing, perhaps it was because everyone had seen the fall too many times to be shocked again—people decided they *liked* the *womp-womp* version of the video. They began to laugh about it. They shared. "We are ALL Floss Natuzzi some days," someone wrote, and suddenly, astoundingly, everyone agreed.

That was when Aston Clipp showed up, calling his name through the door.

When Floss opened it, all Orla could see was a giant cube of jewel-toned flowers. Aston's face was completely covered by them; what she saw first was his hands, golden tan and expertly manicured, cupping the bottom of the vase. The bouquet was too wide to fit through the doorway. Aston barreled in anyway, snapping blooms' necks on the door frame, crushing petals underneath his space-age high-tops.

When he set the flowers down, Orla saw that there was not just one person behind the flowers, but three.

There was Aston, looking just as he did in photos, if slightly smaller. He was easily the best-looking person she had ever seen. His thick black hair fell into his gaze and curled along his jaw, which had a tripod of dimples—both cheeks, and one in his chin. His dark, curved eyes became, as soon as he walked in, the room's magnetic pole.

Behind Aston, bent over picking up flowers, were Craig and Melissa. Craig was a compilation of unappealing parts—mottled skin, baby-blond hair, watery blue eyes, small teeth—who nevertheless carried himself with the pomp of a handsome man. Melissa was startlingly muscular, with a burnt-sienna spray tan and hair about the same shade, shellacked into tight spirals. When they were finished cleaning up, Melissa took all the petals and brushed them into Orla's palms. Orla knew what they thought right away. They took her for Floss's assistant.

"This apartment," Aston said to Floss. "It's special. I've been at the Bowery for months. I hate it. It's, like, *too* nice. They won't stop making my bed." He looked up at the flickering orb by the door, down at the scuffed parquet. "This place is so—*nothing.* But sometimes it's the soulless places that turn out to have the most soul."

"Exactly," purred Floss, whose name wasn't even on the lease. "That's so like you to get it."

Aston pushed off the drywall. He went and stood so close to Floss, the rest of them looked away. "It's over with Paulina," he said. "And I'd love to get to know you. Can I take you to dinner?"

"Omigod, of *course*," Floss whined through her nose.

Craig looked up from the phone he had been assaulting. "Great," he said. "Now that's done. And we come with the deal, Melissa and me." He pointed at himself. "Manager." He pointed at Melissa. "Publicist."

"You mean, like, for the date?" Orla said.

Craig ignored her. He looked slowly from Floss to Aston and back, then turned to Melissa. "I think this will be good. I think this will be huge," he said to her, scratching his jaw. "What do you think?"

Melissa tossed her hair. Orla heard the racket of her hard curls settling on her back. "I think what I always think," she said. "That if we ride the wave and never fight it, there will be good things ahead for all of us."

Aston took Floss to dinner. Orla waited into the night, drinking coffee to keep herself up, thinking that Floss would want to dissect the entire evening when she came home. But the two of them stayed out till sunrise, then slept all day in Floss's room. By day two, Orla still hadn't seen them again, but she had heard the door open and close a few times. The next time she came out of her bedroom, she saw that Aston's things—clusters of glass-bottled essential oils, a remote-control helicopter, great heaps of sneakers—had materialized in the apartment, making it seem young and boyish and smaller right away. After that, he did not leave. Sometimes, Orla minded very much—her back was sore from picking up toys and shoes, and her ears were sore from her earplugs, which covered the sounds of what went on in the bedroom. Other times, she didn't mind at all, because Aston made the place feel kinder, too. He had a tender side he kept indoors, where his fans and foes couldn't access it. Orla had seen him do phone interviews, being uncooperative and unquotably profane, while snuggled under a blanket on the couch, like a child. She had overheard him Skyping with his charity-assigned "little brother," had heard him tell the boy to stay in school (though

Aston himself had quit in ninth grade) and to respect women (though he sometimes showed the kid racy photos of his exes from his phone). When Floss was out or sleeping, Aston would mill in the living room, hanging on Orla. If she had a book in her lap, he would say: "Whatcha readin', bookworm?" If a video was rolling on her laptop screen, he would say, "Whatcha watchin', couch potatah?" Once, when both girls had had enough of his hyperactivity, he retreated good-naturedly to the kitchen and scrubbed the crusted pans they never touched, the ones that came with the place. Then he baked blueberry muffins from scratch.

Three weeks after Aston walked into 6D, he and Floss signed a deal to star in a "docuseries" about falling in love.

Six weeks after that, Floss and Orla took the C train to a gym that had sent them free spinning coupons and found Floss's face writ large in an ad on the subway wall. Sharpie penises prodded at both of her nostrils. They screamed and hugged each other.

A month after that, the show premiered, which was when things went both wrong and right. Right: *Flosston Public* was an instant hit, completing Floss's transformation from heartless sociopath to sympathetic goddess. Wrong: it made Orla famous, too.

———

Flosston Public began with a prank. The show's writer, a tall girl with stringy red hair, explained in her nicotine rasp how things would go. "Floss comes in the front door, Floss yells out 'babe,' Aston springs out from the end of the kitchen and dumps a bucket of flour on her."

No one had invited Orla to the preproduction meeting, but it was a Saturday, so she was home, and she happened to live on location. "Why?" she asked as she refilled the Brita.

"It's a good prank," the writer said. "The audience loves

pranks. Floss and Aston love pranks. It's part of their brand. It's perfect."

"Sick." Aston clapped his hands. "We do love pranks, babe."

The closest thing to a prank Orla had seen Floss and Aston pull was when they had sex on the breakfast bar and knocked her microwaved enchilada to the floor. She looked at Floss dubiously.

"I actually don't love pranks," Floss said. "What if my shirt rides up? I look fat when my shirt rides up."

"Good," the writer snapped. "You could stand to be more relatable. It's nice that you're hot and all, but that only gets you male fans watching you on YouTube without the sound on. You have to make the girls like you."

"But Orla's the only girl who likes me," Floss said. "I get along so much better with men."

"It's true," Aston said. "We get along great." He pulled Floss back down the hall and slammed the bedroom door. The writer rolled her eyes.

"THE PRANK WILL ESTABLISH A SENSE OF PLAY-FULNESS," boomed Mason, the show's producer. He was a puffy man with dark under-eye circles who, in stark contrast to his writer, shouted everything in monotone. He laughed by saying "heh heh heh," doled out precisely, just like that.

"I get that," Orla said. "But why does it have to be *flour*?"

Mason frowned at her and said, "Can you get the talent back out here?"

Before the meeting, Floss and Aston had been holed up in Floss's bedroom, bingeing a TV drama, and now Orla heard the hourly jingle of the theme music wafting from the room. "I'm not their assistant," she said to Mason, sharply. She picked up her laptop from the counter and flopped down to work on the couch, where she assumed she would be out of the shot. Hair and makeup had taken over her bedroom.

This was the truth: she rerouted her whole life by picking the couch instead of the love seat.

"We'll send a cleaning lady to take care of the mess, first thing in the morning, I promise," Mason said.

All night, they threw the flour, setting and resetting the shot, coughing as the air filled up, and in the morning, there was no cleaning lady. Everything Orla touched for the next few days was gritty. When she could stand it no longer, she took a sick day from work and scrubbed the apartment, vacuuming it three times over. Even the insides of the doors on the kitchen cabinets needed to be wiped. It was inside one of them that Orla found a Post-it with Floss's frantic cursive on it. The ink lay in deep grooves on the paper, like Floss had pressed with all her might. "Be relatable!!!!!" the Post-it said.

The next day, the crew descended again. "The audio from that flour scene is complete shit," Mason said. "We need to do it again." He made Orla sit in the same spot on the couch, with her computer. "For continuity," he said. She shrugged, imagining herself foggy in the background, no more part of the action than their Ikea stick lamp. No one told her different.

And then came the premiere.

In episode one, as Floss and Aston pawed at each other, giggling, drawing streaks in the flour dust left on their skin, Orla sat in the background, but not really. Every eye roll of hers had been left in the edit, every sigh made perfectly audible. The dynamic was quickly established: Floss and Aston were idiots, and Orla was the brainy third wheel trapped in their love nest. The response, online, was instant. Bloggers declared Orla the "bitchy heroine" of *Flosston Public*; people turned her sour faces into GIFs. The finger she had swiped across her face to remove a stray crumb became, as it spread across the internet, an emblem of everywoman defiance. **I CAN'T WITH HER!** someone screamed. **QUEEN!** Someone else screenshotted Orla's dismal pout and wrote, **So here for this girl not being here for this.**

Half an hour after the *Flosston Public* premiere ended, someone figured out who Orla was, matching her face to her author pic on Lady-ish.

Forty minutes afterward, she got a text from her dad: **Aunt Marie says you were on television tonight. Maybe you could call your mother and tell her about it?**

Forty-seven minutes afterward, she got an email from her boss. Ingrid kept it short. Subject: **You on Flosston Public.** Body: **The fuck?**

Orla looked up from the email to see Floss watching her from the other couch. They had decorated with streamers and bought André brand champagne—the last cheap champagne they would ever drink—to celebrate the show's debut. Aston had fallen asleep with his head in Floss's lap just after the episode began, and now, as Floss raked his endless hair with her fingers, she glared across the room at Orla. Orla realized she must look happy, thumbing through her own reviews. She quickly changed her face and put her phone down. Ingrid could wait till the morning.

———

But the next morning, when Orla got to the Lady-ish office, her chair was gone. All that was left at her desk was a sinewy clutch of rainbow-colored cables.

"Orla," Ingrid called from her office. She motioned her in and shut the door.

Sitting across from her boss, Orla tried to quiet her pulse by focusing on a fabric-framed photo of Annabella, Ingrid's French bulldog.

Ingrid noticed her looking. She turned the photo facedown protectively. "You're fired," she said. She opened her mouth to say something else, then stacked her hands atop each other on her desk, elbows wide, and placed her forehead on top of them.

Orla stared at the half inch of graying hair on either side of Ingrid's scalp, grasping for something to say. A line from her quitting fantasy came back to her. "Ingrid," she said, "I want to thank you for the opportunity."

Ingrid kept her head down. "You don't strike me as the sell-out type, Orla," she said into her knuckles. "I don't know why you would put me—put all of us—in a position like this."

"What do you mean, position?" Orla said.

Ingrid straightened. She dabbed at the oily crescents on either side of her nose. "The position," she said, "of looking like we let you use Lady-ish to make you and your friend famous."

Orla felt blotches rising on her chest. "Not me," she said. "I wasn't even supposed to be on the show."

"I'm not interested in the details," Ingrid said. "Just go." She checked her phone. "I have interviews for your replacement starting in, like, ten minutes. Oh, and, Orla," she said. "Just so you know. When whatever this is blows up in your face, you can guaran-fucking-tee we will cover it."

———

When Orla got off the elevator at home, she could hear high, messy crying coming from her apartment. She paused just ahead of the door and put her ear to the wall.

Inside, she heard Mason, sounding like he was saying something he'd said a thousand times. "She's all anyone talked about from the first episode. I'm confused—do we not want a show? Do we not want to get *paid*?"

Then Craig: "All right, Mason, but I'm sure—I'm *sure*—you still feel that Floss and Aston are the stars of this show. Don't you, Mason?" Craig exhaled. He rapped on something. "Melissa, will you...*deal* with her?"

Melissa's voice, dull and obligated: "There, there, Floss." Orla had a sudden memory of Melissa the night they celebrated getting green-lit. It was the only time she had ever seen Melissa drunk. She had beaten Craig in arm wrestling, flattening his forearm against the sticky table. Afterward, she growled to no one in particular, "I'm *never* having a baby!"

Floss let out a sob that barely arranged itself into words: "AstonSTOPwiththefuckingBALL!"

A bouncing in the background stopped. "My bad," Aston chirped.

"Floss, I'm sorry," Mason said. "But I'm not here to pimp your ego. I'm here to see that *Flosston* gets a full-season pickup. You want that producer credit? Yeah? Then you should be calling Orla right now to say how great she was."

There was a long, sniffly period where no one spoke. "Fine," Orla heard Floss say. "But she has to be clear on her role."

"For sure," Mason agreed. "You'll see, it'll be funny, kind of like a *Three's Company* vibe that will really endear—"

"That's not what I mean." Orla heard the deliberate click of Floss's heels on the wood, moving closer to the door. "I mean we all know who I'm supposed to be, and we all know who she's supposed to be. Right?"

All of them went around, echoing: "Right."

Except for Aston, who made a lip-trumpet sound and said, "Wha? I'm not following this toxic convo. Who's Orla supposed to be, now?"

There was silence. Orla could picture them, waiting on the talent.

"You know," Floss said finally. "A secondary character."

———

That night, Floss opened Orla's bedroom door. Her eyes were still red from crying. "Let's go out," she said. "Just you and me. We'll do karaoke. We'll celebrate our ratings." The "our" came out, to Orla's ear, like a piece of glass Floss had to gag up.

They went to a place in Koreatown. It was the early side of evening and the bar was bleeding people when they got there, happy hour holdouts stumbling on to search for pizza. The drinkers who were staying, trying to bridge the gap into the real night, blinked and pulled out their phones when they saw the girls walk in.

"They're tweeting that we're here," Floss whispered in Orla's ear. But Orla saw a girl with silver bangles up her arm thrust her phone at her friend. Its screen was glaring white and lined with search results. "See, look," Bangles said triumphantly. "Told you she was someone." She and the friend clutched each other's forearms and moved toward Floss. "Can we get a picture?" Bangles said.

Floss smiled and nodded. She stretched her face forward politely, like a zoo animal accepting food through a fence. Bangles looked at Orla.

"Aren't you—" she began brightly. But then Floss interrupted. "Orla," she said loudly, "would you mind taking the picture?"

Bangles held the phone out. Orla took the phone and backed away from them, counted "one, two, three." By the time she was finished, a guy in a polo oxford, soaked through with sweat from singing, was jamming his greasy phone at her and sidling up to Floss, eyes unabashedly on her breasts.

It went on like that for several minutes—Floss in front of the camera, Orla behind it. By now, by word of mouth or search engine, everyone in the club seemed to know who Floss was. "Where's Aston?" someone shouted. "Where's the bitchy girl?" somebody else said, and Orla thought, *For fuck's sake, I'm right here*.

When there was no one left who wanted her, Floss took Orla's hand and tugged her toward the stairs to the basement. A second earlier, Orla had been annoyed, close to walking out of the bar. But now she looked down at Floss's fingers clamped over hers, pulling her through the bodies. She had seen girls do this before in packed bars—hold hands to keep the mob from separating them—and she had always, always, always wanted someone to do that with her.

In the basement, they ducked into a private room. It had a huge TV with blurry footage of people dancing and was sound-proofed with ugly padding in burgundy and blush. A binder of laminated pages, songs and their six-digit codes, stuck to a ring-stained table. Floss picked up the binder and flipped through it, jabbed a code into the remote.

The song's intro began, all simpleton chords and synthetic drums. It was familiar, either a song Orla knew or one that sounded like everything. She was hardly listening, anyway. She was thinking of how Floss had said the word *secondary* that af-ternoon, the consonants bitter and violent. Orla gathered her anger back and tried to believe she could do it—she could say to Floss, right now, *I heard you, why would you, after all we, you bitch.*

The song went on and Orla remembered it. It belonged to a star who she had since forgotten was once famous for music, one who went on to play in a reality romance and make mid-priced shoes for chain stores. The lyrics came up on the screen, blue rippling across them in time, and Orla found she still knew every word. She remembered herself during a lazy middle-school summer, using Catherine's landline phone to call a video request channel called The Box, pressing in the digits for this overdone ballad. Catherine wringing her hands, Orla rolling her eyes and telling her to relax, that her parents wouldn't notice the charge.

Then Floss began to sing, and Orla's thoughts fell apart. Floss's voice, the real one, the one she abandoned so often in pursuit of something put-on, was phenomenal. It was deep, and ribbed, and searingly on-pitch, demolishing notes out of standard human reach. Floss pushed her hair into a knot on top of her head, care-lessly, as if she was fed up with it keeping her from something.

Orla was thinking of Floss's faceless mother, doubting her daughter's talents, when she blurted, "You're so good, Floss, God. Wouldn't you have rather been a singer than a…?"

Floss waited for her to finish and smiled sadly when she didn't. "I tried to be a singer, at first," she said. "But *how* do you be a singer? It's not like what we're doing. There's no formula." She shrugged. "Maybe if the show gets big enough, they'll let me do a single."

"You could have tried harder," Orla said. "You still could. We could forget the other stuff."

The song was over. Floss put down the microphone and picked up her drink. She stuck the little red straw in the corner of her mouth. "I don't want to," she said. "It just isn't a practical dream."

———

Several Saturdays later, after three subsequent episodes of *Flosston Public* had aired to a growing audience, Orla had plans with her mother. Gayle was coming into the city to see *Jersey Boys* with some of her friends from Zumba. It was not the first time for any of them. Orla was hungover, but she forced herself to try to write beforehand. She held down different keys, creating little pictures in her manuscript that began as procrastination but sort of started to seem like something, perhaps a meaningful graphic that could be worked into the story. Orla highlighted a crude sailboat she had made of lowercase *r*'s and called up its word count. Thirty-nine. Not bad.

Orla could tell from the moment she saw her that Gayle had more news about Danny. Her mother practically glittered when she was holding fresh gossip.

Orla herded Gayle and her friends onto the C train, then the B train. She led them aboveground and toward Mulberry Street. They ambled down the sidewalk five across, mortifying her, and succumbed to the first Little Italy loudmouth who beckoned to them from his doorway. They sat down and ate pasta drowned in sludgy red sauce. Everyone but Orla declared it "heavenly."

Orla tried to settle herself into a place of indifference. The more she wanted to hear about Danny, the longer Gayle would hold back. So Orla smiled as one of her mother's friends performed a long retelling of an episode of *King of Queens*. When another asked Orla if "they still call it the Big Apple," she treated the question thoughtfully. When a third screamed and knocked back her chair, claiming to have seen a roach—it turned out to be a tile scuff, but the woman sniffed that they should still get a discount, for the scare—Orla apologized on New York's behalf. Finally, the girls from Zumba rose to go to the bathroom. Orla and her mother stayed behind.

Gayle drew her credit card out of the leather billfold with a flourish. "They're getting a divorce," she said. "Maybe you should reach out."

Orla blushed, feeling caught. "Why would I reach out?" she said.

Her mother rolled her eyes. "Not to Danny. To Catherine. To offer your condolences." She shook her head. "I never got why you turned so cold to her. Maybe if you'd kept her in your life, you wouldn't be..."

The waiter refilled their waters, unnecessarily.

"I wouldn't be *what*?" Orla felt her heart closing up. They were going to waste time that could be put to use parsing the details of this divorce revelation—*Was Gayle sure? Who told her? When?*—on Orla's entanglement with Floss. This confrontation had been brewing for months, Orla knew, as Gayle's texts and emails grew terser. Even before Orla got fired, her mother stopped posting her work on Facebook.

"You wouldn't be— Well, what do you call what you're doing?" Gayle leaned forward. "I saw the clips of you on TV. You looked so *unpleasant*." Her mother's friends were beginning to file out of the restroom, negotiating their way back to the table. "I thought," Gayle said, "you wanted to be a writer."

"Is that what you thought I was before?" Orla squashed the paper sleeve from her straw beneath her thumb. "Because honestly, what I'm doing is pretty much the same as my old job. Now I'm just on the other side."

Gayle opened her purse and began rearranging it. She was in charge of the tickets, and Orla knew that Gayle would not fully relax until each Zumba girl had been seated in the theater. "Being part of what Floss is doing," Orla went on, "meeting the people I'm meeting—trust me, Mom, that's the fastest way for me to get to be a writer."

Gayle looked up then. She zipped her purse shut. "I'm going to tell you the same thing I've been telling you since you were ten years old, Orla," she said quietly, like she was trying not to embarrass her. "It's not good to be a follower."

"I'm *not*," Orla said. The second word came out just as she did when she was ten: a squeaking, two-syllable opera. "Look, Mom, I'm sorry, but you don't get what it's like, handling all this."

"When I was your age," Gayle said slowly, "I already had you. And a job at State Farm."

"That's exactly what I mean," Orla said. "You don't get how things work in the real world."

Gayle blinked then, revealing a face Orla had never seen on her mother: damaged, blown back, her skin utterly smooth, like a calm before a storm. Her mouth began to tremble.

"Is that right?" she said. "You think you're so great, up here, where everybody under*stands* you. And they do! That's the joke of it, if you ask me." She pulled her chair in to let one of the women pass, and Orla startled as the leg scraped the floor. "You really believe it," Gayle hissed. "That whatever you're doing is more important than what people do everywhere else. Just because you're doing it in a city where, when we come to visit you, we see rats eating on park benches and people shitting on the subway!"

"That was one time," Orla said, though the shitting had been twice.

"Let me tell you something," Gayle said, leaning in. "I'm more interesting at home in my kitchen than you'll ever be in this city."

She jerked backward as soon as she said it, as if she had slapped Orla. But she didn't apologize; she didn't say another word. The girls from Zumba took over the space around them, rounding up their bags, arguing loudly over who had seen *Jersey Boys* first.

Orla still took them to the theater. She knew her mother wanted her to, even if they were no longer able to look at each other. Now she understood why her parents always peered at her with worry in their eyes: despite never having said it, they thought she was doing nothing. This, what she was doing at this moment, was what Gayle believed to be the sum return on their investment in her: she knew her way around Manhattan. She knew to look to the still-new tower to go south, and how to find the Hudson as soon as she climbed aboveground. Phones could do as much these days, but there was a certain pride in knowing how to do it on your own. This was what Orla had amounted to, in her mother's eyes: an expensive collection of instincts, useless on the other side of the river.

———

It took a while for Orla's official *Flosston Public* offer, the deal that would make her a regular part of the cast, to come through—the studio had to approve it, then the network. When Orla asked Craig what was taking so long, he went on about holidays. To hear Craig tell it, there was always a festive reason he couldn't reach someone in Hollywood. The Fourth of July gave way to Labor Day. Rosh Hashanah turned into Yom Kippur, which put everyone "out of pocket." He wouldn't call anyone with an Italian last name for a full week surrounding Columbus Day.

Finally, the contract arrived. Orla would make sixteen thousand dollars an episode—"really decent for a minor player," Craig said. Orla just nodded—she had no way to tell otherwise. She hesitated with the pen in her hand, thinking of her mother's angry gaze, then of Floss in the karaoke room, so sure her real dream wasn't worth it. It wasn't forever, this show, Orla reminded herself. The show would pay her rent, and give her a platform—a place to start when she was ready to send her book out and be an author. Once her book sold, *Flosston Public* would become trivia, moving steadily down her Wikipedia page as the years and her accomplishments piled up. She would laugh about it later, on a stage somewhere, as an author *in conversation*.

After she signed the papers, Aston gave her a high five and a wet willy.

Melissa emailed her a summary of her fees, ending the message, "Of course, I know you can't afford me now, but for the future." She tacked on a winky-face emoji. Orla looked across 6D, at Melissa's actual face. It was trained on her phone and stony.

Mason handed Orla a pair of glasses—glossy, gaping, black. She held them awkwardly, the pads of her fingers pressed into the lenses.

"But I see fine," she said.

Mason nodded. "Yeah, we think it helps establish your character," he said. "You know, your corner of the brains-brawn-beauty trinity. Heh heh heh." Orla didn't have to ask which corner was hers. She put the glasses on and everything looked the same.

Floss was draped on a chair, letting someone touch her up before her next shot. She winked at Orla and said, in the voice she used to only use on other people, "I love you in glasses. This is gonna be *so* fun."

———

When the New Year began, *Flosston Public* was the biggest thing on TV. The one-sheet Melissa always used to describe it summed up the gimmick thus: "A wackadoodle, white-hot celebrity couple and the sarcastic schlump who shares their living space." Orla's name appeared, in parentheses, after the word *schlump*.

Money accumulated meaninglessly. Floss and Aston did big things, like chartering a yacht to watch a rare comet (but everyone got drunk and forgot to look for it). Orla did small things, like running up four-digit bills at Saks, pushing away the sense that she would be exposed as a fraud, asked to give her items back, by the time she reached the golden doors.

Though Orla and Floss could have afforded to, they didn't move. They stayed in the little apartment, where the paparazzi knew to find them. The five of them—Orla, Floss, Aston, Craig, and Melissa—were nearly always in 6D, five coworkers, each with their own dress codes. Floss never changed out of lingerie, Aston tramped around in designer tank tops, Orla wore yoga pants and hoodies, and Craig and Melissa dressed respectably, in pants that zipped closed. Melissa arrived first, at nine sharp, bringing coffees for herself and Floss and Aston, as if walking into a room of four people with three coffees was the most natural thing in the world. Aston would take his and pull himself up cross-legged on a bar stool, arranging his crystals and chanting. Floss would review the selfies they had taken in bed that morning, usually ones with her breasts artfully hidden by the sheets, and ask Melissa which one she thought she should post. (She almost never used Melissa's choice.) Melissa would give Floss and Aston what she called "their assignment" for the day—she might ask them to take a slow stroll through the Bronx Zoo in matching beanies, or to scoop corn at a soup kitchen in the East Village for fifteen minutes. In the pictures, Floss slipped and fell near the lizards, sneaked theatrical tastes of the corn. When her Post-it—**Be relatable!!!!!**—lost its tack and fluttered down from the cabinet, she used tape to put it back up.

Craig would walk in midmorning, often with a box of strawberry shortcake ice cream bars from the Gristedes next door. Aston ate around four of the bars every day. Craig would shove the box in the freezer, then cast an irritated look at Orla. "Is there coffee?" They would all sit together and go through the press clips and the tweets. Floss would bite her nails over anything mean, but Aston would just bellow "ooooooh," like someone else had been called to the principal's office.

Then Mason and the crew would materialize in the hallway, ready to shoot until lunchtime. Orla noticed, as time went on, that almost all the scenes were the same: Aston would say something grossly sexual to Floss, Floss would throw a pillow at him, and Orla would snort and say "you *guys*" from what had become her mark—the cushion Mason liked her to sit on had a little X of tape on it now. The only note she ever got was to make her eye rolls bigger, to exaggerate the motion for camera.

In the afternoons, there was nothing to do, but Orla got nothing else done. Her book was always there on the screen before her, but distractions were everywhere, endless. Now, in addition to watching Danny, she had to watch Floss, and herself. She would sort through Twitter and Instagram to see who was down at their door; at any given time, up to a dozen fans stood at the barricade, hoping for a glimpse of them. Now they brought squash out of love—and Melissa, in her opportunistic wisdom, had begun having Floss, trailed by paparazzi Melissa called to come, walk the squash down the street to a shelter. (At least, that was what they did until the shelter begged them: please, no more squash.) Now they just threw it away.

Orla would end up, often, going down to see the fans in person. She would put on foundation and lipstick and pretend to have somewhere to be. She would act surprised to find people waiting for her. She would lean in for their selfies. She could not deny the warm feeling it gave her, all these people glad to see her, even if she knew she was a distant third on their list. Once, ten minutes after meeting a girl who told Orla she was her "spirit animal," Orla stood in line behind her at the Jamba Juice down the block. "Yeah, it sucks," the girl was saying, on the phone to someone at home. "But we did see the roommate. I forget her name."

One March day she was doing this, squeezing hands and

moving down the line, when she came all the way to the back of it and—impossibly—there he was. He was pressed against the metal barricade, grinning and clutching the bar so hard his fingers had turned white. *In the flesh* was the phrase that came to her mind, and she understood it for the first time. She had to keep double-checking his face, his body, to make sure it was really him. And it was, and now every doubt Orla had felt, fixing her fate to Floss's, dissolved. So a model had fallen. So her book wasn't done. So she had been fired. So her mother wasn't proud. So what? He was here. It had all come true.

"Hey there, star," he said, and she could tell he had practiced it. But she didn't care.

Orla reached up and took off the sunglasses she had recently paid three hundred dollars for. Floss had sat on the counter at Bergdorf's, legs swinging, egging her on. "But what if I break them?" Orla had said. "Then you get another pair," Floss had answered.

Orla pulled him out of line with everyone watching, some of them calling her name, all of them raising their phones. She knew she should have waited until they walked inside, but she found she couldn't wait another second. She hugged him, the sun bleeding into her eyes as she rested her chin on his shoulder. When she heard herself speak, she found it wasn't just Floss who had tweaked her natural vocals. This was her voice from home. She hadn't heard it in ages.

"Danny," she said, the way she used to sound catching in her throat. "Danny. Hi."

CHAPTER TEN

Marlow

New York, New York
2051

When Marlow opened her eyes, she was in New York, the sky a glum lavender outside the tablet-shaped windows of the plane. The pilot came on and told them it was 5:44 in the morning. Marlow, who had never left California before, felt a punch of giddiness at the time. No matter what they did, everyone in Constellation would be three hours behind her. She had outrun them into the next day.

It hadn't been easy. Her car was not familiar with the concept of a getaway. No matter how she shouted and pounded, it took long rests at every stop sign on their way out of town. It dropped down to a prim ten miles per hour as it rolled beneath the vine-draped wooden arch at the edge of the enclave. *Welcome to Constellation*, said the side of the arch that faced the rest of the state, as if the place was open to the public. As she approached the edge of the enclave, Marlow tensed every muscle in her body, bracing for—what? A bullet? An armored truck skidding sideways to block her path? As she reached the guard post, a uniformed man looked her right in the eye. When he raised his arm, it was only to flick his device at her, snapping photos as he leaned out of his booth's little window, watching her leaving town.

Just the other side of the border was Constellation's miniature airport. Marlow got out of her car at the curb. "Go home," she told it, sharply, and it lurched off like an obedient pet.

In the ladies' room, she changed into jeans and a black gauzy sweater. She rolled the yellow dress into a ball and left it under the sinks. Then she pulled out the stack of cash she and Ellis had brought to exchange for pesos and marched to the check-in desk.

The bot behind it, though, had no idea what to do with paper money. It summoned a weary-looking human attendant, who sighed when Marlow held out the bills. "It's been about a hundred years since you could buy airfare with cash," she said to Marlow coolly, "and besides—to New York, you said?" She counted it clumsily. "You don't have enough here for round trip." The woman shuffled the bills into a pile and poked at her gray-screened tablet. She frowned. "We don't have an approved itinerary for you on file here from the network."

Marlow smiled and tilted her head, even as her heartbeat picked up. The cash had to work; she had no device to access her credit, and anyway, she was sure the network had frozen her accounts by now. "You know," she said slowly, "my husband was supposed to take care of it for me, since he travels so often. Ellis Trieste?"

It was funny, the way the woman's face changed. It softened, but not in the glad way it would if, say, Ellis was the type to wink and thank everyone each time he flew. It softened in a way that made the woman look fearful, reminding Marlow that the whole world saw her husband the same way: not as someone worth accommodating because he was kind, but because he was important, and not afraid to act it.

"Of course," the attendant said. She dropped her eyes quickly. "He's a valued Freebird Platinum Access customer. I'm sure the itinerary's on its way. Let's get you all set with a one-way ticket." She scooped up the bills dramatically, using her whole forearm, then handed a smaller pile, Marlow's change, back to her. "I'll see that someone processes this payment." She tapped her tablet once more and nodded. "Flight 1361 to JFK. Seat 18A. I've added your name to the manifest. Have a safe flight."

Marlow walked to the place near the gate, where everyone else seemed to know how to stand. They shuffled toward a retina scanner. As each person was successfully identified, a bot nodded and waved them through.

So they would know she had gone to New York—her name was there on the list, her eyes would be checked and accounted for. But after that, she reassured herself, she would move about unmarked. She noticed, just as she got into the line, a bot approaching the human attendant. It was holding its own tablet and trying to show what it said to the woman. "Urgent security bulletin from the Constellation Network," Marlow heard it say. But then the woman, who was double-checking her count of Marlow's cash, held up a hand and said: "Mute. I'm trying to focus— Oh, for crying out loud. Now I've got to start over."

She was still counting when Marlow thudded down the corridor to the waiting jet.

Then she was alone in the eighteenth row of a sparsely attended flight. Marlow's stomach felt vaguely jumpy; she had never been on a plane. She found both ends of her seat belt and clicked them firmly into place. Then she closed her eyes, forgetting her naked wrist, and intuited: *How do I fly?*

There was no voice to answer. It was only then, hours after she had torn herself away from every person she knew, that Marlow felt alone.

Someone touched her shoulder as she waited on the curb for a taxi. Marlow turned to find two women staring at her. The younger of the two, a teenager in a low-cut dress all wrong for her age and the time of day, was fidgeting in her heels as she looked at Marlow, uncertainty and exhilaration competing for control of her expression. The older one, fiftysomething, had on a dour look and an I ♥ NY shirt that reached her knees. As the younger one's hand drifted toward Marlow's arm, the older one glared at what must have been her daughter. "You can't touch them," she whispered. "There are rules."

Marlow stood there, feeling naked, clutching her duffel over her torso. These were people—real people—who had never met her, but knew who she was. Followers in the flesh. She supposed that on some level, she had never believed it, that behind those millions of screen names were humans with heartbeats and luggage, like her.

The girl withdrew her hand. "I'm a huge fan," she said. "I used to give myself eraser burns a zillion times a day, but you know." She gestured at Marlow. "I'm good now."

Marlow felt a little streak of triumph shoot through her; this, she was prepared for. There were dozens of phrases she used to respond to followers who sent her messages of their own mental health plights; they had been scripted by the network's advertorial team, massaged by Ellis on behalf of Antidote, and signed off on by standards at the network.

"Isn't it amazing what we can conquer," Marlow said to the girl, "with willpower plus a little help from Hysteryl?"

The mother snorted. The girl looked confused. "Huh?" she said.

"And—I'm glad you're feeling better," Marlow rushed to add, her face growing hot. "I mean, eraser burns—those really hurt." It wasn't part of the approved verbiage, she thought, but she was far away now from anyone who would care. At the thought, something lifted in front of her. The sky seemed to lighten. This was it—this was the world where people didn't live on camera. She was in it. Her audience, right now, was two. She let her duffel drift back to her side.

The girl stepped closer to Marlow and planted one high-heeled foot into the concrete. She jutted her hip out petulantly. "But what happened at the rest of your sowing?" she said. "Your feed is down. It's killing me!"

Her mother shot her a look. "That's enough, Donna," she said. She looked for something with which to tug her daughter back, but the girl's dress was so skimpy, her mother's fingers kept finding skin.

The girl pressed on, batting her mother's hand away. "Really," she said, squinting. "What are you doing here? Where's Ellis?"

Marlow felt like her heart was at the base of her throat, trying to climb to the light. The girl said Ellis's name just like she did—as if she had known him forever.

"Mom, she's not answering," the girl complained after a moment. "Will the baby be a boy or a girl?" she said to Marlow. "You could at least tell us that."

Marlow could not think of one thing to say. She stood there, frozen, as the girl's face turned disappointed, then annoyed, before her mother forced her away, dragging both of their bags herself. Marlow turned toward the line of cabs, pretending not to hear the rest of their conversation.

"Just not my cup of tea," the mother was saying. "You know, the other girl still has the most terrible scar."

Marlow felt a stab of cold rip straight through her chest. She saw crimped black at the edge of her vision. Anger closed in on the other things she was trying to hold on to: reminders of her age and privilege and the benefits of the high road. There would be more of these people. They were everywhere, her followers, fragile by definition. She couldn't go around mouthing off to all of them.

But maybe just this once.

She turned around and called after the women. "Who has a *scar* in this day and age?" she shouted, stopping them instantly. The mother pulled her daughter to her side, protectively, as they looked back at her. But Marlow didn't lower her voice. "No one," she went on, loudly. "No one who doesn't want it."

———

Marlow supposed her first impression of Manhattan was an unoriginal one: it was so full of people. Living ones, specifically. She sat in her stalled cab, appalled: real people were doing all the bot work. There was a policeman directing traffic in the midst of a chaotic intersection; there was a woman coaxing trash into a dustpan with a broom. Marlow jumped when a furry blue mascot—she had been sure that at least *this* was animatronic—removed its own torso to reveal a sweating man. He leaned against a stretch of steel fencing.

"Humid as hell out here," she could hear the man mutter to a costumed superhero.

The superhero shrugged. "That March heat," she said.

Alone in the taxi, Marlow listened to them talk. Otherwise, New York was quiet. Her cab, like the others, inched and idled in polite silence, waiting for the clogged lane to clear. A fire truck—the kind that was lofted in order to straddle lanes of traffic—approached from behind so soundlessly that Marlow only noticed it when it glided over her head, making things dark for an instant. The people shuffling down Thirty-Seventh Street were mostly lost in their devices, bobbing their heads to music she couldn't hear, mouthing words to people she couldn't see. She noticed their slack jaws, their bad posture, their stomachs blooming loose. This was what it looked like, she realized, when people moved through the world unfilmed. She watched a harried woman burst out of a Mickey D's Fresh, dragging a gray dog with one hand and eating a lettuce wrap with the other. All the while, she rolled her eyes and kicked her feet impatiently, annoyed with whoever she was talking to on her device. At one point, the woman, forgetting her food, threw her hand up in exasperation. Lettuce sprayed across the sidewalk. A glob of dressing landed on the woman's chest. She stood there, wearing the stain. The sight made Marlow nervous. She had to remind herself that this woman had no followers, no army of voyeurs who would mercilessly mock the ranch soaking into her shirt. The woman's dog, meanwhile—Marlow gasped and clapped a hand to her mouth—her dog was *defecating on the street*. It was a *live* dog, she realized. She was almost offended. What was the point, in this grassless place? Who would scrape poop from the concrete when there were teacup beagle-bots you could power down and put away when you went on vacation?

She reached Times Square, a blinding patchwork of faces from home. The stars of Constellation were everywhere, hovering like ghosts among fashion ads and snack brands in the intersection's famous holograms. A hologram of Jacqueline—her waist thinned substantially, Marlow noticed—sat coquettishly atop a hotel's circular roof, sipping a purplish juice, its logo dancing near her shoulder. On a green mirrored building to the right of Marlow's cab, Ida's miserable face was projected beneath the title of a tabloid magazine app, *Constellation Weekly*. IDA LEAVES HER FAMILY, the headline screamed. Her nose was a story tall. The cab moved up a few inches, and Marlow spotted her own face, peeking out from a faded, peeling still-life billboard. The ad was old. It showed a photo from her wedding day, one Marlow could not remember posing for. She was smiling serenely in Ellis's arms, her head dipped against his shoulder. Marlow + Ellis, read the text beside her left ear. And in larger print, to the right of her chin: "To have and to hold. Happiness—ever after—by Hysteryl."

Suddenly, as Marlow looked on, every image above her head vanished. The sky was suddenly undisturbed blue, the buildings naked concrete. Only then did the New Yorkers look up, bewildered by the blankness. Pedestrians froze in the middle of crossing the street. The lunch crowd on the red plastic stairs held their forks still. They waited, and Marlow waited with them, for the rainbow clutter to come back. Then the Coke Zero hologram, the totem in the center of everything, stuttered back on. A face appeared above its logo.

Her face.

Marlow shrank back into her seat. She clapped her hands over her mouth, peering over the tips of her trembling fingers as the particles of light arranged themselves: her unruly burst of hair, her serious dark blue eyes. She stared at the same image of her face—unsmiling and head-on, like a mug shot—multiplying across the block. She was where Jacqueline had been and where Ida had been. She replaced the clothes and the snacks. There were dozens of her. She was everywhere.

The people stared, too, looking away from the holograms only to exchange bemused glances with each other. A few moved on, shaking off the spectacle with practiced indifference, but most of them simply stood there, waiting to see what would happen next.

The light changed from red to green, but the traffic jam stayed the same.

Then came the banners, rippling across Marlow's software-smoothed forehead in every image. WANTED: MARLOW CLIPP.

A voice from somewhere boomed above the gentle hum of the cab engines.

"Constellation fans!" it cried, female and ecstatic. "This is a special day. It's time for a scavenger hunt! Our own Marlow Clipp is out there somewhere in Manhattan, waiting for you to find her. Spot her, and you'll win serious prizes. Go, stargazers, go!"

Marlow pressed her back into the seat. She slid downward.

Jacqueline was right. The hunts were real.

She hadn't ever believed it, and she hadn't ever had any reason to. No one important enough to truly interrupt programming had ever left Constellation, at least not since Marlow was a child. About two years after the enclave opened, dozens of the original cast tried to defect. Some of them—the Idas, the people no one cared about anyway—were let go, their feeds canceled, their followers suavely redirected to stars with similar looks and lifestyles. Others—the ones with big audiences—were convinced to come back in different ways. The network gave them raises, or held their savings hostage—they all banked with First Constellation, after all. There were a few cases where none of that worked, and Marlow could remember trading myths with other girls during grade-school sleepovers, all of them spooking each other off-camera as they huddled in their parents' Jacuzzi tubs. If you left, the story went, and you mattered, the network would make it look like they just let you go. They wouldn't stop you by force. Then they would blast your photo everywhere, would tell your followers to help them find you. They'd make it look like a game, a stunt for the fans. There would be prizes for tips on your whereabouts, prizes for pictures of you on the run. And a grand prize for whoever actually caught you—for whoever closed in on you, believing you were in on the joke, and grabbed you, and made you go home.

"Total bullshrimp," Floss had said, sitting on Marlow's bed, when Marlow had brought her this story, as a child, and asked her if it was real. "It's true that the network has hunts sometimes, but it really is just a game. Nobody gets hurt. The network is here to protect us."

"But why did all those people want to leave our town, anyway?" Marlow had said.

Floss had paused, thinking. "They lived the other way for too long," she said finally. "They couldn't get used to their followers wanting to be with them all the time."

"But you and Daddy," Marlow said. "You'd never leave, right?"

"Oh, sweetie, of course not," Floss said, tucking the covers around Marlow's shoulders. "Daddy and I love it here."

Marlow could remember the way she had wished her mother had said, instead, *Of course not—we'd never leave you*. She could remember feeling like she couldn't catch her mother's eye as they spoke. She could remember, the next morning, packing her schoolbag across the room and realizing where Floss was looking when she told Marlow not to be scared. Not at Marlow, but into the yellow eye of a daisy sewn onto her headboard—a spot better known, to Marlow, as Bedroom Camera Three.

———

Marlow was so shaken by the sight of herself in Times Square that she forgot where she was going: to 1000 Tenth Avenue, the hospital address Grace had given her. When the cab stopped, it scarfed down Marlow's twenty-dollar bill through a grimy slit in the back seat. She put her hand on the door handle and waited for the rush of people coming down the block to thin out. When the street was as close to empty as she imagined it would ever be, she darted out and toward a dozing vendor on the sidewalk. He was ancient, and possibly blind. His mirrored lenses reminded her of the glasses she had taken from Amadou's house, to remember him after he died. The vendor barely moved as she placed some money on his table, next to an army of tiny souvenir snow globes with bronze helixes twisted inside. Marlow seized an electric blue hijab and a wide pair of tortoiseshell sunglasses. She tugged them on and turned to face the place where she was born.

But it was gone. There was no hospital at 1000 Tenth Avenue. She definitely had the address right, for there it was spelled out in iron, above the gate in the fence that stood between her and something stunning: the enormous, life-size version of the helix inside the snow globes. The structure spiraled into the clouds, an endless chain of bronzed, disembodied, interlocking arms. Each set, Marlow saw as she walked through the gate and moved closer, began at the fingertip, crossed angelically at the elbows, and ended abruptly at the shoulders. When Marlow got up close, she saw that each pair was unique. Some of the arms were burly, with a finish raked to look like hair. Others were delicate and feminine, with brutal, long nails or rings climbing the fingers. And some, Marlow saw with a shiver, were small and smooth. Not quite full-grown.

Marlow put her own hands against the pair of arms in front of her—a woman's hands, clearly, with a tattoo that said AIDEN above the left fourth knuckle. She pulled herself forward to peer over the fingers, to look at the inner edge of the sculpture. There was information stamped inside every right wrist: name, age, hometown. The hand she was holding belonged to Ariel Long, twenty-two, of Fort Pierce, Florida. In the semicircles of grass that flanked the memorial on all sides, people stood still and somber with headsets covering their eyes and ears. Above Marlow's head, tiny drones wove around the chain, hovering above information plates.

A plaque where the chain began read simply: *Each set of hands belongs to an American lost in the wake of the Spill.* Next to the plaque was a pile of handmade tributes—unlit pillar candles, roses gone dry and brown-tinged, and printed, laminated photos piled up on top of each other. A small flag staked into the grass: black, with a graphic of white quilted cubes. NEVER AGAIN, the flag said, beneath the squares.

Something must have sensed Marlow pausing there. A hologram appeared in front of her: an arrow pointing her toward the slender silver mesh building the chain of arms wound around. "Want to learn more about the world before the Spill?" an automated voice asked in a pious hush. "Housed inside our Internet Archive is the former World Wide Web. Programmers have been working for decades on recovering the information lost or damaged in the Spill, and today, we're proud to say, we have on display 97.6 percent of the old internet as it existed from its invention in 1989 until its destruction in 2016."

Marlow stepped into line behind a family of four. All of them were wearing orange ponchos that pictured, on their backs, two gray skyscrapers and an American flag beneath the words THE FIFTIETH ANNIVERSARY OF 9/11. The teenage daughter was having, Marlow could tell, a silent conversation with someone she was attracted to. She kept touching her hair self-consciously, as if the other person could see her. Every ten seconds or so, she giggled at top pitch.

"Time to hang up with your boyfriend and show a little respect, Barbara," the mother snapped. "You're on hallowed ground."

The daughter rolled her eyes. "I've been on hallowed ground all *day*," she muttered. "You promised we would go IRL-shopping."

Marlow walked in behind them. A bot in an eggplant polo—female, at least a generation old, dingy around the eyes, with a whisper of scrubbed-off graffiti at her jaw—nodded at her pleasantly. So here were New York's bots, which made sense. The government was always buying up the old models discarded by industry, installing them in museums and public school classrooms.

"In 2016," the bot said, its voice dull and stiff, "the web was open-publish. Anyone could post whatever they wanted on it. People made up their own passwords, often from meaningful dates or pet names. Sunglasses off, please," it added as Marlow passed. "Just ahead, you'll be walking through our retina scanners. We like to know who's visiting us for security purposes—and so we can customize our museum experience to your interests and needs."

Another retina scanner. Marlow hesitated. With the hunt on, she couldn't risk being tagged here. Then again, if there was as much of the old internet—of her parents' old lives—inside this building as advertised, she might be able to find out who her real father was.

She shuffled toward the red beam. People were crossing it casually here, not pausing their conversations to look straight into it. Children slipped beneath it easily. The secondhand bots all had their backs to it. The scanner seemed like more of a suggestion here than it had at the airport—and so, as she approached it, Marlow pretended to drop something, then ducked beneath the line.

When she straightened up on the other side, nothing happened. No one came to push her back to be counted. No one seemed to notice her at all. Marlow felt a rush of pride; was she *good* at this, being a renegade? Security behind her, she slipped her sunglasses off for just a moment and wiped the sweat from her face.

By the time she put them back on, the teenage daughter from the line was staring at her.

"Mom," the girl was whispering. "Mom—" She cupped her hand to her mouth and leaned into her mother's cloud of hair. After a moment, the woman's eyes slid toward Marlow.

The girl poked her mother, hard. "Stop that," Marlow heard her mother say. "Our tour leaves in five minutes. Hustle."

"But—" the girl said. She reluctantly followed her mother.

Marlow went the other way. She shook herself free from the slow-moving mass and hurried to the right, following a sign that pointed her to "General Searches." Flanking the long hallway on both sides were lines of security bots, all male, all run-down and funnel-shaped, with tight waists and broad shoulders, rendered in a thoughtful variety of skin tones. They wore identical eggplant blazers. Marlow moved through them like a debutante, avoiding their stares as they tracked her, en masse, every pair of eyes rolling left to right until each chin had to follow.

At the end of the hall was a bot with a beard so precise, it could only be software-designed. Its name tag read Mateo. A moment after Marlow passed it, it peeled off from the ranks and trod after her, keeping six feet or so back.

Marlow felt a jittery seed of fear in her stomach. It could be nothing, she told herself. It could be a random security measure. There was no reason for any bot to want her. Bots didn't care about scavenger hunts.

The wide maw of a giant dark room rose up in front of her, and she walked through it, toward one of the lilac squares that beckoned with a graphic: W W W. Marlow settled onto the stool in front of it. Mateo found a spot to rest its back against the wall.

"Welcome," came a crisp voice. "Which year's internet would you like to browse today?"

Marlow hesitated.

"Or would you like to search for a person or place?" the voice continued.

"Floss Natuzzi," Marlow said. "And Aston Clipp."

Instantly: "There are 46 million results for Floss Natuzzi and 51 million results for Aston Clipp," the voice said. "Here are some tags you can use to narrow your search."

In front of Marlow, illuminating the dust in the air, bright boxes with phrases inside them appeared—so many phrases that they crowded the space, forcing each other to shrink. *Aston Clipp New Album. Aston Clipp Lyrics. Aston Clipp Instagram. Aston Clipp Twitter. Aston Clipp Rwanda Comment. Floss Natuzzi Instagram. Floss Natuzzi Brow Tutorial. Floss Natuzzi Paulina Kratz. Floss Natuzzi Dating. Floss Natuzzi Aston Clipp. Floss Natuzzi Flosston Public. Floss Natuzzi Haircut. Floss Natuzzi Anna Salgado. Aston Clipp Fire. Floss Natuzzi Wedding. Floss Natuzzi Pregnant.*

Marlow held her breath, waiting for her own name. But the tags stopped there. Of course. This version of the internet ended at the Spill.

She plunged her fingers into the tags. She called up stories and pictures, trying to keep the dates straight. She was looking for men around her mother, for hints that their genes might be swimming inside her. The more she looked, the less reasonable the task seemed. There were hundreds of men, dozens appearing regularly, and virtually all of them—even the ones she suspected were gay—touched her mother, in pictures, like they'd slept with her. Then again, Aston seemed to always be nearby, not bothered, and not bothering to overplay his claim on the girl they all wanted, because she wanted him.

After a long time looking, Marlow leaned back and rubbed her eyes. The room was beginning to empty of tourists, who trudged off looking worn out by their days. Marlow planned to stay until night, and then what? She had no idea what she would eat, where she would sleep, how she would escape the gaze of everyone on the street who had heard about the hunt.

She had at least a few more hours to kill before it got dark. She decided to try another tactic. She told the hologram to give her her mother chronologically. She went back to the beginning.

A vaguely troubling series of images kept resurfacing: shots of angry young people behind metal bars on a city block, and a visual Marlow didn't quite understand—a short burst of text, next to a little square photo of a young woman, and under that, a photo of an apartment building's double doors. Marlow squinted at the words. Twitter, she realized. This was Twitter, the thing Floss had told her about. **This is where that skank who hurt Paulina lives, if anyone wants to drop by and beat the shit out of her. C'mon world. Don't hold back.** After that: an address.

The skin on Marlow's arms went taut and cold when she read that. She dug into her bag for the paper from Grace and turned it to the side Grace had written on, then realized that she didn't have a pen. She rummaged through her bag for something to scratch with, pushing the folded swimsuits and prenatal vitamins to the side. Then she felt something she hadn't packed: a clear vinyl case. Alone in the dark, Marlow smiled. This always happened. Despite the fact that Marlow never wore anything but a smoothing balm on her face, Floss was always tucking makeup into her bags or her bathroom drawers, as if Marlow might become a new person entirely if Floss only found her the right shade of something.

There was an eyeliner pencil in the kit. Marlow uncapped it and copied the address down, squeezing it in beneath Grace's printing. 303 W 21st St.

The black tip of the pencil crumbled as she wrote. FACE BY FLOSS, it said in copper-colored letters on the side. Her parents' home was crammed with boxes of these old products—mascaras fully fossilized before they could be opened, serums that had long unclotted themselves into thick layers of oil and sediment. All Marlow knew about the line was that it had launched to total silence a year after the Spill. The basement had been filled with back stock for as long as she could remember, her old bikes leaning against the crates stacked to the ceiling.

She put the slip away. She was on the earliest page of search results, lined with the very first glimmers of her mother becoming someone. Marlow reached forward to tap the earliest story. Up popped a soft-focus photo of Floss brushing her eyebrows just the way Marlow always saw her do it: mouth open, eyes stretched wide. The headline read: "Sooo What Does The World's Most Expensive Brow Gel Actually Do? One Instagram It Girl Finds Out." It was strange, Marlow noticed, her eyes drifting down to the space beneath the headline: the name of whoever wrote the piece was missing. After "By," there was only a bar of white space, like something had been erased. Next to it was a tiny headshot of a half-smiling woman. The nameless author, Marlow thought. She leaned closer to the story, the tip of her nose dipping into the hologram. The woman looked familiar.

Marlow went back to the red-carpet photos of Floss and found the woman almost immediately. There she was—next to Floss, but not really. The woman slumped in the shadowed edges of the pictures, waiting and holding two purses while Floss pouted in the center of the shot. She was thin by normal measures, but her waist was still thicker than Floss's, and she was paler, almost gray-looking, next to Marlow's mother. She seemed, Marlow thought with a stab of pity, like nothing but a point of comparison—a reminder, recurring in dozens of photos, of how dismal normal looked next to beautiful. "Floss Natuzzi and guest," read some of the captions. "Floss Natuzzi and friend Orla," read others. Marlow found a video clip in which the woman briefly stood with Floss on the carpet. Floss, twinkling in a gown made of champagne-colored scales, put one of her hands on the woman's shoulder and cupped the other at her mouth. She shouted something toward the cameras, but Marlow couldn't hear it. She was supposed to have her device on—that was how everyone else here was getting audio. She took a step back from the display, frustrated, and squinted at Floss's moving lips, trying to read them.

Suddenly, she felt fingers on her shoulder, tapping. She knew instantly it was a bot; the fingers mimicked the rhythm of someone wanting her attention, but the force of the touch was off. Too hard. It was one of those motions bots struggled with, even after hundreds of updates.

Marlow turned. Mateo was standing there, holding out a basket of plastic blue earpieces. "Happy to help," it said.

Marlow rummaged in the basket. "Do these still work?" she said.

Mateo nodded. "The Archive currently uses them for our guests younger than seven, and our guests whose income indicates that they live below the information line," it said. "In other words, our guests who do not have devices."

Marlow pressed one of the tiny buds into her ear. "Thank you," she said. Mateo nodded again and put its hands behind its back. It didn't retreat. "That, um," Marlow said. "That will be all."

"Of course." Mateo took a few steps backward, never taking its eyes off her.

Marlow felt the buzz of her earbud syncing up with the content in front of her. Floss was frozen, in the frame she had paused on, with her tongue rolled up in the cave of her mouth, about to unfurl. Marlow pressed Play.

"My friend Orla Cadden," Floss cried out. "C-A-D-D-E-N. She's a literary talent—" The ancient cameras, spitting loud clicks and lightning, drowned out the rest of the sentence.

Marlow uncapped the eyeliner again to write the name down. "Search Orla Cadden," she demanded.

In all her years of taking answers for granted, she had never heard the words the voice responded with. It dropped its sunny ting, like she had ruined the fun. "Error 404," it said. "Not found."

CHAPTER ELEVEN

Orla

New York, New York
2016

Within an hour of Danny's arrival, Orla did three things she wasn't proud of.

First, she took him to a bar. Not one of the dozen within walking distance that were considered of the moment, with their bartenders who knew Orla by name and treated her with discretion. No—she wanted to go somewhere terrible, where people would see her and fuss. They went to a cheap box in the East Forties where tourists ate nachos with half-melted cheese and drank volleyball-sized margaritas. They sat in a cream-colored pleather booth with a tall, quilted back. She knew, as they sat there, that she would never forget the sight of him, there across the table. What she didn't know was how memorable the booth itself would prove to be. Less than a year later, when the city was still reeling from the Spill, Orla would pass this place again and find the booths dismembered on the curb, junkyard-bound, part of the design exorcism going on in rooms across America. Everyone was trying to forget white padded walls.

Danny looked up as two girls—both young, both Asian, both with spilled-drink stains on their silk Theory shells—clambered toward their table. They bent, cuddling up to Orla, and extended their arms for selfies.

"I'm a Floss," said the one on Orla's right, sucking her cheeks in as she snapped the photos.

"And I'm an Orla," said the other. She had glasses.

Watching the interaction, Danny touched his face and wagged his head in disbelief. "Whoa," he said.

After one round—he followed her lead and had the prickly pear, on the rocks—their eyes swam in their heads. They smiled at each other.

"Let's get it over with," Orla said. "What happened with Catherine?"

They both groaned theatrically. It was the second thing she felt bad about.

"The truth?" Danny stirred his second drink. "I'm over it. She's over it. I know it's supposed to be more complicated than that, but it's not." He took a long sip and sat back. "Oh, and I wouldn't go to church. Which is exactly what she wanted."

"What do you mean," Orla said, "what she wanted?"

"Catherine's smart these days." Danny dug his elbows into the table. "She's not the little—*oh, who, me?*—she was in high school." He glanced at a table that was staring at them and swallowed. Orla could tell he thought they were looking because he was being loud, but the people were focused on her.

"She didn't want to be married to me anymore," he went on in a lower voice. "But she's not an idiot. She's not going to go and cheat on me—she doesn't want to be the villain. If you're the one who cheats in a town like ours, good luck at the grocery store." He took another sip. "So she gets a church instead. She's at stuff every night, she's at stuff all weekend, she comes home quoting the Bible and looking at me like, 'What, you don't get it?' Like I'm the asshole, all of a sudden, for not wanting a Jesus tattoo."

Orla could see him mentally braking, trying not to fly through the windshield of his rant. He took a long breath. "But I'm lucky, actually," he said. "You have no idea how many times I wanted to come and find you, to tell you..." His face colored and he waved the train of thought away, like he thought he was wasting her time. Then he grinned, the grin she remembered from when they were fifteen. "I always thought you and me could take over the world," he said.

If she had been on her third drink, or even further into her second, Orla might not have felt the sudden sting of intuition: like when he had called her a star at the barricade, this line sounded too planned. But she was not on her first drink, either, so she could push the thought away. She buried the instinct beneath what she wanted. And that made three.

———

When they got back to the building, Danny trailed just far enough behind Orla that the doorman thought they weren't together. He looked into Danny's eyes and flicked his head like the young guy he was, instead of murmuring "Evening" with his eyes down, as usual. He had mistaken Danny, Orla realized, for one of his kind, not hers. Danny shook the doorman's hand and asked him his name. Orla heard it, filed it away, and forgot it again by the elevator.

On the way up, she looked at Danny. He still had a better smile than any actor she'd met that year, and theirs were highly tended to—his had just grown in that way, even and bright. But he had gained weight, considerable weight, and his jeans— crayon blue, with too many pockets—made her want to die a little. His hair was thinning, and she could tell that he worked hard to create the illusion that it wasn't. That hurt to think of, too: him at the mirror, biting his lip, arranging pieces here and there, a man forced to ape grooming motions after a boyhood of effortless looks, of barely a glance in the mirror.

The apartment was empty for once. Floss and Aston were shooting on location, having brunch on a Tuesday afternoon, when nobody served it. The restaurant had been closed for the occasion, stocked with extras who were told to pretend it was Sunday. Mason had called last night to ask that they be prepared to fight. "We're finding in edit that we're a little low on conflict," he said, his voice fizzing out of Floss's iPhone speaker. "So if you guys could work something up, maybe about the way Floss dresses, that girl Aston talked to at the Grammys…" Orla had watched as Floss and Aston both looked at the floor. They used to laugh when Mason asked them to argue, used to have to search for things they didn't agree on. But they had been bickering all week about the same topics Mason suggested. When their fights spilled into the living room, Orla went still on her side of the fake wall, wondering why she was the one trying not to be heard.

Danny's eyes lit up as he came into the apartment. He picked up a mug on the counter, looked at it like it was an artifact, and carefully put it back down exactly where it had been. "It's smaller than I imagined," he said. "But they say it's always like that with TV shows, right?"

"Sort of," Orla said. "This is just where we live, though, so it's a little different." She ran into her room ahead of him and kicked tangles of underwear-inside-yoga-pants under her bed.

Danny followed her in, filling the doorway. Because there was nowhere else to go, she sat down on the bed. So did he. Their shoulders came to rest against each other.

He turned his face toward her. Orla's heart began to pound. "What's she like?" he said.

"Who?" Orla could not believe, could *not* believe, could not *believe* they were this close.

He put his hand over hers, the same way he had in the car, long ago. It was like he had found an old underground wire. The jolt in her skin was still there.

"Floss," he said.

"Oh, um." Orla tried hard to think. "She's just like you imagine. What you see is what you get. Prettier, though. If you can believe that."

Danny twisted around and nodded at the thick ream of paper on Orla's desk. Its top sheet was marked up with red pen. "Oh, there it is," he said. "Your book."

"How did you know about my book?" she said.

He pinched the skin on the top of her hand. "I see it on the show sometimes," he said. "In the background. I knew what it had to be."

Orla felt blood flooding into her cheeks. She had not yet kissed him, she had not yet slept with him, but she realized now that this was the pinnacle: luscious validation. He had been watching her as closely as she was watching him. "You were right," she said. "It's my book."

"Yeah, I knew it," Danny said. "I always knew it." He put his hands on either side of her jaw and pulled her toward him. She felt the pulse of the strobe light at the graduation party. She felt his serious eyes trained on her the first day of school. She heard him asking if she would remember them, the line that had pulled her through years and years, that had sent her the only way she wanted to go: back, by way of special.

When she pulled him onto the mattress, she steered him away from the end of the bed that touched her desk, not wanting to disturb the papers he had marveled at. The pages were full of Microsoft gibberish, lorem ipsum and so on. When production had asked her to print out her book as a prop, she only had, after all this time, forty-nine pages. The heft of them would not hold up on camera. "It's no problem," Mason had said, beckoning to an intern. "We'll make it look like a real thing."

Danny stayed and stayed. He told Orla he had endless days off available, because Catherine didn't like vacations. Orla pretended to be hearing it for the first time when he said he managed the cold-storage facility, though she had known it from Facebook for ages, and she listened as he explained what this meant: tracking the comings and goings of frozen fish and icy medicines, dressed in an industrial-grade parka and usually alone, working long hours that ensured he saw the sun only on Saturdays. She wanted to do nothing less than change his world, to turn it from an unending spool of cold and dark to something filled with light and warmth, and to make sure he knew the glow depended on her. She brought him to everything: a charity gala for which Melissa begrudgingly called in a loaner tux. A Brooklyn arena concert that they watched from a luxury box, Danny's eyes popping at the twinkling private bar. A women's magazine party celebrating female "influencers." Danny asked what the term meant, and Orla shrugged before turning to receive the editor in chief, who murmured in her ear, "If those bottom-feeders at Lady-ish could see you now!"

"Let's get out of here," Danny whispered when the editor floated on. "Let's get pizza." Having him around reminded Orla that she, too, had once felt starving at every fancy event, that there was a time before she could be satisfied by artful bites of almost nothing on crackers.

"We're leaving," she told Floss.

Midselfie, Floss gave a shuddering sigh without looking away from her phone. "Must you make my best friend be lame every night?" she whined in Danny's direction, loud enough that the departing editor glanced discreetly over her shoulder.

Orla flicked her hand at Danny in a way that meant he shouldn't worry about Floss. Floss's attitude toward Danny, Orla sensed, was one of patient disdain, as if Orla had started wearing a tacky hat everywhere, and Floss could only wait for her to outgrow it. If Orla wasn't careful, she could find herself feeling flattered by this show of possessiveness. She had to remind herself that that was what it was: a show. She didn't doubt that she and Floss were best friends, but that only meant she knew Floss very well—well enough to realize that, to Floss, friendship was theater. Floss shrieked with joy when Orla entered a room, and captioned pictures of the two of them with venomous affection—**my best friend is hotter than yours**. The edge of jealousy toward Danny was another one of these pantomimes, the kind that might have seemed genuine to the people in the cheap seats. But Orla, in the front row, saw them for just what they were: distractions sequined over the truth. Floss might have believed she loved Orla, but Orla knew Floss was only for Floss. She knew that Floss was the kind of selfish friend most women could only keep one of. The one they tried hard to love but had to hang up on twice a year, the one they told the rest of their friends about, in sentences that always began, "You know I love her, but..." Orla felt aware that it was risky, having this kind of friend as her only one, with no cushion of other contacts to help metabolize the crazy. But she had lived the alternative, too. She knew it was better than having no one.

It took a blizzard for Floss to soften toward Danny. The storm started up in the middle of the first Friday morning in April, shocking the city with more snow than had fallen all winter. It stranded them as a foursome—Orla and Danny, Floss and Aston—together in 6D, drinking rum mixed with instant cocoa someone found in an out-of-reach cupboard. The power went out, which was quaint. They talked and talked.

"My little liberal here thinks I'm nuts when I say the government wants our guns," Danny said as Orla stroked his hair. "But someday they won't just come after our guns. They'll want to know everything about us, want to track our every move. It's starting already."

"No *shit*, man," Aston said, spreading his arms as he jumped off the couch. "I have this super-rare Uzi at my house in Santa Monica, and it was such a bitch to register. Like, let me do me. I only bring it out at parties, anyway."

"Oh, you two," Floss said fondly. Orla's heart leaped to hear Danny mathematically included in her tone. She smiled at Floss, who looked up from the spray of split ends she had been inspecting and grinned back. *Men*, her eyes seemed to say. Holding her gaze—*me and my best friend, here with our boyfriends*—Orla had never felt so content in her life.

The weeks went on: sex, takeout, events, sex. Photos of Orla and Danny had begun to surface, had made their way into the consciousness of home. It was too much for Mifflin to bear: Orla Cadden becoming ultrafamous-adjacent and then—*get this*—bringing the dude from American Cold Storage along for the ride. Twined together on the couch, Orla and Danny tracked Facebook chatter about themselves. They read aloud to each other from emails they got and never responded to, sent from classmates they laughed at. They weren't trying to be mean; it was just that the existence of other people suddenly struck them as funny.

Orla was careful, though, to never let Danny see her inbox. Gayle emailed a dozen times a day. Orla ignored one message, then another, until there were so many that the idea of reading them overwhelmed her, like an assignment she would rather take a zero on than face. The subject lines piled up in desperate bold:

Have you lost your mind

This has to stop

Please talk to me

We are here for you

When Danny asked casually, after weeks, about her book, Orla started sitting at her laptop in front of him. But she was always stuck, always blocked, and she spent most of the time online shopping. She had learned to enter her credit card digits with a cadence that mimicked prose.

Sometimes, while she sat there, Danny would bring her her glasses. Orla had never explained they were fake. In the beginning, she had forgotten, and now too much time had passed. The truth was more embarrassing than it was important, she thought, so she kept it to herself.

———

One late afternoon as they lay in bed, afterward, their breathing beginning to normalize, Danny extracted his arm from behind Orla's head and sat up. He grabbed his laptop from the windowsill. He got back into bed, set it on his thighs, and opened it so they could both see the screen.

He pulled up a PowerPoint presentation. The first slide read, in blocky font, MERCHANDISING PLAN—FLOSS NATUZZI.

Orla's stomach puckered, a flicker of doom, as he cursed under his breath, trying to cue up some music. "What are you—" she said, but he shushed her as the song began.

He clicked through, being rough on the trackpad, and Orla read in silence: three-bulleted ideas of his for jewelry and clothing and unbreakable athletic water bottles, all of them branded with Floss's name. On the slide detailing cosmetics, *mascara* was spelled with twice as many s's and r's as it needed. There was choppy clip art of lipstick that made her heart sink into her legs.

"I know the music isn't synced up," Danny said, "but you're just practice. I'll have it perfect before I show Floss."

Orla sat up, tugging the sheet around herself, and looked at him. "Please," she whispered. "Don't do that."

"Don't what?" The song continued to play, though the presentation was stuck on its final slide, which read: *AND MUCH MORE IN THE FUTURE!* "I worked really hard on this," he said, darkening. "Floss needs to be licensing. We're leaving a lot of money on the table here." He reached into his beat-up back-pack, which sagged on the floor, and pulled out a book. *Make Your Name Make You Rich: A Primer on Branding & Licensing*, the title read. The cover pictured the author: a Lebanese man in a pin-striped suit and neat magenta pocket square. "It's all here," Danny said, tossing the book at her stomach—a little hard, she thought. "You should read this. It's a business-category best-seller on Amazon."

Orla picked up the book. "I've met this guy," she said. She couldn't look at him. "He handles Floss's licensing personally. They're starting with a skin care line. Face by Floss."

Danny leaned forward and hooked his arms around his drawn-up knees. "Well," he said after a moment. "She still needs some-one on the ground."

Orla put a hand on his back. "It's a huge undertaking," she said. "You couldn't do it with another job."

He looked back at her, harshly. "Maybe I won't have that job much longer," he said. "I'm starting to think about my next move."

Being with him had been perfect, eerily similar to what she imagined, until now. But now she realized that the strange thing about having a life she had built in a dream was that she had only dreamed so far. She had thought hundreds of times about the first time she would see him again, had thought thousands of times about their first kiss. Now she had run out of fantasy. But maybe, she thought, Danny's plans went further than hers. Maybe she wasn't the only one in the bed who knew what it was like to scheme toward something better. Who needed to hear they deserved it.

"That's cool," she said limply.

They didn't talk about the PowerPoint again, but after that

day, something tightened between them. Orla saw the way Danny ground his jaw when the crew bustled through the apartment, skirting him like he was furniture. One day, when he casually stayed next to Orla on the couch as the crew got set to roll, Mason looked up, annoyed, and said, "Hey, Orla, your boyfriend's in the shot. Can we put him somewhere?"

Danny shrugged afterward, wounded, and said, "It's just that I want to be with you all the time."

She looked at the flannel shirt pulling apart at his chest, wearing thin at the elbows, and said, "Okay. I'll fix it."

They went shopping, Amadou shuttling them at Orla's direction. She nodded as the women she knew at each boutique, the ones who let her in the side doors, draped Danny in shawl-collar sweaters, blazers that curved snug around his shoulders, fitted jeans that fell on his scuffed Reeboks all wrong but on the buttery desert boots from the other side of the store just right. Danny hesitantly touched a pale gray cashmere sweater, and Orla nodded emphatically. Then she took him to the man who cut Aston's waves. Danny watched with naked wonder as the stylist whipped his thinning spikes into a head of hair. The man tucked pomade and thickening treatments into a small white bag and handed it to Danny with a smile. "*Much* better," he said. Orla paid with her credit card. She had had it out all day.

After, they met the others at a restaurant on Downing Street. Orla led Danny down a narrow set of stairs to the basement, where the rest of them were already seated in a private, warm room off the kitchen, walled in with colonial brick and walnut. Orla could tell instantly that Floss and Aston were fighting. Floss had her elbow propped on the table. Her head sat in the curve between her thumb and index finger, the rest of her fingers spread, blocking Aston out of her sight. Aston kept rocking back so that the front legs of his chair reared into the air. He was frowning mournfully—until he saw Danny. He pulled him into a headlock. "Looking fresh, my man!" he shouted. Craig and Melissa looked up from their phones at Aston's exclamation, reviewed Danny, and locked eyes with each other. They didn't say anything to Orla, who sank into a chair next to Mason. The second her butt hit the seat, Mason turned to her and said, "Nope."

She spread her napkin across her lap. "What?"

"Orla." Mason took a forceful glug of his wine and grimaced as he swallowed. "I'm not putting him on the show."

"I'm not asking for him to have a starring role." Orla sipped her water—it was flat. She found a bottle of Pellegrino and tipped it into a random empty glass. "I just wanted him to look presentable. So you wouldn't have to shoot around him."

"And thank you *so* much for that," Mason said. "But I'm gonna keep shooting around him."

"*Shh,*" Orla hissed. She thought she saw Danny's ears stiffening toward their conversation. "Why?" she whispered, feeling desperate.

Mason seized a roll—deep brown, with floured white diamonds—from the basket on the table. He tore it apart. "What Danny's doing to you?" he said. "I've seen it a million times."

"What he's doing to *me*?" Orla said. She gestured at Danny, the boy from home, redone in things that she had paid for to make him look like part of her life. "Does it really look to you like he's running the show?" she said to Mason.

Mason dipped his chin apologetically. "Of course it does," he said. "Of course."

She wanted to protest, but Danny was changing seats, making his way around the table toward her. Before he reached her side, she leaned close to Mason, her hair almost falling into his glass, and said, "If you don't need him, maybe you don't need me, either."

Mason stared back plaintively. "That's a possibility."

Floss and Orla and Aston and Danny rode home after dinner together, silent as Amadou wound the SUV north. Floss and Aston sat with space between them in the middle, heads trained out their respective windows, while Orla bounced in the deep back, under Danny's arm.

A red light stopped them outside a shop with a pink-and-white marquee. The headless mannequin propped in the window wore a crisp navy suit. Danny crossed his hand over Orla's neck and pointed, pushing her head uncomfortably to one side, at the dummy. "I like that," he said. "Maybe we'll check that place out tomorrow."

Floss turned around to face them, her flawless features washed in the ghost-story glow of her phone. "You really do have some nice new things, Danny," she said. "Some real investment pieces." She paused. "Now, tell me again. You work in a big fridge, right?"

Orla's face began to heat.

"You get paid by the hour?" Floss pressed.

"Shut up, Floss," Aston snapped.

Danny remained cool. "That's right," he said. "I manage a cold-storage warehouse. But if this is what you're getting at— yeah, the clothes were a gift from Orla. A very generous gift." He kissed Orla's ear.

The car stopped outside the girls' building. Amadou got out and shut his door softly. They waited in silence for him to come around the other side.

Floss was wearing a jacket hung with ivory feathers. The plumage trembled as she raised her finger in the air and moved it in a circle. "*All* of this," she snapped, "is a gift from Orla. You're in our world as her plus-one. Don't forget that."

"Ignore her," Orla ordered him. "She's jealous."

And there it was, crushing her: Danny's face didn't look like it should. He wasn't offended or embarrassed. She could swear hat he almost looked hopeful. All of a sudden, she knew exactly what he thought she meant. The thing she had tried to keep from knowing—*he's using you to get to her*—came tunneling up, unstoppable.

"Not jealous of *me*, for being with you," she said, correcting his mistake. "Jealous of you, for being with me. She used to have me all to herself."

Floss was smirking. She had seen Danny's face, too.

The door of the Escalade clicked open. Floss got out, then the boys, then Orla. She took Amadou's hand. Adrenaline made her feet shake in her latest pair of shoes. They had a column, running up the front, of patent leather bows, deeper blood than the red of the sole, and though the salesgirl swore they were stronger than they looked, the spike beneath Orla's foot felt too flimsy to rest her full weight on.

Floss dawdled on the sidewalk, bitching at Aston as he held her wrists, looking angry. "I'm tired," Orla heard him say. "I'm fucking tired, Floss." A teenage boy passing by did a double take, then fished his phone out and snapped a photo without breaking stride.

In the lobby, Danny ignored the doorman's friendly eye. He followed Orla into the elevator and glared at her as he pushed the button. "You need to apologize to Floss," he said.

Orla looked at his reflection in the smudged metal panel. "You've got to be fucking kidding me," she said.

"You were way out of line." His finger was still on the button, and Orla wondered why. Then the sound of Floss's heels on the tile grew closer, and Orla realized Danny wasn't pressing 6. He was holding down the button that kept the door open. He would hold it, for Floss, for as long as it took.

———

A few days later, Orla got her first injections. She felt like a sellout, but she didn't have much choice after the Met Gala, to which she had worn the wrong gown. Insanely cut, it exposed the outer sides of both her thighs. Lady-ish took the lead on destroying her. Yale Girl had the byline. Her post featured pics of Orla's legs in close-up, ostensibly to show the ugly beading on the dress's crotch-bib hem. But the actual headline was the sight that went unmentioned: Orla's thighs, stark white and pocked with cellulite from hip to knee. **Not sure if her leg is the Titanic or the iceberg, but either way it's fucking huge**, a commenter had written. It was the kind of remark, Orla thought, that Ingrid used to take down instantly. But maybe she had made an exception.

Cellulite, like cockroaches, could not truly be defeated. Orla knew this. Floss had been talked into thousands of dollars' worth of freezing chambers and seaweed wraps, and nothing made the dimples go away. So Orla chose to focus on something she could change—the crease in her forehead—instead.

When Orla returned from her appointment at dusk, face tingling, she could hear Danny and Floss, but she couldn't see them. She realized, listening in the apartment's doorway, that they were both on the other side of the wall. Her wall.

She went to her bedroom and threw open the door. It yielded like a piece of cardboard. "What's going on here?" she demanded.

Floss was sitting on the bed in one of her nighties—leopard print—her legs splayed wide in front of her. Danny knelt on the floor before her, his bulky frame squashed between the mattress and the giant air conditioner. Even finding them like this, hiding from her, Orla had to bite herself back from warning him not to scrape himself on the unit's sharp corner.

On the bed between Floss's legs was Danny's laptop. His too-thick black laptop, with the pretzel crumbs fossilizing in the cracks of the alphabet. An embarrassment among the fleet of sleek and silver everything owned by Floss and Aston and

Orla, so much of it that they couldn't always remember what was whose, or how much they'd gotten for free.

Floss cocked her head. "We're having a presentation," she said to Orla. "Unbreakable water bottles. Did you ever dare to dream, Orla, that my name could be on a water bottle?"

Danny drew the laptop backward, turned it so the screen was facing him. He glared at Orla, like she had ruined things somehow. He looked back and forth, between both girls, as he said, "If you would just let me finish."

Orla let her keys fall from her hand onto the desk. She took a long look at him. He had gone back to putting the shitty gel he brought from home in his hair. Orla could see the screen of the laptop, blinking Danny's final slide—*AND MUCH MORE IN THE FUTURE!*

"It looks like we did let you finish," she said. "It looks like you're actually done."

———

It would have been better if someone could storm out. But Orla couldn't do it. She lived there. And Danny couldn't do it. He had to ask Orla how to connect his laptop to her printer so that he could purchase and print out a bus ticket. By the time they had successfully linked the machines, the tension had slipped from the room.

"Okay, then," Danny said wearily, over the bleats of the inkjets. "Take care."

"Yeah," Orla said. "Good to see you."

"Good to *see* you?" Floss squawked, giggling, thirty minutes later, as they rode the elevator toward the roof. Orla forced herself to join in.

The lock on the Ukrainian man's gate had been removed. Floss had guessed that it would be. "He'll know who we are by now," she had said. "He'll think we have better places to go."

Orla noticed that the toddler car was gone. In the center of the dining table was a pair of small terra-cotta pots with finger painting on them. One said DAD. The other, in wobbly printing, KATYA.

"Don't feel bad," Floss said, passing Orla a bottle of whiskey—something small-batch, limited-edition, much better than whatever they had drunk up here the last time. "I won't have a boyfriend much longer, either." Her eyes followed a cruise ship gliding over the slice of the river they could see, headed south and away from the island. "Aston's a fucking child."

"Well, he kind of is," Orla said. "He's twenty-two." She thought of herself at twenty-two, a year under her belt in New York. She was already waiting for Danny then, and now she felt a pang. She pictured him in line at Port Authority, the smoggy spot she stood when she went home. When she used to go home. She shook Gayle's face out of her head. "The years I wasted," she murmured, trusting Floss to keep up with the subject.

Floss nodded. "I don't know how you could want something all that time," she said, "and not have a plan for getting it."

Orla thought of how carefully Danny had packed all the clothes she bought him. He took his time folding everything, as righteous as if he'd come in with it. There was meanness in that, she thought—the way he didn't mind her seeing what mattered to him just then. Then again, she thought, with a sudden rumble of guilt in her stomach, the clothes might have been the least she could do. Hadn't she, all those years ago, handed him a brainy book to read? Hadn't she believed he was better than he realized, and made him feel that way? Then he had come here and called her bluff, tried to grow into his potential right in front of her. And Orla had shown him the limits of what she really thought of him: he was special and smart, of course—he was better than Mifflin. But not as special and smart and better as she was. *I will finish my book this fucking month*, Orla thought. *And I will go on a date with that guy from Craig's office, the one with the parrot. I will open my mind to this parrot.* She breathed deeply and waited for Floss to wrestle the conversation her way.

"When it's over with Aston, it's *all* over," Floss said quietly a moment later. "People know me as his girlfriend. I'm half a combo name. *Flosston.*"

For the first time, Orla considered the other option. She grinned. "Better than *Ass.*"

Then, suddenly, turning lazily to the distance, Orla spotted her: the girl Floss had aimed her head at all those months ago. The one in her room, in her sports bra, working late on her own dream. Here she was again: again in the bra, again at the computer. Again staring at the screen, brows stern, fingers curled at her lips. Then the girl's face changed. She smiled. Orla watched as she lifted her hand and waved at the screen. She was talking to someone, Orla realized. Not pounding away at a goal. Her eyes moved downward to the girl's stomach. Tiny rolls jumped with each giggle. She looked effortless—the literal opposite of girdles and mink lashes, of photo filters and **Be relatable!!!!!** Post-its. The opposite of everything that kept Orla and Floss busy all day and night. Orla couldn't stop staring; she was beautiful. She was real. A thought began to form in her head.

"What the fuck are you *gazing* at?" Floss said.

Orla looked at her friend. She was far from perfect, but she was the only one up here with her. It counted for something. It always would, even later, when what happened to them should have eclipsed it.

"I know something you could do," Orla said, "to be famous on your own."

Floss clapped her hands together. "Spill," she said. "I'll do anything."

———

It was Melissa who woke Orla twelve hours later. She must have thought that she had roused Orla before she did, because she was already talking when Orla came to, in the middle of her frantic explanation. "A tragedy," Melissa was saying, in a low, stern voice. "And that's the thing with tragedies. Everyone wants someone to blame, fast." She paused and, satisfied that Orla was awake and listening, stopped shaking her and took a step back. "The fact remains," she said, "that she's dead. The fact remains that it's a big fucking deal, and it's only getting bigger. So you need to get up now."

"Who's dead?" Orla said. She propped herself up on one elbow. "What are you talking about?"

It was like Melissa couldn't hear her, like she was going to finish her prepared way of saying this no matter what Orla said or did. "I'm not trying to scare you," she said. "And I'm not saying it's your fault." As Orla watched, she held up her hands like scales, raising one palm, then the other. "At the same time," Melissa concluded, "it's not *not* your fault."

CHAPTER TWELVE

Marlow

New York, New York
2051

Marlow was in the Archive lobby, looking for a human or
bot who could tell her what that code meant—*404, not
found*—when a photo in the slideshow lighting up one wall
stopped her cold.

It was a picture of Honey. Honey, grown, her blond coils loosened into a matrix of salon-sanctioned waves, standing in the
center of a crowd of clapping people. She held a pair of oversize lacquered scissors over a ribbon, ready to snap. The ribbon
stretched across the entrance to the room where Marlow had
just sat, searching for her father.

A caption unfurled itself across the bottom of the image:
"Marquee donor Honey Mitchell unveiling the Mitchell Wing,
a $65 million space devoted entirely to general searches of the
Internet Archive."

Marlow looked back at Honey. The women at the airport had

been right: on the side of her face was a painful-looking starburst of shining, raised skin. Purple at the center, fading pinkish white at the ends. Marlow took a step backward. She felt, suddenly, as doomed as she would if Honey was there in person. Honey, who had always been so lethally resourceful. Honey, whose lair she had naively drifted into.

Forget the error, forget Orla Cadden, forget her real father—it was time to go. Marlow turned and saw the bot from earlier—Mateo—right there, waiting. Standing close enough that she'd have to step around it to run.

"Marlow Clipp," it said, and she felt her whole being rise in fear. It knew who she was. "Marlow Clipp, on behalf of Ms. Mitchell, I'm asking you to follow me."

She looked into its eyes. Mateo blinked pleasantly. She heard the tiny whir of it preparing to repeat itself.

She stepped around the bot and started to run. "Marlow," the bot called after her, without an ounce of urgency.

There was a crowd between her and the doors, a mass of peo-ple she mistook for a shuffling tour until she realized that they were moving toward her.

"There!" cried the girl at the front of the group, and Marlow saw that she was the teenage girl who had identified her earlier. The group behind her wasn't made of tourists. It was made of hunters, coming her way.

Marlow turned and sprinted away from them, skirting Mateo, who made no move to reach out for her, but turned and followed her with placid speed. She heard the girl shouting, rerouting the mob, heard their footsteps squeaking and pounding. When Marlow reached the hallway where the bots stood like knights along the wall, she saw the girl and her band of followers flood-ing into one end of it. She stopped in the middle and looked over her shoulder. Mateo was advancing from the other side, sure and sweatless.

"Marlow Clipp," it said. "Please reduce your speed to avoid injury or confusion."

"C'mon!" the teenage girl barked from the other end of the hall. "Enough with the running. I have a side sticker! I won this hunt fair and square!"

Marlow stumbled toward the wall in front of her, put her left palm flat against it. As she steadied herself, something flicked in her peripheral vision—two words, halfway down the wall, projected in soft blue light: Employees Only.

"The Archive's security force is here for your protection," Mateo called out.

Marlow pushed, and a door gave way, revealing a small room with a table and coffee dispenser. She stood there dumbly for a second, startled to find herself in such a humdrum space in the middle of being pursued. She hurried through it, through the next darkened room with the grid of security footage, toward the door beneath the red EXIT sign.

Then she was out on a block she hadn't seen before, looking left and right and shaking, searching the faces that pushed by her for signs of recognition. No one took a second look at her. No one stepped closer to try to see past her disguise. As she turned around and around, trying to stir up her sense of direction, a man brought his sneaker sole down on the back of her ankle. "Hell outta the way," he mumbled, heaving himself around her.

There was a cab. She stumbled to it, tore open the door, and fell in.

"Please speak slowly while telling me your destination," the cab's soothing automation said.

"Just go," Marlow said sharply. "Just go anywhere."

The voice was silent for a moment. "This vehicle will remain in park until you provide an address."

She looked out the window and saw the hunters pushing their way out the main entrance, pawing their way through people trying to come in, regrouping, shouting, whipping their heads around. The teenage girl was red-faced, petulant—her mother was patting her shoulder, trying to reason with her.

And with them, now, was Mateo. While all the humans around it tried to figure out where Marlow had gone, Mateo was looking straight at her cab, blinking, standing perfectly still.

"Please repeat the address of your destination slowly," the cab prompted.

Her destination. She didn't have one. She just needed to move. Marlow pressed on her temples. An address, any address, she could just make one up, *why could she not come up with one address?* What was the name of this street she was on? Which number would take her to a very distant part of it? She dug in her pocket frantically, finding the slip of wallpaper that she had written the address from the search results on. "Three-oh-three," she shouted. "West Twenty-First Street." The cab lurched away from the curb, through the intersection, away from her followers.

The cab's welcome message started up, the one she had heard already, Mayor Charlotte C. Mezvinsky welcoming her to the city. All the way down to Twenty-First Street, Marlow worked on breathing in and out, persuading her pulse to slow down. She listened to the cab's breezy ads play on loop—including the one that reminded her, every five minutes, of the bounty on her head.

————

Three-oh-three West Twenty-First Street was a block of grimy blond stone with brick designs inlaid, red lines that reminded Marlow of the dried blood on her wrist, where her device had clung to her skin. The apartment building was on the west side of the city (she had figured out that the hazy blue tower was the island's southern point). She could see, a few long blocks down, the shimmering surface of the West Side Canal. The commuters who kayaked up and down it streamed eastward, toward where

Marlow stood in front of a nail salon, unzipping their wetsuits to the chest, shaking water out of their hair.

Marlow went inside and found the mailboxes. She picked the lock and went upstairs, collapsed on the sun-bleached couch in the strange, haunted 6D. She lay there, safe from the hunt for the moment, but not from her own thoughts. Not from Honey.

Marlow had gone over the night that changed her life thousands of times, and that wasn't counting the dreams. Before Hysteryl—and after it, now—she dreamed of it constantly, always waking with a bad taste in her mouth.

She had met Honey Mitchell when they were both fourteen. Honey came through the exchange. Every year, at the start of the school term, Constellation received an eighth grader from somewhere else—usually a struggling, smog-filled town. The literature on the exchange program lauded Constellation's pristine air and unparalleled nutrition—it promised a chance for underprivileged children to breathe and grow and thrive.

But fresh air had nothing to do with it. The exchange was just more marketing for Constellation's ongoing mission: to get more people sharing again. When Honey came to town, it had been almost ten years since the government took over the internet, ten years since Constellation was launched alongside it, to make the new web look good. Yet the federal internet remained, overall, a flop. People had been coaxed, over the decade, to use it for essentials, like messaging and searching and keeping track of each other's locations. But they layered suspicious caution into every interaction they allowed themselves. In emails, they used code words they had agreed on in person. They buried their real search-engine question in nineteen fake ones, obscuring what they really wondered about so the government wouldn't know. Marlow's father explained to her why everyone his age tried to hide their online footprints: they had grown up using an internet that had nothing to do with the government, one that at least pretended not to be watching people. But that was before the Spill, and now the Department of Information was blunt about the reality: yes, on the new internet, data was constantly gathered. It was kept forever, used and shared at the government's discretion. What choice did they have, if they wanted to keep people safe? Her father did a funny impression of the president from back then, declaring that America's new internet would function just like China's.

Fine, people reasoned reluctantly. They got over it the way they'd long ago gotten over taking off their shoes in airports. But they weren't going to share more than they had to. They certainly weren't going back to sharing *socially*. They scoffed at the Department of Info's dorky replacements for their old social-media platforms. The Department filtered silent ads through people's still-new devices and into their minds: *Flick your device-dominant wrist at something fly to snap a photo of it, then post it on Amerigram!* Yet Amerigram, with its red-white-and-blue-striped background, sat sadly, sparsely used. "Lame," Marlow's mother said tartly when she saw the star-spangled graphics.

The social sharing drought was a problem for the government, Aston explained to Marlow. The Department of Info needed companies to buy ads on the internet, to supplement the relatively thin slice of federal budget it had been granted. But companies didn't want to buy ads, because they couldn't tell, as they had in the old days, what people wanted.

"How did they know back then?" Marlow asked her father. His response was a torrent of foreign terms: people "liked" things, people "pinned" things, people discussed things out loud as their smartphones sat there, still and dark, but somehow eavesdropping.

In any case: no matter how the Department of Info pleaded, Americans were keeping their likes to themselves, teaching their kids to do the same. This was the part that truly frightened the government. What if the internet they had built only lasted for one generation? That was where Honey came in. The exchange program was part of the effort to pry teens from the rest of the country away from how they'd been raised. If a kid came to Constellation and spent a year on camera, tasting attention, chances were she wouldn't want to stop sharing her image and her voice when she got home. Maybe she'd start using Amerigram, get her friends hooked on it, too.

It took Marlow years to see the irony in the way they called this program an exchange. Constellation never sent a child anywhere.

Honey came from War, West Virginia. She swore the name of the town was real. She went to one of the spooky religious schools Marlow and her friends had only heard of in stories, the ones with sad-eyed pictures and gory statues in the classrooms—the man on the cross bleeding out of his side, the veiled woman whose virginity was discussed constantly, even by children, even in prayers. Honey's parents technically survived the Spill, but it still killed them. When she was in fourth grade, the two of them drank too much at a party and got into a fight about one of their files. Her father shot her mother, then himself.

Afterward, Honey and her brothers went to live with her grandparents. Her grandfather had been the last in a long line of Mitchell men to work in the Mountain Laurel mine. Now that it had been closed and gutted, he still worked there, in the underground theme park it had been turned into. He wore a red hat that said Mountain Laurel Family Funzone and ran a roller coaster all day long.

Marlow could remember her eighth-grade teacher urging all of them to listen to Honey, saying she could teach them a lot about the history of America: about factories and assets chipped out of the ground, about sooty, grimy means of energy. She could remember Honey fixing the teacher with ice-cold eyes and saying, "It's only history to you because you live out here and aren't poor." Honey wasn't interested in being a counterpoint to clean power. She had come to Constellation in search of another kind of power: absolute.

Her strategy for getting it was ragged at best, but her looks were on her side. When the pawns in question are ninth graders, what can a new girl in town not do? Especially one who has caught them off guard with her beauty. After years of the exchange, the Constellation kids had expectations for the students who came through it: they were usually rough or fat or knobby-kneed, covered in skin that looked like it had lived several lives. Invariably, their teeth overlapped.

But Honey was perfect fruit. Her skin was peach-cream velvet. The hair that tumbled down her back was blond and full of curls that jostled and shone when she giggled. Short as she was, her legs seemed endless, and her breasts were high and formed. Marlow could still remember the sense of respect that overwhelmed her when she first saw those breasts. She believed that the way the girl filled out her bra meant she knew more than the rest of them.

The queens of Marlow's class aimed to become her gatekeepers, the ones who would tell the boys, *Honey hates when you do that* or *Honey thinks you're cute, you might have a shot*. This way, the boys could not afford to neglect them altogether, these still-curveless girls they had grown up with.

But Honey didn't want anything to do with the girls who were popular at school. She wanted the ones who were popular with the audience. Though they were middling players in the eighth grade, Marlow and her best friend, Grace, were well watched across the country that year. As usual, it was hard to tell exactly why; while the appetites of adult Constellation fans were more consistent, the kid viewers treated the network's junior talent like crushes, following and unfollowing them unpredictably. The surge in Grace's numbers might have been because of the acoustic guitar covers she breathed directly into a camera in her bedroom, but it wasn't anything dozens of other kids weren't doing. Though Marlow did everything she could to set herself apart from Floss, the network's cleavage-baring jester—she wore black lipstick, combat boots, and mercilessly tight twin braids—her numbers always seemed to grow in tandem with her mother's, spiking when Floss did a Floss-like thing, such as tripping drunk into a bush or buying a nude sculpture for the front lawn. Whenever her mother did something vulgar, the very next thing she did was check her numbers and Marlow's, muttering like a stage mom: "We're doing so good today, baby."

When Honey walked over to Grace and Marlow, during lunch on her very first day, she held her tray and looked between them, waiting to see who would say something first. Marlow didn't look up from her tofu. She had no interest in Honey Mitchell. The last thing she needed in her life was a peer who, just like her mother, acted bold and nervy and led with her breasts, making Marlow feel flat in every way.

It was Grace who moved over on the bench—a silly thing to do, since their table was, but for them, empty. As Grace scooted down, Marlow watched Honey's eyes moving from the spikes on Marlow's boots to Grace's shy, gapped grin. It was easy to see who was softer, who was more open to being shaped.

Honey sat. She poked at her avocado toast and went on about a thing that had happened in class earlier, while Marlow was in the bathroom—a boy's voice cracking in such a way that he sounded just like their lady principal. As Honey spoke, she faced Grace exclusively, leaving Marlow to stare at her ear. When Marlow tried to chime in, Honey just wiggled her eyebrows at Grace and said, "Yeah, you kind of had to be there."

When school ended that day, Honey followed her host family's son—a shy piano prodigy whom Marlow felt sorry for, having to live with that rack in the next room. Marlow and Grace were walking the other way. Honey called over her shoulder, "Bye, G!"

"G?" Marlow said to Grace.

"For Grace, I guess she means." Her friend studied the ground.

By the next morning, Honey and Grace were a unit that Marlow floated outside of. On weekends, she spotted them from a distance, entering the spa and leaving the frozen yogurt shop. At school, she tried to ignore them quoting jokes she didn't know the roots of. Grace only looked sorry about any of it if she ran into Marlow alone, like the time they were both in the bathroom and Marlow told the lie that set it all on course.

She was washing her hands at the sink when Grace came out of the stall behind her. Their eyes met in the mirror. Grace looked, Marlow noticed, like she would rather turn around and drown in the toilet than talk to her.

"You could come with us to this thing tonight if you want," Grace said, but Marlow could see how hard she was hoping that Marlow would say no.

So she said she couldn't make it, along with the next thing that came into her head: she had plans with someone else.

"Who?" Grace asked.

Marlow felt an anxious flick. "Eva," she said, without thinking. It was the name embossed on the box of pink slime soap bolted to the wall between them.

Grace's eyes shot down to the dispenser, back up. "Eva who?"

Who knew where she got the next part? "Tree," Marlow heard herself say, and then she silently shrieked every curse she could think of, in the order they came to her.

"Eva *Tree*?" Grace extracted from her pocket a tube of tangerine-colored lip gloss. She had been wearing it every day, at Honey's recommendation.

"You don't know her," Marlow said. She ducked over the sink, trying to keep her burning face out of the mirror. "My parents are friends with her parents. She just moved to Pismo Beach. From Paris."

The week after Marlow invented Eva Tree, the school held its first dance of the year. Marlow didn't want to go, but Floss insisted. "It's my job to make you tough," she said. "I'm not going to let you shut yourself in your room just because Grace is being a dick." The logic checked out, parenting-wise, but Marlow saw panic in her mother's eyes. She knew Floss had plans for the night that she didn't want her daughter ruining.

So Marlow went, and stood alone, her back against the cool pocked surface of the gymnasium wall. Honey had decided she and Grace would wear the same dress, and now Marlow watched them walk in, clad in the same strappy thing. The dress had a smattering of tiny pink paisleys and three pearly buttons at the chest.

By the time Grace walked over to Marlow, with an hour left in the dance, Marlow knew what she should say. Meanness had been brewing in her stomach all night. It was time to let it taste the air.

"The same dress as Honey?" she said, looking pointedly at Grace's smooth chest. The top of the dress gapped over it. "I'm guessing that wasn't *your* idea."

Grace lowered her eyes to the shell-shaped toes of her white sneakers. "I came over here to ask if you wanted to hang out after," she said. "If we could go to your place."

It was how they spent Friday nights before Honey came: lying on Marlow's bed, heads flung back over the edge, messaging boys to tease them as their long, thick hair brushed the carpet. Marlow felt her heart surge with unexpected hope. She let the version of herself she was trying out dissolve. "Okay, yeah," she said. "We have lots of chips and stuff. I'm ready to go whenever."

"Great," Grace said. When she looked up from her shoes, there was guilt in her eyes.

"Great," Honey repeated, appearing out of nowhere. She linked arms with Grace. "I'll tell the guys," Honey said, then added, "Tell Eva Tree to come, too."

They walked to Marlow's house in a group of five, Marlow in the lead. Two well-liked boys, boys who had never noticed Marlow and Grace before Honey, came along. Each of them tried walking next to Marlow for a moment, gauging up close whether or not she was of interest. But she was nauseous with dread, too sick to smile or flirt, and soon they drifted backward, away. Once, Grace touched Marlow's arm, and Marlow turned to hear what she had to say for herself. But Honey whined right away—"G, I need you"—and Grace fell back into her shadow.

The group reached Marlow's front door, fanning out behind her on the step. Marlow's thumb was slick with sweat as she punched the code into the keypad. What would her father say when he saw who she was with: Grace in strange lipstick, two boys he didn't know, and a half-woman girl from Appalachia?

But the house was dark. Aston wasn't home. Marlow's stomach knotted as she walked around, waving on lamps. Her father was supposed to be here; she had heard her parents arranging it. She had been sure he would see her face and find a reason to kick them all out. She had been counting on him.

When Marlow turned and padded back to the kitchen, the boys had the fridge door wide open, its otherworldly light and cold leaking into the room as they got out her father's starchy beers and pored over the labels.

"Buncha old-man IPAs," one of the boys muttered, green eyes rolling high. Taylor, his name was. A jock. They both were. The other—Angel, who wore his hair in a boxy flattop—closed the fridge and handed the bottle in his hand to Honey. He hadn't even taken a beer for himself, Marlow realized. Pathetic. She had entertained a crush on Angel earlier that year, and now she had an urge to call up her diary in her head, to swipe away all the passages concerning his smooth biceps and nut-colored eyes. She was forever editing her diary.

Marlow looked over at Grace. She was doing what she always did when she first got to Marlow's house: perching forward on a stool at the kitchen island, rearranging the fruit in the shallow wooden bowl. She would not meet Marlow's eye.

Honey rested the lip of her beer's ridged cap against the island. She angled the bottom of the bottle toward herself and brought the heel of her palm down hard on the cap. It popped off the bottle and fell to the floor. Powdery chips of the counter-top rained down after it.

"So," Honey said, over the trickle of steam. "Is Eva meeting us, or?"

Marlow pulled herself up to sit on the counter. "I texted her and she can't," Marlow said curtly. "She's stuck at home. She has to watch her little brother. Billy," she added, almost giggling at her own recklessness. Where the *fuck* was her dad?

"No big deal," said Honey. She kept her eyes locked on Marlow as she raised the butt of the bottle and started to chug from it. Ten seconds went by, then nearly twenty, and still she didn't stop. The beer trickled out both corners of Honey's mouth and tunneled down her neck to her cleavage. Taylor's eyes tracked the drip hungrily, but Marlow saw that Angel was frowning now, looking away. It was silent in the room but for a series of muffled yelps, like something tiny dying in a bag. It took Marlow a moment to place the sound: Honey's rhythmic swallowing.

Finally, the bottle was empty. Honey lowered it. She burped with a force that rattled her face. Taylor laughed like it was the funniest thing he had ever heard.

"So let's go to her house," Honey said.

"Who?" asked Grace. It was like they couldn't remember life before Honey chugged the beer.

"*Eva*," Honey said impatiently. She tossed the bottle into the sink and walked across the kitchen. She didn't have to ask which door led to the garage. She grabbed the knob right away, like she had been there many times. She must have been a longtime follower, Marlow thought. She must have been a loyal fan.

———

The car Honey chose was one of Aston's favorites, because of-fucking-course it was: a silver vintage Land Rover, retrofitted with autonomous everything.

Honey was in what was still called the driver's seat. Grace went for shotgun, but Honey tilted the world she had built by waving Grace off and summoning Marlow. So Grace was in the back seat, wedged between Angel and Taylor, who set their hands on the upholstery in just such a way that their pinkies grazed her thighs.

"On," Honey said to the car. To Marlow, she said, "What's Eva's address?"

Marlow started to panic. She kept her eyes on the closed garage door.

"Marlow." Marlow felt Grace's fingertips on her shoulder. "Just tell her the truth," she said quietly. "Tell her Eva isn't real."

"What's she talking about, Marlow?" Honey pressed her palms into the wheel so that her arms went straight. She waited.

Marlow tugged at her seat belt. "I don't know the exact address."

Grace sighed.

"Can't you look her up on your map?" Honey said.

"She—" Marlow straightened her spine. She had gone this far, and she rather liked the sound of the fib that came to her next. "Eva doesn't use mapping," she said. "It's a French thing."

In the back seat, Taylor laughed again.

"That's okay." Honey eased the car forward. Marlow's heart began to pound. The garage door sensed the vehicle coming and slid up to let them out. Honey turned left out of the driveway, right onto the main road. "Grace says you claim she lives in Pismo Beach. Pismo Beach," she said, loudly, to the navigation.

"Go home," Marlow countered at the same volume, and the car braked.

"Cancel last command," Honey said. It started moving again.

"Honey." Marlow leaned across the console, hoping no one could see her shake. "I don't know what you think you're doing," she said. "But we are not *stealing* my dad's 2004 Land Rover and taking it to Pismo Beach. Do you know how much trouble we could get in? We're fourteen. We don't know how to drive."

Honey turned and looked at Marlow. She waggled her fingers above the wheel. "What exactly do you think you have to know?"

Something shifted in the car then, the air drying up the same way it had when Honey chugged the beer. Marlow knew that all of them—Grace and Angel and Taylor—had to be thinking the same thing she was: Why hadn't the network intervened yet? She did the mental math—all right, maybe the executives would look the other way on one beer. But grand theft auto? Talent welfare wouldn't let this play out, would they?

Marlow was considering saying something. It would get her in trouble with her parents, it would get them all in trouble with the network, if she referenced, on camera, the fact that they were filming. But Marlow wondered, as Honey put the car on the freeway and pushed it to ninety, if it might save their lives, reminding this girl that people could see her.

Then Honey fluffed both sides of her hair and winked at a spot on the dashboard. A spot where there was a camera embedded.

Marlow's stomach turned to ice. Honey, she realized, *wanted* to be watched. She saw Honey's game laid out as clearly as the road in front of them. She pictured Honey at home, wanting badly to be noticed, having no real way to pursue her goal from her bedroom in West Virginia. Resolving to hijack the country's biggest platform, its capital of fame: Constellation. She had come here to make herself a star, and this was her breakthrough moment.

"Go. Home," Marlow said again to the car, her voice chipping into something uneven.

Honey looked at her like she was the most boring thing on the planet. "Automation off," she said, then gripped the wheel and frowned. "This thing is *dusty.*"

"Uh," said Angel, "what're you doing?"

"Driving," Honey said. "Some of us still know how." And

to prove it, she zigzagged the car in the lane, laughing as they tossed from side to side.

Marlow started to yell then. She started to threaten. She said she would call the cops, then backtracked and said she'd called them already. Aston had antitheft on all of his cars, she cautioned. He had surely been alerted.

"Then I guess he doesn't care," Honey said.

Marlow unbuckled her seat belt. Without thinking, she lunged for the wheel and grabbed it, pulled it toward herself. The front part of the car careened toward the side of the road. Its back end went the other way, bucking toward the middle. Grace screamed, a deafening, unfaltering sound of fear.

Honey put a hand on Marlow's chest and pushed hard, thrusting her back to her side. She righted the car. "Hey, guys?" she said to the others, looking in the rearview mirror. "It's incredibly dangerous for someone who doesn't know what she's doing to be messing with a car at these speeds. I think maybe Marlow is getting hysterical. We need to restrain her, or else we'll crash."

Slumped against her window, Marlow panted.

"What do you mean, restrain her?" Grace said uncertainly. "Maybe we should just pull over."

"That's not going to happen," Honey said smoothly. "So let's just do what's safest." She glanced in the rearview mirror. "I know," she went on. "Why don't you boys put your belts around her hands and feet, so we can keep her safe till she calms down?"

"That's insane," Grace said, her voice wobbling.

"Oh, it's totally not," Honey said. "It's actually what paramedics do in this kind of situation. I swear." She looked at Taylor in the rearview mirror. "You guys do have belts on, right?"

Taylor and Angel looked at each other. "I don't know if—" Angel said.

"It's really the safest thing for all of us," Honey insisted. "It's what's best for her right now." Marlow saw the way Honey moved her face to find Taylor's eyes in the rearview mirror.

'And it's not that much farther to the beach," she said. "I cannot *wait* to get this dress off."

Marlow heard the tinkling of buckles coming apart.

———

'We'll hang out here until you get in touch with Eva," Honey said when she turned the car off. The Land Rover had tackled the dunes with ease and settled on a dark stretch of sand near the water.

"Just tell her," Grace whispered for the hundredth time, curling over her lap to talk into Marlow's ear. She was holding Marlow's head between her palms. Marlow didn't answer. She had decided not to say another word. The last time she checked her followers, they had grown tenfold. Let the rest of them, Grace included, look like the biggest fucking assholes. Marlow would remain still and innocent. She focused all of her energy on trying to suck her stomach in, trying to find a way to hold her body, as they laid her across the back seat and left her, that wouldn't look horrific on camera.

"Everybody out," Marlow heard Honey say. "She'll feel better after she rests." Then Marlow was alone in the car, counting four doors slamming, listening through glass to the thrum of the ocean. She was lying on the back seat with her wrists, which were tied with Angel's brown belt, resting on her stomach in front of her. She grunted and lifted her feet into view. Taylor's black belt was binding her ankles. After a while, she sat up, her stomach muscles burning with the effort, and saw that Honey had misjudged the tide. The waves were starting to lap at the car, foam collapsing in the tread of the tires.

Down the beach, she saw Grace, on the sand by herself, arms wrapped around her knees. Angel squatted at the edge of the surf, his face tucked down on his chest, poking at the ground with a stick. Taylor was in the water with Honey. True to her word, she had taken off her dress. She jumped in and out of the waves in her sodden bra and underwear, her whole body quaking every few seconds. *The Pacific's cold, moron*, Marlow thought. She remembered learning about the Atlantic in third grade. The outspoken teacher had taken some liberties, like the East Coast's ocean was a rival team: "Brown, full of trash, piss-warm," he had scoffed.

She gingerly raised her arms, watching her wrists move as one. Her skin was starting to chafe beneath the leather. Outside, Honey jumped into Taylor's arms suddenly, and he stumbled under her weight.

Marlow remembered that it was dangerous to leave a child in the car with the windows up. Did that still apply to her? She didn't feel like a child at the moment, but she was sure none of them were adults. If they were adults, they wouldn't be here now—one of them would have been brave enough to speak up. She thought of the teacher who talked shit on the Atlantic. He had been dismissed that same year, disappearing from the enclave, for being too frank with her class about the Spill. She remembered what he said about why so many of the lives lost belonged to teenagers. It wasn't just that they did everything online, he said. It wasn't just that, unlike their parents, they didn't know life before technology. It had nothing to do with their habits or the point in time when they were born. They died mostly because of factors that hadn't changed over the course of human history—their still-developing brains and the manic chemicals pooled inside them. "Teenagers don't really get that there's a life beyond the moment," the teacher said. "You know that phrase *I'd rather die*? Teenagers actually would."

———

Marlow fell asleep sitting up. She woke up sometime later to a chorus of ragged breathing. Everyone was back in the car. She could just make out their forms: Honey and Taylor were crammed together beneath the wheel, lying back, reclined. Angel was folded neat and straight into the passenger seat. Grace

at in the back with Marlow, her cheek smashed on the opposite window.

Marlow heard sloshing somewhere near her hips; the water
must have reached the car's wheel wells. Her device leaned suddenly into her wrist to let her know she had lost service. She
wondered if, here, in the ocean's shallow end, the car's cameras
had lost signal, too.

She looked out the window, which was the same thing as
closing her eyes. It was distant-from-anything dark outside. No
lights on the beach. No moon. So this was what it was like, she
thought, to feel abandoned. Marlow loved her parents—she did.
She loved her father with ease and loved her mother with effort.
But from a young age, perhaps from the first time she had seen
how disappointed they looked when she stole out of bed and
slipped into their parties, she had understood that both of them,
as parents, topped out at half-functioning. She was able to love
them anyway, because she knew there was a third thing keeping her safe: the network. Her followers. When Floss claimed to
be *stopping by a thing* and came back two days later with a yacht-
front sunburn, or when Aston got a message that he claimed was
from his mother, but grinned in a way Marlow felt she shouldn't
see, she felt like the cameras were there, standing with her. It
was the same at night, when her parents were usually gone; it
was up to Marlow to put herself to bed, to shut down the house,
and she never figured out a way to do it that didn't mean she
had to pass through some rooms in the dark. But she was never
really afraid, the same way, when she got older, she was never
afraid to walk down an empty street or to be caught, at a party,
with the wrong boy on the wrong side of a closing door. Her
whole life, Marlow had been sure that if she got into trouble,
the network would protect her. But here she was, tied up in a
drowning car, and no one was doing anything.

She told herself the cameras weren't working. They couldn't
be. If the network knew, they wouldn't leave her. They prized

drama, but not at this cost. She was sure. They'd have a place-holder card splashed over her feed, brightly claiming technical difficulties, as they tried to figure out how to help her.

There was the sound of something landing on the roof.

The others stirred but didn't wake. Marlow listened. Whatever was on top of them was crawling the length of the car now. Two legs? Four? She counted. No, five. She looked up just as the thing dragged its silver belly over the moonroof. There was the *toonk* of glass on glass, and Marlow saw it then: an eye, all inky pupil, looking in at them.

Suddenly, there was blinding light. Marlow saw everything she couldn't see before: the way Taylor's and Honey's hair, nearly the same shade of blond, wove together and shone. The way Grace's face had dried pink and brown, as if she had cried for hours. The way Angel's hair rose, like a shadow, over the headrest.

The thing on the roof had a voice that boomed through the glass. "This car has been identified as stolen," it said. "Get out of the vehicle. Put your hands in the air."

The others were wriggling, turning pale, untangling themselves. But Marlow saw that Honey was frozen still, terrified. "Whatisitwhatisit," she screamed, covering her eyes. "Police drone," Taylor was saying over and over, until he was shouting it, furious. The explanation only seemed to scare Honey more. The drone slithered down the driver's side window, looking for a culprit, and the next thing Marlow knew, Honey had hurled herself into the back seat. She huddled next to Marlow, shaking.

"Get the fuck off me," Marlow said. The swear word felt good, a small pocket of pressure deflating, and she let herself have another one—she was that sure she wasn't being broadcast. "Untie me, bitch," she snapped at Honey, knocking her with her shoulder, but Honey only screeched and burrowed deeper into her. The others were tumbling out at the drone's command, were wading with their arms up toward the human cops movng toward them, rifles raised. More cops skimmed the sand in a tank, its looped tires flattening the beach beneath them. Behind the tank, struggling mightily, was Aston's low-slung red Porsche. Marlow watched as the car spun its wheels and gave up. It was still on, headlights shining, when her father got out of it. The sea breeze and the wind of the drone whipped his hair straight back from his face. A moment later, the Porsche's passenger door opened, in several tentative movements, and a woman stepped out. Marlow couldn't see her well, but she could tell that she was thin and staying out of things. So it definitely wasn't her mother.

The water began seeping into the car where Grace hadn't closed the door right. Marlow looked down at it, pooling around their feet, and spit at Honey, "What, you've never seen a police drone?"

You piece of redneck trash. She didn't have to say that part; her tone left it curdling in the air. And she could tell that Honey heard it, that she knew the sound of words like that being meant without being said.

"No," Honey answered softly. For a moment, she sounded as young as the rest of them. But then she stared out the window for a long, rapt moment and turned back to Marlow with the look of a gun with one bullet left in the chamber.

"Who's that lady with your dad?" she said. She leaned so close that her nose brushed Marlow's. A fleck of her spit landed on Marlow's lower lip as she spoke—a fleck that Marlow had to let sit there, bound as she was. Two cops were running toward the car, the beams of their flashlights passing gold through Honey's curls.

Honey slid her face against Marlow's until she was speaking right into her ear. "I mean," Honey whispered, "if Aston even is your real dad. You don't look anything like him, and your mom's always been such a slut."

Marlow strained her arms and legs, trying one more time to

break the belts. There was something rising in her. It reminded her of the time that sewage had backed up into their house through a drain in the basement floor. Aston had stood above a plumber and said, "Can't we just cover the drain?" The plumber had squinted up at him like he was everything he was—rich, clueless, impatient with reality—and said, "You can cover this one. But the crap will find another way out."

The leather on her wrists and ankles didn't budge, and Marlow saw that Honey was laughing. She was laughing as she started sitting back. "Such a slut," she said, pulling away.

Marlow opened her mouth like she was going to scream, then closed it, hard and fast, on Honey's face. Her teeth sank into the pad of flesh between the spot where Honey rubbed blush on her cheek and the long curve of her jaw. Marlow heard Honey gasp. She felt her jerk and go still. Honey screeched, her words warped, like she was the one with a mouthful. "Marlow, fuck, stop it!" When Honey pushed away, something tore and stayed behind. It was still in Marlow's mouth when she saw Honey looking horrified, scrambling backward to the seat's other side. There was an oily pink patch on her face with tattered, uneven edges. Blood was rising, more than running, from it.

Honey's skin was still in her mouth as the police reached the car and pulled Honey out first. Marlow waited her turn. The throbbing scrap in her teeth waited, too, for her to spit or swallow.

———

Most of the cameras in the car hadn't been working. One by one, as Honey drove them farther and farther from Constellation, they had lost their signals and gone off-line. But there was a camera in the dashboard—a sort of emergency option, with low-grade definition and no audio at all—that had still been transmitting video. Its angle missed the painful way Marlow's hands and feet were cuffed. All the viewers could see was her head in Grace's lap—all it seemed like, without the sound, was two friends fooling around. The camera was not as generous to the moment Marlow lunged at Honey. It captured Honey, looking terrified of the police drone, shaking and curling into Marlow. And then, in a violent flash, like a wildlife film, Marlow attacking, leading with her teeth, followed by Honey falling back, bitten. Marlow herself felt bile in the back of her mouth when a talent welfare officer played the scene for her, afterward. She had never seen herself on camera before—Constellation stars were prohibited from watching any of the content they made—and so at first she could almost convince herself it was someone else, someone who looked a bit like her, clamping down on Honey's face. But she knew, deep down, she had done it; she remembered the taste.

Kick her off the air! one of Marlow's followers wrote. **I check my feeds after a long day of REAL work in REAL America. I tune in for a laugh, not to see twisted little psychos.**

Heard that one girl was "eating" another one on camera and I'm pretty disappointed it was this LOL, said another.

Someone else just wrote: **Ur a monster.**

Everyone wanted Marlow's family out. Marlow was turned away, the next week, at school. Parents stood in a line in the parking lot, keeping her from the doors. "Jealous *nobodies*!" Floss shrieked at them, purple-faced, bucking the car into reverse as Marlow slumped in the back seat. Aston was at City Hall that morning, getting reamed out by the network.

"We'll just move somewhere else," he said when he got home. "We'll go back to LA or New York, and…"

"And get jobs?" Floss said. Marlow was sitting at the kitchen table with her head down. She heard the way Floss said "jobs." Her voice was thick with uncertainty, the same way it sounded when she pretended to know French. She watched her mother get up and walk out the door.

For days after that, Marlow stayed in her room and thought about that—the sound of her mother saying "jobs." It brought back things she didn't know she knew: vague memories of life before Constellation. She could see, in blurry hindsight, the hotels they had lived in when she was a little kid: the fancy ones, at first, where Floss loved being recognized, then the dingy ones where, when people came up to her, she pretended to be someone else. She recalled games of hide-and-seek, Aston springing at her from behind the ice machine, Floss holding her on rusted pool chairs late at night. Floss would sing to Marlow, to help her fall asleep—but then she'd seem insulted when Marlow did. "I only sing for you, you know," Floss would say, annoyed. "Don't you think Mommy has a pretty voice?" Marlow thought her mother had a beautiful voice, but she didn't know then this was special. She figured all mothers had beautiful voices—it was nothing worth staying awake for. So she would nod off to the songs, then the sound of what they gave way to: Floss trying to talk herself into going on. "Look at this girl in your arms," she would mutter. "She's beautiful, and she's yours. Hashtag blessed. So toughen up for her, Floss. Fucking toughen up *now*."

She remembered the hotels getting worse and worse until they landed in one so dirty, Floss tore the bedspreads off the beds and stuffed them right out the broken window. Floss took towels from the maid's cart and laid them on the floor, mapping a path from the bed to the bathroom, forbidding Marlow to step anywhere else. She asked Aston, when she thought that Marlow was asleep, "What about your mother?" And he said: "Oh, no problem. I'll just have to divorce you first. What about yours?" Floss didn't answer.

Marlow remembered feeling like that last motel room was swelling like a balloon, like she could see the walls warping outward from the pressure building inside them. And then, one day, at the height of the tension, Floss banged in with a brand-new look on her face and a brand-new bag on her arm. She stood in the doorway with her hands on her hips. She said to Marlow and Aston, "We're in."

"They liked the footage?" Aston said skeptically. He and Marlow had been playing scat on the walnut nightstand, laying discards down on top of the curse-word mosaic scratched into it. (The first time her father saw the profanity, he had turned to Marlow and sighed, "You can't read yet, right? Let's keep it that way. Don't be trying to sound this stuff out.")

Floss dug her fists into her hips like a superhero. She had left the door to the room open and was silhouetted, now, against the hazy arid hills, the moping California traffic. "They *loved* it," she said.

Marlow looked down at her cards. They meant nothing to her; usually, she needed Aston to peer over the edge of her hand and tell her if she was close to twenty-one. Even when he saw her cards, he played on in good faith, like he hadn't.

Floss kicked the towels on the floor out of her way and walked across the room to them. "That birthday party was worth every penny," she said as she sank down onto Marlow's bed.

Marlow put her arm around her mother's waist. Privately, she disagreed. Her fifth birthday party, a few months before, had been an odd affair, with hushed lighting and down-tempo music. The guests were all children she had never met who seemed uncertain as to why they were there. A frightening cluster of men with cameras documented everything. Marlow noticed that, though it was her party, they seemed more interested in following her mother. This suspicion had been confirmed afterward, when she saw the footage, which her mother watched obsessively for weeks—searching for what, Marlow still couldn't say.

"We're going to move to a new town," Floss told Marlow, squeezing her. "A place no one's ever lived before. They built it just for us. And when we get to our new house, we'll be famous again. You, too."

Marlow said nothing at the time. The statement did not seem outrageous. Floss talked about past fame and current fame and strategies for future fame as easily and as often as other mothers referenced being out of milk.

After they were settled in their new home on Pitt Street, Marlow sat at the kitchen table with Stella, the rainbow-haired clown who tried to explain Constellation to its children. Everywhere in America, she told Marlow, people were watching her. Rooting for her. "Even people I don't know?" Marlow asked, her stomach an uneasy jumble. Stella put down her star-topped wand and cupped Marlow's face reassuringly. "You may not know them like you know your mom and dad," she breathed, "but your followers are your friends—your very special friends. The happier and brighter you act, the more special friends you'll get—and the more special friends you get, the happier and brighter your life will be." Stella's pancake makeup fractured into tiny white fissures as she smiled. "No one loves you more than your followers," the clown said.

———

A few weeks after Marlow bit Honey, Floss came into her bedroom. Her face looked the same determined way it did when she came back to the motel years ago, to tell them they had made the cut for Constellation. "Get up," she said to Marlow. Then she went into Marlow's closet and chose an outfit: a starchy petal-pink dress Marlow had never worn, a white cardigan she had outgrown. When Marlow protested, Floss ignored her. She slid a white headband into Marlow's hair. Marlow's cowlicks rejected it instantly, pushing it back down her forehead.

They drove to Mountain View and slowed at the guarded road for Antidote Pharmaceutical. A network exec and a writer met them in the parking lot. They didn't look at Marlow; they wouldn't stand too close. They profusely thanked the man from Antidote who joined them in the conference room. When Floss spoke, they took turns cutting her off.

"Marlow's never done anything like this before," Floss said.

'She's never been angry. She's never been violent. I mean, she, like, threw her helmet at a softball game, once, when she was younger, but I think she was just caught up in the vibe. Softball girls are like—" Floss held her arms out, curved at her sides, and made a guttural sound.

The female executive, who wore her dark hair snipped short, leaned forward to block the Antidote rep's view of Floss. "Marlow has always been an exemplary student," she said. "And she's made excellent content for us. Normally, to be frank, an incident like this would be grounds for terminating a talent contract." The executive smiled at the rep, who was leaning back in his chair, fingers steepled and touching his lips. "But Antidote has always been such a valued partner. And when we heard about your troubles with marketing Hysteryl, we thought a bit of fate might be at play here."

The man's chair squeaked as he leaned forward. He studied Marlow for a long time.

"Hi, Marlow," he said, as if she had just sat down. "So you like softball?"

"No, I quit," she said.

"She does ballet," Floss cut in.

"I hate that, too," Marlow said.

The man smiled. "I get it," he said. "Marlow, do you ever feel like—" He paused, as if searching for the right words. "Like life is just too much?"

"What?" Marlow looked around the table. All the faces were carefully neutral, not willing to help her with the answer. Floss blinked at her almost pleasantly, like she was watching her play the piano.

"I think I have a good life," Marlow said slowly.

The man nodded thoughtfully. "But even a good life can be so hard, can't it?" he said. "Life will always be hard. We can't do much about that. But you're so lucky to live in this day and age: we can control how you feel about it." He waved his hand over his shoulder. A screen on the wall behind him flicked on. Marlow watched as a boy her age clapped a capsule into his mouth, washed it down with a swig from his water bottle, and charged out onto a baseball field. His mother looked on sagely from the bleachers. A tagline layered over the image addressed the mother: "What if your son's best self was his only one?"

"This pill us grown-ups are talking about, Hysteryl," the man said, "is like— Well, you know how you get upgrades for your device, for the system that runs your home functions? Think of Hysteryl as an upgrade for your feelings. And our feelings sure do have a lot of bugs, don't they?"

The adults laughed, and Marlow imagined clunking all their heads together. The headband slipped down to her eyebrows for the thousandth time since the day began. She pushed it back again.

"Hysteryl is made especially for people your age," the man went on. "It's made to grow with you. We here at Antidote envision a future in which your entire generation, having on-boarded Hysteryl as teenagers, becomes the happiest, most well-adjusted, most confident generation of Americans ever."

The network exec turned to Marlow and waggled her eyebrows happily, like the man was outlining dessert options.

"But new things can seem scary," the man went on. "People always have their reservations about change, even when change is the best thing for them." He looked down for a reverent moment, pressing his lips together. He ticked off a list on his fingers: "My college roommate, the week before graduation. The youngest in the family I grew up down the street from. My mother's favorite student."

Marlow straightened in her seat and tucked her chin down, the way children were taught to do when adults talked about the Spill.

"If we'd had Hysteryl back in the twenty-teens, the twenty-twenties," the man said, "they'd still be here."

From beneath her lowered lids, Marlow saw the exec jut her elbow into the writer's. The writer nodded and rapped on the table.

"Maybe all people need is a story," the writer said. "To see the way this drug can help a child. A child they already know and love. To follow her journey from rage and insecurity to—" the writer waved one hand through the air "—happiness. By Hysteryl."

The man nodded. He thought about it. He smiled and swiveled his chair toward Marlow. "Has a nice ring," he said. "Doesn't it?"

Marlow turned to her mother. She wondered what sort of deal Floss imagined they were coming here for. Not this, she had to believe—not her own veins as a venue for product placement. She sat back and waited for her mother to yell, to call them a pack of lunatics.

But then she heard, to her horror, Floss reciting the sentence she had practiced in the bathroom that morning, as she brushed on what only she would call "a subtle look for day."

"We feel lucky you would even consider Marlow for such an opportunity," her mother said, covering Marlow's hand with hers. "I think it sounds *amazing*."

CHAPTER THIRTEEN

Orla

New York, New York
2016

When Orla came into the living room, Craig was handing out bagels prepared in batshit combinations. He pressed a blueberry with scallion into Orla's hands. Two everythings with raisin walnut sat on the couch, in the wide space between Floss and Aston, who had crept into 6D sometime after Orla went to bed.

"What's going on?" Orla said. "Who's dead? What the fuck?"

Melissa looked at Craig. "Craig, we have to tell them now," she said. "Do you think you can stop with the bagels?"

Craig was staring at a chocolate chip bagel with a neon strip of lox between its halves. "This isn't right," he muttered. "This isn't what I ordered."

Melissa sighed and turned away from him. "We got word about an hour ago," she said, "about a really unfortunate incident." She looked at Floss and Aston and Orla. "What we all need to remember, as the next few days unfold, is that Floss intended her photos to be a celebration of the female form. An empowering message of real beauty to real girls everywhere. Right, Floss?"

"Exactly." Floss already sounded defensive. "Orla said—"

"No." Melissa held up her hand. "Orla had nothing to do with the idea. That's gonna be important."

Orla set her bagel down next to the television. "Of course I did," she said. The ideas were always hers. Didn't they all know their roles by now?

Three minutes. That was all it had taken for Floss's naked pictures to crash Instagram. Floss wasn't even dressed yet when Orla reloaded the feed on Floss's phone and the screen gave her a gray, broken face. "Done," she said. "You're officially famous on your own. You didn't need Aston. You didn't even need clothes."

"Yay," Floss had said. A moment later, a box popped up on Floss's phone, telling her she'd been suspended from Instagram. So Orla gave Floss her laptop and her password. Floss logged into Instagram as Orla to watch the reaction unfold. When Orla went to bed, Floss was still up on the other side of the wall, drinking Moët and refreshing the mentions.

———

Now they sat in silence as Melissa read the reports out loud. No outlet seemed to have the full story, but each one was still breathlessly brandishing what they could find. It was up to them, in the quiet apartment, to put it all together.

Anna Salgado was seventeen, and lived on Staten Island.

She had been having a rough time anyway. Everyone, from her own crying parents to the sober-faced reporters, was quick to point this out. She had not been asked to the prom. She had tried to ask someone herself, a boy she had liked since freshman year. He told Anna he already had a date, then rushed to ask someone else: Anna's best friend. He invited the girl over hasty text, accidentally copying Anna on the chain. But neither he nor Anna's friend realized she was there, that she could see her best friend writing back **But aren't u going w Anna?** and the boy responding **Uh NO**. He added an emoji, a little yellow face with full, rosy cheeks and a double chin. It was the shorthand kids were using to call each other fat.

Anna told her parents she wasn't going to prom because it was a tool of the patriarchy.

When they asked her gently, the night of, if she wanted to go to California Pizza Kitchen—her favorite restaurant—she said no, thanks. She would read in her room. That evening, as Anna gripped her phone, scrolling through shots of her friends in their gowns and barrel curls, something arresting poked through all the posed shots: Floss, naked. Anna stared at the dimples on Floss's thigh, at the outrageous curve of her hips, and felt a kinship. Floss looked nothing like the skinny girls at Anna's school who monopolized the boys' idea of hot.

Anna was inspired. She must have decided she wanted to make a tribute, her own version of what Floss did. She stripped herself down, propped her phone on a stack of dystopian paperbacks, and stood as Floss had. She had never sucked her cheeks like that before, her mother pointed out later—for a second, she didn't know it was her daughter in the picture. Anna hesitated, but only for a moment. Then she posted the photos on Instagram.

Like every tragedy, it was all in the timing. Anna's naked body lasted ten minutes online—longer than it should have, longer than Floss's, perhaps because the chaos Floss set off had left the platform scrambling, behind. If everyone Anna knew hadn't been in the same place, pausing from their sweaty, sex-adjacent dancing to hunch over their phones and laugh, the photos might not have spread so quickly. If her classmates hadn't been wild from adrenaline and malt drinks bought by older cousins, their comments might not have been as harsh. If the school lock-in that followed the prom hadn't been so boring, their teachers trying to tempt them with cornhole and *Jenga*, they might not have lingered on the story so long, ravaging Anna's social-media accounts long after her shots had been wiped.

And then there was the comment Floss made.

"Comment?" Floss reeled her head back when Melissa said it. "I didn't leave any comment."

Melissa was looking at the empty champagne bottle on the counter when she said, "Yes, you did."

Someone had screenshotted the picture of Anna before it had been pulled down. **Loving Floss Natuzzi for repping REAL Latina bodies**, Anna had captioned the shot. **I want to meet her in person one day! #queen #naturallyperfect #womensrightsarehumanrights.**

There had been dozens of comments, but the screenshot homed in on two in a row.

yungrebel2016: kill yourself THOT you look so fat

orlajcadden: this is floss and i agree. you should!

Orla stared at her name, sitting somewhere she had not put it, next to words that were not her own. She had forgotten that Floss had used her account the night before, after her own was suspended because of the nudes. The comment had been liked two hundred eight times.

"'I agree,'" Melissa quoted aloud. "'You should.'"

"I was talking about her caption," Floss said. Color climbed from her clavicle upward. "That she should come meet me!"

Craig was at the sink, tearing the bagels to pieces, forcing the pieces down the drain. He whirled toward her. "But that isn't how she fucking took it, Floss," he said, "*is* it?"

Floss's mouth was hanging open. She looked from each of them to the next. "It was a mistake," she said, her voice trembling.

"Balls," Aston said quietly. He pulled his cap down over his eyes.

"It wasn't just about what Floss wrote," Melissa said. "People just piled on after that. Kids she knew. Kids she didn't know." She showed them more comments, and Orla had to turn away.

Anna's parents didn't want to make her feel like they were checking on her, so Mrs. Salgado didn't crack her daughter's door till after 3:00 a.m., on her way to bed herself after dozing on the couch. Anna was in bed with the covers pulled up. Everything looked as it should, but a mother knows when things only seem right. Mrs. Salgado turned on the light and saw the empty bottles on the floor—the vodka that Anna, who never drank, was holding for a friend. Mr. Salgado's post-root-canal Percocet. The doctor had prescribed more than Mr. Salgado needed.

Melissa turned to Orla. She picked up the remote like it was ticking. "Sometimes when details are slow to come out," she said, "the media focuses on stupid shit." She turned the television on. She told them she had gotten an email from the producer of a morning news show. The producer wanted to give her a heads-up: they were doing a segment on Orla, "the woman behind" the Instagram handle that Floss Natuzzi used to tell a girl to kill herself. "They're hitting it hard," Melissa said, "the whole angle of you writing about Floss while you were at Lady-ish. Exploiting the site to make her famous. Not that this is new information."

Orla looked at the television, at the muted ad, innocent footage of an old man riding a chair lift up a flight of stairs. "It's not new information," she repeated. "Lots of people know this—people tweet me about it. Why is it a big deal now?"

"I suppose because it speaks to your character," Melissa sighed. "And because now a girl is dead. Now everything's a big deal." She glanced down at her phone. "They say they've booked three major players from your life," she said. "Who could it be?"

Orla had no idea. "I have to call my parents," she said. But the show was already coming back from commercial.

"Turn it up," Craig said dully.

On-screen, Ingrid and Yale Girl sat opposite a stern blonde

anchor. Orla noticed that Ingrid had switched her bright lipsticks for tasteful nude, but Yale Girl seemed determined to stand out. She wore glittery eye shadow and a lime-colored blouse with a teardrop cutout above her cleavage.

The chyron at the bottom of the screen read: TEEN NATUZZI WANNABE CYBERBULLYING SUICIDE.

"This morning," the anchor said, "in the wake of Anna Salgado's suicide, Lady-ish published a statement saying that they will no longer cover Floss Natuzzi. Isn't that a little like Weather.com swearing off thunderstorms?"

"It is, Kate," Yale Girl said, nodding earnestly. "But Floss Natuzzi—she hasn't released a statement yet, by the way, Kate—has, we feel, now proven beyond the pale to be damaging to young women out there. And that's our core audience, Kate."

On the TV, Ingrid cleared her throat. "We feel we have a special duty to take a stand here," she said. "You see, Lady-ish—" She faltered for a minute, her mouth tightening, then started up again. "Lady-ish, unfortunately, played a pivotal role in the Floss Natuzzi phenomenon."

Orla watched, feeling outside herself, as her own photo fell like grains of sand into place on the screen.

"The woman you're looking at," said the anchor in voice-over, "is Orla Cadden, a former Lady-ish blogger who now, what, costars on the reality show? Recognize her name? It was her Instagram handle Natuzzi used to encourage the girl to kill herself."

"I think what she actually—" Ingrid began, at the same time Yale Girl said, "Exactly."

A millisecond's flicker of annoyance crossed Ingrid's face. "Orla used to write for us," she went on. "She wrote for us about Floss Natuzzi when, unbeknownst to us, she had already befriended Natuzzi and was colluding with her to help her get famous. She used her platform as a blogger to give Floss press when Floss was just starting out. Orla now appears on *Flosston Public*. She's sort of a sidekick."

"We fired her over it," Yale Girl blurted. Ingrid put a hand down in front of Yale Girl on the desk.

The anchor shook her head, the clipped ends of her hair swinging in perfect coordination. "So," she said, as the camera cut to her alone, "what kind of person *does* a thing like that? Mmm." She took a breath. "We have an old friend of Orla Cadden's joining us now."

"Oh, God," Orla said. "Danny."

But it wasn't. The camera pulled out, revealing a third woman at the table. She pulled self-consciously at an ill-fitting blazer as the anchor nodded at her and said, "Thank you for being with us today."

"Sure thing," Catherine said. Her face was blazing red.

——

It became the thing she feared most in the world, her name. And it was everywhere.

One time Orla sat in a cab, stuck in traffic on her way to the prissy crisis counselor Craig had prescribed, and watched her name ripple over the Times Square crawler of a national news network. That time it was just her last name, at the end of an ominous headline, one sandwiched between stories on the presidential race she was paying no attention to: SALGADO FAMILY MAY PRESS CHARGES AGAINST NATUZZI, CADDEN. Orla's face had gone limp with shame, thinking of her parents. Their name looked just the same on-screen as it did on the driftwood sign above their stove: THE CADDEN FAMILY, EST. WITH LOVE 1985, MIFFLIN, PA. She hadn't talked to Gayle and Jerry since Anna Salgado died, and she would only be able to if they showed up and pressed the buzzer at her door, which they hadn't so far. Orla had set her phone to airplane mode. She wasn't checking her email. She deleted her social-media accounts. She stopped watching television—first because she couldn't fathom that she was on the news, and then because she couldn't fathom that she wasn't anymore. How dare the world move on and leave her to live out this ending alone?

The people who recognized her on the street now looked at her sharply and called her a cunt. She had been called that so many times on the internet, she thought the word had lost its sucker punch. But hearing it out loud, unexpected, when she was in sweats and just picking up toilet paper, was a whole new kind of injury. Once, as Orla was hurrying home, past the nail salon under her apartment building, a woman standing on the sidewalk in her toe separators hissed the word and spit at her. Then she went right back to being on the phone, as if the gesture was routine. As if it took nothing out of her.

After that, Melissa bought her a Yankees cap and said not to leave the building without it. She banged the hat against Orla's desk, then set a tennis ball beneath it, squeezing the brim into an arch over the ball and wrapping a rubber band around to make it stay. "So that it doesn't look so new," she said. Orla nodded in silence, looking at her, thinking that Melissa looked fat. Orla knew she hadn't worked out since Anna's death, nearly a month ago, and that, apparently, was enough time to melt the marble curves that took her years to carve.

As for the rest of them: Mason still reported to the apartment each day. He was afraid to tell his husband that the network had suspended *Flosston Public* indefinitely, that they were ignoring Craig's pleading follow-ups. Craig still came to 6D most days, too, for no discernible reason. He puttered around like a broken toy, chattering or sinking into hour-long silences. He missed the mug when he tried to pour coffee. He opened cabinet doors and left them that way. He had to be reminded, every day, that Aston wasn't there.

Aston had gone back to the Bowery Hotel, and he wouldn't leave his room. He would not return calls or texts from anyone, but he tweeted constantly.

Anna S was a beauty. Coulda seen her in one of my videos (after 18th bday, obvs)

My true heart goes out to her family and friends

It's so loud in my head why should I be quiet

I thought I was eating the world but the world ate me, the money, the money made a monster out of me

But the money will be gone son

SOON

Hey ASTONished Nation—Don't forget to download my app! It's free all month! Let's get this to number one on the App Store!

FUCK THAT LAST TWEET I been hacked

"You weren't hacked," Melissa said, when she somehow got him on the line. "It's a preset promotional tweet. Please put your phone down, I'm begging you. Aren't you on your way?" They were all waiting in the apartment, Amadou, too, his hand resting on Floss's pile of suitcases. Floss and Aston and Mason were scheduled to begin a trip to Bali from Teterboro in an hour. Though the network was freezing them out, Mason had agreed to finance the shooting trip himself, to the tune of twenty-one thousand dollars, in hopes that the network execs would look at the footage and remember why they used to like them.

"Put Aston on speaker," Floss said to Melissa now. Melissa shook her head, but she did it. "Aston, baby," Floss purred. "I know it's a tough time, but we need to be together right now."

Aston ignored her. "Is Craig there?" he said, sounding yelpy and frail.

"Yeah, I'm here, buddy, what's up," Craig tittered.

"I heard they might sue," Aston said. "Anna's parents."

Craig opened his mouth, but Melissa held up her hand. "Don't worry about that, Aston," she said. "That's our job."

"I'm not worried about it," Aston said. "I want to be named. As a—" There was the sound of him fumbling, checking something. "As a defendant," he finished.

"What do you mean, pal?" Craig covered his eyes with his hand. "The suit, um. I mean the suit probably won't happen, but they were only talking about Floss. And Orla, I guess, because the comment came from her account."

"Orla wouldn't be involved if she didn't know Floss," Aston said flatly. "And Floss wouldn't be famous if she didn't know me. So if you think about it, it's actually all my fault." There was the sound of rustling paper. "I called Harry."

"*You* called your accountant?" Craig dropped his hand. His eyes bugged.

"Yes," Aston said, a hint of pride sneaking into his wobbling voice. "Harry says I have fifty-nine million dollars."

"You're *worth* fifty-nine million dollars," Craig said. "It's different."

"I started doing stupid shit online, and now I have fifty-nine million dollars," Aston said dreamily. Instinctively, Orla grimaced. Her shoulders tensed and crept up toward her ears. When she looked around the room, she saw the rest of them doing it, too, as if they were hearing the first crash of thunder in a storm. "Fifty-nine *million* dollars," Aston repeated. "Anna did something stupid online—one thing! And she's dead. It isn't right, it isn't—"

There was a muffled grunt, and the sound of something breaking on a wall. In 6D, everyone flinched.

"I want them to have my money," Aston babbled. "Her family. I'm done with it. I don't want it. I don't deserve it. She's dead. Do you know what it's like in my head? Is it not like this in *all your heads*?" There was a pause; Aston's breathing sounded so childlike, Orla felt she might cry. "Fifty-nine million dollars," Aston said. "If they won't sue me, I'll Venmo it to them."

What the fuck, Melissa mouthed at Craig. She cleared her throat. "Such a kind thought, Aston," she said soothingly. "But we can't be making donations to the Salgado family just now. With the legal proceedings, it might muddy—"

Mason piped up: "Can we talk about this in person, Aston? Please. The plane is waiting."

"What plane?" Aston sounded annoyed.

"Bali, babe." Floss leaned toward the phone. She was using her sexy-baby voice, but Orla could see that she was shaking. "We need this trip so badly."

Aston laughed, an empty, disbelieving sound. "I'm not going to Bali," he said. "With you?" He kept laughing. "I'm not going to fucking Bali."

There was the sound, on the phone, of a light, distant knock, then of Aston dropping the phone. A faraway voice, hotel-polite, asked him something. "No," they heard Aston answer. "Everything's *not* all right. A girl is dead 'cause I'm famous. And your Wi-Fi here fucking sucks."

———

Later that day, Orla was alone in the apartment. Mason and Floss left for Bali without Aston. Craig and Melissa wandered home. Orla lay down to take a nap. Since Anna's death, her sleeping hours had begun to almost outnumber her waking ones.

Every once in a while, as a form of penance, she listened to one of the voice mails her phone filled up with. There was always more cunt talk, and sometimes a creative variation: people surmising that she didn't have a soul, or offering to rape her with a two-by-four.

One day, the message she chose was so formal and hateless, it sounded foreign. "Orla Cadden?" said a woman, sounding befuddled, like she was reading Orla's name off something she hadn't seen before. "I've been— You sent me an email earlier this year," the woman said. "Or rather, it was last year. It was at least a year ago. I'm sorry to be getting back to you so much later. But if you still don't have representation, let's set up a time to talk." She paused. "Oh—this is Marie Jacinto. I'm a literary agent."

———

Marie's assistant told Orla to come in the next day at eleven. In the morning, Orla put on a pair of black ponte pants that were snugger than she remembered, despite the fact that she had barely been able to eat lately, and a freebie owl-print blouse from a hipster store that once mistook her for larger and quirkier than she was. She put on the Yankees cap.

Outside, the air was warm, the sun beating. Orla registered for the first time that it was June, then realized, with a startled glance at the clock in the drugstore window, that it was actually almost July.

In the wake of Anna's death, a crowd had gathered again outside their building. People who wanted to yell at them mixed with loyal fans shouting support. After the fuss died down, the police removed the barricade for good. For the first time in nearly a year, the whole width of the sidewalk on Twenty-First Street was open. Now it looked as it had when Orla lived here without Floss.

Today, though, Orla peeked under the curved brim of her hat and saw a woman sitting where the line used to be. She looked about fifty, and familiar. She was Latina, with woolly hair dyed brassy orange and eyes rimmed in smudged electric blue. Her soft upper arms shook slightly as she scratched at a sudoku. She had brought, Orla saw, her own chair, the kind of padded metal folding chair Gayle would have dragged to the table if they had an extra person for dinner. The woman looked up when Orla walked out of the building. She closed her book of puzzles.

Orla had time to stop at Starbucks. Hypothetically, she wanted coffee, but she found that the thought of actually drinking it made her queasy. She was, she supposed, nervous. She stood beneath the mermaid marquee, trying to decide what to do. Suddenly, in the glass, she saw the woman from the chair. She was standing still behind her, two sidewalk squares back. Orla started walking again, heading north. She crossed Twenty-Third Street and glanced over her shoulder. The woman was still there, following her. She looked Orla right in the eye.

Orla started to sweat. She wanted to raise her hand, hail a cab, escape, but she could see the cars jammed end to end, up to Madison Square Garden. She would have to take the subway to make her meeting on time. She sped up and crossed Eighth Avenue, headed for Seventh. The woman kept up with no effort, practically floating after her.

Underground at Twenty-Eighth Street, the woman gave Orla space, pacing two columns down on the platform. Just before the 1 train crawled into the station, Orla stole a look at her and tried to figure out where she'd seen her before. In a flash, she saw the woman on television, sitting with her eyes cast down, a man's arm around her shoulders as she hiccuped and broke into tears. The rest of the memory flooded to the surface, shocking Orla into dizziness. The train's doors opened, and she forgot, until they were closing again, to step on. She pressed in just in time. The woman was already seated at the other end of the car, with her sudoku back out again. It was Mrs. Salgado. Anna's mother.

CHAPTER FOURTEEN

Marlow

New York, New York
2051

Marlow was still sitting in 6D, thinking of Honey and staring at the stationery with her name on it, when she heard the footsteps in the hallway, evenly pounding her way. She stood up. She watched the handle on the front door turn. *Human or bot? Bot or human?*

Bot. It was Mateo, from the Archive, and Marlow sputtered indiscriminately in protest as she took a step back from it, toward the apartment's artless window. If Mateo belonged to the Archive, how could it be all the way down here?

And then she saw that an explanation must be on the way. Mateo was holding the door for someone.

It was strange: she didn't hear a single footstep before Honey Mitchell appeared—she seemed to just materialize out of stray, sparkling atoms in the apartment's doorway. Honey just stood there for a second, taking in everything in front of her, resting her unimpressed gaze on the sofa, the stick lamp, the matted, faded rug. Somewhere in her survey—between the counters and the busted intercom, hanging off the wall near the door—she glanced at Marlow, with no more or no less interest than she had shown for any other thing using space in the room.

Finally, Honey cleared her throat. "Let's not be in here too long," she said briskly. "All this grime makes me nervous."

As if she had spoken a command it recognized, Mateo slid its own jacket off, draping it over the seat of a bar stool. Honey climbed up carefully. Marlow watched her, watched everything that wasn't her face. That part, she was putting off. Honey wore a crisp white blouse tucked into white riding pants and a white cashmere shawl wrapped several times around her shoulders. There was a white hat, vaguely Western with its white braided cord, cocked above the fat blond bun at the back of her head. On her hands, she wore white leather gloves; on her feet, white leather cowboy boots, perfectly unblemished. Even Marlow, who had been in New York for less than a day, understood what sort of privilege spotless shoes meant here. Above the backs of her sneakers, Marlow's Achilles tendons were gray from the who-knew-what rising out of these streets.

Finally, she confronted the scar. It seemed, in the room, almost pretty—a shining spot, designed to catch the light. But she knew that might be temporary. Marlow, once, in a fit of regret-tinged interest, had asked her device endless questions about scarring. She had learned that the color of scars could change, could rise and fade with the hour, could vary with emotion. That some never lost their angry hue completely. Perhaps Honey's was only white right now because she was—and she did seem—very calm.

"How did you know about this place?" Marlow said. She was still standing, frozen, just a few steps in front of the couch, unsure of what else to do, whether to sit. Her intruders seemed more comfortable than she did. "How did you know I was here?"

Honey frowned at the gray spots on the fingers of her gloves marking where she had gripped the bar stool. "I knew you were in New York because everyone knows, now," she said, sweeping one hand toward the street below. "Then I heard about your near miss being hunted at the Archive, so I had them go back through the footage to see what you were doing. They'll do that for me, you know. I've been very generous." Honey smiled at Mateo, but the bot missed the gesture. It stared politely into the distance. "I saw you in our search room, writing down this address," Honey said. "The cameras could just make it out."

Marlow felt herself reddening. With all the people walking hunched and chewing ugly in New York, she had figured the city was light on surveillance. But their nonchalance, she realized now, only signified that no one cared to watch what they were doing. That didn't mean they weren't being filmed.

"That's invasive," Marlow snapped.

Honey laughed, a glittering cackle that filled the apartment, making it feel, just for a moment, like a place people might have once lived. Then her face turned thoughtful. She studied Marlow now, as if Marlow had just come alive, had finally become more interesting than all the dust-coated furniture. "I'm glad you think so," she said. Then she stood and clapped her hands together. "Let's get going, then," she said. "I'm sure someone in Archive security has sold a tip on you being here by now."

Marlow had never felt so angry with herself. She had to write this address *down*? She couldn't have memorized it? (No, she knew instinctively. Since the day she'd strapped on her device, she'd never had to memorize anything, and now she couldn't. That part of her brain was out of shape.) Her instincts had been right: no good came of paper. She picked up the cursive letter from where it still sat on the couch, folded it awkwardly, and jammed it into her jeans pocket. "The last time I went somewhere with you," she said to Honey, "it basically ruined my life."

"Didn't turn out so hot for me, either," Honey said. "And

yet, here I am, trying to help you." She hopped down from the bar stool and walked Marlow to the window. Below, on Eighth Avenue, people scurried, looking goal-oriented, seemingly unconcerned with Marlow's whereabouts. But then she saw a cab pass—two, actually, in quick succession—with holograms of her face shimmering above their roofs.

"So, to recap," Honey said. "People already know you're at this address. And I think you know what will happen if you try to leave on your own. My car's around the corner, at the freight entrance. I know you don't trust me. But I'm your only good option."

Marlow turned her back on the window and looked up at the ceiling, pretending to weigh her nonexistent options. She noticed then the strangest thing above their heads: running across the ceiling, just above their heads, was a row of white jagged bits, shaped like teeth, jutting downward. Sharp remnants of a wall that had been shattered, or blown away—a wall that must have once protected the couch from the sunlight that ruined it eventually.

Honey was watching her. Marlow met her eye. "I'd feel better about this," she said, "if you'd just tell me what you want. What your angle is."

Honey rolled her eyes. "You Constellation folks," she said. "You can't see past plot. Out here in the real world, sometimes we do things just to do them, and see what happens later."

Marlow remembered, suddenly, a middle-school lesson on local culture. The teacher had been going on about someplace where people ate chili on top of spaghetti—this factoid conjured blank looks, since Constellation kids had never tasted either— when a student asked the teacher what she would say Constellation had. What people did only there. Being filmed and broadcast all day to millions was the obvious reply, of course. But since the teacher couldn't say that on-camera, she launched into a speech on the town's architecture. Marlow had another answer, though she didn't raise her hand to offer it. *We see story,* she thought, crystal clear. *We see arcs everywhere. That's what comes from living this way. That's what's ours.*

And maybe, Marlow thought now, she could use that to her advantage. Because usually, she knew, the simplest plot was the right one. Twists only put off the inevitable. This was easy: Marlow had destroyed Honey's face. Even if Honey wouldn't say it, she had to be after revenge. And as long as Marlow knew that, she could stay one step ahead of the story. Honey would be a character in hers, she told herself, firmly. Not the other way around.

"All right," she said to Honey. "Let's go." She added, reluctantly: "Thank you." When they walked behind Mateo to the elevators, Marlow made sure to keep Honey where she could see her. That was the key to getting through this, she decided: following from behind. Never letting Honey out of her sight.

———

Honey's building was a mirrored rose-gold spike, her apartment its very top shelf. The walls were all glass, an effect that wrapped sky around the whole place. Everything inside it was white. There were white bleached wood floors covered in white shag rugs with white suede sofas sitting on top. The dining, coffee and end tables were cubes of blinding concrete topped with swirled marble. There were gigantic, freestanding fireplaces made of white steel on both sides of the room. The appliances in the kitchen were luminescent pearl. Marlow could see a man bent in front of the fridge, buffing at it with an air of great crisis. When he saw them, he straightened and hid the rag behind his back, as if it was something unsightly.

"Hello, David," Honey called to him brightly. "This is Marlow. She took a chunk out of my face, back in the day."

Marlow turned to stare at Honey.

But David only nodded politely. "Hello, Miss Marlow," he said. He gestured at the fridge. "Water? Club soda?"

She asked for water, and when David brought it, Marlow stared at the red lines in his eyes, at the uneven coast of his hairline. What must it have cost Honey, keeping human help? You almost never saw that now. Marlow knew Honey was a pundit—Jacqueline, who voraciously cataloged the ups and downs of every person they'd ever met, had informed Marlow years ago that Honey was "some sort of white-trash Jesus—she preaches to people, you know, tells them they should live a certain way." Marlow had asked what way Jacqueline meant—what did Honey stand for? Jacqueline couldn't remember. Whatever it was, Marlow thought, taking a sip of her water, it evidently paid well.

Honey pulled out a chair for Marlow at the kitchen table. As they sat, she called to David: "Would you start us up some cheeseburgers? Marlow's never had one."

"Of course I have," Marlow said.

Honey ignored her. A mousy makeup artist, dark-skinned, all bird legs and face-hiding curls, approached and seized Honey's arm. "Hi, Elsa, darling," Honey said to the girl. "Have you met Marlow? She bit me in the face."

Elsa took a quick, sharp breath, Marlow noticed, but she didn't look up from her work—she was carefully removing Honey's device with rubbing alcohol. That was the way to do it painlessly, Marlow remembered, if you weren't in a rush. "Lovely to meet you," Elsa said flatly.

"Nice to meet you, too," Marlow said. "I was provoked."

"Of course!" Honey laughed. "Oh, I was very provocative back then."

Elsa didn't respond. She handed Honey's device to David, who took it into the kitchen and put it in a drawer. Then she began to rub the white square of skin where Honey's device had been with a sponge soaked in tan liquid.

"Anyway," Honey said to Marlow. "You think you've had

a cheeseburger? You've had smashed-up crickets with fortified cashews on a quinoa bun. Who here," she said, twisting around in her chair, "would kill themselves if you lived in a place where people called *that* a cheeseburger?" Elsa and David raised their hands, rote, like this was all part of their job.

Marlow felt the onslaught of pettiness creeping in like a headache. "I don't see what's so great about meat," she snapped, "unless you only *want* to live to eighty." She heard how humorless she sounded, how much heavier she seemed than all the other people buzzing lightly in the room. But meat—really, it was disgusting. This was something she had always known.

So why was she desperately inhaling the smell—burning, metallic, carnal somehow—that rose out of the sizzling pan on the stove?

David put the burgers in front of them. The patty wept a clear, fast ooze—pinkish-clear, like blood and water—that pooled around its bun on the plate. Marlow's stomach spasmed, begging her to take it in. She lifted the burger and sank her teeth into the bread and then the beef, all salty give. The cheese stretched luxuriously as she pulled away. She took another bite and then another, tipping her chin this way and that to get good angles on the sandwich. When she saw that the burger had dwindled to a third of its size in her hands, she felt a plummeting sorrow. She looked up and saw Honey watching her, amused but somewhat on guard, as if Marlow was an animal that, against her better judgment, she had brought inside. "My goodness," she murmured, her eyes twinkling.

"You're right," Marlow admitted, through the meat. "It's— I've *never*." When she was finished, she wiped her mouth and said, trying to sound casual, "I'm assuming that, like with our burgers, people usually just eat one?"

Honey laughed and signaled to David to bring Marlow another. "Not a bad idea," she said. "You'll need your energy for the party tonight."

Marlow watched David slide another portion onto her plate—glossy bun, bright toppings. It was hard to look away from it. "Party?" she said to Honey. "I'm not going to any party. I'm here to hide."

Honey shrugged. "Oh, don't worry. We wear masks." She waved her wrist, which Elsa had finished working on. The paleness where her device had been was completely blended away. "And no devices. So no one'll know it's you, and even if they do, they can't call you in anyway."

"I'd rather stay in my room," Marlow said firmly. Then, feeling rude, the nudge of her duffel bag still at her toes, she added, "I mean, if I have one."

Honey laughed. "You have a room. But my parties tend to—spread. There isn't really anywhere to hide. You're better off masked, among the masses." She stood up and went into the kitchen. She and David began discussing party details; he showed her a set of cocktail glasses, she told him why they were all wrong.

Marlow bit into her second burger. *Masked*—she clung to that word. She saw herself killing time, anonymously, at the party—maybe even killing enough time that people outside lost interest in the hunt. She saw herself, if opportunity or necessity called for it, slipping out of Honey's apartment with some other party-goers, her next move protected by the crowd and her mask and the middle of the night. She saw herself in a taxi, making up addresses in neighboring states—*figure out what states are around here*, she noted to herself—until it drove her far away, out of sight.

The party was a start, she decided, even if she didn't know of what. And the idea of being unseen, disguised as everyone else—it appealed. What would it feel like? she wondered. Perhaps a bit like being behind the scenes.

Elsa was still at the table with her, unpacking pots and brushes from vinyl cases, waiting for Honey to sit back down so she could resume her work.

"Are you going?" Marlow asked her. "To the party."

Elsa blinked at her, then looked quickly over her shoulder. Honey and David were lost in a linens debate. When Elsa met Marlow's eye again, her meekness had evaporated. She had almost a wicked look in her eye as she ran two fingers gently down the side of her own face, tracing her flawless black skin. "Me?" she said to Marlow, smirking. "I don't think so. I would clash."

CHAPTER FIFTEEN

Orla

New York, New York
2016

"I'm sorry," Marie Jacinto said through a mouthful of cheese filling. She was eating a Danish as Orla sat across from her. "I had a *morning*. Didn't get to breakfast yet."

"That's all right," Orla said. She smoothed the kink the cap had left around the crown of her head. She stared at the gaps in Marie's thinning red hair as the agent bent over her manuscript, which Orla had emailed to her assistant the day before. She hoped Marie took all day. When Orla headed toward the building's revolving door, Mrs. Salgado had walked into the Lady Foot Locker next door. Orla was pretty sure no one had ever gone into Lady Foot Locker to do anything other than wait

Marie took a zealous bite of her Danish. Flakes sprayed across Orla's pages. "So," Marie said. "This is…"

"It's, um, a novella." Orla leaned forward, willing the pitch she had prepared out of her mouth. "Originally, I conceived it as a full-length novel, but I think the brevity actually suits the subject matter, because it's about a girl who believes she'll have an extraordinary life, but she hasn't done much at all."

Marie scrunched up her face like she was waiting for a sharp pain to pass.

"I used to have a character in there who was raised Orthodox Jewish," Orla added. "I could definitely put that back, if you think…"

Marie sat back and flattened her hand on the paper. "This is my fault," she said. "I thought, when you agreed to take this meeting, that you might be pitching a different project. I mean, I know who you are, Orla. I know you haven't given any interviews."

Orla sat there, her stomach sinking and hot. "You mean," she said, "you thought I'd want to write a book about Floss? And Aston? And…" She dropped her voice to a whisper, in case a vent in Marie's office led straight to one in the Lady Foot Locker. "Anna?"

Marie leaned forward and folded her hands. "Well," she said, "why would you write about a fictional girl that nothing's ever happened to, when you could write about you—a real girl, with an extremely dynamic real life?"

Orla shook her head. "That stuff isn't my life," she said. "It's just some weird things that happened. A weird year." She pointed at her book. "Maybe if I tell you about some of the themes behind—"

"Oh, but I'm just not interested," Marie said, in the same tone she might have used to say that her Danish wasn't blueberry. "Though I'd love to talk about this other idea."

Orla looked down at her lap. Her pants were stretched so tight across her thighs, the fabric shone. "It's just this book," she said. "That's all there is."

Marie took her time chewing and swallowing. "If you change your mind," she said, "you have my card."

Mrs. Salgado followed her all the way home. Orla watched her settle back in her chair and went inside without saying anything. She found Melissa in the apartment, cleaning it vigorously.

"This place is a fucking dump," she told Orla, showing her the rust-brown paper towel she had been rubbing along the counter. "And your fridge is full of rotting food." She held up a blue-and-white container—months-old chicken from Gayle, Orla realized, feeling suddenly like she could cry. She turned away, trying to find air from elsewhere. It was like Melissa had angered every festering thing in the apartment by poking around in her yellow gloves, and suddenly Orla could smell it all: the shower curtain growing moldy down the hall, the overstuffed trash warming under the sink, the putrid chicken desiccating in Melissa's hand.

"Anna's mother is following me," she said.

Melissa put the chicken down. "What?"

"She's down there sitting on a chair." Orla pointed toward the window. "And when I left, she went with me. All the way there. All the way back."

Instead of going to look, Melissa took off her gloves and placed them gently in the sink. After a moment, she turned back to Orla. "My advice?" she said softly. "Just let it go."

"Let it go?" Tears rose in Orla's eyes. She had been counting on an answer from the Melissa who calmly deconstructed problems.

"People grieve in different ways." Melissa went to the coffee maker, which she had cleaned and set to brew. She pulled two mugs down from the cupboard above it and filled them carefully. "She's not going to hurt you, or she would have done it already. She's clearly trying to make a point, and we don't know what it is, but after what we put her—after what she's been through?" She took a sip from one of the mugs and pushed the other toward Orla. "Trust me—just be respectful."

Orla picked up the coffee, sniffed it, and threw up into the sink.

"What?" Melissa said, as if Orla had spoken, not vomited. "Are you sick?"

Orla shook her head. "It's the coffee," she said shakily. "The smell of it."

She watched horror rise upward, like steam, in Melissa's face. First her jaw set; then she frowned; then her eyes went wide and sober.

"No, it's not that. I can't be." Orla's heart was thrumming in her ears. "It wouldn't make any sense." Every time with Danny—night, day, drunk, drunker, blissful, angry, bored—whirled through her head. No single instance stood out like the start of something new.

Melissa picked up Orla's coffee and poured it down the sink. "And yet," she sighed, "you obviously are."

———

Melissa stayed with her that day. Orla let her lead her around, let her make arrangements. Melissa picked through the kitchen, throwing out things Orla couldn't have: deli turkey, Brie, weird peas Aston left behind. She held her hand out for Orla's insurance card and helped her find a doctor. When Orla grew tired again—the exhaustion made stinging sense now—she told her to sleep on her side, not her back.

"How do you know all this stuff?" Orla asked, pausing in the doorway of her room.

Melissa hesitated. "I was pregnant once," she said. Orla remembered her in the bar, shouting about not having a baby. She let the moment pass.

When she woke up from her nap, Melissa was sitting at the counter, working. A bag from Duane Reade sat beside her. "Prenatals," she said, nodding at it. "And saltines. They help with the nausea."

Orla slid onto a stool beside her. "Did you see her?" she said. "Anna's mother."

Melissa nodded. She looked at Orla over the rim of her laptop.

"Did she say anything to you?" Orla asked miserably.

"No." Melissa shook her head once, a hard jerk of her chin to the left. "She was painting her nails," she said, with a sound that was almost a laugh.

Orla's phone buzzed under her hand. She turned it over. It was Gayle.

Melissa saw it, too. "You should talk to your parents," she said. "Your appointment's not until Wednesday. Why don't you go see them? I think it would make you feel better."

Orla had a sudden vision of herself sitting at her parents' table, looking out the bay window. She imagined Mrs. Salgado picking her way through the trees by the bank. "You don't think—" she said.

Melissa shook her head. "No, Orla," she said. "I don't think she'll follow you to Pennsylvania."

———

Just to be on the safe side, Orla left the building through the freight entrance. Linus, the super's son, directed her to it with city-kid sureness.

Downstairs at Port Authority, she got in line at gate nineteen. She stood behind a couple who gazed at an old backlit ad for the Greyhound bus, striped in blue and gray and parked proudly at a grassy curb. "What a lovely photo," the man said. His voice had a trace of a Polish accent, and not a note of sarcasm.

Orla pulled out her phone and texted her mother. **Hi Mom** she typed. **I'm coming home.** She watched the gray bubble that meant Gayle was responding ripple back and forth. Finally her answer came through: **OK. Your father will pick you up.**

Orla's parents seldom drank, so that wasn't a problem. But in some bizarre upending of a life's worth of expectation, Gayle had purchased sushi for dinner. She had gone to a new restaurant on Mifflin's main drag to get it. "It doesn't have any windows," she reported. "I don't trust a restaurant I can't see out of." But she had bought the sushi all the same, and now she put down her fork and stared at Orla, who was moving a yellowtail roll around her plate.

"I thought this is what you liked," Gayle said.

"Your mother's nervous," Jerry mumbled.

"That's ridiculous." Gayle peeled a California roll open and sniffed its contents. "I am not."

"I do like sushi," Orla said. "I'm just not feeling well."

Gayle and Jerry looked at each other. Then Gayle reached across the table and rubbed Orla's forearm.

"I know, honey," she said, and then she drew herself up in a way that told Orla she was about to say something she had rehearsed. "I may never understand why you hitched your wagon to that girl," Gayle said. "But I know you, and I know you must have seen a way to your dream." She glanced at Jerry, who nodded encouragingly. "And you will find your dream another way, Orla," she said. "This will pass and you *will* start fresh. Here, in New York, wherever you want. You will be special wherever you are." She said the last part emphatically, doting on each syllable, and Orla knew her mother was thinking of that day in the restaurant. She had probably been planning this speech ever since. This was how it worked, Orla saw now: being a parent meant that, sometimes, you got to apologize without apologizing, and being a child meant that, sometimes, you got to not apologize at all.

Jerry put one hand on Orla's and the other on Gayle's. Orla looked at their hands on hers, their faces turned toward hers, toward where she sat, at the place that had always been hers.

She was the point toward which they had aimed their hopes and modest resources for twenty-nine years. She had forgotten this feeling—the feeling of being someone's primary focus, rather than a secondary character.

Her mother smiled and said, "I made chicken cacciatore, too. Would you rather have that?"

Orla nodded, though just the thought of chicken cacciatore made acid rise from her stomach, and she knew then that she could never tell them she was pregnant. She was not finished being their child. They had been sitting here every night since she left for college, trying not to look at her empty chair, and all that time she was mostly ducking their calls, mostly ignoring their texts. She owed them, at the very least, the absence of heartache. She owed them permission to keep hoping that she would amount to something, even if—she thought of Marie Jacinto, her tongue streaked with cheese filling as she rejected Orla's efforts—she never actually did.

After dinner, Orla went up to her childhood bedroom and threw up into her Tweety Bird trash can. She sat back, when she was finished, and looked through her watering eyes at her bedroom door. Over the last decade, Gayle had slowly replaced her bedroom fixtures with things that were more mature, corralling Orla's old collages and photo negatives into linen cubes, replacing her Joe Boxer bedding. But Gayle had left the door alone. Still stuck to it, with aging loops of masking tape, were wallet-sized school photos of people Orla didn't talk to anymore. There was Ian, who had the parties; there was JC Kraus, a handsome year-older quarterback who once tossed a handful of his pictures into the air and watched the girls scramble for them. And in a larger-sized photo—indicative of their best-friend status—there was Catherine, her blond hair worn down for picture day, arranged in two neat swaths on her shoulders. Her smile was extreme, uncharacteristic, but Orla remembered

244

he had wanted to show her teeth off that year. The braces that Orla still pictured her in had been removed over the summer.

What was it Catherine had said about her on television, the morning after Anna died? The sight of her former friend nodding into the camera was so disorienting, Orla almost fainted. "So she was sort of a shady character, even then?" the anchor had cut in, impatient with Catherine's rambling. "Yep," Catherine had answered. "She always acted so innocent, but..." Catherine tucked her hair behind her ears and narrowed her eyes at the anchor. "She thought she was better than everyone else. That she deserved more. She was ruthless, in her own way."

Beneath Catherine's picture on the door was Danny's. He wore a blue Structure T-shirt with a thick red stripe across the front. Orla smiled at the stripe. She could see the younger version of him pointing at it, hear him saying, "Yeah, this is my fancy T-shirt."

Of course it had been easy to long for him then, when maintaining their personas was their full-time job, when the right quip or band tee or book in common was enough to make them fall for each other. She saw now that she had built her life around a flawed hypothesis. She had believed that Danny had reached for her hand in his car that night because he knew, deep down, they were meant for each other. But really— realistically—it could have been anything. Boredom. Blanket horniness. Whatever he'd drunk. It could have even been an accident.

She saw, too, why she was able to leave him alone for a decade, even when she thought she was pining for him: because his, the school-picture Danny, was the one she had wanted. Why would she want to keep up with him, to hear how things were going? Things only went one way.

Orla turned the picture over. She felt sure that he had signed it, inscribing a reference to an inside joke. But except for the photographer's watermark, the back of the photo was blank.

Orla went back to New York the morning of her doctor's appointment. Gayle and Jerry hugged her tightly as the bus belched gas behind them. "Whatever you need, sweetie," Gayle kept saying. "We're here."

Mrs. Salgado's folding chair stood sentry, empty, at the doorway to Orla's building. Orla dashed inside. Anna's mother was probably in the bodega across the street, buying a Diet Mountain Dew. Orla had seen her in there before, laughing with the cashier.

Upstairs, Floss was sprawled in the living room, back from Bali. When Orla came in, she leaped off the couch, spilling a full bag of chips onto the floor, and threw her arms around Orla's neck. "I missed you so much," she said. She was wearing a shroud-like dress, moss green, in a canvas kind of material. "Isn't this madness?" Floss said when she noticed Orla looking at it. "Like forty blind nuns made it or something."

"Wow," Orla said. "So Bali was good?"

"Bali was *life*-changing." Floss whirled in a circle and dropped herself back onto the couch. "You have to go. I mean, you'll have a reason to go, because I'm almost definitely moving there."

Orla put the bag of leftovers from her mother down on the counter. It had been straining against her hand all the way back from the subway, the plastic handles pulling apart like taffy. "Did you get some good footage?" she said.

Floss shrugged. "We did this thing where I pretended to lose my pendant on the beach," she said. "Mason made me cry. But like, by the time it airs no one will believe it, because it'll seem so materialistic, and after this trip, I'm telling you, I'm over possessions." Floss's eyes went wide and her mouth dropped open. "Omigod," she said. "What's wrong?"

Orla realized she was crying, tears falling fast on the front of the Mifflin Panthers T-shirt she had worn back from home.

he pressed her palms to her eyes. When she took them away,
loss was frozen, staring at her.

"I'm pregnant," Orla said. "I'm fucking pregnant."

Floss didn't hesitate. She put her arms around Orla. She let her
ry into the work of the forty blind nuns. "We'll figure some-
hing out," she said. "We always do."

———

)rla had imagined that, at the appointment, she would have
er stomach spread with jelly and see something like a tadpole
lickering on a screen. But there was no jelly or tadpole—there
vasn't even a doctor. Just a gravel-voiced nurse who made her
ign dozens of forms, then stacked them hard when Orla was
inished. She gave Orla a folder of badly photocopied handouts
vith spaced-out women and storks on them. She asked Orla the
.ate of her last period, then flicked a small cardboard wheel that
eminded Orla of the one her guidance counselor had used in
.igh school, to tell her what she should be when she grew up.
'Something in forestry, distribution, or otherwise concerning
.ata and things," the counselor had said. "Things?" Orla had
epeated.)

The nurse held the wheel up to her glasses and said, "Eleven
veeks. Almost three months along already. You're due Christ-
ias Day!"

Orla raised her hand, as if she was in class, and said, "Is eleven
veeks too late to…?"

The nurse looked at her. She took off her glasses and rubbed
iem on the hem of her scrubs. "No," she said. "No, you have
ime. I can—" She rummaged in a drawer and found another
andout. She pushed it across the desk: a single sheet, sober black
nd white. "There you go. Some resources."

Orla nodded and stood to go. She gathered all the papers.
You don't need to take the rest of those, if," the nurse said.
)rla put them back down.

Across the subway car on the way home, Mrs. Salgado looked lik
she was curious about where they had just been. They walked i
tandem back to the building. Orla, so dazed she forgot to be afrai
of the woman following her, let her eyes meet Anna's mother's a
she reached to open the door. "See you later," she murmured.

Mrs. Salgado nodded and spoke to her for the first time, he
Staten Island accent filing down the *r* in Orla's name. "Good
bye, Orla," she said.

———

The sun had just set on the night before Orla's abortion whe
Floss burst into her room, rattling the partition, and said, "Loo
at this shit." She held up her phone.

Together, on Orla's bed, they watched Aston crying live to a
audience of millions. He was sitting on a small rug somewhere
staring straight into a mounted camera. "Spent every penny I ha
on this place," he was saying. "In memory of Anna. I mean, it
true I need somewhere to live for a while. It's true that me an
the Bowery Hotel…parted ways. But I'm not gonna live here fo
long. I'm gonna give this place to Anna's family. They could liv
here. They could sell it. They could come for vacation and shi
I dunno." Aston chewed on his lip. "I haven't heard back fror
them. I guess they hate my guts right now." Aston got up an
disappeared for a moment. The camera wobbled, then panne
around the apartment. Orla held the screen closer to her face
The apartment was empty except for dozens—no, hundreds—
of burning candles, sitting right on the floor, wax pooling an
rolling down them. Beyond the flames, Orla could see the jag
ged outlines of a breathtaking Midtown view.

"He bought a place at One Fifty-Seven," Floss said dryly
reading Orla's mind. "He has *lost* it." Orla knew the buildin
It was a bratty new fixture on the skyline, crystal clear and bui
to dizzy heights over Central Park.

Aston sat back down in front of the camera. He glared int

t. "You see that?" he said. "A candle for every one of you assholes who liked the comment about Anna killing herself." His
voice began to wobble. "Two hundred and eight. Monsters."
He tore his shirt off and flung it out of frame, pulled his knees
up to his chest, and sobbed.

Abruptly, Floss forced the phone down to Orla's comforter.
"I can't be here right now," she said. And Orla, who had been
torturing herself by wondering if the quakes in her stomach were
the work of a desperate fetus, sending up flares, felt the same.
When Floss headed for the door without mentioning where she
was going, Orla got up and went with her.

———

They ended up at the rooftop bar where they used to eat brunch
before they knew better. They sat at their old table in their new
Yankees caps—Floss had one, too, it turned out, though she
wouldn't pull it down as Melissa had instructed. They ordered
drinks from the same waiter who had seethed on the day that
they sat there forever, then skipped out on the check.

"He doesn't remember us," Orla said, after the man took their
orders with a smile.

"He doesn't recognize us, either," Floss said. "But they do.
These hats don't do shit." She nodded at a group of good-looking
Middle Eastern guys. The tallest one was pointing out Floss and
Orla to a bachelorette party of Southern blondes. Orla heard one
of the girls' voices trailing toward them across the banquettes.
"You wouldn't think they'd be *out*," she said. "They're, like,
villains now, right?"

The waiter returned with their drinks, and Floss held hers up.
"To being a villain, I guess," she said tonelessly.

Orla touched her gin and tonic to Floss's tequila, but couldn't
bring herself to take a sip. She watched the men and the bach-
lorette girls flirt. One of the women was wearing a sash that
said "#TeamBride." She was pointing at something beyond the

wall with great excitement, and now the rest of the girls clus
tered in on her to see. The men did, too, pressing against them

"It's a bachelorette party," Orla said to Floss. "Who *isn't* Team
Bride?"

Floss didn't answer. She was perfectly still, her mouth slack
her eyes tracking the stare of the bachelorette girls and the guys
who were buying their drinks. Orla twisted around. Everyone
in the bar was now looking north, past Team Bride's finger, at
a building twenty blocks or so up. The tower, thin and glassy
could hardly be distinguished from the twilight. Most of its units
were dark, so the sky bled into the bedrooms and kitchens, turn
ing the building bluish gray from top to bottom—nearly. Just
beneath the penthouse, the tower had a wound: one square was
startling orange. Inside it, a fire ebbed and raged.

Floss stood up suddenly, knocking her chair into the one
behind it. "That's—" she said. She looked at Orla wildly. She
pumped her arm in the direction of the burning building.

"What?" Orla stood, too, frightened by Floss's flailing hand
By the time she was on her feet, she had put it together herself

"Aston's building," Floss said. "The candles."

Orla grabbed Floss's phone from the table and took herself back
to the browser, back to the window where they left Aston crying
on the floor. **This livestream has ended.** She thumbed the screen
She tried to call him instead. Voice mail picked up promptly
"Aston? It's Orla," she said into the phone, raising her voice above
a sudden chorus of sirens below. "Aston—we're worried."

Across the roof, Team Bride crossed herself with great fan
fare, then turned and sobbed into the blazer of one of the Mid
dle Eastern guys. "It just looks *so* much like 9/11," she warbled
then drew her face back, sniffling, and peered up at the man
"No offense."

Orla watched the girl who was getting married lift her drug
store veil from her eyes. "Y'all, I know it's fucked up," she said
softly. "But from here, it's kind of beautiful, too."

CHAPTER SIXTEEN

Marlow

At eight thirty, Honey tapped the door of the guest room and pushed in without waiting for an answer. Marlow, who had been dozing, uncurled herself and looked at her. Honey was wearing a strapless white jersey jumpsuit. Her hair had been ironed and slicked straight back. She carefully set down on the bed a gold tray that held a clear drink, a pair of white leather ankle boots, a folded square of white silk—a dress, Marlow supposed—half a dozen silver tubes of lipstick, which wobbled as the tray touched down, and a white mask, the kind that covered just the top half of the face, with winged ends pointing upward on either side.

Marlow sat up and touched one finger, gently, to the rim of the glass. The smell of mint and lime rose from it as the ice cubes gently rearranged themselves. "I'd rather red wine, if you have it," she said.

Honey snorted. "And risk a spill?" she said. "You can't afford to reupholster my couch." She nodded at the lipsticks. "If you use any of these, please do it over a sink."

Marlow looked at the lipsticks—beautiful, all of them, in dark raisin and eggplant and pewter and even an old-fashioned red. "I don't wear lipstick," she said. "Not a fan."

"No?" Honey raised her eyebrows. "And you decided that?"

Marlow rolled her eyes. "Yes, Honey, I decided that." Such a believable assertion—*I decide what I like and I don't*—and yet she had a feeling Honey could tell it wasn't true. Marlow had been in the midst of deciding whether or not she was a lipstick kind of person when she met Ellis, years ago. He had mentioned nonchalantly, on one of their early dates, that he couldn't stand lipstick, that it reminded him of Stella the clown, that fixture of Constellation childhoods. His vote had made up her mind. But her followers were skeptical. **That whole lipstick speech he gave you?** one of them commented after the date. **BullSHIT. His last girlfriend SLEPT in the stuff. Homeboy's just toeing the company line. Think about it: the Hysteryl peeps don't want you drawing ANY attention to your mouth—brings back memories, CHOMP! I mean, why do you think you don't wear lipstick already? Floss has only given it to you 128,913,291,00 times!!!!!!!** *Because I don't really like it*, Marlow thought, but then something else occurred to her: one of the things that turned her off about lipstick was that she always seemed to lose it. Later on, she thought of this again, after they were married and Ellis complained about a clear gloss she put on. That night, she had stolen out of the house during off-camera time and sneaked into her parents' home, where she went into her old bedroom and cleared out her glitter-stuck dresser drawers. She found plenty of other things that she was sure had disappeared, but she didn't come across a single lipstick.

Uneasy, Marlow picked up her drink and tasted it. Ice-cold, vaguely minty, and strong. Strong enough to make her gums ing. Maybe she'd have just the one, to put her at ease, to blur the last two days. She drained half the glass in a sip.

Honey nodded approvingly. The sounds of the apartment beginning to fill with people—whispering, laughing, finding each other in bursts of happy recognition—wafted down the hall. Honey got up and smoothed the front of her jumpsuit. "See you out there," she said, almost grimly, then strode away with the gait of a woman on a mission, spike heels pummeling the dark floors.

Marlow got dressed, worming her feet into Honey's shoes, tugging gently at the dress's purring zipper. The mask was rubbery and warm. It had neat cutouts for her eyes, so she could keep Honey in her sights. It left her nose and mouth free, too. Technically, she could breathe easy.

———

David intercepted Marlow at the end of the hallway, just before the living room. He held out a gray-screen tablet with minuscule printing—a contract—and asked her to sign with her finger.

"Standard nondisclosure," he said. "Nothing leaves this room. There's no recording, no messaging, no mapping allowed at Honey's gatherings. No devices at all, actually. No one's to tell anyone they're here." He nodded, approvingly, at Marlow's bloodied wrist.

"And no one can say I was here," Marlow said.

David nodded. "Not if they don't want Honey's lawyers to ruin their lives." He lifted her hand to the tablet gently and pointed at the empty line.

There were about fifty people in the living room, waiting, fidgeting, gripping their drinks. Like her, they were all wearing white, and the masks. It took her a moment to place what the room was missing. Every guest, to a one—she thought of Elsa's smirk—was pale-skinned. When Marlow emerged from the hall, they all looked up at the sight of someone entering the room, dropping their conversations instantly. She braced herself for the looks of recognition, afraid that the mask she was wearing wasn't enough to hide who she was, that the temptation to cash in on the hunt would trump some partygoer's fear of Honey's NDA. But all she saw was disappointment; she was not who they were waiting for. It was somehow true, she thought, her mood warming with the booze—she was safe. The best place to hide in New York was in a crowd that only cared about Honey.

And then Honey was there, making them roar, stepping into a spotlight that swung toward her from somewhere unseen. The people began to clap. Marlow edged into a space along the wall and watched them. Men were misty-eyed. Women bounced in their shoes. Honey held up her glass to them.

"My friends," she said. "So good to see you."

As if prayer had begun, every head tucked downward.

"I remember privacy," Honey said. She slid her free hand into her jumpsuit pocket and began to sway slightly. "I was born right before the Spill. The federal internet didn't start till I was five, in 2021. Yes—I'm *old*." She gestured, with her drink, at a cluster of twentysomething girls. They tittered. "My parents didn't trust it like most people," Honey went on. "Though they did like the mapping." She smiled with practiced mischief. "There was an old sycamore tree on my uncle's land my mama wouldn't *never* let me climb," she said. "But I used to sneak right past her and climb that dang tree anyway. That tree gave me courage. That tree made me strong. But once the new internet came along, the government always knew where everyone was. And my mama always knew where I was. I never climbed that tree again."

Marlow glanced around to see if anyone else had noticed that Honey had just begun speaking in a heavy Southern accent. But the people were shaking their heads, as if this business with the tree was the most tragic thing they'd ever heard.

"And then, when I was fourteen," Honey said, "I went out to Constellation. Y'all remember what happened there, don't you?"

Marlow froze. Around her, the people were murmuring sympathetically. One woman pressed all ten fingers to her lips and blew a pained kiss Honey's way.

"I was saved," Honey said, her eyes glittering. "Saved from the life I thought I wanted. Everywhere I looked, I saw those old ads, you remember 'em? 'Share American Stories Again.' And I was a young girl with a nice set of tits coming in, and I thought—well, I thought what so many girls think when they decide more people should be looking at them. I thought, 'Why *not* me? Why shouldn't *I* be famous?'" Honey laughed. She stroked the scar on her face. "But that night, on that beach, with all of you watching, I sure got my comeuppance. And I realized the government was wrong. I realized that sharing isn't the way. I realized what my true calling is: to bring privacy back to America. And that's why you're here tonight, right?"

Whoops from the crowd. Bodies shimmying slightly, thrilled to hear Honey ramping up.

"You've been lied to all your life," Honey said softly. "You were lied to when you were told the only way another Spill could be prevented was if the government ran the web, and if all of you kept sharing on it. You were lied to when you were told that, because your smartphone was cooking your brains, you'd be better off with a device—something *that would speak right into your brain*. That could look, too. That would talk like it's you! '*I* should take five steps east—*I* need to replenish my skin's moisture levels.' Those aren't *your* thoughts." Honey let her mouth fall open, as if she had just thought of this, shocking herself. She continued: "And what does your life look like now? Well." She thrust one hip out. "For one thing, we know from the color of your public profile just how much money you have. That part doesn't bother me, exactly. Mine's a nice shade of platinum."

Thunderous laughter. Honey waited it out, licking her lips. "But I've got my gripes, too. My device was always telling my doctor, 'Wah, Honey had gnocchi again! With extra Parmesan!' My device was always telling my boyfriends, 'You know, Honey faked that orgasm.' Look, I'm a busy lady." Honey threw her hands up, faux-exasperated. "If I wanna fake it and get on with my day, that's my business!"

Sheepish looks from the men. Shrieks so loud from the women, Marlow almost covered her ears.

"That's why I quit my device," Honey declared. "Quit sharing years ago."

Marlow looked across the room, at the kitchen drawer where she had seen David tuck Honey's device, sliding it beneath folded white dish towels. She took a sip of her drink, finishing it, and caught another as a waiter sailed by.

"That's why I went private," Honey said. She raised a fist and pumped it with each word that came next. "You. Can. Too."

Applause—applause like they had been holding it in the whole night, their whole lives.

"Living only the part of your life you would if your grandma was watching," Honey said. "Does that sound like the land of the free? The home of the brave?"

"No!"

"Would you like to see what freedom's really like?"

"Yes."

"Are you ready to experience privacy?"

"Yes!"

"Okay, then," Honey said. She tapped her lip with a finger as if she was trying to think of something. "Let's see. You've removed your devices. We've disabled every bit of technology in this apartment, down to the security sensors." She held one hand up to her mouth, stage-muttering a secret. "I'd like to rip the goddamn things out of the walls," she said. "But alas, I'm just a renter. Sometimes I'm tempted to pour tequila on the sensors— you know that's how you break them, right? Or so I'm told. The tequila I keep around is too damn good to waste on such things." She clapped her hands together. "What am I forgetting?"

Marlow jumped a little as they all said it together, without hesitation: *"The drapes!"*

Honey nodded. She raised a finger in the air. "The drapes!"

Ivory velvet began to descend over every pane of glass. Marlow stepped forward as one of the curtains swished, ghostlike, against her on its way to the floor. She looked at the glass in her hand. This one was empty now, too. The network had a two-drink maximum for talent, unless intoxication had been prescribed for the sake of a storyline. If a star tried to go for a third drink—Jacqueline attempted it constantly—a stagehand would be dispatched to crouch-run past the talent in their own home, wiping the glass the moment it was set down.

If she were at home, she would have to stop.

But she wasn't at home, Marlow thought, holding the gaze of the waitress coming toward her. She didn't have to stop.

———

She woke the next morning in her own pajamas, tucked as primly into the guest bed as if she had fallen asleep reading. But her hairline was drenched and her stomach was throbbing as if it had its own pulse. And her mind—she groped, but her mind was blank. The hours between Honey's speech and the dawn taking reluctant gray shape outside her window—they had fallen into a hole.

She sucked in her breath and tried to put the night together.

People started to figure out who she was, even with the mask. They wished her luck evading the hunt. They shared their Hysteryl stories. "I started taking it after I didn't win homecoming king, which was bullshit," one guy said. "This other dude who hated me totally rigged the system." He paused and finished his beer. "Joke was on the other dude, anyway. My parents had the same crown made for me custom."

At some point, she got boxed into the kitchen by two men, both stocky and thick-browed, cut from the same pattern.

"What are you doing here?" one said. "Mom would kill you."

"What are *you* doing here, Barry?" the other retorted.

The first one shifted closer and hissed, "I'm not Barry in here. It's Shane."

A woman with a terrible voice sang over the music, her own song, in a corner. She faced the drapes.

Someone turned to Marlow and said, "I think you're mental, but you should still hit this."

Marlow took whatever it was, something slim and black and rocket-shaped, and sucked from the slit. The air she took in tasted earthy and sour.

In the center of the room was an all-white cardboard model of a planned privacy community, a place where people would give up tracking each other, where they would take off their devices and literally keep their thoughts to themselves. "It just looks like a town," a twentysomething blonde girl said, distressed, and Marlow laughed without knowing why. Within a few minutes, she and the blonde were drinking mojitos with their elbows linked. "I think I could really do it, though," the blonde said when they lowered their glasses. "Go totally private."

Her tall friend tossed her hair and said, "Yeah, right, Jenna. You don't even know your address without your device. Can't see you doing the full 404."

"404," Marlow had repeated. She knew it meant something to her, but the thought was trapped behind cloudy glass. "What does that mean?" she said.

The tall one began to answer—but then Jenna, the blonde, stumbled into the model, her palm crushing a whole street flat.

Honey mingled, reprising her pitch in pieces all night. She waved a shrimp tail, empty of the curl she had sucked down already, and reminded people that if they liked how they felt tonight, and if they wanted to feel this way all the time, they should join one of the fifty gated communities currently being built. Living there would feel, Honey promised, like being toally off the grid. No more devices. No more federal internet. All interactions with the government—taxes and the like—would be handled discreetly by the main office, a service built into the residents' HOA fee, alongside mowing and snow removal.

"A privacy town in every state," Honey said. "Sea to shining sea. David can explain more about packages and pricing." There was also a more affordable option, Marlow heard David say as he took over: you could keep living where you were and simply give up communication as you knew it. For $1,399, you'd get a box of materials meant to coach you through withdrawal: Honey's books on going private, videos of her lectures, and a bulky machine that would play the oily-looking discs the videos came on.

A while later, when the woman with the terrible voice was still singing, Marlow looked down at her own feet and arms and realized she was dancing. On a table. A man—one of the brothers from earlier—laughed when he saw her horrified expression. He reached his hand up to help her down. "Shane," he said hotly in her ear.

He propped her against a wall. "Did you ever think about how weird it is that babies are born, like, whenever they want, like a Tuesday when everyone's at work?" he said. "Or how people can die on a sunny day when kids are playing next door?" His mask had slipped a bit and she couldn't find his eyes, but the way his jaw ground made him seem angry at her, like she, specifically, should have sorted out these indignities. She let Jenna pull her down the hallway, and watched Shane-not-Barry's hands clutch dumbly at the air where she had been.

In the bathroom, Marlow let Jenna go first. She raised her mask and looked at herself in the mirror. Her hair looked like she had slept on a balloon. The color of her skin, beneath her sweat, alarmed her; it was slightly gray, as if concealing a shadow cast from the inside. She looked like someone old, doing something she was too old to do, and she suddenly felt like she could not keep her eyes open for one more moment. She told Jenna she would be right out and climbed carefully into the slippery concrete bowl of the tub. She put her head back.

The door swung open again. Shane-not-Barry was moving from the dim hallway into the bathroom's starched light. "You trying to ditch me?" he said. "You can't ditch me."

She remembered him climbing in. She remembered laughing at the fact that the tub was inconvenient, even though she didn't feel like laughing. She remembered when he let out a sound—*mmm*—and put more of his weight on her. She remembered that she had mumbled something to stop him after waiting what might have been too long. *Maybe not the best idea.* She remembered that Shane-not-Barry had giggled and turned on the faucet over her face, let her sputter in the stream for a moment. "Live a little," he said.

In the guest bed, now, her heart went cold as she remembered how it ended.

Her anger had saved her.

How strange, she thought, that so many livelihoods—hers, her parents', Ellis's, his coworkers', network staffers'—had depended on her moving through every day complacent. All that effort and money spent on making sure she stayed sweet and even, when the real hero inside her, all along, was this other thing. The thing she was meant to tamp down.

Something in Marlow snapped when Shane turned on the faucet. It wasn't about the water that shoved her breath back down inside her. It was about the way he yanked the faucet knob: without hesitation, like there was no chance he wouldn't get away with it.

Marlow rose out of the stream and wrapped her hands around his neck. She could remember thinking *just for a few seconds just so he knows I'm for real*—but she couldn't remember actually counting.

Then Honey was there, on her knees, peeling Marlow's fingers back one at a time. Shane-not-Barry flopped out of the tub like a fish, screaming *you crazy bitch*. He threatened things, but Honey just held up a hand and reminded him of what he had signed. Tall men came in to remove him. "And give him a pill first," Honey told them. "David knows which ones."

Marlow remembered muttering that she wanted to go to bed. But Honey ignored her, pushed her toward the party, wouldn't let her fix her hair.

"Please don't touch it," she said. "It's perfect."

Then they were back in the living room, the people all turning to face them. Honey held Marlow's limp form triumphantly—by the armpits, as if she had hunted her—and ripped off her mask. There was a gasp as the party took in this star they had streamed for years, this talent looking ill and worn and desperate. "See?" Honey shouted into the crowd. "See what comes from a life of being watched?"

———

There was more meat for breakfast. Actually, Marlow corrected herself, as she surveyed Honey's kitchen table, there was only meat for breakfast. There was sausage and bacon and ham. Honey, inexplicably, was eating fried chicken. Before Marlow could speak, she sucked glistening fat from her thumb and stood up. "Good morning, sunshine," she said. "Make a plate and bring it with. I want to show you something."

Marlow followed Honey to a door at the back of the apartment, then up the stairs to the roof. "No way," she said, when she saw what was parked there. It was a drone, the million-dollar, person-carrying kind, a giant muscled bug with a storm-gray glass windshield. The sight of its vicious little propellers made Marlow's gut lurch.

Honey grinned at her. "Who's afraid of drones now?" She climbed inside, white robe billowing in the wind behind her, and patted the passenger seat.

As they lifted off, Honey searched Marlow's face, then nodded as if she was satisfied. "Good," she said. She stole a sausage from Marlow's plate. "I was worried you'd be mad at me for using you as an example."

"I am mad," Marlow said. "Or I'll be mad, later. Right now I'm just working on not throwing up." They were passing a tower that reminded her of a telescope she had as a child: round and stacked with narrowing layers, seemingly ready to collapse into itself.

"I figured you're used to it," Honey pressed. "Being used to sell something. You really changed the world, you know that, Marlow? Kids never kill themselves these days. You'd sooner hear of a child dying of cancer."

Marlow wanted to eat a piece of bacon, just to give herself time to think up a response while she chewed, but she couldn't—she knew it would come back up. "Kids don't kill themselves for a lot of reasons," she said. "They're built not to, now." She thought, with a jolt of nausea, of the mock-up of her and Ellis's baby, the one they had left unfinished. "And they don't have secrets anymore," she added.

"You say that like it's a good thing." Honey smirked. "But admit it. You didn't mind a little privacy last night." She turned toward Marlow conspiratorially and pulled her knees up, like they were best friends at a sleepover. "You seemed to be enjoying yourself."

Marlow looked at Honey. She felt her anger resurfacing. "Oh, yeah, it was a thrill," she snapped. "I liked the part where I almost got raped."

Honey pinched the last piece of bacon from Marlow's plate. "Don't be dramatic," she said. "You shut that down just fine. I'm sure no one's ever bothered to say this to you, they've been too busy making you eat pills and wear cardigans, but—Marlow, you can take care of yourself."

Marlow jerked her face away, toward the window. She didn't

want Honey to see how much it meant to her, to hear someone say something like that, even someone who didn't really care about her. It would shift everything between them Honey's way.

Honey took both plates and tucked them somewhere out of sight. "You know, I went to Constellation specifically to fuck with you people," she said, the way someone else might have said *I went out there to major in mechanical engineering.* "Back when we were kids, I mean."

"Yeah, I picked up on that," Marlow said. "Right around the time you drove my dad's car into the ocean." Her heart pricked at the word *dad*. But that was still Aston, wasn't it? Even when she learned who her father was, it would be too late for that person to be her dad.

"And it wouldn't have made sense to go home afterward." They were drifting toward the Statue of Liberty, and Marlow swore she saw Honey give the statue a curt nod, like she was a coworker. "I had momentum," Honey said. "I was famous, all of a sudden. But fame was not enough, you know? I wanted something else. I couldn't have come up with the word, back then, but I'm big-time now, I have a good vocab." She smiled. "Influence. That's what I wanted."

She kept talking, and, theoretically, Marlow was dying to cut her off. But another one of her just-unearthed feelings was perking: curiosity. She was parched for details. So she let Honey go on, and Honey went on: after Marlow bit her, she didn't go back to War, back to the brothers and uncles and the boys she would have married, all of them with the same frowns, the same dark dust in their wrinkles. She wouldn't go back to the rancher with its squinting, shutterless windows. She wouldn't go back to the creek—the *crick*, as she said it—at the back of the property, the one that had dried up so bad over the years, it didn't cover her parents' ashes when she chucked them in. Age nine, straw-armed, she had to go back to the house to fill a bucket at the laundry room sink.

Instead of going home, she came to the island passing beneath their feet, where television anchors in creased lipstick sat across from her, asking questions. They all wanted to see her right away, before she healed too much. They asked her what was going through her mind when she realized what Marlow was doing. They asked her whether she thought Constellation, that grand and indulgent experiment designed to lift the country's Spill-ravaged spirits, to glamorize sharing again, was actually—and here they paused and raised their perfect eyebrows—dangerous.

Their questions didn't really matter. Honey had already decided on her answers. "I studied old interviews," she told Marlow. "I learned what to do, how to just say what you want to say, no matter what they're asking." She grabbed the H-shaped wheel of the drone, even though it was flying independently, and jerked it side to side. "Pivot, pivot, pivot," she chanted.

She stole her talking points from people who stopped her on the street, to tell her they were sorry she got bitten. Constellation was ten years old by then, a juggernaut, ripe for backlash. Now there was a reason to pounce: Constellation had hurt Honey—a young girl, an innocent girl (so they thought)—and it wasn't all Marlow's fault, was it? Marlow was clearly unhinged, but that wasn't the whole story. Of course it was bound to go bad, this world where people were filmed all day. It was their fault, too, as followers—they had gotten addicted to watching. And they had let their guards down. Though they refused to use things like Amerigram, they were slipping into sharing, weren't they, when they partook in the Constellation Network feeds? If they liked a star's necklace or catchphrase, they said it. They parted, when they commented, with just a bit of themselves. They handed it over to the government. Now, looking at the wound on Honey's face—seeing what had happened to her when she'd put herself out there, sharing as much as anyone could—they felt the suspicions they'd had all along about this new web re-heating, demanding action.

Oh, they should let her go, they told Honey, gripping her arm. But before they did: Did she ever think that maybe they'd all be better off off-line? Without any internet, period? The way people were in the 1900s?

Honey listened keenly, and heard the plea between their words: they were desperate for someone to lead the way, to help them escape the internet. America needed an antisharing renegade, a patron saint of privacy. And if she could be that saint, she bet, she wouldn't have to go back to West Virginia.

So when journalists asked about Marlow, Honey pivoted fiercely. She talked about how badly she'd wanted to be known, like the kids in Constellation, about how she had bought into the post-Spill propaganda—sharing was good now, sharing was safe now. She wondered aloud whether the government was really any better at protecting data now than Facebook and Twitter and banks and insurance companies had been before the Spill. She used the word *privacy* over and over; sometimes she just said, firmly, "Privacy good. Sharing bad." She said, raising her voice to distract from the fact that she was only fourteen years old, "The only way to know what you share with the government is safe is not to share with the government at all."

It worked. She was young and blue-eyed, scrappy and freshly maimed, and people called her brave. They said the questions she asked were theirs, too. Honey was invited to speak to clubs of troubled teens, to attend galas, to sit as an honorary junior member on the boards of various charities. She was given an hour to shout at the camera each night on a cable-news station. Publications put her name on lists of the year's most interesting people—"me," she told Marlow now, thumping the second button of her pajamas, "*me*." A woman with children to feed quickly wrote a book for Honey to call hers, and Honey promoted it hard. She did late-night-show karaoke games and kids' programs where drones pelted her with sticky green goop. But mostly, she went on repeating herself until she grew bigger than a star. She was not just someone people looked at. She became someone they obeyed.

The man who ran the network that aired her news show took her in. He and his wife lived on Central Park South. "I had my own bathroom," Honey said. "It blew my mind, that bathroom." The couple had never had children, and though Honey was seventeen by the time they got it formalized, they adopted her. She called them Papa Bob and Mama Brynn. She had her twenty-first birthday party at the Plaza Hotel. They only denied her once: when she asked for plastic surgery. Mama Brynn touched Honey's scar and said, "Darling, it's part of who you are." Papa Bob was less nuanced.

"He said it was my brand," Honey said. "And it has been, ever since."

Marlow noticed now, since Honey hadn't washed her face since the party, that she applied her makeup around the scar, not over it. "Why are you telling me all of this?" she said.

Honey looked at her so sharply, she startled. "Because I'm trying to show you how hard I had to work to get what was handed to you," she hissed. "All your millions of followers that you got just for growing up in the right neighborhood. You didn't do *shit*. So yes, Marlow, sure. Some of my fans, some of the people who want to go private, who come to my parties—like the gentleman you ended up in the tub with..." Honey exhaled, a weary breath. "They have—traditional values. Of course privacy is going to appeal to people who have things to hide." She leaned over and pressed a finger into Marlow's chest. "But this movement, these people, my place in this world—this is all I have, Marlow. So if I have to look the other way sometimes, then I *do*. I know it means that, as we used to say in Catholic school, my soul is not as clean and white as a milk bottle. But I can live with a couple spots, Marlow. I just can, to have what I have."

Marlow laughed, a sharp sound that made the back of her

266

throat burn. "You can live with spots on your soul?" she said. "You can't handle spots on your *couch*."

To her surprise, then her fear, Honey laughed, too.

The drone wove between the buildings. The spires on top of them made Marlow think of the needle in the fairy tale, the one with the princess who pricked herself on something inevitable and missed everything for years, her whole life. "Are they still around, your Papa Bob and Mama Brynn?" she said.

Honey flicked her hand at the buildings below. "Not really," she said curtly. "Fog. They're in a home down there."

"Mine, too," Marlow said. "Well, my dad. He's been gone for years. My mom is better off. She can live on her own."

Honey shook her head. "Funny how that works," she said, and Marlow noticed her voice was wobbling. "And my Mama Brynn—she did everything they said to do to try to keep it away. The meditating, the eye masks, the board games. All we ever ate was sweet potatoes. She wouldn't so much as look at the display on an alarm clock. But Papa Bob never quit. He kept his screens till the day he forgot how to use them. And they ended up exactly the same."

"Do they eat?" Marlow said. "My dad doesn't eat. I actually daydream sometimes about him eating a sandwich, or a big bowl of soup—about how nice it would be to see that." Her face felt suddenly warm. She had wanted, many times, to confess this to her mother, but never found a moment off camera. She couldn't say it otherwise; she knew it would embarrass Aston if she told the world something like that.

"I don't know if they eat," Honey sighed. "I never go. They don't know the difference, and you have to remember—" She raised her eyes defiantly to Marlow's, staving off judgment. "I already lost one set of parents. No one should have to do it twice."

Marlow looked away, straight ahead at the Statue. She hadn't realized they were so close. The Lady's dusty mint gaze filled the windshield, one blank eye trained on each of them. "I'm sorry, Honey," she said. She said it because this was a good spot to say it, with lost parents having come up. But Marlow meant more than the formality. She meant that, though she had spent her whole life defending the bite to herself—*she provoked me, I had no choice, my hands were literally tied*—she had been wrong. She was grown now, she saw both sides of the story, and she understood: of course she had been wrong. She wanted to say all of this, to clarify what she was apologizing for. But something pride-shaped was lodged in her throat.

"That's the thing about real people," Honey said, shrugging. "They get sick. They forget your face. They die. They disappoint you." Honey paused and looked out. The sun had wrestled the morning from the clouds, turning the sky around the Lady's head a hopeful peach. "I would never turn you in, Marlow," Honey said. "But I think you'd be dumb not to go back to Constellation. You're out here, giving up all those followers, to look for real people? Your real parents? Real people are so *impractical*."

"Just the one parent," Marlow said. "Just my real father."

Honey frowned. She twisted away from Marlow and reached her hand between her seat and the wall of the drone, feeling for something in the pocket on the door. "I don't know about that," Honey said.

When she turned back to Marlow, she was holding the letter from Orla Cadden's apartment. Marlow felt her mouth go bone-dry.

"Now, don't have a fit," Honey said quickly. "It fell out of your jeans last night, when I was looking for your jammies."

Marlow snatched for the envelope, and Honey let her take it—let her take it with the slightly giddy smugness of someone who already knew what it said. "But you can't read it," Marlow protested, when she saw how Honey's face looked. "It's in cursive."

"See, that hurts my feelings," Honey sighed. "I've been following you since we were kids. I know every damn thing about you. But you can't keep anything straight about me. I just told you I went to Catholic school."

Marlow said, "And what the hell does that have to do with anything?"

As it turned out: plenty.

CHAPTER SEVENTEEN

Orla

New York, New York
2016

The night Aston burned his new fifty-nine-million-dollar apartment black, Orla and Floss waited in the sickly pink hospital wing, in a room the nurses gave them after their presence proved a distraction. They dozed on plastic chairs with their heads together. In the morning, a nurse came and woke them, choosing Orla's shoulder to touch. They went in to see Aston. The doctor said he was lucky, but Orla didn't think he looked it. Lee Kumon sat in a chair by the window, glaring them out of the room, glaring harder when a cell phone rang and it took Orla too long to realize it was hers. She was still getting used to its ping—she had only recently taken it off silent, as the hatred that lit it up for weeks finally trailed off. Orla stepped out to listen to the voice mail. Before the woman on the recording even started talking, Orla looked up, saw the clock for the first time that day, and knew what the message would be. She had missed her appointment.

She was about to call back to reschedule when Floss came into the hallway, crying. She shoved her own phone under Orla's nose, showing her an email. "The network," she said. "We're canceled, officially. I mean, I know they pretty much decided it the second that girl died but—" She flicked her chin at the doorway to Aston's room, spoke bitterly. "Now, with all his drama—they say they're just thinking of our mental *health*."

A nurse passing by glanced back and shook her head at Orla once, an unwavering, split-second judgment of the entirety of her, like Orla should have known better than to be where and who and with whom she was.

Orla pushed Floss's phone away. "That's what you're worried about right now—the show?" she said. "God, don't you ever get sick of yourself?"

Floss hiccuped. She blinked, wounded. "Why are you pissed at me?" she warbled, snot clogging her words.

"It isn't *real*." Orla snapped her fingers in the air, grabbing, pinching. "Nothing you do is—none of it is anything, don't you get that? It's *nothing*."

Floss was letting her tears run unchecked into her mouth, then letting them run right back out. Her ugly-cry was famous for good reason. "The show is your job, too, in case you forgot," she blubbered. "I guess you don't care if we lose it, 'cause you still think you're different, right? You're supposed to be a writer?"

"I will be a writer." Orla heard something desperate, high and thin, in her voice. She ignored it. "This ends for me. You might be talent, but I *have* a talent. That's the difference between you and me."

Floss whirled on her heel and stomped off, the backs of her mule sandals slapping up and down. The doors at the end of the hall said RESTRICTED—STAFF ONLY. But she pushed right through them, and was gone.

Aston's mother poked her angry face out of his room, reached for the door, and slammed it closed.

Orla flattened her hands into her sacrum and leaned against the wall's chair rail, massaging her aching back. *You're right*, she thought, a command to her confidence—she was already, automatically, doubting herself. *Everything you said was right.*

But that wasn't true. One thing she said was wrong. She had been wrong to say this would end for her, that she could walk back into her old life, unmarked. The reality was the opposite. However this ended, Floss would be fine. Aston, the doctors assured them, would be fine. Craig would be fine. Melissa would be fine. Danny would be fine. There was only one bit of inescapable proof of the way they had lived this last year. It was the size of an avocado this week, and it lived inside of Orla.

———

There were so many ways what happened next might not have happened.

If she had made it to her abortion.

If she had rescheduled her abortion, instead of hanging up every time the receptionist put her on hold, over and over until finally she was five months along, and the abortion just wasn't going to happen. Not because she wanted the baby, not because she felt guilty, but for the same reason most things happened to her: she could not make a choice.

If the social worker she had seen about adoption hadn't done a double take at her face, at her name on the form. If she hadn't said with a sigh, halfway through their meeting, "The couples won't know who you are at first, but eventually you'll meet them, and so you'll have to address—things—then."

If Marie Jacinto had agreed to sell her book instead of tossing it out with her Danish wrapper.

If Danny had loved her.

If she had loved Danny.

But none of that had happened. What happened, instead, three weeks after the fire, was that Aston took an Uber from the hospital to their apartment and collapsed in Floss's lap like a child. Orla listened from her room for an hour as the two of them wept. Then she listened from her room for a month while they got back into their old awful rhythms, defiling all the spots Orla had Cloroxed after their breakup, all the spaces she thought were finally safe. Sometimes she heard them, in Floss's room, planning their next act. They whispered so she couldn't hear, and she felt both hurt and relieved. At long last, she was on the outside.

One day, her Google alerts pointed her to a new television interview Floss and Aston had done. Orla hit Play, keeping the volume low on her laptop so Floss and Aston wouldn't know she was watching. Floss, sitting against a black backdrop, looked shattered and subdued, and Orla half wondered if she might open a cabinet later to find a new Post-it—Seem sorry!!!!

"I was responsible for everything, the night that Anna died," Floss said, when the reporter pressed the issue. "My friend Orla had nothing to do with it."

The reporter touched a pen to her lips, then posed to Floss one of the many questions Orla had never dared to ask. "Why do this at all, Floss?" the reporter said. "Why did you want to be a reality star, to get all these followers—what's the point, in your mind? What did you want?"

"What did I want?" Floss repeated. She glanced at Aston, who was staring down at his lap. Though Orla couldn't see him from the waist down, she bet his leg was jiggling.

"Were you bullied as a child?" The reporter leaned in. "Distant from your parents? What made you crave this approval, this attention?"

Floss inhaled. When she answered, it was in what Orla knew Floss thought of as her smart voice, which made what she said sound even worse. "It's not so much that I craved it," she said.

"I thought I deserved it. I think I'm fun, I have an interesting life. I think I'm special."

Aston looked up at the reporter, into the camera, above it. He grimaced.

The reporter smiled, a tight show of teeth. "You're just being honest, of course," she said.

"I mean, everyone is special in their own way," Floss said quickly. She blushed and started pulling at her hair. "But the more people followed me, the better I felt. I mean—anyone would do this if they could, wouldn't they?" She looked genuinely confused as she cocked her head at the reporter. "Right? Wouldn't you?"

———

The interview seemed to work. Orla scanned the comments, the blog posts analyzing it; Floss had reclaimed her relatability, because Floss had been so honest. Everyone did, as it turned out, think they were special in their own way. Everyone was again Floss Natuzzi some days. Orla heard Floss and Aston leaving again, often, sounding like they really had places to go and needed to be on time. They were no longer people who could afford to make others wait.

One morning, Floss skipped into Orla's room as if they had never fought. She threw an arm over her head and dropped into a squat, writhing like a stripper on an invisible pole. "Guess who you're having lunch with today?" she said.

"Whom," Orla said. "And no one."

"Wrong." Floss popped up and swiveled her hips. "Polly Cummings."

Orla sat up straight. "You don't know Polly Cummings."

"The agent. Big lady, blonde, Parisian vibe?" Floss swayed from one foot to the other. "I met her last night at a thing. I told her about your book. I told her all about you, actually, except for the part where you've been, like, jerking off to her business card since you were little."

Orla's heart was pounding. "You're disgusting," she said. "I don't believe you."

"Excuse me, I know book people," Floss said. "I read."

Floss owned, Orla knew, exactly three books. They sat on the windowsill in her bedroom. They were all by an heiress who wore stretchy dresses and dispensed tips on having it all. When Orla opened one of them once, its spine crackled with newness.

"What did I say back in the day?" Floss said. "An agent would come to you. Now get up. Lunch is an hour. We have to find you an outfit."

———

Orla ended up wearing the same thing she had worn to meet Marie Jacinto. It was not ideal. The black pants had to be held shut with a shoelace Floss threaded through the fly, and the owl-printed blouse was so snug that the outline of Orla's belly button bled through. Her flats honked with each step, fighting the swell of her feet. When Orla saw Mrs. Salgado dozing on her chair outside, she tiptoed to make the shoes silent.

Orla spotted Polly Cummings as soon as she stepped inside the restaurant. Polly was seated at the back of the sunken, blush-lit dining room, facing away. Her fierce blond bob swung forward over her menu. Her linebacker shoulders were wrapped in an olive-colored scarf. Orla took a moment to will her sweating to stop as the maître d' stood eyeing her. She could tell he took her for someone who wasn't staying, who only wanted to use the bathroom. She lifted her head and walked past him.

Then she was standing at Polly's table, looking at the woman she had only seen in the trades and watermarked party pictures. Polly looked up and snapped her menu shut. "Orla Cadden," she said. "Sit."

Under Polly's menu was a stack of papers with a Post-it on top, and on the Post-it was Orla's name. Orla looked at the page, the paragraphs that spread around the sticky note, and felt a streak of dizziness. It was her book. Floss must have gone on her laptop and emailed Polly the manuscript, without asking or telling Orla.

Orla sat down hard. Across the table, Polly seemed to be counting each flyaway buzzing on top of Orla's head, each pill dangling from Orla's blouse. When Polly's eyes moved down to her stomach, Orla blurted, mostly to bring up her gaze, "I'm so honored to meet you, but I have to say one thing up front, based on, ah, past experience."

Polly blinked at her through her glasses, the frames of which were green and heavy-looking, like they were carved out of stone. "Go ahead," she said.

The busboy poured their waters, holding his tie with one elegant hand. "I don't want to write about Floss," Orla said. "Natuzzi," she added, blushing, in case Polly didn't watch TV.

Polly nodded. "Thank you, Darrell," she said to the busboy, and then to Orla, "That's fine. I'm not interested in that from you." She tapped the papers in front of her. "I see promise here," she said. Orla almost laughed. It was the same thing Polly's assistant had said about the pages years ago, back when Orla was seventeen. Back when she knew how to finish things.

"I like the first chapter," Polly went on. "And there are certainly some bold choices. The experimental elements—the drawings, the lyrics. The Orthodox Jewish character who metaphorically remains to be filled in—I found that quite interesting, though we'll have to find another way into it. 'TK,' that's too inside baseball, don't you think?"

Orla felt like her stomach was dropping through her legs. *The experimental elements.* Floss must have sent an old version, a wild version, maybe from as far back as when Danny was around, filled with padding and errors and gaps and, she remembered, feeling like she might pass out, a sailboat made of lowercase *r*'s.

"Oh," she said weakly, "I should explain what—"

"I think this could be quite a debut," Polly said. "I don't like the words 'next big thing,' I think they're crass, but…" She raised her eyebrows. "Perhaps, just for scale, think in those terms."

"Are you kidding?" Orla stared at her.

Polly shook her head. She lowered her eyes to the salad the waiter was placing in front of her. The waiter did not look at Orla or ask if she wanted to eat. Polly frowned at the arugula, then picked up her fork with a sigh. "Though I do think," she said, stabbing a tomato, "you may have some logistical issues." Her eyes scrolled downward again.

Orla pulled her napkin up over her stomach. "This, you mean? Pregnant?" she stuttered. "Sorry. I don't know what…"

Polly wiped her mouth. "I guess I just want to know," she said, "how serious you are about becoming an author. If you're making arrangements to have the time to be an author."

Orla weighed her options. She wondered how Polly would respond if she let the whole truth roll out of her mouth. *I am as serious about becoming an author as I am about being alive*, she wanted to say. *It's the reason I've stuck it out here for years. It's the reason I made myself blog about booty shorts. I used to be a girl who wrote after school until her legs got numb. And recently, yes—I got lazy. And distracted and lonely and pregnant. But I have only been this way for such a short part of my life. And I have been that other girl forever.*

"I have a two o'clock," Polly said coolly.

"I'm serious," Orla said quickly. "Very serious." It was suddenly clear to her, clear as the empty whisper-thin wineglasses cluttering their table: she would do whatever was best for this book, whatever worked for Polly Cummings. She had been giving things up for so long: Danny to Catherine, a decade to cyberstalking Danny, just about all she had to Floss. She had one thing left—her long-lost dream—and she was going to keep it. This was the truth, no matter who it made her: she couldn't give it up.

Orla looked Polly in the eye and said, "I'll figure something out."

To her surprise, Amadou was at the curb when she came out. She hadn't seen him since they cut back on expenses after Anna's death, when they weren't going anywhere anyway.

"What are you doing here?" she said, hugging him, watching herself in his mirrored glasses.

"Miss Floss asked me to come get you," Amadou said. "For a surprise."

In the back seat of his Escalade, she found some earrings in the well beneath the door handle. "I haven't been driving any one client regular," Amadou said quickly, as if it might make Orla feel bad to hear that he had replaced them. "No one special." He nosed the car onto Forty-Second Street.

When he turned onto the FDR, Orla leaned forward. "Where are we going?"

"Oh," Amadou sighed. He adjusted his GPS unit as it slipped down the inside of the windshield. "Somewhere new."

———

Orla had never been to Brooklyn Heights. It was eerily quiet, with flat-faced, shuttered houses and streetlights out of a storybook.

Amadou pulled over in front of a massive three-story home. It had gray clapboard siding and a navy door flanked by thick white columns. Ferns, lime green and deep maroon, spilled out of the window boxes.

Orla got out of the car and walked around to the sidewalk, which was made of small, smooth slates, so unlike Chelsea's shit-streaked concrete. She looked to her left and was surprised to find that, just a block away, the street dropped off and the river rose up to where she could see it. Past that, across the water, were the tall blocks of the Financial District. "What is this place?" she said.

Amadou answered literally. "Thirteen Pineapple Street."

As he spoke, the front door swung open and Floss leaned over the threshold. She had on a bizarre dress: strawberry pink, with a high, square neckline, a flouncy skirt, and little puffed sleeves. She had rolled her dark hair back on both sides and secured it with rhinestone-dotted combs. There were white leather pumps on her feet. The overall effect reminded Orla of her great-aunts in the sixties, smoking at parties in pictures.

"Welcome." Floss did a sort of curtsy.

"To what?" Orla said, climbing the stoop.

"To our new home." Floss let her in, and shut the door behind them.

Orla stood in the foyer, her head turning slowly. In front of her were stairs, wide and walnut, leading up to a second-floor landing with a small hexagonal window above it. To her right was a living room with heavy gold draperies and a long velvet sofa, emerald green. A fire burned beneath the mantel, which was engraved with dozens of icons—fruit and wheat and men in wigs. To her left was a dining room, a blizzard of blue and white—chinoiserie vases on the round, polished table, royal-and-cream-striped curtains, aqua crystal and milk glass held in the triangular cabinets built into the corners. A discordant flash of green inside one of the cabinets caught Orla's eye. It was the urn with Biscuit's ashes, she realized.

Orla looked at Floss, who was watching her carefully. "If this is a prank," she said, "I'm not in the mood."

Aston came padding barefoot down the thick runner in the hallway then, headed straight for her. Orla blushed fiercely, because—why had she assumed that by "our," Floss still meant Floss and *her*?

Aston was wearing pants and a zip-up sweater, both cut from pale gray cashmere. Above where the zipper ended, Orla saw the new pink flesh of the scars on his chest. "Shouldn't you be in, like, the best mood ever?" he said. "Miss new bestselling author! Polly just called Floss a minute ago."

"She did?" Orla looked between them.

"Oh, yeah, you know Polly," Floss said vaguely. She grabbed Orla's hand and pulled her down the hallway. "Hope you didn't fill up. I made lunch."

They came into the kind of kitchen Orla thought did not exist in New York, not even for the rich; it was so deceitfully suburban. There was endless counter space, a full-size dishwasher, a real stove with lemon-patterned tiles behind it. At the far end of the room was a wall of windows, looking out on a narrow, sloping yard, and a long bench, padded in flowered fabric and bolted to the wall. Floss motioned for Orla to sit down there. Aston pulled the table back so that it didn't squeeze her belly.

Floss brought things to the table, an endless parade of food off-limits to pregnant women—mayo-drenched seafood salad and sliced-turkey sandwiches that she left in their containers, not bothering with presentation. They talked about Polly. Floss would not apologize for sending the manuscript without Orla's permission—"Because I was *right*—she loves you!" Aston wanted to know if Orla could give him the "TLDR" version of her book. "Like a shorter version of the story, because I have this thing where I can't get through books," he said, bouncing on his seat. "TLDR means 'Too Long, Didn't Read.'"

Could she even believe it, they asked, over and over, and later she thought that they must have been checking to see if she actually did.

Floss brought three champagne flutes to the table and sat down. She slid the one with the darker liquid toward Orla. "Sparkling apple juice."

Orla flicked her glass. "Just this once, I'll take the real stuff," she said. "One glass of champagne won't kill the baby."

Floss and Aston grew quiet. They looked at each other.

"Whoa," Orla said. "You guys are different in Brooklyn. Fine. Half a glass."

"I'd rather you didn't," Aston said. He sounded like a child playing grown-up.

Floss lifted one puff-sleeved shoulder. "Maybe better safe than sorry?"

Orla rolled her eyes and reached for the bottle. Floss gripped its neck and tugged it back. She got up, skirt whirling, and set it on the counter, as if that settled that.

"Okay." Orla leaned as close to the table as her stomach would allow. "What the fuck is going on here?"

"Let's just get to it," Aston grumbled to Floss. His shoulders slumped. "It's just Orla. I don't know why we had to make a big show." He pushed aside a vase of carnations blocking his face from Orla's view.

"Because," Floss said. "It's, like, a big deal, and I wanted it to feel special."

Floss and Aston interlaced their fingers and put their hands on the table together. Orla gasped. Between the house and Floss's costume, she somehow hadn't seen it: a teardrop-shaped choking hazard of a diamond, covering Floss's left ring finger all the way across.

Floss and Aston began taking turns talking, like nervous bridesmaids sharing a toast.

"We're getting married," Floss said. "Soon."

"It's more than that, though," Aston said. "We're, like, new people."

"Literally *new*," said Floss. "You were so right, Orla, that day at the hospital. I needed to take a hard look at myself. To learn what was real. So I did that, and then we got this place—we just, like, want to simplify. We rented it furnished," she added, in a tone that made *we rented it furnished* sound like *we built it brick by brick and hewed the table before you by hand*.

"This is where our new life begins," Aston said.

Orla looked at Floss. "So you're moving out of 6D?" she said.

Floss nodded. "My movers will come get the rest of my stuff tomorrow."

There was more. There was so much more. They had quit drinking, they said proudly, except for wine and champagne at meals, of course. They were getting acupuncture. They had had their auras photographed. They were immersing themselves completely in the study of cathartic movement.

"Is that exercise?" Orla said.

Sharply, they both answered, *"No."* They said they went thrice weekly to a loft in Tribeca, to beat their hands against their thighs and scream about what they deserved. Floss thrust out her phone to show Orla a picture of the class's teacher. It took Orla a long moment to remember where she'd seen the face before. Their teacher was the anxious, overdressed waif from the red carpet where Orla met Floss. She thought of telling Floss this, but Aston was deep into a story that had the pink lines on his chest pulsing, catching the chandelier's light.

"So class is over, right," he said, "and Floss and I are just standing there. We're exhausted. Our throats are raw. Our tunics are see-through, we're so sweaty. Everyone else has left the room. And we're just staring at each other. We were thinking the same thing. Then we said it, at the same time." He beamed. "'Let's have a baby.'"

"We told Emily—that's the teacher—what happened," Floss said. She flapped her hands. "And she was just like, 'Oh, you had a shared revelation? That's just another Tuesday in here! Happens all the time!'"

"So anyway," Aston said. He put his arm around Floss, who leaned into him. "We're going for it."

"Well, cool," Orla said after a moment. "I mean, congratulations. So, you're…pregnant, too?"

Aston gave a somber shake of his head, and Floss bit her lip. "No," she said. "I had surgery when I was young, to get a cyst out, and something went wrong. The doctor was a douchebag. The point is, I can't."

"And I want to adopt anyway," Aston jumped in. "I'd *rather*. I love kids so much, Orla. Like, I relate to them *more*." He reached across the table and put his hand on top of hers. "I think I'd be a really good dad."

This was the part in the story, when Orla looked back, where things slowed to a surreal pace. The part where she could remember all the details in high definition—every one of Floss's lashes its own blade against her skin, the way Aston's sweater puckered each time he breathed. It probably wasn't true that she actually knew these things. It was probably her mind combing for things to cling to, to prove that what happened had actually happened, that Floss really took a breath and said: "And we were thinking that this could be perfect, since you meant to abort yours, anyway."

It was so quiet, Orla could hear the strokes of the clock above the cabinets. Her heart beat twice to each tick.

"But I didn't," she said. "I'm not."

"But you would have," Aston said. "If I wasn't in the hospital. So maybe you could just, like, still pretend that you did, in a way."

"*What?*" Orla said.

Floss shot him a look. "We know it's unorthodox," she tried.

Orla stood up. She forgot that she was pregnant and on the tighter side of a booth. The table's edge forced her back down. "I know that you went to a lot of trouble," she said, "buying these sandwiches. But no. No! I feel like I shouldn't have to say this—I'm not giving you my baby."

Floss made her voice sympathetic. "When we discussed it with Emily—"

"*When you discussed it with Emily?*" The bitch from the red carpet, reincarnated as an expert on glutes and fate, discussing *her*

283

baby with Floss and Aston. "I swear to God, Floss," Orla said. "You have no filter!"

"It's not like I told her your name or anything," Floss said, raising a shoulder defensively. "I called you Pat, like our fake publicist from the old days."

"I don't mean what gets out," Orla said. "I mean you'll let just anyone in."

The truth of it swelled inside her. Every scheme they brought to life together, every drink they shared without wiping the other's spit from the bottle, every drunk ride home with their feet in each other's laps—to Orla it had been everything, an end, but to Floss it had only been means.

This time, Orla shoved the table into their chests as she stood.

It was Aston who came after her, soundless on the rug, so that she didn't know he had followed her until his hand shot past hers to hold the door closed. "All we're asking," he said, "is that you give it some thought. This is a big moment for you, with Polly and the book. We know you've been looking for a solution, and—well, we're family already, you and me and Floss. Is it really that crazy? Worse than giving her to strangers?"

Orla stared at his hand on the door. She noticed yet another scar for the first time: a beet-red swath of skin across his knuckles, scattered with deep white pockmarks. "I don't know the gender," she said. "I didn't find out."

"Well, I think it's a girl," Aston said. There was a warmth to his voice that knocked Orla back for a second. The unwanted thought that came to her then was: he would be a better dad than Danny. It made no sense on the surface, she knew. To the naked eye, Danny was salt of the earth, Aston a sizable tumble in America's cultural downfall. But he would be better. She was sure. She pushed the thought away and pushed past Aston out the door. He let her go. She heard him call, as she went down the stairs, "Hold the railing—careful."

The street outside was empty, the surprise ride from Ama-

Jou evidently a one-way arrangement. Orla looked both ways for one of the globes that signaled the train. She pulled out her phone and tried to focus on the slow-loading map. On her way out of the kitchen, she had noticed the orange bodega tag on the bottle of apple juice. Three ninety-nine, that was all it cost, and they hadn't even taken the sticker off. Orla fluffed up her indignation, trying to make it put out the feeling sparking like an ember beneath it. The sensation that suddenly, if she wanted it—she had found a way out.

CHAPTER EIGHTEEN

Marlow

New York, New York
2051

In the drone, in the sky, in the Statue's shadow, Honey decoded cursive and read the letter out loud to Marlow.

January 5, 2022

Orla—
Serious question: Who the fuck do you think you are?

No, really—I'd love to know what your plan was. What were you gonna do, sit with the kids while they ate their cake and tell them your sad little story?

Who were you planning to tell the birthday girl you were? That's the part—the thought of you going up to Marlow—that makes me want to track you down and slap you. It'd be well worth the price of a flight. Fuck, I'd even fly coach. So you're lucky that

I don't know where you are. (Which is bananas, by the way. I gave you the goddamn apartment! Live there! It's free! You're free!!)

Also, Orla, this stationery. I mean, what? I'm only using it now so you understand it's in my hands, not hers.

I'm not trying to be a bitch. I ripped up the first version of this letter because it was coming off super mean, and I know you must think it was mean of me to have you thrown out of the party. But I'm a mother, Orla, and that's what mothers do—they don't fuck around when they think someone's hurting their child.

I would think you of all people would get that?!?

(Now I'm thinking that was harsher than anything in the first letter. But my hand is starting to cramp, so whatever. I'm not starting over again.)

There's something else I want to say to you. It's not exactly "sorry." I'm not much of a "sorry" person—I live with no regrets. Unlike Aston. He still never shuts up about Anna, by the way. He'd still be trying to give her family money if we had any. Which we don't, at the moment, but I'm not out of ideas. They think I'm finished, but I'm not. We're waiting to hear back on a project right now, in fact, something that could change everything. I will give her a great life, and then you'll see.

Back to what I wanted to tell you. The way things went down—I see now that it sucked for you. But can I be honest for a second? It was a programming decision. You and I were used to them. The network showed what they wanted to show. People saw what they wanted to see. You didn't wear glasses, but you wore them. We were getting Marlow from you one way or another, and I guess I didn't think the details mattered. I thought the wedding would be like all the things we did together. Another lie we were both okay with.

It's funny—I think I miss you, sometimes. Sometimes I think I miss you a lot. But then I saw you at the party, and your face— it hurt my feelings, Orla. I realized that you've switched it all around in your head. You set this situation in motion when you made a choice for yourself. But now you think you were the victim, or the hero, or both. Even though you—let's not forget—are the one who literally almost killed her. (←Proud of me for using "literally" right?!?)

You're so much smarter than me, but there's one thing I get that you never have. There aren't actually heroes or victims or villains. Not in our story, and probably not in anyone else's. I know you know this deep down: it's all in the edit.

Floss

"How do I know this really says what you say?" Marlow snapped as soon as Honey stopped talking. "Are you fucking with me? Because if you are, I'll make that thing on your face look like the day I was nice to you."

Honey raised her hands slowly, like Marlow was not to be startled. "I'm not fucking with you," she said.

Marlow's temples pulsed. She imagined her mother, a younger version of her, sitting down, writing this letter.

Her mother who was *not* her mother, if Marlow was hearing things right.

But Grace had said nothing about *Floss* not being her biological mother—

Because Marlow had told the designers to ignore her mother's genes

So all that Grace had seen was that her father was not her father.

All she had seen was half of the picture.

And this woman, Orla Cadden? The one who, at the Archive that day, had prompted the eerie search result message: *404, no found*. Marlow was putting it together: Orla had been her mother's friend, her roommate, an extra in Floss's life. And she had come to Marlow's— Which birthday party? Oh, yes. Marlow remembered. The one that Floss had filmed, for the footage that got them

288

to Constellation. It gave Marlow chills to think Orla had been here, just across the lobby, close enough to touch.

That woman was her real mother? Not Floss?

Marlow bunched and smoothed the pages, staring at the script. "Do you know what 404 means?" she asked Honey.

Honey pointed at the letter. "Her? She's 404?" When Marlow nodded, she sighed. "It means she lives in Atlantis," she said. "It isn't far from here. But of course, it's impossible to get to." Marlow must have looked blank. Honey said, "You know about Atlantis, don't you?"

Marlow searched her mind, but nothing came up.

"Well," Honey added, "maybe you don't. They probably don't teach you about it, out there. I suppose it would be counter-productive."

Marlow ran her thumb over the daisies at the top of the letter.

"What are you thinking?" Honey said softly.

The stationery looked different, Marlow thought, than it had on Twenty-First Street, back when it was something stolen. Now she knew it was a gift. It was meant to belong to her. Now she was thinking that, when she was small, she would have loved this paper.

———

Back in Honey's place, at Honey's command, David spent the rest of the afternoon pressing comforting measures on Marlow. He had brought her so many herbal somethings to eat and sip and be rubbed with, she was beginning to feel allergic to herself.

Atlantis. She was turning the word over and over in her head, along with what Honey had said: it was close to here. She didn't know how she would get there, only that she had to. She started packing.

Honey came in to check on her, took one look at her things and her face, and said: "I'll arrange it."

"You don't have to," Marlow began, but stopped when Honey

lunged toward her. It was a violent motion, a frightening one. Somehow, between the lunge and her hand coming up, Honey recalibrated her force. She chucked Marlow on the shoulder in a lighthearted, friendly way, though Marlow noticed the fist she made was so tight, the color drained from her knuckles.

Honey gave a canned half laugh. "Oh," she said, a little too loudly. "Do *you* know how to get into Atlantis? I didn't think so."

She had a guy who could do it, she said, who could take Marlow to Orla. The plan was that the guy would pick her up before sunrise the next day. They would pass at dawn into Atlantis, gliding over the land border without the guard's face even changing, all because the car had been sent by Honey Mitchell, privacy princess. The leaders of Atlantis appreciated her work, even if it was a thin, commercial knockoff of theirs.

The guy came to the apartment that afternoon. He gave Marlow a sober nod as he shook her hand. He handed her a little paper map of the tristate area and traced the path that they would travel with a chapped, thick finger. He told her about contingency plans, about public transportation she could take and where to find it, on the off chance that something went wrong, separating them along the way. When the guy got up to leave, Honey thanked him. "I'm eager for Marlow to see Atlantis," she said. "I've told her how beautiful it is." The second the door closed behind him, she turned back to Marlow. "It's a shithole," she said. "And I say that as someone who grew up without indoor plumbing. But there you go, it's all set. Anything you need for the trip, go out now and get it on me. There's a silicone press of my thumbprint in the drawer next to the stove. Sunglasses on my vanity. My wig closet's in the hallway, third door on the right. Don't worry," Honey said. "Everything will go according to plan."

And as far as Marlow knew, everything else did. But she did not. Instead, she waited in the dark until she was sure that Honey

as asleep. Then she did several things she had never done before, all in a thrilling row:

She found Honey's expensive tequila and poured it, slowly,
over the security system sensor by the front door, the one that
would have told Honey she was going. She watched the sensor's
blue light flicker and die.

She sneaked out.

She made a person on the street stop and meet her eye. It
took several tries, several frustrating episodes of her pleading
and shuffling her feet. Finally, someone paused, looking put
out, and told her where to get the bus.

She saw a bus.

———

She had not gone along with the plan because, shortly after her
Atlantis escort left, Marlow decided to take Honey up on the
shopping. She lifted a pair of sunglasses—a chunky, shapeless
set that hid the whole top third of her face—from a felt-covered
bar in Honey's room. She stood in front of the wig closet, marveling at the strands that rippled from ceiling to floor, quivering like ghosts when she opened the door, and wondered what
Orla Cadden's hair looked like. In the end, she chose a sleek
bob in silver, piled her hair on top of her head, and pulled the
wig down hard.

Marlow was halfway to the block of shops David had directed her to when she realized: she had forgotten the silicone
print of Honey's thumb, the one she could slip on to use her
credit account.

She was on Hudson Street, headed back, when she spotted
Honey. She was doing the strangest thing: walking, instead of
being driven. She was on the opposite side of the street, headed
north, wearing a blinding getup: white sneakers, white wide-
legged pants, white turtleneck, white headscarf, white-framed
aviators. A disguise about as subtle as an extra exclamation point.

Somewhere in Marlow's mind, a soft bell went off.

She took up Honey's route, keeping half a block back an[d] close to the storefronts, so that she could duck into one if Hone[y] turned around. She followed her until Honey turned abrupt[ly] in the middle of a block, and disappeared into a wall.

When Marlow got closer, she saw that Honey had walke[d] through the gate of a garden sprouting out of nowhere. Sh[e] peered down a gravel path that was shaded by curving, whit[e] flowered branches. At the end of the path was a bench th[at] leaned on a fat column of brick. Honey sat down on the benc[h.] She spread her arms and legs, taking up all the space. She too[k] the hard, impatient breath of a person kept waiting.

Marlow circled the block, looking for another entrance, an[d] found a gate on Barrow Street. She spotted the brick colum[n.] By the time she had flattened herself against the other side [of] it, out of Honey's view, Honey was no longer waiting. Marlo[w] could hear her talking to someone. "Just think there's a lot [of] upside here," she was saying. "For both of us."

There was a pause. Then a man spoke up. "I'm grateful yo[u] got in touch with me," he said. "I want to be—cooperative. B[ut] I'm not sure how."

A shiver shot down Marlow's neck, her back, her legs. Sh[e] clapped a hand to her mouth. There, just around the corner fro[m] her, was her husband. Ellis.

"Here's what I'm thinking," Honey said. "When Marlo[w] comes back to Constellation, she'll get pregnant. Then she['ll] breastfeed. Maybe do it all again right afterward, if your bab[y] ratings are good."

"So…" Ellis sounded impatient already.

"So Marlow will be off Hysteryl for the foreseeable futur[e.] She'll need a new sponsor. And I was thinking, if I turn h[er] over to you—" Honey drew in her breath. "Her new spons[or] could be me."

There was a long pause. "You?" Ellis said finally. How strang[e]

Marlow thought as she tried to picture the encounter, that his features were blurred in her mind, impossible to pin down. Whereas Honey's were crystal clear, down to her scar's ragged borders. "You're a privacy advocate," Ellis said slowly, like he found Honey mind-bendingly stupid. "And you'd like me to hand you a major ad campaign on the Constellation Network, which *exists* to promote sharing."

Marlow heard the soft scrape of sneakers on the ground. Honey was on her feet, pitching him, undeterred by his response. "Easy," she said. "All you need is a story, and half of it's played out already. Marlow and I meet, after all these years. We make amends. She sees what I do. She has a revelation. She's moved to consider the merits of privacy."

Ellis scoffed, but said, with audible curiosity: "Then what?"

"In the end, she doesn't go private," Honey said. "She goes back home. She chooses Constellation, but she's been *changed* by what I told her. She feels it's only right her followers—her sixteen-point-three million followers, last I checked—get to make the same choice themselves. So I become her sponsor, and her followers get to hear all about me, all about privacy." There was a small spray of gravel; Marlow pictured Honey turning to look down on Ellis.

"Can you explain to me," Ellis snapped, impatient, "what exactly is in this for me? I mean, what do I really need you for? She won't last out here, with the hunt on. She *will* come home on her own."

"I think you underestimate her," Honey said. "I've spent the last few days with Marlow, and guess what? She likes privacy. She was angry that I filmed her writing down information at the archive. She went completely wild at this off-line party I had last night. I think you're in danger of losing her permanently."

"We are not," Ellis scoffed, and Marlow almost had to laugh. The "we" meant that Ellis had taken Honey's comment to mean that the network was in danger of losing Marlow. Whether he would lose her, too, seemed to him less pressing a question.

"How's it *going* out there, Ellis?" Honey's voice had grown lower, threatening. "Because here's what I see. I've been watching Antidote's stock since Marlow ran. Your company is tanking—because of your wife. How's that playing, at work? What does Liberty think of this whole mess? Let me guess—the merger's on hold? And Hysteryl prescriptions? I hear they're dropping already. People see it didn't fix her crazy after all." Honey whistled, a low, piercing sound. "A shitshow of Broadway proportions, Ellis. And your name's on the marquee."

"The hunt will take care of—" Ellis said.

"The hunt," Honey cried, "is a failure! Two measly tips, in a city of millions. It's obvious: I'm the only one who knows where Marlow is. And as that person, may I just say: I don't think she's coming home on her own."

Marlow held her breath. The sun was setting, sinking into the crevice where she stood. She closed her eyes and let it wash over her, balled herself against the wall.

"You're right about everything," Ellis said. "Except the last part. I don't underestimate Marlow. I estimate her exactly right. have her eggs. Did you think of that? No? Well, she will, soone or later. At the end of the day, she's a woman. She's not going to abandon her children."

Honey snorted. "Eggs are hardly *children*."

"Try making children without them," Ellis said calmly.

Marlow was shaking so hard against the brick, it began t scratch pulls in her sweater. She thought of Ellis with her at th doctor's office. In her physical long-term absence, one form sh had signed said, he was authorized to deal with her frozen egg as he saw fit.

"If you don't take my deal," Honey said, "and I let Marlo go to Atlantis, she will not get back out. You'll never see h again. Your current shitshow? That becomes permanent. B

y the word, and when her driver shows up tomorrow, I'll send
m to your hotel instead."

"She won't go through with Atlantis," Ellis said.

"That is a stupid bet," Honey said. "I told you, it appears that
r biological mother is there. Marlow wants to find her. Biol-
y is a powerful motivator."

"Biology's power to motivate," Ellis said, "is precisely what
n betting on." It seemed to Marlow his voice was fading. He
ust have been walking away. "I'm sure she'd like to meet her
other, or whoever this woman is," he said. "But not at the
pense of meeting her child."

"Ellis," Honey called after him. "What if Marlow doesn't
ant a child?"

The question rang in Marlow's ears as she wrapped her arms
ound herself. What if she didn't? What did it say that she didn't
ow, that she hadn't thought once of her eggs, defrosting on
e opposite coast? They would not keep forever. Shouldn't that
ve made her panic and turn back, as Ellis expected? Mar-
w felt around in the dark well of her thoughts, searching for
stinct. When nothing surfaced, she felt her fury turning on
rself for the first time. She dug her teeth into her lip. *Decide!*
Ellis had warned her, right up front: he liked exploiting the
ws in things. And now he read her thoughts through the wall.

"Maybe she doesn't want them," he said, and Marlow knew,
om his tone, he was smiling. "But she won't be able to tell.
nat's the thing about her, that's how I know she'll fall in line.
e doesn't *know* how to know what she wants. The girl needs
me direction."

CHAPTER NINETEEN

Orla

Gros Islet, St. Lucia
2016

Orla left for St. Lucia on December 23, the night befor Floss and Aston's wedding. In the dark, per the agreeme she had signed.

Amadou drove her right up to the stairs of the little whi plane that was waiting at Teterboro. She struggled out of th door he opened and let him take her arm. They climbed th stairs to the mouth of the plane, their faces and Orla's swo len stomach pressing into the wind. She could feel Amadou concern, his reluctance to let her go. But Orla had to go. Flo had insisted, had cajoled a doctor into agreeing with her, in scribbling a note. "You're be flying private," Floss said to Orl "and you'll have a doctor with you 24/7. You'll be totally sa and besides, like, who says pregnant women can't fly this lat Women can do anything."

After Amadou helped her step onto the aircraft, after the do

d been closed, Orla sat and nodded while the pilot showed her
e map. It was Orla's first time to the Caribbean, and she had
nagined all the countries bunched together. But she saw, as the
an pointed to St. Lucia, that the one she was headed to was
rther than she thought, almost all the way to South America.
iter, she would be certain that this—the long distance—was
hy Floss had chosen the island.

———

rla hadn't said yes right away. She had ignored Floss and Aston
r weeks, even though they wrote her daily: short, pleading
xts that also asked after her health, and long, pleading emails
out their metamorphosis into grounded people, about the
ostairs room they were saving, in case. Floss attached a photo
ice, and Orla couldn't resist. The room was tiny, and already
render. It had a round stained-glass window with a rose carved
to its middle.

Aston had been right: the baby was a girl. A nurse had slipped
and called it "she" at Orla's six-month checkup. "I'm so
rry," she had gasped, looking like she might cry. "But how do
u feel, now that you know?" She wiped the goo from Orla's
omach. "A girl is wonderful, isn't it?" Orla had nodded. But
she felt was fear, and an understanding of why she had de-
ed this moment. It made everything real.

Randomly, Floss and Aston sent her pink peonies that same
ernoon. No message on the card, just their names. Orla shoved
e glass cube to one end of the counter and set her laptop down.
e thought she might Facebook-message Danny. She was think-
g she should tell him the truth. Then she made the mistake of
oking at some new pictures he'd posted. Being from Mifflin,
e got the logic behind them: it was his penance for spending
ne in her fancy world, acting this much like a hick. Orla saw
at he had bought a pickup truck and raised it high off its tires.

The rear windshield had a decal that said, "Jack 'Em Up—F[...]
Girls Can't Jump."

"No," she said aloud when she saw it. That was the end [...]
telling Danny.

Polly sent her notes on Orla's book by messenger. Red in[...]
filled the pages—brutal double-circles, incredulous questio[...]
marks. Orla's eyes swam. She slid the papers back into their o[...]
ange envelope. She turned the envelope over and saw that the[...]
was another piece of mail stuck in its seam: her rent check f[...]
the next month.

Downstairs, the super, Manny, was sitting with his son, Linu[...]
who had just come home from school. Orla watched the bo[...]
eyes flit down toward her breasts as she asked why her che[...]
had been returned.

"Because your roommate bought the apartment." Mann[...]
smirked, his lip twisting up over a graying incisor. "How [...]
you not know this?"

I just didn't want you to worry about rent and stuff, Flo[...]
wrote when Orla asked if it was true. **Consider it yours f[...]
life.** *"I,"* Orla thought. *Not "we."* She had suspected, the mi[...]
ute she stepped onto Pineapple Street, that it was Floss's mon[...]
behind this. Renting big houses in Brooklyn, buying dinge[...]
up Chelsea units—Floss had been forcing down free vodka a[...]
borrowing dresses for years now, acting like she wasn't payi[...]
any attention to what she was doing. But Floss was always pa[...]
ing attention. She had been saving up for just the right thing[...]

No matter what you decide, Floss added, when Orla did[...]
respond.

OK, Orla finally wrote. She walked down the hall and look[...]
into Floss's room for the first time since the movers had be[...]
there. It was so big, and she had been there before Floss. W[...]
hadn't she ever thought to take it for herself?

Like Aston said, Floss went on. **Your family.**

Orla's thumbs couldn't help themselves. **It's you're.**

I think its your

It's IT'S and it's YOU'RE

I know I'm just fucking with you now

Orla didn't know what to say next. Floss was starting another
ought, her little gray text bubble wavering, disappearing, re-
pearing. When she couldn't watch anymore, Orla went back
the lobby. Manny was gone, but Linus was there, spinning
owly on his father's stool.

"I want to get the wall taken down in my apartment, the one
put up to make it a two-bedroom," she said to him. "Do you
now what your dad tells people for that?"

Linus reached into a slot in the desk. He passed her a business
rd. "This guy," he said. "I think it's twelve hundred dollars."

"Oh, no." Orla shook her head. "I paid that up front."

"Yeah." Linus smiled ruefully. "They charge you twelve hun-
ed to put it up, twelve hundred to take it back down."

"You've got to be fucking kidding me," Orla said, then,
orry." She had forgotten for a minute that he was just a kid.
Hey," she said, changing her tone and leaning over, tipping
r cleavage forward. "Completely unrelated—could I borrow
ur dad's ax?"

An hour later, the wall was gone. It lay on the floor in pieces
at had chimed improbably as they fell. A jagged edge remained
ong the walls and ceiling, hinting at what had been there. The
r was misty with flecks of drywall, bouncing in the sunlight
at hit Orla's living room furniture—her couch, her rug—for
e first time ever. Everything was even more worn and cheap-
oking than she thought.

Her phone buzzed. Orla pulled down the silk Hermès scarf
e had been using as a makeshift mask, wiped her fingers on

her sweatpants, and picked it up. A column of messages fro
Floss, delivered while Orla hacked at the wall, was waiting.

**Don't want to overstep but I thought of a cool name, if
it's a girl. Wanna hear**

Marlow

Because it has all the letters of your name

Like you'd always be with her

Just a suggestion, of course

Orla began to cry. She cried the way she hadn't since sl
started living with roommates. Her weeping echoed off th
walls of the newly empty apartment. It came to Orla sudden
the key that had eluded her all her life. There was only one tri
to making a choice, and that was doing it fast.

I like Marlow, Orla texted back. **And the baby is a girl.**
Then, before she could think better of it:

Actually

Can you come over?

———

The time between then and now had been a blur of paperwo
and meetings and consent. Over and over, Orla consented. Sl
signed all the standard contracts surrendering her parental righ
and she signed plenty of other things that had been drawn
just for them. When she got to the agreement that called f
her to stay inside for the last two months of her pregnancy, O

looked up from her place at the table, where she sat alone. "This seems intense," she said.

Every face on the other side—Floss and Aston's legal team ran six deep—smiled. Someone patiently explained. It was presumed that the three of them would do a magazine cover after Marlow was born, with an exclusive tell-all on their "extraordinary arrangement," as Melissa had them calling it. A stray paparazzi shot of Orla would complicate the negotiations. They had been lucky that there hadn't been any so far.

So Orla stayed inside. She confronted Polly's notes and worked on adding to her manuscript. When she ran out of things to do and went down to get her junk mail, she tilted her head against the front door's glass and checked for Mrs. Salgado. Orla never left anymore, and neither did Anna's mother. She just sat in her lawn chair and knit. Sometimes, when the wind blew down Twenty-First Street, the end of her work would lift and flutter across the door, so Orla could see it from the lobby. The scarf that Mrs. Salgado was making was coming along nicely.

——

On the plane to St. Lucia, Orla's pretending to sleep finally turned into sleeping. She woke to the doctor gently shaking her arm. She blinked her eyes open and looked at him. He was younger than she expected, maybe in his early forties, tall, Indian, with a neat, trim waist and dark eyes that he held politely at half-mast as he roused her.

"Orla," he said. "I'm Dr. Kodali. Do you mind if I check your vitals? And I'd like to have you stand, for a minute, to help your circulation." He offered his arm formally, with a hint of a smile, like he was asking her to dance.

Soon, they were on the ground, saying goodbye to the pilot, descending to a waiting town car. It sped off as soon as Dr. Kodali pulled the door shut. The car clung to the tight curves that wound up the island's mountains. The baby shifted inside Orla, following the pull of the wheels.

They moved, after a long while, back toward the ground, and passed the long lanes to several brand-name resorts. The driver braked his way down a hill. Banana tree fronds brushed the roof of the car. When the trees parted, they were in the brick driveway of a cream-colored, Spanish-style building. A woman in a perfectly pressed white polo emerged and got Orla's bag from the trunk, then Dr. Kodali's. Carrying the bags as if they weighed nothing, she skirted the blue-tiled fountain and led them down a footpath, toward a villa set apart from the resort's main house. The woman spoke quietly the whole time. Orla could tell that she was imparting information about the resort and how to enjoy it, but she couldn't hear a word and didn't think she would need it, anyway. She was under strict orders to remain indoors or on her balcony, resting, and to call Dr. Kodali first if she needed to go anywhere.

The woman stopped under the bulb that lit the villa's vestibule. She handed each of them a key. Dr. Kodali's door was to the left, Orla's to the right.

"Second floor there is a hot tub on each of your verandas," the woman whispered.

"You can't use that," Dr. Kodali said to Orla.

Orla nodded. "I know." She had not yet turned her phone back on. She asked what time it was.

"11:30 p.m.," the woman said. "One hour ahead of New York."

Orla thanked her and touched her key to the door. Back in the city, she thought, Floss and Aston would be going to sleep. Their wedding was scheduled for nine in the morning, with a brunch reception to follow. Getting married first thing on a Friday, and they couldn't have been happier. Floss had been flushed with pleasure when she told Orla the news at her ultrasound: a cable network had agreed to air the wedding live. Flosston was back on camera.

———

The drapes in the villa were blackout, and Orla was never not tired now. She might have slept right through the wedding if not for a calf muscle spasm. She looked at the clock on the nightstand, heaving, as the pain started to fade, and saw that the wedding was due to begin in exactly seven minutes.

The gummy bears in the villa's minibar were eleven dollars, but she figured she was celebrating. She grabbed them and sat down on the bed in her bra, resting the bag on her planetary middle. Her skin was stretched so taut it was translucent. It seemed there were a thousand veins just beneath its surface. The only thing more unbelievable than a life growing large inside her, Orla thought, was the idea of it sliding out of her body, leaving her one person again.

She turned on the television, one of those low-definition models that only hotels still seemed to have, and found the channel. Two anchors, the male and female version of each other—thin, tanned, tawny highlights, teeth so white they were almost blue—sat in high canvas chairs at the back of a tall, open space. Behind them, people in black bustled by, looking frantic, while people in furs and glitter ambled toward their seats, pretending not to realize when they sashayed into frame.

The first thing that told Orla something was wrong was the straw. There were bales of hay stacked everywhere. She couldn't locate the ornate curves of the Plaza ballroom Floss had shown her weeks before. "My theme is retro holiday chic," Floss had declared, circling her mouse over the massive chandelier. "Red and green and gold and crystal and brocade. Very Jackie Kennedy holiday White House party. The dress is super Jackie, don't you think?" Floss's dress had a bodice so sheer, she had to have her stomach waxed. There was a time when Orla would have pointed this out, but instead she had only nodded. She was never not tired.

A minute later, the anchors identified themselves—Gianna

and Chip—and trilled that they were "broadcasting live from The Foundry in Long Island City, New York." Orla stopped chewing the stale green bear between her teeth and checked her phone. There was no word from Floss or Aston, but something must have gone wrong—a paparazzi invasion at the Plaza, perhaps, or a burst pipe at the last minute.

On-screen, Gianna's eyes were watery and red. "We understand that this wedding will coincide with a major announcement from the couple." She sniffed, then added, "My apologies to all of you at home—I'm allergic to hay. We didn't know there would be hay."

"Indeed we didn't, Gianna," Chip chortled. "What are we thinking here, about this theme? Farmhouse chic?"

"I guess probably yes, Chip," Gianna said, wheezing.

The show cut to commercial. Orla texted Floss: **Just saw you're at The Foundry. Hope everything's OK**. She paused—she wanted to add a warm wish of some sort, but what was the thing to say to someone whose wedding was mostly being watched by stay-at-home moms on their second coffee? **Break a leg and enjoy every second**, she wrote, feeling generic and distant. The dialogue told her the message had been read, but Floss did not respond.

Orla peed, and decided while washing her hands that she had to pee again. By the time she came out, the network was playing a pretaped package about "Flosston's high-drama road to forever." Then the montage faded and was replaced by a live shot of the empty altar: a crude wooden structure, also filled with straw.

"We're interrupting our package," said Gianna with the air of a war reporter, "because there's something happening here at The Foundry, where the wedding of Aston Clipp and Floss Natuzzi is just about to begin." She paused. "A small horse—a pony—"

"I believe it's a donkey," Chip shrieked. "Donkey!"

"A donkey is being led down the aisle here," Gianna went on.

The camera whirled. A heavyset woman led a donkey, gray and groomed, down the aisle by a red leash.

"I am," Chip said, "*so* confused, Gianna."

Gianna put a finger to her earpiece. "I'm being told that the donkey is being followed by an ox and several sheep."

"Yes, we can see them now," Chip said. "There they are. So perhaps this is a zoo theme?"

"*Adore* that," Gianna sighed.

The bag of gummy bears crinkled under Orla's tailbone as she leaned forward, trying to figure out for herself what was happening.

"And now we see the groom proceeding down the aisle," Chip said. The camera followed Aston approaching the altar. He was wearing a long-sleeved tunic that fell to his knees and laced up the chest. It was made of something that looked like burlap. On his feet were simple brown sandals.

Gianna flipped the cue card in her hand and looked at Chip. "We were told that Aston would be in a Gucci tux," she said. "I'm not sure what's…"

She trailed off as a whooshing gasp went through the crowd. Chip and Gianna both raised themselves out of their chairs, trying to see what was happening. Gianna looked uncertainly at someone off camera while Chip hopped up, took a few steps out of frame, and quickly returned, panting. As he climbed back into his chair, the cuff of his pants rode up, exposing his leg above his sock. Orla saw his real skin—it was pasty, half the color of his made-up face and hands. "This is unbelievable," Chip said, breathless. "Even for *this* couple, this is a stunt beyond— Hold on, we're working on getting you all a shot here—"

Orla's heart began to pound. The photographers, who had been behaving at the edges of the ceremony, were now rushing the center aisle, blocking the shot. Orla saw the broad, gray-suited shoulders of security moving into the frame. They swept the paparazzi away. Finally, her mouth falling open, Orla saw Floss at the back of the aisle.

She was lit from behind like an angel, and she wasn't wearing her slutty dress. Instead she wore a plain white column of silk, a braided gold rope around its empire waistline. Her veil was thick and floor-length, opaque, bird's egg blue. On her feet were the same type of sandals Aston wore.

Floss took a step and all the fabric moved, shifting to reveal that when she came forward, her stomach came first. Her stomach was high and round and full. Like Orla's.

Forgetting her state, Orla leaped to her feet and stumbled to the screen. She put her face right up to it. The glass pixels made her eyes water. Could it be distorting things, this shitty TV?

Then she heard Gianna say, "Folks, it's unbelievable. Floss Natuzzi has somehow managed to keep from the entire world that she is with child, and now the theme of this wedding, I finally get it: it's the Christmas story of Jesus's birth." She laughed. "No pressure, kid!"

"And guess what, Gianna." Chip waved another cue card in the air. "Sounds like our bosses were in on the whole thing, those scamps. I'm now being told what the major announcement we've been waiting on is: Floss and Aston will return to television this winter with the brand-new docuseries, *Flosston With Child*."

Orla thought she must be hallucinating as a graphic bubbled up in the corner of the screen: Aston and Floss, alien-airbrushed, a pink faceless bundle between them.

Orla backed toward the bed and collapsed on its edge, slid down to the floor.

On-screen, Floss proceeded down the aisle, hands folded beneath the round of her stomach. She nodded beatifically at people as they applauded—they were *applauding*, Orla realized. When Floss reached the altar, Aston picked up her hands, taking a moment to look lovingly down at her belly. Craig stepped between them, grinning. This was the only detail that remained intact from the version of the wedding Orla knew: Craig would officiate. Melissa should have been in the front row. But Orla saw, as the camera swept the scene, that Melissa wasn't there. She could spot the seat-filler summoned to take Melissa's chair—an unfamiliar, fidgety blonde with too much eye makeup and too little skirt—from where she was, two thousand miles away.

"Fuck all of you," Orla yelled. She threw her empty bottle of minibar water at the screen. It hit the bride square in the nose. Floss smiled.

Orla turned her back on the TV and seized her phone. Twitter was exploding. In the midst of the swelling pile of drivel, a real-looking headline caught Orla's eye.

THIS JUST IN: FLOSS IS ALSO WRITING A BOOK.

She clicked on it and waited. "Come on come on come on," she muttered, shaking her phone.

A press release filled the screen of her phone. At the top was the cozy logo of a publishing house. "Floss Natuzzi, Reality Star, Influencer and Mother-to-Be, to Pen Book of Essays and 'Life Wisdom,'" the top line trumpeted.

The seven-figure deal had been brokered by Polly Cummings.

The tan phone on Orla's nightstand rang so loudly, she dropped her cell on the duvet. She picked the rattling handset up, trembling. "Hello?"

"It's Melissa." Orla could hear that she had been crying. "They only told me this morning, and I quit right away. They're monsters."

"But why are they doing this?" Orla put her mouth right on the phone. "Why?"

"It's the network," Melissa said. "Craig the dickless wonder—

he laid the whole thing out for me. Months ago, Floss and Aston went to the network. They begged for another chance. They asked what it would take. They *brainstormed*. A reinvention. A new chapter. A family. A baby. They were impatient. They wouldn't listen to Craig about adoption, or working with Floss's, whatever, condition. Your baby was right there, they said. They said your baby was *ready*." Melissa blew a bitter breath into the phone. "And then, Polly," she said. "I hate telling you this part. They brought Polly in on it."

"What do you mean?" Orla's eyes slid to the screen. Craig was stepping back. Floss and Aston were kissing.

Melissa sighed. "Polly knew a book by Floss would make fucking millions," she said. "She would have done whatever they asked. And they figured if *you* thought you were finally going to get to be an author, you'd be more likely—to go along with it. So Polly helped them. She said she'd pretend to represent you. She set you up. Oh, God," Melissa whimpered. "I need you to go on your laptop right now and email me what you signed. *Everything* you signed. Okay?"

"But I did what they wanted," Orla said. "They got everything they wanted. Why are they pretending she's the pregnant one?"

"Oh, that." Melissa laughed. Orla heard what Melissa wished in that laugh: that her whole life had been different. That she never met Orla, never got into publicity, never liked English more than math. "Because the network didn't *love* the storyline," Melissa said. "They didn't love the idea of someone else's baby. They told Floss and Aston to fix it. And as you see, they did."

Orla gripped the phone. "So she'll never know," she whispered. "They'll never tell her she's mine."

Melissa's breath was ragged on the other end. "Oh, I'm sure *that's* not true," she said. "It's just TV. I'm sure in real life…"

Orla hung up. She put on the only shoes that still fit her. She lugged her suitcase to the door.

It took Dr. Kodali a moment to answer her knock. When he did, he was tying a hotel robe over a pair of swim trunks. Water rolled off his shins and pooled on the burnt-orange tile. "I apologize for the delay," he said. "I was testing out the hot tub. Is everything all right?"

"We're going home," Orla told him. "Now."

———

People asked, after awful days that split time, turning present into long-gone past overnight, "Where were you when it happened?" When the first plane hit the World Trade Center, Orla was in first period, ninth-grade geometry. "A shame," said the teacher, squinting, bent over a beige computer that faced away from the students. "Sounds like a little two-seater ran into a building in New York. Or something. Now, where'd we leave off yesterday? Prisms."

With the Spill, things were different. The question would always be: "What were you looking at?"

For Orla, it was the microwave. She remembered the last time she saw it before: 6:17 p.m. She had just gotten home from St. Lucia. She was sitting on the couch, watching television. All that seemed to qualify as news, it being Christmas Eve, were recaps of Floss and Aston's wedding. The reveal of Floss's belly. Aston's crazy toast: he said, with a verve that made him seem unhinged, that he and Floss were "reclaiming the story of Jesus's birth—we make it hot. We make it sexy." At that, Craig clapped him on the back and took the mic.

As Orla was watching, her phone rang on her bed. When she heard the rippling chime that meant she had a new voice mail, she made herself get up. Her impossibly low-slung stomach rubbed along the tops of her thighs. She thought about the way Floss had danced in the clips from the wedding. She had jumped right off the ground during "Shout." Had no one found that suspicious, with her presenting as any-moment-now? Had no one at the wedding ever been pregnant before?

Orla's voice mail was from the bride. Floss spoke over the sound of muffled conversation, Aston talking to someone in the merry voice he used to make service workers think he was like them. "Just thinking of you," Floss said. "We missed you at the wedding. Did you watch? I'm not sure if you could get it in St. Lucia." She paused and coughed. "If you did, you might have noticed we went in a different direction."

Might! Orla thought. *Have noticed!*

Floss went on. "The network and Mason, I dunno. They got weird at the last minute. They said we needed to do it like this or else it'd look like we exploited you. *I* didn't want to do it. I mean, did you see that belly? I cried. Who wants to look fat on their wedding day?" Floss sniffled. "Anyway, I hope you're not pissed, and I hope you're having fun at the resort. You're probably getting a luscious prenatal massage or something. It's snowing in New York. It's freezing. We just got to our suite at the St. Reege, and I'm wearing like the biggest sweater. All right. Give Marlow a kiss from Mommy."

Orla went to her window. Floss was right. It was snowing. The air was thick with lazy flakes. Orla leaned on the windowsill, the edge of the air-conditioning unit pressing into her belly, and watched the people on Eighth Avenue, hustling with their collars up. She caught the sight of her reflection and was startled by all the space behind her. She kept forgetting her old fake wall was gone; she could see all the way back to the kitchen, with its ghoulish overhead light. The apartment felt hollowed out. There had been so much in here, not long ago: people and their shoes and their phones and their cords and their food and their fights and their crying. Floss's blankets pooled carelessly on the couch. Aston's strawberry shortcake bars growing frost in the freezer. Craig's gym bag blocking the door. Melissa's laptop hogging the counter. The free things from publicists and the wilting bouquets from asskissers and the fridge full of drawings from fans, mailed to the building or passed through the barricade. The television—always on, so often blaring their own voices back at them.

"It's kind of sad," Orla said out loud, remembering that she should talk to the baby. "After what she tried to pull, she still thinks she's gonna be your mommy."

Tomorrow would be Christmas, a day of clear sidewalks and out-of-office messages. There was no chance that Orla could find a photographer or get a blogger on the phone. But she had decided that, the day after Christmas, she would find someone— she'd throw herself at Ingrid's feet, if she had to—and she would tell them everything. *Due any second! A girl. Marlow. What's that? I know! I had no idea Floss was pregnant, either! I guess we'll see how that turns out.*

Let them trash and harass her. Let them sic their lawyers. Orla wasn't afraid. She knew the truth: they were nothing to be afraid of. Just a few people who had mistaken their small dreams for big ones.

She slipped her phone into the pocket of her sweatshirt, lay down on the couch, and closed her eyes.

She never knew how long she slept, exactly. The sound of banging on her door woke her up sometime later, and the first thing she saw, lying on her side, was the faraway microwave clock. The shape of its numbers was off, vaguely unsettling. Her first thought was that there had been some sort of outage. But the lights were still on.

She yelled to the person knocking that she'd be right there and waddled over, her bloated feet leaving prints in the drywall dust from when she knocked down the wall. It reminded her of the flour that had been all over 6D that first day of shooting. No matter what she did, it wasn't coming up.

Before she reached the door, she glanced again at the microwave. The shape of its hard-edged, little green numbers stopped her in her tracks.

The time said 6:66.

CHAPTER TWENTY

Marlow

New York, New York
'051

Marlow stayed in the park until it was empty and nearly dark, and she still didn't know what she felt about her eggs. But she figured out something else: she was finished taking direction.

So she sneaked out and found the bus while Honey slept in the next room, while Ellis slept uptown. She didn't know how their deal turned out, and surprised herself by not really caring. The farther she got from Honey's apartment, the smaller they seemed in her mind.

The bus took her to a train. The train took her out of New York, under the river and through a nameless stretch of New Jersey, all graffiti-chalked cliffs and buildings with the glass punched out of them. She wore Honey's silver wig, even though it was the middle of the night, and she was glad that she did when she looked to her right and saw, somewhere around the middle of the state, a hologram billboard for the hunt. There was a photo of her that must have been the one the girl at the Archive took. There was an update saying that the grand prize had been tripled. The bright ad played between two notices of wanted criminals, as if whoever programmed these things had been smart enough to see there was no difference.

Marlow rode to the place where the tracks dried up, disappearing into a weedy endcap station marked Absecon. Then she started walking. She traced the route—south and east from New York toward what people called "the Shore"—from the little paper map the guy Honey knew had given her. She didn't need the map for long. The formidable concrete horseshoe that wrapped around Atlantis was everywhere, impossible to miss. The basin of the U-shaped wall wrapped around Atlantis on land, sealing it off from the rest of the state. The wall's long sides extended hundreds of yards into the ocean, maritime borders slicing right through the waves. A smattering of buoys bobbed between the ends of the U. Just beyond them, small, mint-colored boats drifted. ATLANTIS COAST GUARD was painted on their sides.

The towers inside the wall were clustered together, the ancient logos at their tops mostly cracked or fallen away. Marlow glanced at the people around her. It was easy to tell who also meant to sneak over the border. Their faces were carefully neutral, their eyes firmly on the ground. Their paces were prim and measured, engineered to deflect all attention. Marlow fell into step next to a couple, quick for their age. They looked to be eighty-something and were fusing into one set of looks, both of them wide-hipped with brown skin and thick white hair. When the man nodded at Marlow, she noticed the front of his cap. Bars of every color and, in yellow stitching, KOREA II. Together but not, Marlow and the couple aimed themselves at the border wall's right side, where it curved and stretched out into the sea.

Ventnor, the last town before the wall, was a strange mix of vacation kitsch and border-town glumness. The concrete hotels on Marlow's right were streaked with rust. Bright beach owels hung from their balconies. On her left were tiny booths with flimsy plastic pulled over their wares for the night. She got closer to one of the booths and peered inside, squinting into the light of the bare security bulb. There were shot glasses and Christmas-tree ornaments painted with this still-new American border, the sand and the sea and the wall rising over them, casting a long, dour shadow. There were T-shirts that said, in artless printing, TELL MY GIRL DON'T BOTHER MESSAGING—GONE TO ATLANTIS. There were ballpoint pens filled with water. Inside them, a tiny guard with a rifle and neon-yellow sunglasses floated back and forth. Marlow whirled round suddenly, spooked by the suggestion. But the only uniformed man for miles seemed to be concentrating hard on not seeing her. When their eyes met at random, he turned and took several steps in the other direction.

The wall was a block away when Marlow and the couple she was following found themselves in the dark. Marlow looked up to see the illumidrone that had been bouncing over her head, lighting her path, idling a hundred feet up. When she took another step toward the wall, it thrust forward once, then fell back as if it had struck something. It turned and flew away, back inland. Marlow stood there, letting her eyes adjust to the miserly gleam of the streetlamp, and waited to see what the couple would do next. They paused, then continued toward a shack at the end of the street. Marlow couldn't read the sign on it—until, suddenly, a light over the shack turned on and blinked three times, slowly, before going off again. Her eyes put it together in the flashes: The Drinks-at-Dawn Express, the sign said. A booze cruise. The couple hurried toward it, glancing around. Marlow did, too.

A woman in a wetsuit stood behind the counter. She looked alert and pleasant, as if it was the middle of the day and she was conducting normal business. She held her palm out. Marlow wasn't sure how much cash she handed over. It was dark,

which meant the woman couldn't count it, either. She slipped i
somewhere out of sight, beneath the splintering ledge she leane
against. "Meet on the beach at Dudley Avenue," she said. "Tw
blocks that way. Wait until it's almost light."

Marlow killed an hour with her back against the rear wall o
the stand, dozing and watching seagulls collect dropped pizz
crusts. When the sky turned a thin, easy gray, she stood up an
went to the beach.

The boat, moored several yards into the waves, looked like
life-size version of a toy: pale blue and white, plasticky, with
skull-and-crossbones flag hanging flaccid above the cabin an
a whiskered pirate, eye patch and all, painted on the side. "Arr
You Ready?" the pirate asked in a sloppily drawn thought bub
ble.

Marlow took her shoes off and hurried down to where a sma
group had gathered around the woman in the wetsuit. Th
woman was gesturing expansively at the boat and the life jacke
in her hand and not actually talking about either of them. Sh
was telling them, instead, how they would cross. The Drinks
at-Dawn Express would take them straight out to a sandbar. A
boat bringing supplies to Atlantis from a British shipping barg
would pass by precisely twenty minutes after they dropped an
chor at the sandbar. "We'll get on the boat," she said. "Quickl
It'll continue on to Atlantis and dock there, near a restaurar
that overlooks the marina. I'll lead you into the basement of th
restaurant, where you'll change into standard waitstaff uniform
The owners of the restaurant, they used to live in Connecticu
Never got over missing their parents, their brothers and sister:
They've been helping us for years." She looked around the grou|
"After that, you're on your own."

A Jeep rumbled their way in the sand, its driver uniforme
and bleary-eyed. VENTNOR BEACH BORDER PATROL
the lettering on the door said. Sighting it, the woman swivele
her hips and whooped. "Now, who's ready to get *faced*?" sh

hrieked. "Sorry about that," she mumbled when the vehicle had assed. "Last thing: the fine print. I assume you all know this if ou're here, but I have to say it anyway. The US State Department forbids travel to or from the territory now called Atlantis, ormerly known as Atlantic City, New Jersey. You are aware hat you're here to do something illegal. You are about to cross nto a foreign country with which America has no diplomatic elations. If you're caught over here, you'll go to jail. If you're aught over there, you'll never get back home." She flicked her ead over her shoulder at the wall, a few hundred yards down ne beach. "Look how far out it goes," she said, and Marlow did, ollowing the slab as far as she could see into the water. "And et," the woman said. She smiled at them, and Marlow saw that ne had a gold tooth, like the pirate on the boat. "And yet," the voman repeated. "We can still get around it, can't we? That's ne problem with a wall. It has to end somewhere."

On the boat, Marlow stood at a deck railing, holding one f the cocktails they were all pretending to drink. As the light ame up, she pulled off the wig and dropped it into the waves. he checked to see if anyone recognized her. But each passener was staring resolutely at the sky as they gripped their giant lasses, pretending to be lost in the sunrise. For them, it was art of the ruse.

But Marlow really was mesmerized. She watched the colors of ne sunrise bleed upward from the water. She pictured her father a his room. She pictured her mother ugly-crying over Marw with her good side turned to the camera, and even though ne meant the thought to be nasty, she found herself, suddenly, iissing Floss so much that she almost sank to her knees. She vondered if Ellis had broken down and called Honey, if he'd elt doubt molding in his airtight analysis of Marlow and deided to take the deal after all. She pictured Honey in her pajaias, flapping around her gorgeous lobby—what did the driver iean, Marlow hadn't shown up? Her mother and husband and famous acquaintance—they would all be thinking the same thing. Where could Marlow possibly be, besides where she'd been told to go?

Here. Here, cutting through choppy, silt-filled water, away from all of them and closer to the truth. Marlow had been taught that being watched put food on the table, that there wasn't a better way to live. But she had seen, on the sidewalks of New York, all the happy nobodies—people whose days weren't built around lengthening the trail of attention spans floating behind them. They were paunchy and muttering and somehow more alive, and they made Marlow feel sorry for Floss and Ellis, with their endless performing, and Honey, with her army of dark-hearted disciples. They might have had all the followers, but they were never finished chasing.

Marlow was done being looked at. Now she was doing the looking, and finally seeing things differently. She found, in the sunrise, all the colors the pills had kept from her for years: a shade of orange she loved. A yellow that reminded her of when it was her favorite. A pink that might have been fine after all. She was hearing something, too, in the space her device used to fill: a brand-new voice inside her head, telling her to keep going.

She leaned over the boat's railing, into the spray, and listened to the voice. She was almost positive it sounded like herself.

CHAPTER TWENTY-ONE

Orla

New York, New York
2016

Orla followed her super, Manny, off the elevator, toward his place, 1A. "Most of the building is gone for Christmas," he said. "So we've got enough space for anyone who doesn't have a watch. I think it's better we stick together, as a precaution. Seems like it might be the whole block."

"And none of the clocks are working?" Orla said. "Yours say the same thing, too?"

Manny nodded. "If it plugs in, it's fucked."

She remembered her phone then, patting for it, and slid it out of her belly pocket. "But we can use—" she said, trailing off when she saw the screen. Her background—a photo of her and Floss from the year before—had been replaced by a strange, fuzzy graphic. The screen was filled with white, rounded-corner squares—a white padded wall, Orla realized, like the ones lining cells in mental institutions. There was no time, no date, no prompts. Just the white squares, keeping them locked out instead of in. "Look at this," she said, and showed Manny.

He grimaced. "Yeah. They all look like that." He opened the door. When they went in, Orla noticed he locked it behind them.

Manny's kitchen gave her déjà vu. It was the same as hers had been her first two years in the building, before men came through and updated it: yellow light even worse than the hard white that came after, cabinets with faux-pine picture frame edges.

Orla took a few steps in. There were about a dozen of her neighbors in the apartment, huddled around the kitchen table, shifting to make room for each other on the burgundy sofa. Sunk into the center of the couch was the angry old woman who spent her days on the lobby's leather bench, jabbering at the doormen. "Punks, or some sort of glitch," she muttered now, to no one in particular. "Talk about an overreaction."

Leaning against the green speckled counter was the fifty-something man from the second floor, the one whose Boston terrier carried rolled newspapers in his mouth. "Exactly," the man said. "I lived downtown breathing dead people for a year. So you'll excuse me for thinking not knowing the *time* is not the end of the world."

In the living room were the children from the fourth floor, a boy and a girl whose ages were indiscernible to Orla and whose bright toys were always splitting into pieces in the elevator. They were staring at the television—which, Orla saw, her pulse picking up, had the same white squares as her phone. The children's mother twisted around to look at her. She was wearing the same candy-cane pajamas as her kids. "It's been like this for a while," she said. "But we're keeping it on just in case."

The Latin, muscled guy who used to leave for work the same time as Orla was helping Manny's son, Linus, move the Christmas tree farther into the corner, so that it took up less of the room. Orla nodded at Linus, but he wouldn't meet her eye. She thought it might have had to do with him being spooked by her giant breasts, until he raised his face and she saw that his eyes were red from crying. He was scared.

Manny came over then. He put his hands on his boy's shoulders. "So we don't know much," he called out to the room. "The electric's still working, but someone's messing with the time somehow. Everything's got this six-six-six. The internet's gone, the TV's gone. All sorts of shit is just…frozen. No one's had any luck with their phone, right?"

They all tried, screen-punching hungrily, and shook their heads. No.

"Lucky for you all," he said cheerily, "this old bastard's still got a landline. I'll get the cops over here to check it out." He took the phone off the wall and listened, then frowned and put it back quietly.

"Miss," a man said softly, behind Orla. "Would you like to sit?"

Orla turned around. In a wingback chair with a doily draped over it sat a broad-shouldered white man. He wore silver-rimmed glasses over his calm, wide-set eyes. Beneath his rumpled white shirt, Orla could see the collar of a yellowing undershirt and pale brown chest hair curling over it. It took her a moment to place him: he was the Ukrainian man from the penthouse, the one whose deck they had borrowed long ago, Floss emboldened by her perfect ass, and Orla emboldened by Floss. She thanked him and took his seat.

There was a weak knock. Everyone turned. Manny looked through the peephole. He was already shaking his head as he opened the door. "I'm sorry," Orla heard him say. "I gotta think of people in the building."

"I understand," a woman's voice replied. "But just for a while, to get warm. I live on Staten Island. I can't get home.

Everything's shut down. The buses, the trains. The tunnels, th
bridges. No one's allowed on the roads."

"Is that true?" someone whispered behind Orla. "Jesus."

"I can't do it," Manny said.

"Please."

The woman sounded familiar. Orla stood and shuffled right
trying to see who she was. She saw a puff of dyed hair abov
a fleece headband. She went to the door and touched Manny'
shoulder.

Mrs. Salgado watched her, blank-faced. Expecting nothing

"She's with me," Orla said.

Manny curled his lip at her. "We can't get started with that,
he said. But then he sighed and ignored the hot gaze of his wife
He let Anna's mother in.

———

Together, they stayed up all night, waiting for something t
change.

Manny went out when the sun came up. He came back wit
sliced bread, peanut butter, and bits of disorienting news, gath
ered from cops and jumpy cashiers making change by hand. Th
police all used the same term: multipronged hack. GPS signal
they said, had been snuffed out. All the major cable and phon
and internet companies were ravaged, backups upon backup
defeated. One cop told Manny that in a sleepy town upstat
where some people still used a local web provider, there wer
still a few people online, trying all the websites they could thin
of and finding them broken and gone.

The power grid—that was the part that scared everyone, be
cause it meant they were dealing with artists. The hackers ha
found a way to tweak the electrical current. That was why eve
old and dusty plugged-in things were no longer counting mo
ments right. Manny heard that the NYPD, the FBI, the mayo
and the governor—they had all set up shop at Grand Central

beneath the old clock with its four opal faces. And Mrs. Salgado was right: no one was going anywhere. Stoplights' timers were fried. Trains were dark and useless. Planes were either grounded or circling, waiting for air traffic control to triple-check their paper maps.

The streets were mostly empty, Manny said. People were hunkering down the way they might have anyway, considering it was still snowing. But he admitted, with lots of shrugging to keep from alarming them, that he had skipped the closest grocery store because of "just a little looting."

Then the lights went out. The room became the same blue-gray of the outside's overcast morning.

They went a long time without talking, like the lights might come back if they didn't mention the darkness. But finally, it seemed official, and the Ukrainian man gave a sigh. "Well," he said, scratching his ear. "It's Christmas."

———

Everyone could sense Manny's wife needed space. She had been picking up people's water glasses and putting them in the sink. So they mumbled about going back to their own places for a while. They would bathe and rest, while it was light. They could reconvene at sunset.

The feel of Mrs. Salgado following her was so routine, it took Orla a minute to realize that the woman meant to come with her into her apartment. But where else would she have gone? Orla let her shower first. She handed her yoga pants and a Lehigh sweatshirt to change into.

Mrs. Salgado took the clothes and looked at Orla's swollen ankles. "You'd better lie down and put your feet up," she said. "When are you due?"

"Today," Orla said. "But it won't be today. I don't feel any different." She said it firmly; she wanted the baby to hear. She was still determined to keep Marlow in there until this was all

over. Until the photographers returned and the internet cam
back and people were not too preoccupied to hear what she ha
to say: Floss tried to steal her baby.

Mrs. Salgado looked at her. Her lips twitched. "Is that wha
you think it'll be like?" she said. "You'll wake up one day an
feel like a mother?"

"I just mean," Orla said, "I don't have contractions."

"You never will, just so you know," Mrs. Salgado said. "Th
baby will come, and you'll wait to feel different. You'll wai
for years and years. You'll always think you'll change one day
That you'll wake up and feel—" She flicked the bathroom
light switch up and down, to no effect. "Capable," she said
"Capable of protecting this precious little thing. But it neve
happens. So you keep being scared that you'll fail. And then
one day, you do."

Orla looked at Mrs. Salgado's face. It was dry and crepe
and grooved, and so dark around the eyes. She wondered hov
much of that face had come from Anna living, and how much
had come from her dying. She wondered what marks she ha
helped to put there herself.

"Why have you been following me?" Orla said.

Mrs. Salgado tilted her head to one side and tugged the ban
from her matted hair. She made a face like she was looking at th
sun. "I wanted to try to make you less of a monster," she said
"I've only seen you on TV. I thought if I watched you walkin
or riding the subway or buying your groceries, I don't know—
maybe stepping in a puddle or something, it might make yo
seem more real. I was trying to think of you as someone else
daughter."

Orla's heart clutched in on itself. She thought of her parents
They were nearly finished with a six-week European tour tha
Orla had surprised them with, despite the fact that it nearl
doubled the mean red number on her credit card statement. Sh
had booked the trip months ago, wanting them far away for he

third trimester, never the wiser as she went from pregnant to not so, one way or another. Gayle had been highly suspicious—"thirty-seven isn't a big anniversary, honey"—but she had gone along with the gift.

"Did it work?" Orla said to Mrs. Salgado.

The woman put her hand on Orla's arm. She patted it, rubbed it. She said, "Not at all."

————

After her shower, Orla slept, the sort of light and troubled sleep in which she heard her own moans. When it was dark again, Mrs. Salgado woke her. They went back downstairs. Orla noticed on their way out that one of Floss's heiress books, which she had left behind when she moved, was sitting on the counter. Mrs. Salgado had tucked a take-out menu into it where she left off, like she planned to come back.

The crowd of neighbors was thinner on Christmas night: just Orla, Mrs. Salgado, the old woman, the Ukrainian man, and Manny's family sat around the table, eating the pernil Manny's wife had cooked on the gas stove. She kept mumbling that it wasn't enough for all of them, how could she have known, and they kept mumbling back that sure it was, and of course she couldn't have, and anyway, it was delicious. The Ukrainian man brought a bottle of vodka and poured drinks for everyone but Orla, even Linus. Linus looked at his mother. She surprised them all by saying, "If you can get it down, go for it." She was wearing jewelry she hadn't had on that morning—a platter of a necklace, dripping earrings, thick bracelet—and it seemed to improve her mood slightly. Orla was grateful that Manny had shopped well, and early.

They cleaned up together. Orla dried dishes until Mrs. Salgado took the towel from her hands and told her, firmly, to sit. The Ukrainian man carried the old woman, who was drowsy and flushed from the liquor, to the couch.

They were all just settling in, thinking the same thing, Orla could tell—*what do we do now?*—when they heard a roar coming from outside. It came in waves, rising and dying, and there was an intimidating force to the sound. But they were more stir-crazy than they were frightened, so they held the super's Bic lighter to the wicks of his wife's tapers. They went outside.

It turned out to be singing.

Eighth Avenue was crammed with people facing east, looking up at a man leaning precariously out his window on the third floor of a low-rise. He wore flashing Christmas-tree novelty glasses. He was leading the crowd in song with wild, wide-armed gestures. In one hand, he held an oversize martini glass, its liquid sloshing onto the street. In the other, he held an oversize dildo, purple and illuminated. He slashed it back and forth as he led the crowd in "O Holy Night."

"That's nice," Manny said, grinning. His wife countered, with a sharp look at the dildo, "No, it's not."

Orla looked down the block. Someone had ransacked the Starbucks. The mermaid that usually dangled from a post above the door was facedown on the sidewalk, wires sticking out her back. Farther north, the screens on Madison Square Garden were black and quiet. The Empire State Building was snuffed out, its dark spire slicing the moon. The sounds Orla was used to had evaporated—no horns, no sirens, no engines. It was almost comforting to see the wild-eyed man from the corner of Twenty-Sixth Street shouldering through the crowd, still yelling about Jesus. "It's too late!" he was saying to the singers. "Too late!"

When he got to Orla, he stopped and stared at her. Instinctively, she took a step back. "You're wet," the man said, in a completely normal voice.

"What?" She wrapped her arms across her midsection.

"I said you're wet," he repeated. "Your pants are wet."

She thought he meant at the bottom, from the way her cuffs dragged in the slush, but then Mrs. Salgado lowered her candle.

Orla saw that her sweatpants were soaked in the crotch, darkening down her leg.

"Your water broke, Orla," Mrs. Salgado said. "We need to get you to a hospital."

"No," Orla said. Tonight was not the night, so this had to be something else. Then there was a hot push going through her back, filling her vision with sparkling pain. "I want to wait," she said.

But no one heard her. Mrs. Salgado was calling to Manny, who was calling, over the music, to a cop. Orla heard his voice woven into the chorus, the masses and her super competing. *Yo, night divine, need some help over here, oh night divine, gotta lady in labor. Oh night divine.*

———

The generators at Mount Sinai West were already sagging. The lobby went black, then blinding, then black, like the kind of nightclubs Floss had always loved and Orla had always hated. Mrs. Salgado was beside her as she made her way to the desk.

The power seized again as a nurse led Orla and Mrs. Salgado past the nursery. Babies, no babies. Babies, no babies. The newborns, indistinguishable in their caps and cotton wrappings, seemed not to notice the blinking.

A new pain hit as Orla settled into bed. "Breathe," someone said, but she held in all the air she could get. A nurse with a snarl of watches in a small bin handed one to Mrs. Salgado. Mickey Mouse's white-gloved hands claimed it was eight fifteen. "You're in charge of contractions," the nurse said to Anna's mother.

The doctor stood next to Orla's bed with her hands in the pockets of her lab coat. "Sorry, honey, no epidural," she said. "We're short-staffed. But you can do this. Millions of women have done this. You have your mother here with you. It's gonna be fine."

"I'm forty-*six*," Mrs. Salgado sniffed.

The doctor stuck her fingers inside Orla, who tried not to gasp. "Three centimeters," the doctor said.

Three hours later, it was only four, and the baby's heart rate was slowing. The doctor called in another one. The two of them conferred in the corner, near a yoga ball that hung from the ceiling in a large mesh hammock.

"All right," the first one said to Orla. She clapped her hands together. "We have to do a C-section. That means," she went on in doctor singsong, "you get some anesthesia! Finally, right?"

When they were about to wheel her in, Mrs. Salgado bent over the gurney. "If this watch is right, it's still Christmas," she said to Orla. "Your baby will be here before midnight—you won't believe how fast it goes. I had a C, too." She reached down, tentatively, and smoothed the tiny curls at Orla's hairline back. The lights went out again. The little OR-bound parade stopped and waited.

"I'm sorry," Orla said into the darkness. "I'm so sorry."

It was silent for a moment. Then the nurse over Orla's left shoulder said, "Funny—it's usually the husbands who say that up here."

When the lights came back on, Mrs. Salgado was gone.

"It's all right," the nurse said, as Orla lifted her head, looking. "She'll be there when you get out."

But she wasn't. Mrs. Salgado tried to stay. But she had to go when her mind filled with thoughts of Anna—Anna being lifted out of her, as she lay on a table just like the one they cut Orla open on, Anna's first fierce sound, Anna's slick and pumping fists, Anna's reddish-purple chest, swelling with her first breath. No one told Orla any of this. By the time she woke up in recovery and let them put Marlow on her chest, no one had to. She was a mother. She understood.

All that was left of Mrs. Salgado was a neat stack of wool on the chair in Orla's room: tiny pants, tiny sweater, tiny hat. Orla knew the yarn. She was sure it had been a scarf unspooling over

Mrs. Salgado's hands these last several weeks, outside her building. But she also knew, from having a mother who knit, that an experienced purler could change her design, if she just changed her mind in time.

———

On the first day of Marlow's life, the world was still timeless and frightening. But in Orla's room, everything was perfect. Marlow slept, prompting relieved looks from the overworked nurses. Marlow ate, prompting a grin and a loud "praise *be*" from the nosy lactation consultant. Orla beamed right back at her. Look what she had made. She would never be alone again.

Normally, they wouldn't have left her alone with Marlow so much. Normally, there would have been baths and tests and admonitions that Orla stay in bed, so that the deep slit in her belly could heal. *But under the circumstances*, they kept saying, and what they meant was: they weren't watching. They told Orla to be careful when she got up. They showed her how to remove and replace the canvas pumps strapped around her legs, coaxing her blood to flow evenly. They told her to buzz if she was lightheaded, and to be patient if they didn't come quickly. They told her to, above all, listen to her body.

Only because there was nothing to do, Orla figured out the outages. They happened every twenty minutes or so, and lasted for about thirty seconds. Each time the shadow and hush fell over the floor, the nurses would rush from their stations toward patients who had something crucial plugged into them. Then the generator would kick back up, the power would return, and everything would go back to normal.

Later that day, while Marlow slept in the clear bassinet, Orla swore that she heard the bouncing lilt of a cell phone. She went to her door, cracked it, and looked out at the nurses' station. All of the nurses were huddled around the brunette with the feathered hair, the one who had made Orla blow into a cylinder just a few minutes before.

The brunette was holding her phone. Orla could see, from the blue light in the grease on the woman's chin, that the phone was on, its image moving. A video. Behind the brunette, two nurses exchanged looks. They backed away.

"What?" the brunette shouted suddenly. She was talking to the phone like someone was on the other end. But clearly, nobody was. "Ava is seeing this?" she said. "What the— Oh, no, oh *fuck*!" She stood up. The other nurses scattered like pigeons. The brunette walked to the stairs in her soundless shoes and slapped the door open with both hands.

"Was her phone working?" the girl in the room next to Orla's called out.

"Back in your rooms, please, everyone," another nurse snapped, and Orla realized that it wasn't just her—everyone was watching. She got back in bed and strapped her pumps back on. Five minutes later, a nurse she hadn't seen yet—baby-faced, with dimetight black curls—came into the room. She didn't look at Orla as she picked up the foam block from the ledge of the dry-erase board. She wiped away the brunette's name and replaced it with her own. Then she left the room and went back with the rest of them, cloistered behind the high walls of the cubicles, whispering together—*what the fuck just happened?*

It had been two feedings, a change, and the better part of Marlow's next nap when Orla realized that no one, not the young nurse or anyone else, had been in to see them in hours. She was sure she was overdue for her small white cup of pain pills; the flesh on her stomach was burning around her incision and aching underneath. It seemed, Orla thought, like she and Marlow had slipped through the cracks.

She was about to press the call button and beg for someone to bring her a painkiller when a thought shot through her. A crazy thought, an unthinkable thought. But that only meant it matched the state of things.

She took her finger off of the call button.

"Just ran right out of here," her nurse was saying, outside the door, to someone who had just come on shift. "Something about a video, and Ava seeing it. Isn't Ava, like, nine?"

Orla rose slowly, gripping the bed's bars, and went into the bathroom. She looked at herself in the mirror. She was thinking that maybe this crack they slipped through was actually an opening.

She winced as she pulled her clothes on, over the white medical corset and the bandages beneath it. She swept all the supplies from the bathroom into her bag, even the things she didn't understand: cold packs that stretched the length of her crotch, the comically oversize maxi pads, the soft plastic bottle with its nozzle top. Then she moved to the bassinet and packed everything from there, too: the diapers, the wipes, the little snapped shirts that bloomed around the baby's seven-pound body, the extra hat, the tiny comb, the bulb for sucking her nose clean. She stopped to lean over Marlow, to make sure she was all right. The closeness of her breath made the baby flinch and wrinkle her nose.

Orla went to her door, hung the laminated sign that said she was breastfeeding and not to be disturbed, and closed it softly.

She unwrapped Marlow on the bed, marveling again at the tiny limbs that sprang wide when she opened the blanket, at the firm little belly with its lingering nub, pupil black, of the cord that connected them. Marlow was still as Orla changed her diaper, fumbling the yellow tabs over and over. "Good girl," Orla said.

The pants that Mrs. Salgado had made, she saw gratefully, were footed. She pulled the sweater inch by inch over Marlow's head.

"We're going home," she whispered to Marlow. She put her back in the bassinet.

She hauled her overnight bag up onto the nest of sheets, the motion like a knife running straight across her middle. The things she had brought, the things she was taking—almost all of it, fortunately, amounted to padding. She pushed everything to the sides of the bag, making a well in the middle.

She picked up Marlow and waited for the next round of darkness.

The plastic bracelets both of them wore had matching numbers and a sensor. If either of them went through the swinging unit doors before discharge, the sensors would sound an alarm, a nurse had told her. The hospital would lock down. "Except," the nurse said in a low voice, "during these goddamn generator fails. But we're talking seconds at a time. What are the odds, you know?"

Finally, the lamp over Orla's bed flickered out. The room cooled and quieted.

Orla opened the door and stuck her head out. She looked at the nurses' station. All of the women were up and jogging toward the rooms that needed them. A chorus of "How we doin' in here?" rang up and down the hall.

Orla shut the door, went back and picked up Marlow. She placed the baby gently in the bag and zipped it an inch short of all the way shut.

She walked briskly down the hallway, her torso blaring with every step. She kept her eyes on the exit. As the doors got closer, she asked herself, panicked, what the fuck she was doing and got the answer swiftly, pure intuition. She was listening to her body.

Her hand touched down and pushed. They were through. She braced for something terrible, but the only sound behind them was the swish of the closing doors.

She had made it to ground level, to the sign that said EXIT TO STREET, when the lights came back on. She already had the door open. And then she was out, they were out, on the wet sidewalk that now seemed miraculous, beneath the scaffolding that now looked like majesty, in the damp city chill that now felt like new life. Free and clear on Fifty-Eighth Street.

There was less snow and fewer cops on the street now than when Orla went in. And there was a man walking toward her, wearing a suit, which no one did in an emergency, she thought. He was holding a banana. A banana! Like it was any other day, like he had to eat on the run. Looking at the fruit, she almost wept.

And here was another yellow miracle: a cab, all alone on the street, coming down the block right toward her. Reflexively, she put her arm into the air.

"I had to get out of the house, man," the driver said as she got in. He pointed at the meter. Its screen was blank. "I won't charge you, but no Brooklyn, no Queens. I got a quarter tank of gas and I gotta make it last. Shit, the techpocalypse couldn't go down *before* my mother-in-law flew in?"

"No problem," Orla said. "Twenty-First and Eighth." Her plan was to go back to Manny's, to hide there until she found a way out of the city, back to Pennsylvania. Gayle and Jerry weren't back from their trip yet, but she could go home and let herself in. She imagined her and Marlow, safe behind the screen door of her parents' enclosed porch. She imagined sliding the spare key out of the fake hydrangea on the plant stand. It was funny, how she used to think she knew what it was to want something. She had never felt the kind of burn that ran through her now when she pictured that key in her hand.

She unzipped the bag and looked, heart pounding, at Marlow, nestled inside. The baby's eyes were closed, but when Orla put a finger to her mouth, she sucked it instantly. "That's my girl," Orla whispered. "That's my girl."

The cabbie stopped at every block, checking for crosstown traffic, but it was still the fastest ride home from Midtown Orla ever had. The bars and restaurants on Ninth were all packed, even this early, spilling people out their narrow doors. What

Orla thought, as the cab crept past a painted storefront, was that she had never seen so many people with their heads held straight up. She had never looked into a bar and not seen squares of lit screens. The people in the bar were looking at a tall, bearded guy who stood atop the bar. He was singing, and strumming a guitar, and bending his knees just slightly, so that his head wouldn't graze the ceiling. Orla watched through the window as the crowd threw their hands up in happy unison. Even with the windows rolled up, Orla knew what it was: the man had started playing a song that everybody knew.

On the seat next to her, Marlow cracked an eye and sighed. Her tiny fist gripped the seam of a pair of the massive mesh hospital underwear. Orla stroked Marlow's cheek with a finger. "A little farther up," she said, when the cabbie pulled over half a block before her door. Any other day, in any other year, she would have gotten out wherever. But now she spoke for two people. Mrs. Salgado had been wrong, she thought. Already, she was different.

The cabbie seemed not to have heard her. His head was down, and Orla realized, suddenly, what he was looking at: his phone, which had shed its white tiles and was showing him a document. Even from the back seat, she could see its truncated lines, its clots of carets and single-spaced text—it was an email chain. He was thumbing through it furiously.

"Sir?" she said. "I really appreciate the ride. If you wouldn't mind—"

The man got out of the car. He left the engine running, and his door wide open. He began to walk toward Ninth. Orla turned to watch him through the smudged rear windshield. When he got to the old firehouse building, he stopped and turned, dramatically, to face the curved red door that had once let horses and buggies pass through. The cabbie hesitated for a moment. Then he lunged—kicking the door, punching the door. The flag above it quivered.

Orla got herself and Marlow out of the car as fast as her cut would allow. Before she walked into her building, she remembered the man was saving his gas. She reached in the driver's side and shut off the ignition, leaving the warm keys dangling.

———

Manny wasn't answering. Orla rocked Marlow back and forth as she slapped at the door, waiting. Soon, Marlow began to wail.

"Shh, Marlow," she said. "Shh, baby, shh."

"Orla." She turned and saw the Ukrainian man at the end of the hall, walking toward her. He had a plastic bag of groceries in his hand. She didn't know he knew her name; she still did not know his. He looked down at Marlow, then back at her. "They're gone," he said.

"Gone?" Orla bent her knees and straightened them, trying to soothe the baby, whose cries were growing louder. "Where would they go?"

The Ukrainian man nodded. "You've been in hospital, of course," he said. "Things out here, well. Everything is moving pieces." He put the groceries down and rolled up his sleeves, unfurled his forearms toward her. "All right," he said, over Marlow's crescendo. "Let's go. We take our time."

She stared back at him, not understanding.

"I'll hold you," he said. "You hold her."

"The thing is, I can't go to my apartment," Orla said. She pictured Floss at the door, waiting, drumming her nails on folded arms.

The Ukrainian man took a step forward and began to lift her gingerly. "We go to my place, then," he said.

"The penthouse?" Orla said, as her feet left the ground.

He breathed with force, like a weight lifter, as he curled them into his chest. "Just nine floors," he said.

"Okay." Orla clutched Marlow close. Somehow, it had always

seemed higher. On the way to the stairs, she looked down and saw, strewn in the hallway, the jewels Manny gave his wife for Christmas. The necklace was slumped against a strip of vinyl trim, the bracelet turned metal belly-up on the carpet. One earring crunched beneath the Ukrainian man's foot, and another lay just ahead, waiting. As if someone angry had hurled it down, a second after its match.

———

The man's name, it turned out, was Andriy. The first thing Orla noticed, when he put her and the baby down just inside his apartment, was the alarm clock on the card table near his sofa. It read 11:18 a.m. Orla gasped and pointed at it. "Is that real?" she said.

Andriy nodded, grinning. "They got control of the current earlier," he said, when he caught his breath. "My clock was blinking twelve when I woke up. I took it out on the street and asked someone the time, and when I set it, it keeps track."

Orla lowered the baby toward it. "Marlow, look," she said.

Andriy gestured to the television. The padded wall remained. "They say this is next," he said. "We can hope."

"Where did Manny and his family go?" Orla asked. Marlow began to fuss again. She stuck her thumb in Marlow's mouth, wondering where she would feed the baby in this strange man's apartment.

Andriy stopped smiling. "That is the thing I am not getting yet. The rumor that there is more to this. That time, power, data all going away, this was nothing. Just curtain for them to work behind. This morning, when I went out with my clock, Manny and his wife are shouting. I hear it even in the stairs." Andriy raised his hands, as if to show he had nothing to do with it. "And then when I go outside, I see this again. People yelling, people crying. People whose phones have come back."

He told her what he saw when he went looking for the time. People stopping in their tracks at the sounds in their pockets,

ounds that had long been so familiar they were more like flicks
in their brains, sounds that nonetheless were startling after the
last few days. He widened his eyes and dropped his jaw, aping
the shock of those who thought they were blessed when their
things came back on. Bystanders gathered around the twinkling
machines, peered over their owners' shoulders. What happened
next, Andriy said, was always the same: the screen would light
up already cued to a text. Or an email, or an image, or a document, a video or audio file. And the owner's delirious relief
would harden into something else—fear, or panic, or anger.
One young woman he had seen, Andriy said, peeled the rubber bunny backing off her phone and smashed it on the rim of
a metal trash can. Then she sat in a snowdrift and cried.

"I try to console her," he said, adding wistfully, "My daughter has same case."

In the grocery store, he found more of the same. The cashier behind the belt where Andriy plunked down his order, a
inky redhead with an asymmetrical haircut, ran away halfway
through the transaction. The man's phone, sitting next to the
register, had begun to emit moans and gasps. Andriy looked
down to see a sex tape playing at top volume. "Two men, both
have gray hair, equivalent penis size," he reported to Orla. "I
was not staring. The quality was very good."

When the cashier left, Andriy said, he took his things into
the next lane, to a Hispanic girl with doorknocker earrings
who was pretending not to watch her coworker. She rung up
Andriy's things without making eye contact, snapping her gum.
Suddenly, a ding rang out from her midsection. She looked
down. A square of white light shone through the thin purple
cotton of her apron.

The girl pulled the phone out slowly and looked at it. Swiped
once, twice. Put the phone back and picked up Andriy's bag of
trail mix.

"What are you seeing?" he asked her. "What makes every one go so crazy?"

"Not the same thing for everyone," the girl said. "I hear the got stuff for everybody."

"What stuff?" Andriy said. "Who is they?"

The girl shrugged. "Nobody knows," she said. "Had a gu in here, FBI or something. Said that everybody who has stu turning back on, it's weird. The first thing you see is some thing you don't want *nobody* to see, and then you see where the sent it." She was dragging items over her scanner even thoug it wasn't working. "Like for me, they say they sent my mom lotta shit I talked on her, like a *lotta* lotta shit. I said I fantasiz about her dying."

"You said this in a text?" Andriy asked.

The girl, he said, had shaken her head. She was oddly caln Only the gold in her ears shook. "Copies of notes from m shrink," she said, and she showed him. "Apparently, that's a bi one. They're in the medical systems. It's like they know how to look for secrets." She punched at her calculator, held up th total, closed her hand on his exact change. "So if you got some thing fucked up, man, spill it now. Before they do it for you.'

———

Andriy was very sorry; in the three-bedroom penthouse, ther were no beds. Floss was right, all those months ago—he live in Delaware, close to his ex-wife and daughter, and when h stayed in the city for work, he slept on the couch. But ther was a beanbag in the corner of the largest bedroom, so Orla sa there, her whole body screaming from the lack of support. She le Marlow eat and looked around uneasily. The room's walls wer covered with the sort of posters Orla remembered from dorr rooms—models in shreds of swimsuits and lingerie, kneelin seaside or draped over beds. At college, boys stuck them to th cinder block with putty, but Andriy had framed and hung his

338

He made Orla eggs, scrambled and dry. Next to her plate, he set down two Advil. It was all he had, he said. It was better than nothing, she answered.

They sat and ate the eggs while Marlow slept on the couch, the pillows in a makeshift fortress around her. They were almost finished when the screen of the television went black, then blue, then, suddenly: it was all back, confusing Orla's eyes. The channel guide stared at them like it had never left. Andriy jumped up. He lunged for the remote on the coffee table. Orla watched, half-aware her mouth was full of eggs and open, as he fumbled, pressing buttons with both thumbs.

Most of the stations had not recovered. They were dark or rainbow-blocked or frozen on something from before. When Andriy came to a news channel, they both yelped like children—the image was moving. They could see the face of a grim man at a desk. They could hear his voice, too. The usual cable-news trimmings—the chyrons, the ticker, the little clock in the corner—were nowhere to be found. It made the man look naked. On the desk next to him was a drugstore alarm clock, brown faux wood with red numbers.

"Emotional terrorism," he was saying. He stopped and picked up his papers. He waited a few moments. "If you're just joining us," he said, "we have returned to live broadcast after almost three days of being off the air. It is December 27, 2016, and—" He checked his clock proudly. "It is 1:20 p.m. here in New York."

Orla got up and crossed to the couch. She sank down next to Andriy, taking care not to jostle Marlow.

"The nation is in the midst of an unprecedented attack," the man said. "On our power grid, our communications systems, and, as it's now becoming clear, our personal privacy and security. Let's review." The man waited a beat, blinking. "Debra," he said, when nothing happened, "do we not have that graphic?"

He sighed and flipped up the top page on his pile. On it, some one had hand-drawn a timeline.

"Here," he said, tapping the sketch. "Here's what we know. I the late hours of December 24, hackers launched a multipronge attack on America, marked by the quote-unquote stoppage time. These perpetrators were able to sabotage our power gri in such a way that they could tweak the electrical current th devices use to keep time." He splayed out his fingers to coun "At the same time: they were hacking into the operations major internet, cable, and phone service providers. They wei infiltrating medical records systems, banks, and other large scale keepers of personal information. They were disabling, tampering with, GPS satellite communication. The assault w swift, comprehensive, and devastating. And now we seem be in the midst of another phase of the sabotage. We're gettir dozens of reports about people finding their phones and oth devices finally and mysteriously unlocked—only to learn th the hackers have leaked personal, and often humiliating, info mation about them. Leaking it to the people around them, the people directly concerned by the matter. 'Emotional terro ism' is the term we've been—"

The man was interrupted by a distant ringtone: vague aquatic, like plinking rain. He looked up and past the camer "Mine?" he said. He sounded afraid. He stood up.

A moment later, a woman in not enough makeup, her ha limp and stuck to her skull, slid into his seat. "I'm Dana Ma shall," she said. "I'll be taking over for Bill. My husband ju found out I lied about having breast cancer. So you can bet I be with you all day." She rolled around, collecting Bill's papei They had scattered when he pushed out of his chair.

Orla looked down at Marlow and found that the baby ha awoken without making a sound. Her eyes were the widest Or had seen them yet, and she locked them on Orla's. They star at each other, and Orla felt, though the clocks were back, time slipping away from her again.

Sounding over the voice coming from the TV: three hard knocks on the door.

Orla curled her body over Marlow. She looked at Andriy, who clicked off the television. He held a finger to his lips. Slowly, silently, he opened a drawer in the coffee table and took out a small switchblade. He went to the door. He leaned his eye to the peephole.

When he turned back to Orla, he was trembling with relief. He clutched his chest with one hand. "Jesus," he said with a smile. "She is crazy, your friend."

There was no time to explain, no time to cry out *don't*. All Orla could think to do was sweep the baby into one arm and reach for the patio door with the other. She had to yank it three times, hard. When they got out onto the roof, she looked down and saw her shirt was soaked in blood. Her incision had burst.

She banged Andriy's patio gate aside and ran across the roof, toward the door that led to the elevator. By the time she pulled the handle and felt it go nowhere—*locked*—Floss's face was in the glass. She was behind her.

Orla turned around. "Get back," she yelped. "Get away from us."

The wind whipped Floss's hair across her face, trapping strands of it in her lip gloss. She clawed them away. "She shouldn't be out here. It's cold," she said. She turned her face this way and that, examining Marlow. Orla could tell Floss wanted to grab the baby but wasn't sure how to hold her.

"No," Orla said. "No, no, no." She tightened her grip.

"Orla." Floss backed her toward the door. "Stop being insane. This was the deal, and you know it."

"How did you find us?" Orla said, her voice quaking. She pressed Marlow's face into her chest, to keep her warm and one inch farther from Floss. "How did you know I left the hospital—how did you even know I had her?"

Floss was calm. "The cops said they would search our whole building," she said. "I knew you had her, I knew you left, because the hospital tracked me down. One of your nurses follows me on Twitter. She saw me tweet, before all this shit went down, that me and Aston were at the St. Regis."

"But why," Orla spit, "would they call *you*?"

Floss bent her finger up and down in a tiny wave at Marlow. "You put me down when you preregistered at the hospital," she said. "I'm your emergency contact. They didn't call me because you took Marlow. They called me because you went missing."

Andriy and a policeman reached them then—what had taken them so long? Orla would never know, just as she would never know why the cop took Floss's side. She could guess. He was young, younger than them, and frightened by Floss, by the envelope of contracts she had with her, under her fur-collared parka, by the way she looked familiar-famous and carried herself like who she was—someone who didn't mind ruining people. Orla knew, too, that the way she bled from her middle must have made her look crazy, and that it couldn't have helped, the way Marlow started howling in a way that sounded scared. She knew it made things even worse when Andriy kept stammering, over and over, that he really didn't know these girls at all. She knew it made a difference, the way the cop didn't have any backup, because the backup was all needed somewhere else. Everywhere else.

The cop lifted Marlow from Orla's arms. He kept repeating that it was standard procedure: he had to check the baby out.

"Support her head," Orla choked out as she let Marlow slip from her arms. The cop nodded, then asked Andriy to please come with him back inside. The men walked away with the baby.

Orla and Floss stood alone, together, apart, waiting to see what would happen, on the smaller side of the roof. The part for everyone else.

CHAPTER TWENTY-TWO

Orla

Atlantis
2051

At the age of sixty-two, Orla has made peace with her hair. It's funny; now that it is old, her hair is the loveliest, the most tolerable, it has ever been. She still has so much of it, and its youthful frizz and bulk has mellowed, leaving her with mermaid kinks and more natural volume than most women her age. Not that anyone else has settled for natural. Most of Orla's friends, those former revolutionaries, have quietly taken advantage of science. Their hair and faces look almost the same as they did when they came to Atlantis. But that's one of the things Orla has always missed here: old people. There is something so un-certain, so home-alone-feeling, about a world without anyone white-haired. So, now that she can, she lets herself become an old woman. And Kyle swears he doesn't mind.

Kyle is a good man, but he is still a man. It is why he doesn't understand, even after he shows Orla how it would boost the store's profits, why she refuses to diversify into baby gifts, stocking tiny smocked dresses and soft pink shoes. It is why he doesn't notice that she always goes straight to a restroom when another woman, half joking, tells Orla she is lucky to not have any daughters. It is why he has to ask her where her mind is when her eyes glaze over each Christmas morning, only at a time that's convenient for everyone. She is a mother—she knows how to keep her own thoughts waiting until everyone else has had breakfast.

If Kyle were a woman, he would intuit all of this. But he is a man, so he would tell anyone who asked that they know everything there is to know about each other, he and his wife. And he does know that, long ago, Orla had a baby girl. He knows that the baby was taken away. He thinks it is an old story. But for Orla, the story never ends.

———

After Floss and the cop took Marlow, Orla lasted two and a half more months in New York. She fantasized that another cop—an Irish-looking lady cop with a sturdy bosom, that was what she always pictured—would knock on the door of 6D one day and present her with her baby. She would say she had been looking after Marlow herself, whispering every night in her ear that she'd see her mother soon. She also had a more realistic fantasy: that Floss would come back one day and thrust Marlow over the threshold, broken from putting up with her crying and begging to go back on the deal.

Besides wait and dream, there wasn't much to do. Orla's phone still didn't work; the internet was still dark. She was afraid to go to the police, who might know, when they tapped her name into a computer, that she had kidnapped her own child from the hospital. Orla dug a damp, warped phone book out from the back behind the building's foyer door and pored over it, looking for groups and agencies that had "children" or "parents" or "family" in the name. She walked to their offices, even when it took hours, just to find locked doors and wary staff. Did she *really* think, at a time like *this*, they could— *What* was it she wanted, again? She went back to the lawyer's office where she had signed all the papers and found a note taped to the front desk: GONE UNTIL FURTHER NOTICE. Not closed, she thought, staring at it. Gone.

She went twice to the house in Brooklyn Heights. Both times, every window was dark.

January brought more files—that was what they called them, the things their phones came back on displaying, the photos and videos and texts and emails that ruined their lives—and the return of the late-night shows. When the programs came back. their studio audiences rose with tears in their eyes. At home and ravaged by hormones, Orla cried, too. But the attempt at normalcy proved premature. Within the month, all the hosts would be ruined. The last man to go, the perkiest one, was called away in the middle of his monologue one night. His lapel mic picked up the frantic whispers of the producer who rushed into his shot. "Your home computer turned on," he said. "I don't know what it said, but I just got a call that Rachel's locked herself in the bathroom. She says—she says she's going to—"

The host hurried off the stage. The band stood there, agape. Their horns swung silent by their sides.

Orla knew what the end of the producer's sentence was. She had recently seen the newspaper story about Jordie, the freckle publicist from the pet party, jumping off his nineteenth-floor balcony. He would be remembered as the first, but there were hundreds right on his heels. Experts warned of uncharted territory.

In February, there were almost nine thousand. The next few years would be bad, but there would never be a month worse than that.

The government sprang into action. Bridges were wrapped

ncing, patrolled by men with rifles who scared jumpers back
the land. Prescription pads—the paper ones—were phased
it altogether. The system that replaced them filtered its input
rough Homeland Security. Drugstores put glass over every-
ing from Lysol to Wite-Out. Certain trees—ones that peo-
e somehow identified as doing the trick, if the driver held the
heel just right and kept his foot bravely on the gas—became
orbid sensations, then mulch, when the police had them cut
wn. The wooded roads in Orla's hometown, the ones that
ed to worry parents on graduation night, were now lined with
imps and filled with sunlight.

Weapon sales were halted by emergency mandate, which left
ople who already owned them to decide: Should they turn
eirs in, or wait for someone desperate for a gun to break in
d take it? People whose back doors had stickers that warned
how they handled intruders—*Nothing in this house is worth
ting shot over*—got putty knives and oiled goo and scratched
em off the glass.

The hangings were harder to stop. No one knew how to leg-
ate rope. But at each hardware store in the country, there was
extra worker in jeans and a red vest, looking like all the rest
them as he glanced into people's shopping carts and struck up
easant talk—what were they working on, today, with their cord
their box cutter? The worker was always named Jeff, and he
is never a worker named Jeff. He was something brand-new.
store marshal.

In March, Orla got herself drunk one night. She watched
e antisuicide channel for a while, the looped urgings to per-
t from the actress with the pink cheeks who used to do in-
rance commercials. "Our country has been challenged," she
d, ninety-six times a day. "But our bravest people are work-
g hard to end this trying time. If your file has already leaked,
d you need help, please call the number below. If your file

remains private, please: stay calm and stay positive. Know th
these evil people will be caught soon. Do not give up hope.'

But for Orla, it was time to give up hope. She started packin

———

Then she was back in her childhood room, all but ten poun
the same, like none of it had ever happened—Marlow, Flo
fame, 6D, the last ten years of her life. She told her parer
everything. They listened. They never said a word about h
breaking their hearts. The only way Orla knew her mother w
ashamed: Gayle drew the blinds the day she got home and ke
them that way forever.

Together, the three of them watched Dana Marshall every nig
Dana—the woman Orla had first seen in Andriy's apartment, fi
ing in for her runaway colleague—had become the on-air star
the Spill. No one had known her before, and people would quick
forget her after, but for the moment they hung on her every wo
and sometimes copied her hairstyle.

Dana Marshall told them, one day, that she had a major u
date. That when they thought of this time as something th
would end when some people were arrested, they were se
ing things all wrong. Hackers weren't in an office somewhe
finding and leaking files daily, she said. No: the Spill mann
itself. For nearly a decade, the hackers had worked on bots th
could root through data of anyone who shared anything o
line, who texted or emailed or backed things up on servers th
didn't own or used a screen instead of a pen at the doctor's
fice. They located lies and debts and vices with search-engi
speed and detached precision. The bots chewed through fir
walls and curled up on infrastructure. They caught rides in
people's Twitter accounts via the fake-follower generators peo
like Floss used. They swan-dove into Facebook's endless oce
of data, snatching up user profiles, shaking them out, colle
ing liabilities that came loose like coins. They spit out huma

sounding DMs on Instagram, ravaging anyone who wrote back to the flattery. And then, when they had all the information they needed, they simply automated common sense. They could find a mistress easily: she would be nowhere in a man's email, absent from his thousands of photos, but her number would be saved as something laughably benign, called briefly at the same time each week. The bots sifted bank statements for discrepancies in money going in and money going out. They turned up searches for ghastly porn and at-home abortion how-tos. They found names that appeared in cruel text chains, then went and found the same names in contacts. They copied and pasted. They hit Send.

The only reason all the files had not been released at once, Dana Marshall concluded, was presumably to keep the country down as long as possible.

"It turns out we're all so boring," she sighed. "So alike in our cells and desires. So limited in our insults and strategies. You know how many times I googled 'physical appearance, stage four breast cancer' when I was lying to my husband? That's how they got me." This was why everyone liked Dana Marshall. She always editorialized, and she was just as fucked up as the rest of them.

In April, Orla started leaving the house—only on errands Jerry invented to coax her out, and only late at night. She was on such an errand when she heard about Andriy. At least, she figured it was him, though she knew neither his last name nor his hometown. But there was a forty-eight-year-old Andriy in Delaware who had stabbed his daughter's pediatrician, after a file told him that the man kept photos of her on his laptop. When Orla heard this story, buzzing soberly through the radio speaker of the Taurus, she was leaning over the dashboard outside the twenty-four-hour Rite Aid. She was looking across the parking lot at the entrance to the TGI Fridays. Outside it, Danny and Catherine were pressed against the wall, making out like they had just met. Catherine wore a stiff satin cocktail dress and brassy chandelier earrings that brushed her bare shoulders. She looked strange. But then, Orla thought, people could be strange when they wanted someone. And where else was Catherine going to wear a dress like that, anyway?

It was the same weekend that, the year before, it had snowed and Danny got her pregnant. This year, April was the month of her driving her parents everywhere, trying to decode the symptoms they had begun to complain of. Sometime toward the end of the month, a hobbled version of the internet flickered back on. People began posting rumors about whose files said what. Dark secrets piled up, easily searched, easily browsed. Orla found the deepest shames of everyone she knew in the time it used to take her to locate the closest burrito.

Mason, the producer, must have caught hell at home. For decades, he told his husband that they were mentoring a poor boy from Camden, New Jersey, chipping away at his needs, college and books and security deposits. It turned out that the boy was actually a prostitute Mason had frequented for a short time and been blackmailed by for a long time. The checks and the Venmo exchanges, email chains that were several kinds of heated—the bots sent it off to Mason's husband with their standard note: **Apologies.**

Craig had an affair with a seventeen-year-old, ten years before, when he was twenty-nine. The texts released in his file, Orla thought, colored him improbably likable. He had wanted the girl to marry him. Orla wouldn't have said as much, but she couldn't help thinking it: take away the ages, and this was a story of ordinary meanness—a lonely, besotted guy and the girl less in love, taunting him.

Danny, before he ever came to find Orla, had bought a bunch of domains with beauty-related takes on Floss's name: styledbyfloss.com, flossgloss.com, looklikefloss.com. He wanted flossy.com, too—badly—and tracked down the person who owned it. His file contained the emails he had sent the woman, which moved from middle-school formal (**To Whom It May Concern**) to desperate (**Can you AT LEAST let me know you are getting these?**) to threatening (**Seriously bitch you need to get back to me...please don't make me come after you other ways**). It bothered Orla, but not as much as the file's final email exchange, the dates of which fell within his stay in her room. After she told him about Floss's skin care line, he had hurried to try to get facebyfloss.com for himself.

Catherine had stolen a science test's answers for her whole soccer team in college. Orla noted how old this information was, how far back the hackers had to go to find Catherine being her harmless worst.

Ingrid, decades before, had misunderstood eBay and bid extravagantly on vintage fashion items, then panicked when she learned what she was expected to pay and backed out of all of the deals. She must have been, Orla thought, the kindest person she knew.

Melissa had undercut her best friend back when they were both assistants at a publicity firm, writing a long (and drunk, Orla guessed as she pored over the file) email to her boss about why she should get a promotion, not her friend. The week after her file dropped, Melissa died. A short story on her death conceded that she might have slipped—she had been dressed for hiking, after all, in a forest filled with slippery ledges. But Orla was sure she did it on purpose. The people she knew who were dying then—besides Melissa, they were all friends of friends, or cousins of cousins—they all had one thing in common, and it wasn't that they'd done something terrible. It was that they had mouldered shining reputations, from kindergarten into adulthood. The people who had been known as good—they were the ones who, frequently, could not survive their own bad.

Aston's file said he stiffed people who worked for him, over and over again. But the revelation was dull compared to what

Aston—who Instagrammed his own stools as a teen and who was once seen making the eating-pussy sign at the Vietnam Veterans Memorial—had always done in the open.

That, to an extent, was the same reason Floss's and Orla's files flopped. Oh, their devices turned on, blaring terrible shit—it just wasn't anything new. Orla saw that the bots had gleefully salvaged Floss's naked pics and thrown them back into the world. But who hadn't seen that already? As for Orla: one morning, months after she came home to Pennsylvania, her iPad lit up and showed her an endless compilation. It was all there: early tweets of Floss's the bots could tell had come from Orla's IP address. The Lady-ish posts Orla had written, declaring Floss famous. The emails they had signed from Pat White. Photos of them, clips from the show, all of it culminating in the Instagram comment from Orla's account, the one Floss left on Anna Salgado's picture: **this is floss and i agree. you should!** The effect the bots intended was clear: whatever Orla had been going for, she had done more harm than good. She owed the world a life. Orla's file, a snide addendum from the bots said, had been forwarded to Anna's family. **Apologies.**

Orla reviewed it all calmly, then tossed the tablet into a drawer without turning it off. This was the glitch in the bots' lethal system: they couldn't tell when the worst in someone had already come to light.

———

Three years later, the files were finished, but people were still losing jobs, leaving spouses, killing themselves. Life grew in around death. Graveyards were hopelessly backlogged. High schools had more memorial scholarships than seniors to receive them. Jumpy parents sneaked baby monitors into their teenagers' rooms. Orla had four dresses just for funerals; and even as they got sicker, Gayle and Jerry insisted that they go to so many. "We want good turnout at ours," Gayle sniffed. They were always spook ing room-temperature macaroni salad onto plastic plates. They were always making small talk with devastated people. Orla was tired of hearing bad news, tired of passing it on. Tired of listening to last wishes and of ginning up nice things to say. Tired of pitching in to help clean out the apartments of the dead. Tired of the cards with that day's deceased pictured over Bible verses or silly Irish platitudes. Tired of not knowing when it was all right to throw the cards away. Sometimes she wanted to shout, *I lost someone, too. My daughter. Where's my fucking luncheon?*

She got it—she got two—the next year. Gayle and Jerry died within eight months of each other—first him, then her—from bone cancer that swept through the house like a cough. Soon afterward, when Orla was visited by a lawyer—a girl younger than her, trembling, whose pearl studs did not distract from her night-before eyeliner—she learned what was likely to blame. While Orla was away, in college, the CoreStates Bank had changed names several times and finally been torn down to make way for a flame-resistant fabric factory. "Good *American* jobs," Orla could remember Gayle saying proudly. Something in the product's chemical coating had been seeping into her parents' groundwater for years. Now they and two more Hidden Ponds residents were dead, and young lawyers were asking around. In any other time, Orla imagined, this would have set Mifflin ablaze with uproar, but the people who came to Gayle's and Jerry's funerals were bored. Cancer, these days, seemed vanilla, regardless of how it was caught. The people were accustomed to dramatic ends, and they had all become wake connoisseurs. "Oh, the TGI Fridays?" Orla's Aunt Marge said, dismayed, when Orla told her about Jerry's funeral. "The back room at Applebee's is so much more intimate."

Without knowing where she was going, Orla got ready to leave her home. She peeled the photos off her bedroom door and put her trophies out for the recycling. She paid men, from her parents' checkbook, to replace the bathroom sinks and strip the kitchen's ivy-patterned wallpaper. She did some things herself.

She caulked trim that had pulled away. She fixed a door her late beagle had scratched the finish off in the nineties.

She ate Pizza Hut and Apple Jacks and watched the news alone. She listened to a congressman on a morning show, pitching a new and better version of the web, one the government would facilitate, one that would protect Americans instead of leaving them vulnerable. "The private sector had their chance," the congressman said. "People don't like the idea of the government running the internet? They don't like the government watching them? Let me tell you something: nobody ever had privacy. Privacy was an illusion. Believing that we had it is what left us open to attack. On this version of the web, we *will* be watching you—so that we can watch out for you. Now we need Americans to come together, to say that you'll support this. That you'll use it the way you used to—for banking, for getting directions, for talking to each other. We need everyone to unite and pledge to share data in order to keep this country safe. If you don't share, how can we protect you? I urge all Americans: come into the light."

Shortly after that, Orla watched a report about Atlantic City. People who didn't like the sound of coming into the light were gathering there by the thousands. They said they were building a protest movement. They crushed their phones while people filmed it on other phones. They said they were starting their own new world, off the government's internet, outside the government's eye.

Orla sold her parents' house just before Christmas. She didn't clean it out. Her parents would have been so angry at that, her leaving their snacks and underwear for strangers to have to sort through, but she found that she couldn't face her mother's closet, or her father's garage. The last thing she did before she left home for the last time was pull up all the blinds that Gayle had put down.

"Join us!" a wild-eyed girl on the TV report about Atlantic

354

City had shouted as she swung from a streetlight. "But know that you must come with nothing! You must leave your world behind!" *That works for me*, Orla had thought. And how often did that happen—her résumé lining up with revolution?

As Orla prepared to walk out the door, leaving her keys for the new owner, she realized that she had left the TV on. As she grabbed for the remote, she heard it: Marlow's name. Orla looked up and saw Floss's face. The trashy entertainment show that ran before the news was doing a preview package on Marlow's fifth birthday party. A camera followed Floss through a dusky new Hollywood hotel.

When Orla had finished watching, she pulled the front door shut behind her. She drove into town. She cleaned out her measly bank account, stuffing the white envelope in her bag, then walked across the street, to the shop where Gayle bought cards. She waited while a man went into the back and cranked metal down on the paper. She sprang for the navy-lined envelopes. Then she drove to the Philadelphia Airport, bid the Taurus farewell in lot E, and repeated her itinerary several times for the man behind the desk. Philly to LA, LA to Atlantic City.

Two days later, she stood in the trendy hotel, holding her box of notes, hearing kids scream the way sugar makes them, knowing that one was hers.

Twin security giants blocked her view of the party. "The balls on her, omigod," Orla could hear Floss saying from somewhere just out of sight.

"It's not gonna happen," one of the guards said to Orla, his baritone blending with the music. "You gotta go."

Orla stood there a little longer anyway, hoping to see a flash of Marlow. But she could tell from the sound of the children's shrieks that they were across the room. Finally, she left, thinking of Floss at the pet party, years ago, passing her a drink through the bars. All these years later, Orla thought, she still couldn't get in.

The early days, when Atlantis was still Atlantic City, were routinely borderline terrifying. The protesters spit at the local police, and the police gassed them back. Boardwalk merchants got out of town quickly when they saw what was happening. Their shops were raided immediately—people tore plywood off the windows and shattered the glass to get in. Orla subsisted on stolen saltwater taffy and bottled water shipped in by antiestablishment billionaires. The electricity had been turned off in all of the buildings they huddled in; the only light they had at night came from weak solar lanterns. For reasons Orla could not understand, there was always a fire somewhere.

The news cameras came to watch them. The panel of faux-hippie students who had anointed themselves the leadership—most of them not a decade removed from their elite prep school days—sent a messenger with a letter to the closest federal government outpost: a US representative's office on Brighton Avenue. The note was written on Tropicana hotel stationery. It demanded that the government give up control of the internet, or prepare to watch a revolution by the sea. They chanted for the cameras: "Stay out of our information, or we'll start a brand-new nation!" The news painted the effort as rebellious and high-minded, something to be taken seriously. But Orla saw chaos everywhere, and secretly, she thought the whole thing would soon burn itself out. And then what? She'd have to start over, at least online. She felt breathless and anxious when she thought of what had happened the day she arrived. The boy who checked her in, in the lobby of the old Caesars Palace, had taken her phone and laptop and said they would not be returned. "But I didn't back up to the cloud," she told him automatically.

"The *cloud*," he said, "isn't welcome here."

Orla had moved, feeling naked, to the girl at the second card table. The girl asked for her name, had her confirm which social media profiles had been hers before the Spill, then showed her what she was doing: deleting every search result for Orla on the internet. Orla watched as the girl pulled up an old Lady-ish post of hers, then somehow made her byline evaporate. "From now on," the girl said proudly, "when someone searches for you, they won't find a thing. In fact, they'll know you're one of us because we're using a code. As soon as they search for your name, they'll get that error—404, not found."

"Like a dead link?" Orla said.

"Exactly." The girl's eyes were shining. "Except now you're truly alive."

It was the first time Orla felt, in Atlantis, like maybe she was at the wrong party. A party full of people who made her feel ancient at thirty-three, who insisted on natural deodorant even when it didn't work, who were handy at Big Brother poster board puns, but frighteningly bad at focusing.

She was assigned to Housing, the committee tasked with turning the old gambling hangars into livable neighborhoods. At the first meeting Orla attended, seven of the eight other members got bored of discussing how to achieve running water and began fighting over what to set up in the common rooms—foosball tables, or pool?

The eighth other person in the meeting was Kyle. He met Orla's worried gaze across the table and nodded in sympathy. She noticed, with great relief, that his beard was partially gray.

She was in his room a few days later when the boy who had taken her laptop that first day stopped and poked his head in. Then, they were keeping the doors to the hotel rooms propped open, college-dorm-style, since the only real way to communicate was to go and find each other. The boy looked hyper. He grabbed both sides of Kyle's door frame and swung his chest into the room. "Did you hear?" he said. "We're not gonna be Americans anymore."

Kyle handed Orla her shirt. They got up and followed the

357

boy down the hall, to where a crowd was gathering around the floor's one rabbit-eared television.

The president was reading from a teleprompter, squinting his pin-dot eyes like he found his own words suspicious. "And so," he was saying, "as Atlantic City has become a hotbed of violent crime and, really, an enormous burden on the state of New Jersey and its taxpayers—and it used to be a great town, Atlantic City, it was a fantastic town when I was there—I am asking Congress to grant the big wish of the disloyal protesters there."

"Big wish!" someone burst out, mocking, and someone else hissed, *"Shhh."*

"They are doing dangerous things, very dangerous things, these people," the president went on. "Smashing windows and other terrible, terrible things. Rape. They don't want to be protected against bad attacks, like the one Mexico did to us? They want a brand-new nation? They want to secede? Maybe I should let 'em. Revoke their citizenships. It's treason, folks. Treason."

Orla looked at Kyle. "But we don't *really* want to secede," she said, "do we?"

Kyle looked pale as he held his middle finger up to the blurry screen. "No, we're just being symbolic," he said. "Secession is impossible, anyway." He slapped the side of his face lightly, as if to snap himself out of something. "And for the thousandth time," he muttered at the president, "the Spill wasn't Mexico. It was Russia."

Orla shook her head. "Did you hear how he said 'rape,' just like, on its own?"

They went back to their rooms. They laughed about it. A few weeks later, the windowless buses began pulling in, beneath the decrepit Taj Mahal. Lines of people without luggage shuffled off them, blinking into the seaside sunlight. "We are so proud," the president said on television the next day, "to say that we have done it. We are deporting thousands of illegals. We're getting them out of America, folks. And now we're going to build tha wall—I always said we'd have a beautiful wall, didn't I? We might be putting it in a different place than we thought we would, but it's still going to be beautiful, I can guarantee that. And it won't just keep out illegals. It'll keep out traitors, too. The Atlantic City sissies, I call them. You know they're scared of computers? The internet, our tremendous new internet—it scares them. They're losers."

All that Orla and anyone around her could tell from that speech was: the people who had come on the buses were undocumented immigrants. Kyle went out one day to ask questions and came back with a theory that turned out to be right. "The whole secession thing," he told Orla, "nobody counted on that really happening. I mean—secession just *doesn't happen*. Unless the government wants it to." He went to the window and looked out at the view: a slice of dank bay, some golden marsh. "Do you know how hard it is to deport people by the thousands?" he said. "Very hard—if you're sending them back to another country. But if you just ship them to Atlantic City and then make *that* another country—" He turned back to face her. "Then you've done it, haven't you?"

Orla stared at him. It took her a moment. When she understood, she half rose out of her chair, urgently, not knowing where she meant to go or what she meant to do. She stayed like that, awkwardly, her legs beginning to burn, and said, "But what about us? Are we…?"

"Apparently, it'll be like it was with Cuba," Kyle said flatly. "We can't go back home. They really are taking our citizenship. And the US won't let anyone from the outside come in here."

After the buses stopped bringing people, the construction trucks rolled in. Work on the wall around Atlantic City's borders went on day and night. Orla and the rest of them watched as the arc of concrete went up, sealing them off from the rest of America. It went all along Atlantic City's city limits and reached far out into the water on either side of the town. The beach that had always run uninterrupted up and down New Jersey's coast now ended abruptly, at its southern point, in Ventnor, where one side of the wall was planted into the sand, just behind a tiki bar.

The kids in the old casinos were subdued and scared. But Orla felt the calmest she had in years. While Kyle slept through the sounds of construction, she kept herself awake to watch. She stayed up one night till dawn, feeling oddly choked up as the last bolts went in. The wall was just what she needed, she thought: a barrier to her doubts. Something to fix her firmly, and finally, in her place.

———

After that, there was nothing left to do but put together a life— a blessedly boring life filled with learning to cook with Kyle and helping to draw up zoning rules and making sure her sons' water bottles had been washed by the time they had to leave for lacrosse.

She and Kyle got married on the beach, like everyone else. This was a common joke around Atlantis: "We're doing a beach wedding!" There were no other options. And there were no families, few friends. So they all went to each other's weddings, merrily filling out the crowd. After she and Kyle said their vows, Orla stood receiving her guests, learning some of their names for the first time.

She and Kyle were thirty-five then, and eager for children. They moved out of the Revel and found a real house off the boardwalk, on Florida Avenue. The house was a white-brick two-story with mud-brown trim, a building that had been abandoned for years next to a strip club that had been abandoned for years. A black curved awning with a fuchsia silhouette of a naked dancer still hung next door. Their front door opened into a narrow hallway. There were three small bedrooms stacked at the front, a tiny living room in the middle, and a large, box kitchen in the rear with a slim wooden screen door that close into its frame with loud slaps. It would be the soundtrack to the next two decades of Orla's life, the slap of that door. She knew what it sounded like from every spot in the house—behind her as she walked in, from the living room, where she sat waiting for Kyle to come home from work, from their bedroom, late at night, when the boys were teenagers who both ignored the rules, who didn't fear their parents enough to even muffle the sounds of them breaking curfew.

The boys. She was thirty-six when she had Frank, thirty-nine when she had Gary. They wanted to give them names no one in Atlantis ever heard anymore.

The boys arrived with such ease, compared to Marlow, that the experiences seemed completely separate from each other. "Are you going to attempt a VBAC?" the obstetrician had asked at a late-term appointment with Frank. After the doctor explained what it was, Kyle turned to Orla, confused. "After cesarean?" he said. "What cesarean?" He claimed to have never noticed her scar, and she believed him. Once an angry purple scrawl, it had faded, over the years, to a whisper of shine and white.

Kyle took it fine. Of course he did. He was Kyle. He was buoyant, with a son on the way. He held her hand as she spoke. He called Danny a world-class asshole, Floss and Aston animals. Orla softened the part where she sneaked Marlow out. She and Kyle never talked of it again.

She didn't become a writer, and she didn't particularly mind. In the evenings, she sometimes looked around the table, at Kyle and Frank and Gary, all of them nibbling their different dinners, and thought: *I am truly nothing special, no one but his wife and their mother and a halfway decent citizen. And they like me. They love me.*

Still, she needed something else. When Gary started kindergarten, Orla petitioned to open the store. Their little economy, which ran on the old plastic gambling chips that had become Atlantis's currency, was still so fragile that no one launched a business without group input. But everyone liked Orla's idea right away. They had been without their phones for a decade, and the idea of a store full of books—it was decadent. America wouldn't trade with them, but Europe didn't mind. Twice a month, a cargo barge out of the UK dropped anchor near the old Bally's and sent in parcels from the outside world. (This was why Orla's sons, who lived within view of the Garden State Parkway, grew up wearing Arsenal jerseys and eating Cadbury bars.)

So Orla made some calls, on a landline phone, from the business center at the Golden Nugget. She placed orders with a few publishers. She supplemented the shipments, at first, with books collected from neighbors who had brought a few along in the beginning and had read them too many times since. Orla stood on a ladder before the strip club awning next door and modified the dancer. She painted her a high-necked red dress and a pair of thick black glasses. She drew a book in the hand the woman had thrust over her head. Atlantic Books, she printed, beneath the high-heeled feet.

———

One day, she saw a new entry among the squashed lines of a distributor's catalog: a magazine called *Constellation Weekly*. Orla knew about Constellation, the all-celebrity town where the people were always on camera. It took shape just after she came to Atlantis, in 2022, and Orla remembered what she had thought the first time she ever heard about it: *Floss would do anything to get in there.*

She held her finger over the item number for *Constellation Weekly* and, with her other hand, picked up the phone.

"Magazines?" her sales rep said. "I can look into it. But thought you all didn't use technology there."

"We don't," Orla said. "I mean the print editions."

"The *print* editions?" The woman sputtered. "Orla. Betwee

paying for print, and sourcing them through the UK, do you know how expensive that would be?"

"I'm aware," Orla said. "I thought I'd start with just one title. *Constellation Weekly*."

"A weekly, no less." Her contact sighed. "I feel compelled to tell you: you won't make your money back on this. How many copies?" Orla heard the clicking of fingers on a keyboard. She missed that sound, still. And she missed, sometimes, the power she had felt when she was young, with a phone in her hand, pretending. Pretending Floss was famous, pretending Danny was important, pretending her skin glowed golden tan with the help of a button on Instagram. Pretending followers meant something. Once in a while, she still got phantom urges: to look down at something in her hand when she found herself alone at a table, to fix her face in a way that would work for a photograph taken at arm's length, to conjure a stream of updates on how other people were doing. But every time she remembered her phone wasn't there, she felt relieved, and free all over again. Like she'd been given more life to live.

"I'll take the minimum number of copies," she said. "Whatever it is."

"I'll get back to you with a price."

"Don't bother," Orla said. "Just go ahead and place the order."

So that was how she saw Marlow, in the magazines that cost her—it was insane—two hundred ten dollars a week. They came in every Friday. Orla would make herself save them until the store was empty. Then she would tear through them quickly, searching. Most weeks, Marlow wasn't in them. But roughly every other month, she would find her. Sometimes, she even spotted Amadou, escorting Marlow to a restaurant or ballet class. It was an image so comforting that, the first time she saw it, she put her head down on the counter and sobbed.

Orla wondered what they had told Marlow, or what they would someday. She was a teenager, old enough to ask about her looks, not a trace of which seemed like Floss or Aston. Marlow had Orla's hair, the rough near-curls. But otherwise, she looked like Danny, with her strong jaw and dark blue eyes. Orla loved the way those eyes looked back at the camera. Marlow always seemed to be peering, looking skeptically into the lens—as if to say, *Who's out there?*

Orla would stroke the page and think, *Me.*

CHAPTER TWENTY-THREE

Marlow, Orla & Floss

Atlantis
2051

n the last row of the restaurant's basement locker room, there are the dry clothes the woman who led them here promised. The white button-down shirt is too small, and the black nylon skirt is too big, but she pulls them on, along with the black, tall boots that fit perfectly. When she climbs a flight of stairs and exits beneath the door marked for staff, she looks like anyone else who has just finished working the breakfast shift.

The door takes her into a lobby. The lobby empties into a huge room where children are sitting on stools before old, unlit slot machines with levers on the side. Plywood squares have been nailed down over their surfaces. The children set their pens and notebooks on them. They swivel to face their teacher, who paces the aisle's loud carpet.

Marlow spots the sea across the room and walks toward the doors, then through them, scattering the pigeons outside who stab at a fallen muffin. She steps onto the boardwalk and waits for a group of men with sandals and briefcases, headed toward the green glass tower on the pier, to pass. Then she crosses to the metal railing and looks out at the Atlantic. The morning is stiff and cold, the sky above the water so blue that Marlow can't look right at it. She turns her back on the surf and watches people, trying to decide who to ask about Orla. She needs someone who won't run to the closest cop—their uniforms are mint green, the same color as the coast guard boats, and make her think of the Statue—if they suspect her of crossing illegally. She rules out the man with the wraparound sunglasses and fiercely angular haircut. The woman jogging toward her looks promising at first, but Marlow doesn't trust her exercise clothing, which is frighteningly coordinated. She is also—Marlow can tell—swinging her ponytail on purpose. This seems like a bad sign.

The crowd on the boardwalk thins. All the people with anxious workday foreheads have filtered into the tower. The last straggling children have ducked inside the school, beneath the arm of a smiling monitor who swings the door open to greet them.

Marlow sees a woman coming out of the peach stucco building next door. A banner hangs above the building's entrance: NEW UNITS, 55+. The woman hurries under it, still pulling on one sleeve of her sweater. Her hair is wet. As she jerks at her sleeve her bag lets loose an eruption of books. The woman is wearing sunglasses, but Marlow can tell she is rolling her eyes, because she uses her whole face to do it, circling her chin west to east.

She is clearly running late, and Marlow knows the polite thing to do is not stop her. But she walks toward her anyway, because there is something about this woman that makes Marlow sure she isn't the ratting type. The woman has long, defiant gray hair.

"Excuse me," Marlow says when she reaches her. She kneels down and picks up two books.

The woman squints up at her. Slowly, she takes her sunglasses off.

"I just wondered if you could tell me—" Marlow starts, but the woman is on her feet now, staring. She doesn't seem to notice when her bag falls again. She puts her hands on either side of Marlow's face, pressing her thumbs so hard into Marlow's cheeks that Marlow's eyes prickle with tears. The woman pulls Marlow in and holds her. While Marlow is wondering how to react, the wind picks up behind her. It splits her hair at the back of her head and blows it forward, into the woman's. She sees that, except for the color, their hair is exactly the same. She stands there, letting herself be held, letting her waves whip after Orla's.

———

Orla looks up from where she squats on the boardwalk and sees her, drawn in black and gray against the brilliant sky. The world is so bright behind the girl that her face is mostly in shadow, but Orla doesn't have to look twice.

She wants to laugh. It is Wednesday morning. She has dropped some books. She overslept. She didn't dry her hair. She is still not used to this damn retirement complex Kyle loves so much, and so, on top of everything else, she took the wrong elevator—up, not down. There might be a line of people outside the shop—not to mention boxes. Wednesday is when most things come in.

This is how it happens? She wants to laugh.

But instead she stands, against her knees' wishes, and reaches for the face she has seen in the magazine. She almost expects it to feel, when she puts her hands on it, like that silky paper. But Marlow's skin is warm and soft, faintly beating like her heart is everywhere beneath it. She is all right. She is all right. She is all right.

———

Marlow sits down on the bench Orla points to. The hot sugared doughnuts came in a set of three, and Orla hands her two in the same motion with which she takes them out of their white bag, like she doesn't have to think about how to share them.

"I can't believe I just bumped into you," Marlow keeps repeating, because she can't. How she found Orla—it couldn't have been better if it was scripted. "Something like that has never happened to me before," she says. "It's like…" She struggles to think of the word she wants. She wishes, for a moment, that she had her device. It's been gone long enough now that the marks it left have healed. She has a little bit of new skin.

Orla smiles. She tries to be helpful. "Fate?" she says. "Destiny?"

"No." Marlow has the word. It makes her cry. "A coincidence," she says.

Orla seems to think about how to put it, what she says to Marlow next. Gently, she asks, "Does your mother know where you are?"

Marlow shrugs. She looks at Orla. She notices the way Orla's skin crinkles softly around her mouth and eyes. The effect is so comforting, she almost climbs into her lap. Instead she swallows the last of her doughnut and says, "Do you think I should have a baby?"

Orla considers it, squinting. "Have you done everything else?"

Marlow pictures her wedding-day face, drab and peeling, in Times Square. She thinks of what everyone agrees on: she has always gone along. "No," she says. "I don't think I even know what everything else is yet."

Orla leans forward. She takes Marlow's wax paper out of her lap and brushes the crumbs off her skirt. "Having a baby is one of the best parts of life," she says. "But still. It's only one of them."

———

This boardwalk, Floss thinks. *Why would anyone, it's like—ho about a road, but shitty, and worse?* She grasps her thigh with both hands and yanks her heel out of yet another groove.

A man with a surfboard (and a gut that makes it seem like a prop) balks when Floss says she is looking for Orla, that she has come here from California to find her. He shifts his weight and asks: "So you're an alien?" Floss senses she should open her purse. She finds a pair of bills so old and soft, they seem on the verge of crumbling, and prays that these privacy freaks still like American cash. It works. The man holds out his meaty palm and tells her about a bookstore, points her down the boardwalk and says to get off at the third ramp. It almost makes Floss sad, how little money she has to give him. Some people don't know how to live.

She goes the way he told her, but it has only been a block before she sees them. Both of them. Together. On a bench. It's so *random*. The truth is, Floss wasn't sure that either of them would be here. All she had to go on for Marlow was the idea that had sat in her chest all these years: someday Marlow would figure it out, and then, in an instant, be gone. All she had to go on for Orla was what always came up when Floss searched for her: *404. Not found.*

Found you now, Floss thinks, closing in on them. She is pleased to see that Marlow looks different. As beautiful as always, but something else: more awake. Maybe she's started to use the serums that Floss is always trying to give her.

Orla looks the same, except for the gray hair. *We get it, Orla,* Floss thinks. *You're different.* Then she straightens her spine and reminds herself, as both of them look up and see her: in the minds of her daughter and old friend, she is the agreed-upon asshole. Best not to come in too hot.

She has not been the world's greatest mom. She can admit that. But *she* is the mom. Her. She pretends her heel is stuck again, just to buy some time. She says a silent prayer that Marlow and Orla will grade her on a curve. At the very least, she deserves full credit for completion.

———

Orla has to stop herself from touching Marlow. She wants to put her mouth on her, to grab her by the scruff and carry her away. Marlow scratches her neck, like she can feel Orla's thought. Then she shades her eyes and says, "Are you kidding me?"

Orla follows her gaze. It takes her a moment to recognize the woman coming toward them. There is no way around it; Floss is twice the size she used to be. *Well, good for her*, Orla thinks. *She put her time in being thin*. Still, it must be a lot to carry around on five-inch heels.

A group of ladies power walking stops when they see Floss. They flap their hands. They remember her, from long ago, before they came here. Floss lights up and dawdles, talking with them longer than she should, considering her runaway daughter is waiting just a few yards away.

Orla looks at Marlow. The girl is frowning, with narrowed eyes, as Floss poses and kisses the air around the walkers' cheeks. For the first time, Orla sees something of herself in Marlow's face.

She puts her arm around her. She tries to block out a blinding flash of memory—this same person in her arms. She is so angry for a moment; she has been cheated of this body. Of the smell of its head at three, resting on her shoulder, of the sight of its legs at nine, scrambling after a basketball, of the feel of its waist beneath a wedding dress. She forces herself to breathe, to say what she was going to. What she has to. "Marlow," she says. "There's no way of knowing if I would have been any better."

Marlow softens her jaw. Floss leaves the women and runs toward her daughter, somehow, without falling. Floss grabs Marlow and rubs her back. As if she can't help herself, she reaches out her other hand and pulls Orla in, too. All three of them are stiff-limbed at first, holding something back. Then Orla fee the air between them loosening, just a little. They pull back and look at each other. They take the same shuddering breath. There is a sudden possibility, if only a small one, that none of them are all bad.

———

"I can't picture you on that pirate boat," Orla says to Floss. Marlow was about to say the same thing, but in a much brinier tone.

Floss sniffs. "What pirate boat?" she says. "I flew to London and chartered a yacht from Southampton. There was some sort of mess with the coast guard on the way in, about my American passport—" here, Floss smiles, like *isn't the coast guard darling* "—but I just answered all their questions, took the ticket, and said I'd deal with it later."

"The *ticket*?" Orla says. "Floss, it's a felony charge, crossing the border. You're looking at jail time when you go back."

"My *daughter* was missing," Floss says. Marlow hears the possessive way she leans on the word. "I didn't think about felony charges. I didn't think about anything. I just tried to *find* her."

It is the kind of line Marlow can imagine her mother saying for the camera, except the tone is off. Floss has a performance voice, and this—this isn't it. She sounds exhausted, punched through by worry and adrenaline, and she looks the oldest she ever has. Suddenly, Marlow realizes it: Floss is not wearing makeup.

Orla looks around nervously. "You haven't talked to anyone else here, have you?"

"No," Floss says. Then she snaps her fingers. "Oh, there was a guy who told me how to get to your store. He wasn't happy to hear that I came from California, but don't worry. I paid him off."

Orla's mouth hangs open, but Marlow laughs—she's not surprised. She thinks of herself, of her great lengths to get here: marching to Ventnor in the dark, sneaking over the border. Of course Floss had sailed right up to the wall. Of course she had forced her way in.

"Marlow," Orla says. "Is she all right?"

Marlow looks over and sees that Floss is shrinking into a fog. Orla's face is white. She isn't used to seeing this. She doesn't have fog, she says, and only knows a few people who do. It's less common, in Atlantis. Giving up their screens when they came here seemed to save their minds just in time.

Orla says they should come up to her apartment. When Marlow helps Floss start walking, Orla hesitates. Then she takes Floss's other arm.

———

Floss would like to know: Who is the dipshit who planned a red carpet on a boardwalk?

She is tripping every five seconds, despite the fact that Orla holds her on her left, and an assistant of Melissa's is on her right.

She sees the bank of photographers coming up, all of them squawking at her: *Over here.*

She braces herself for the part when they yell at Orla to step aside. It always makes Floss uneasy, though she can't quite work out why. To be the sole thing in the picture—isn't it what she has worked so hard for? But she can never stand the sound of it *And now, Floss alone.*

She is the talent, she reminds herself. She can do whatever she wants. This time, when Orla is told to move, Floss is going to hold on to her.

———

Orla knows that when she lets Marlow and Floss into her new home, it will be messy. It follows that, as soon as she and Kyb downsized, both of their sons came careening home, claiming a crisis each—the wrong job, the wrong girl.

372

Kyle was eager to unload the old house next door to her bookstore, to get into a smaller, newer place on the boardwalk. He trotted ahead of Orla, like an eager puppy, when they went to look at the old-person units.

"It's in a former ballroom," the realtor told them proudly, like Atlantis wasn't lousy with those.

"You're going to love the view," Kyle promised Orla, and when they got into the unit, she did.

"But I said I want a two-bedroom," she added.

Kyle danced over to the wall. He pulled a handle. A crinkled divider emerged, sealing the rest of the place off from a narrow space near the window.

"There you go," he said. "Two-bedroom."

Orla shook her head as Kyle struggled with the handle, trying to figure out how it clipped into the wall on the other side. "That doesn't count," she said.

———

The boys Orla introduces her to don't get up until Orla tells them to, sharply. Marlow takes their hands, sweaty from holding their books open, in hers. They are handsome, with charming smiles that burst quickly across their faces, even when their mother is making them be polite. Marlow can feel the gulf between them, can remember how old thirty-five sounded when she was in her twenties. She can tell, too, that they don't know who she is. Orla only tells them her name.

She thinks that they look nothing like her. Then Orla says, "They have our hair, too, but they've always worn it this way." Frank and Gary both have shaved heads.

Marlow asks, a while later, when Floss has dozed off in her chair, to see a picture of the boys as children. Orla goes into another room and comes back with a printed one: Frank and Gary on the beach, heads ducked over their buckets. They are off-center in the photo; they only take up the left side. Orla points to the empty sand next to them, studded with toys and half-formed castles, and says, "Right there. That's where I imagined you."

It is exactly, for some reason, what Marlow needs to hear.

She wants to offer Orla something, too. So she takes a plastic bag out of her pocket and shows her the letter from Floss she found. Orla takes the envelope. She checks the address and the date. She hands it back. "That's okay," she says. "Why don't you just keep it?"

———

Floss is only pretending to be asleep. It's a bad look, sixty-three and fat and dozing in a chair in an unfamiliar home, but it is not as embarrassing as being awake and ignored for hours on end. Marlow and Orla are asking each other questions Floss knows all the answers to. Like someone who saw the movie already, she is dying to ruin their endings. She knows so much more about both of these women than they will ever know about each other, no matter how long they sit at Orla's table, matching up their notes. But they don't want to hear from her, she knows. She knows they both have the same thought, when it comes to her—*she never cared about me at all*—but that isn't true. She has fucked up plenty, has hurt people, has built a career on looking like she enjoys being completely self-absorbed. She understands why, whenever she has tried to show these women that she loves them, they have looked at her with suspicion: *What is her angle? What is she after?* And often, she does have an angle. Often, they are right. When she betrayed Orla, she was selfish and scared, and too dubious of her own strength to believe she could really ruin a life. When she betrayed Marlow, putting her on those pills, she was too dubious of her own strength to believe she could really protect one. It's possible that her loving Orla and Marlow has, overall, made their lives worse. But it ha made her a better person. Not a good one, she knows. Just better

She forgets that she is asleep and raises one eyebrow high a

374

she listens. Oh, these bitches are editing heavily. Orla skips the part of her story where she stole Marlow from the hospital. Marlow skips the part of hers where she attacked that girl.

Hey, Marlow, Floss imagines yelling. *Orla almost aborted you! Oh, and, Orla—Marlow bit someone. Exactly—like a dog!*

But then Floss hears Orla showing Marlow another picture, one that must be of Orla and Floss. Marlow says they are beautiful. Orla corrects her: they're young. Maybe because she's actually listening, for once, Floss hears exactly the way Orla says it. Like their age explains everything.

So she decides to test the theory—to see if she can be different now that decades have gone by. To see if she can do, in this moment, the best thing for her daughter, which is to just keep her mouth shut. To let both of them believe that the other is as pure and perfect as they've imagined. She tries it for five seconds, then ten, then twenty. She keeps on counting.

———

Somehow, the afternoon goes by. Orla tells Marlow about Danny.

"Did you love him?" Marlow asks her.

"No," Orla says. "I was obsessed with him. And I don't mean it in the way your mother says 'obsessed,' if she still throws that word around. I mean it literally, and I'm not using 'literally' here, either, the way she does."

"Danny was a loser," Floss says simply. "And bald. Be glad you got your hair from your mother's side."

After that, they all look into their glasses awkwardly. Orla examines the water in hers and realizes that this may be the problem: water.

As if on cue, Kyle comes home from work and starts to mix drinks. When he hears who the women in his kitchen are, his eyebrows nearly exit his face. But by the time he gets the shaker down, he has taken it all in stride. Five minutes later, Floss fawns over his vodka martini, sounding relieved. Kyle smiles and bows, then picks up the phone to order pizza. Orla laughs as Marlow gawks at the piece of buttoned plastic. She gets up to touch its cord.

It gets dark and the boys go out, to wherever they go. When he's done eating, Kyle excuses himself. He says he has work to do. He means to give them space, but Orla feels panicked as he moves down the hall. When she looks back at Floss and Marlow, she sees them watching wistfully, too. Maybe they all need a break.

Orla shows Marlow how to use the shower. Then she goes into the living room and unfolds the futon near the window. She stands back so Floss can lie down.

Floss's hair spreads out on the pillow behind her. "I thought you would hate me," she says, in yet another voice of hers that Orla doesn't know: older, quiet, but clear as a bell.

"I do hate you," Orla says. She makes it sound like a joke they have had forever. They are still laughing when Marlow comes in, clean and shining in Orla's best nightgown, and climbs into bed with her mother. Orla pulls the partition. She goes down the hall, to the room that is hers.

———

But none of them can sleep. First Floss, then Marlow, then Orla, who wakes to the suck of the sliding door—they all step out onto the veranda.

The next day, Floss will sigh on the sofa. She should head back to the States, take her punishment like a big girl, she will say with a pout. She will say this every morning for weeks, for months, until she doesn't bother anymore. An immigration enforcement agent, following up on a tip from someone who saw Floss, will knock on the door just once. Orla will go to her bedroom while the agent sits Floss down at the table, and will hear, in disbelief, how quickly the encounter turns to Floss putting on a show and the agent laughing along. No one will bother them again.

One morning, Floss will come to breakfast in a sheer purple nightie, and Frank and Gary will evacuate for good the same day. One evening, Kyle will snap at Floss, "If you want martinis, maybe pick up some olives. We're out." Orla will tire of her, too, of the way Floss's fabric wall blocks the natural light from the rest of her home. Every day, she will vow to talk to Floss about a timeline for her moving out. And every day—for a year, until the woman across the hall blessedly dies and Floss can be coaxed over there, like a cat—she will end up letting it go. She will turn on the lamps instead.

On the fourth day that Floss fails to leave, Marlow will reach out and take a key from Orla's hand.

She will sail back out of Atlantis on the restaurant-supply boat, this time meeting a water-skiing operation at the sandbar to return her to Ventnor. From there, she will go to New York, back to the place on Twenty-First Street where Floss and Orla lived. Floss still owns it. When she sees the super who watched her pick the lock, she will call him by the name Orla gave her—Linus—and tell him who she is. He will surprise her greatly by crying when he hears. They will become friends, Marlow and Linus and Linus's wife, and then they will become family. Marlow will spend dinnertime and holidays with them, the three of them sharing a joint as they wash the dishes after the children go to sleep. The kids are half-grown; the youngest is eight. But they have never had an aunt before, and Marlow is pleased to find that being theirs is more than enough for her.

She will tweak her appearance until no one knows her anymore. This means growing older, and applying a shy dose of makeup, and dyeing her hair darker—thinking, when she picks the color, of the photo Orla showed her, the one of her and Floss in their twenties. But even though she can see the image clearly—their barely grown faces tipped smugly together, like nothing could ever divide them—she will not be able to remember which one of them had it, the shade she wants.

She will wait months to buy a new device, under the name *M. Cadden*, which she will use to start over. She will follow Jacqueline—just Jacqueline—for a few days. She will watch her throw a party for neon-patterned leggings. She will see Ida, back in the picture, her restlessness quenched by a back tattoo, and a new woman, giggly and pregnant, in her own old seat on Jacqueline's sofa. She will tune in just in time to hear the woman say "Ellis" in a tone of plush ownership, and she will realize that this person has replaced her elsewhere, too. She will think about trying to find out more: who the new wife is, what flaws of hers Ellis is counting on. But then the sight of Jacqueline shimmying in tights will make her homesick, and she will quickly tell her mind to delete all Constellation Network feeds. She will never go back to where she grew up, not even when Aston dies. She will pay to have his ashes shipped and sift them into the Hudson. When she walks near the water, it's strange—she will think not of him, but of the baby she once thought might inherit his looks. At first, she will worry she chose wrong, leaving her eggs. But as the years pass, Marlow is certain: she has a good life. And she doesn't need to share it.

She will become a waitress, hoisting bowls of glossy ziti in an amber-lit cave of a place on Tenth Avenue. She will fall in love with the job—with holding the warm plates and knowing the table numbers by heart and feeling the kitchen's steamed urgency. She will love the way people's faces turn toward her as she approaches their tables, then turn away as soon as their business is finished, pleasantly forgetting her. She will feel the least seen and the most important, she ever has in her life. She will take extra shifts when her friends have auditions, her friends who dream of bigger things and can't believe she doesn't. They cannot fathom that this is enough to make her happy; they want so much to be famous.

Honey, one day, will come into the restaurant, seeing instantly past Marlow's makeover. She will sputter. She will ask how Marlow has been. Marlow will say "fine, thanks" and segue fast into morels and pesto. Honey will tip her enormously, and say that they should grab lunch. But the voice in Marlow's head, the one she always hears first now, will recommend moving on. So she will, to the table that needs her.

She will never go back on Hysteryl.

She will make the city her own. She will buy a new couch to replace the sun-bleached one. She will discover the building's roof, with its rotted fencing and rusted bench, and she will convince the building's management to let her fill it with the grasses and wildflowers that live atop the homes in Constellation. She will learn that the mailboxes still work, downstairs—a postman comes twice a week—and she will find a store on Christopher Street to sell her white sheets with blue-lined envelopes. (She has settled on her favorite color: the sky in New York, in the autumn especially, makes it an easy contest.) She will write to her mothers, both of them, mailing the notes through one of Orla's sales reps in the UK, and they will write back. The letters from Orla are always longer, and not just because they have catching up to do. Orla is better at telling the stories; Floss is better at being in them.

She will learn to fall asleep in 6D, though not before the Empire State Building's lights go off at midnight—she will never find a way to close her eyes against those beams. She will drag her bed to the front of her apartment, because she likes that window better and she can do what she wants—she's alone. She is gloriously alone, except for when Linus and his wife go away once a year and the kids come to stay with her, dragging their sleeping bags. One time, Linus's daughter will bring a lipstick, too, and offer it to Marlow, saying, "Try it. You could be hot, auntie M!" Her mother will swat at her, but Marlow will be touched by the girl's way of seeing her: there is potential. There is still time. She will take the lipstick and wear it and never lose it once.

But none of them—not Marlow, not Orla, not Floss—know any of this yet. They stand on the balcony in Atlantis and lean into the breeze. Orla says she agreed to the place because she loves the view. Marlow nods politely, but doesn't understand why. The ocean is miles away, out of sight. Orla's home faces the land she left behind.

The three women gaze at the windmills, at the cars escaping the marsh. They watch a flock of illumidrones find the wall and bounce back toward America. It's the kind of night when no one misses their man-made glow. The moon stands high and silver white above the little sovereignty. Floss and Orla are thinking the same thing, though neither of them knows it. The light is right on their girl.

ACKNOWLEDGEMENTS

I've had the benefit of enormous privilege in my life. That might be a weird way to start this off, but if you don't acknowledge it in something literally called "acknowledgments," when are you gonna do it? I've gotten breaks that not everyone gets because I am on the lucky end of an entrenched system. And I'm trying to keep my eyes open now, for ways I can call these things out and make up the differences.

I didn't know if I could write a book. I didn't know if I could write this book. Without Stefanie Lieberman and Molly Steinblatt, who tenaciously saw *Followers* through a thousand lives, I would still be wondering. I can never thank the two of them enough.

A million thanks to Brittany Lavery, my editor at Graydon House, for listening, for knowing what I was trying to say and for helping me say it—both in this book and in the process of publishing it.

Thank you to Rufi Thorpe and Catapult for the course "The Novel: Chapter 1," which is where *Followers* took root. Thank you to the writers I met in that class, who gave me notes on the first versions of this book: Katie Runde, Andrea Arnold, Meg Duell, Norah Brzyski, and Veronica Gorodetskaya.

For thoughtful early reads and help with details, thank you to: Lauren Smith Brody, Caitlin Brody, Emma Caruso, Adam Hellegers, Suzannah Bentley, Mindy Steinblatt, Jennifer Close, Jessica Liebman, Hugh King, Scott Curry, Jen Curry. Thank you to Brian Marcus, Rachel Debuque, and Justin Plakas for design feedback.

Jovanna Tosello's cover art has inspired more delighted gasps than I can count, but none have been as giddy as mine was when I first saw it. Thank you, Jovanna.

To the team at Graydon House/Harlequin—Susan Swinwood, Dianne Moggy, Linette Kim, Heather Connor, Lisa Wray, Laura Gianino, Erin Craig, Pamela Osti, Ana Luxton, Amy Jones— thank you for being so welcoming and steering this book into the world.

Thank you to Kathleen Carter for making magical mentions happen.

For vouching for this story, thank you to Abbi Jacobson, whose endorsement I am so grateful for, as well as Christina Dalcher, Jennifer Close, and Rufi Thorpe. And thank you to Tarryn Fisher, whose mind-blowing social-media support I am slowly paying back, in my low-tech way, by recommending *The Wives* to people, one at a time, at the grocery store and in barre class.

Thank you to Charlotte Mursell at Harlequin UK for ferrying this book safely across the pond.

And for general support of me and of *Followers* (sorry for the bland categorizing—it doesn't make you any less indispensable!) thank you to Emily Rose, Doug Johnson, Olivia Blaustein, Michelle Kroes, Adam Hobbins, Zoe Nelson, Claire Dippel, Dawn Prestwich, Nicole Yorkin, Kenya Barris, Jamila Hunter, Ann Weisband, and Erynn Sampson.

Thank you to the teachers who helped me become and stay writer: the faculty at St. Isidore School, at Quakertown Community Senior High School (especially Tracy Houston), and Villanova University (especially Jeff Silverman and Mary Beth Simmons).

This is the paragraph for all the people in my life who always say, "It IS a big deal!" when I start a sentence by saying, "It's not a big deal, but…" Thank you to my friends from Quakertown

Villanova, and New York, and to my whole family, especially Mark and Ashley Angelo, Greg and Tessa Angelo, Tom and Peggy Castronova, and Janie Calvo.

Thank you to my parents, Ed and Mary Ann Angelo, to whom this book is dedicated, for getting me a typewriter when I was little, for watching my kids when I got big, and for every step in between that got me here.

Thank you to my children for being patient while I wrote this. I mean, I know you didn't look, act, or sound patient, but somehow this got done. So I think, deep down, you were.

And thank you to Parker, who always said he'd let me sleep on his couch, and still does.

ONE PLACE. MANY STORIES

Bold, innovative and
empowering publishing.

FOLLOW US ON:

@HQStories